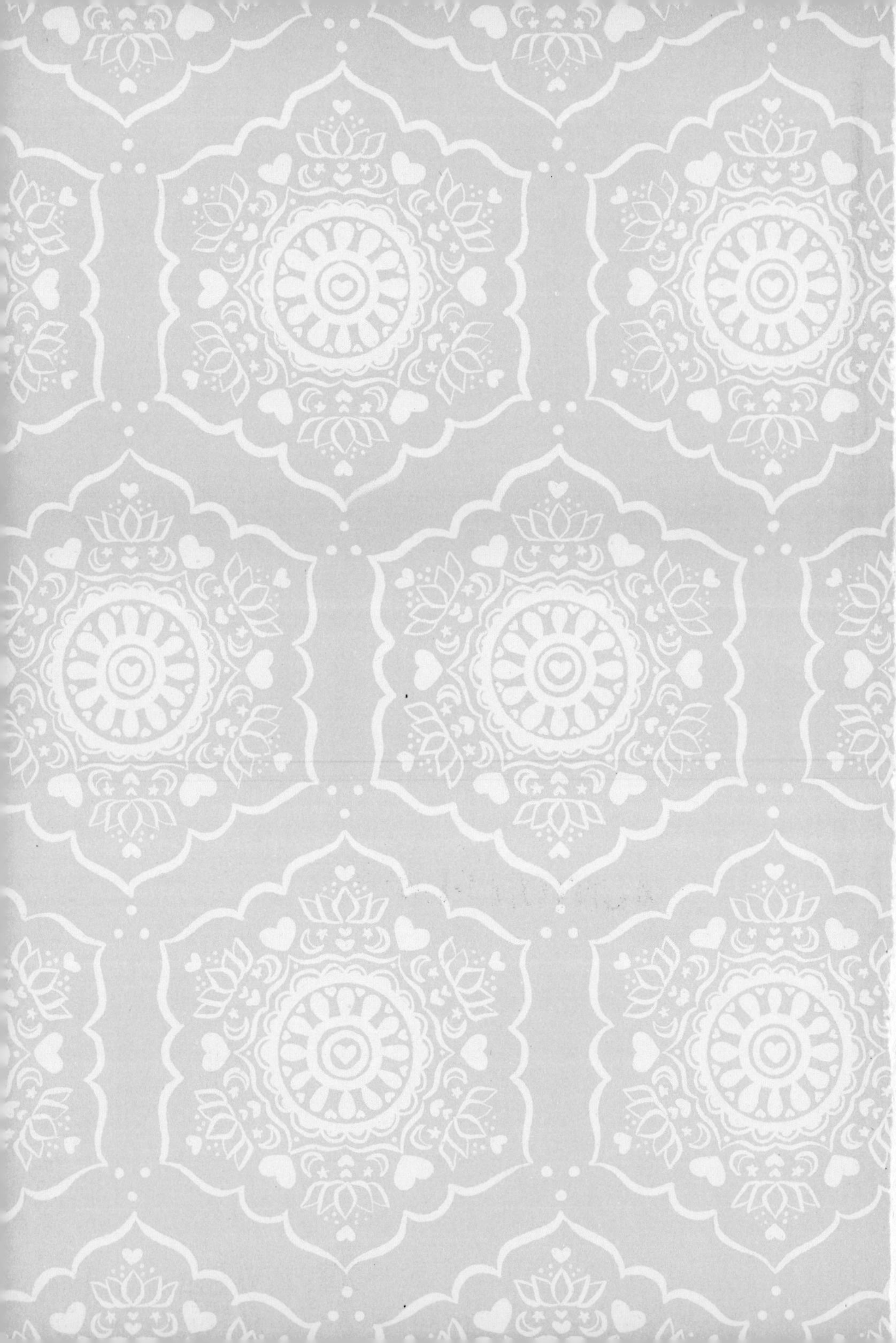

PIECE *by* PIECE

THE STORY OF NISRIN'S HIJAB

PRIYA HUQ

AMULET BOOKS · NEW YORK

CONTENT NOTE: This book contains portrayals of racism and violence, which some readers may find distressing.

Library of Congress Control Number 2020952013

Hardcover ISBN 978-1-4197-4016-9
Paperback ISBN 978-1-4197-4019-0

Printed and bound in China
10 9 8 7 6 5 4 3 2

Amulet Books are available at special discounts when purchased in quantity for premiums and promotions as well as fundraising or educational use. Special editions can also be created to specification. For details, contact specialsales@abramsbooks.com or the address below.

Amulet Books® is a registered trademark of Harry N. Abrams, Inc.

ABRAMS The Art of Books
195 Broadway, New York, NY 10007
abramsbooks.com

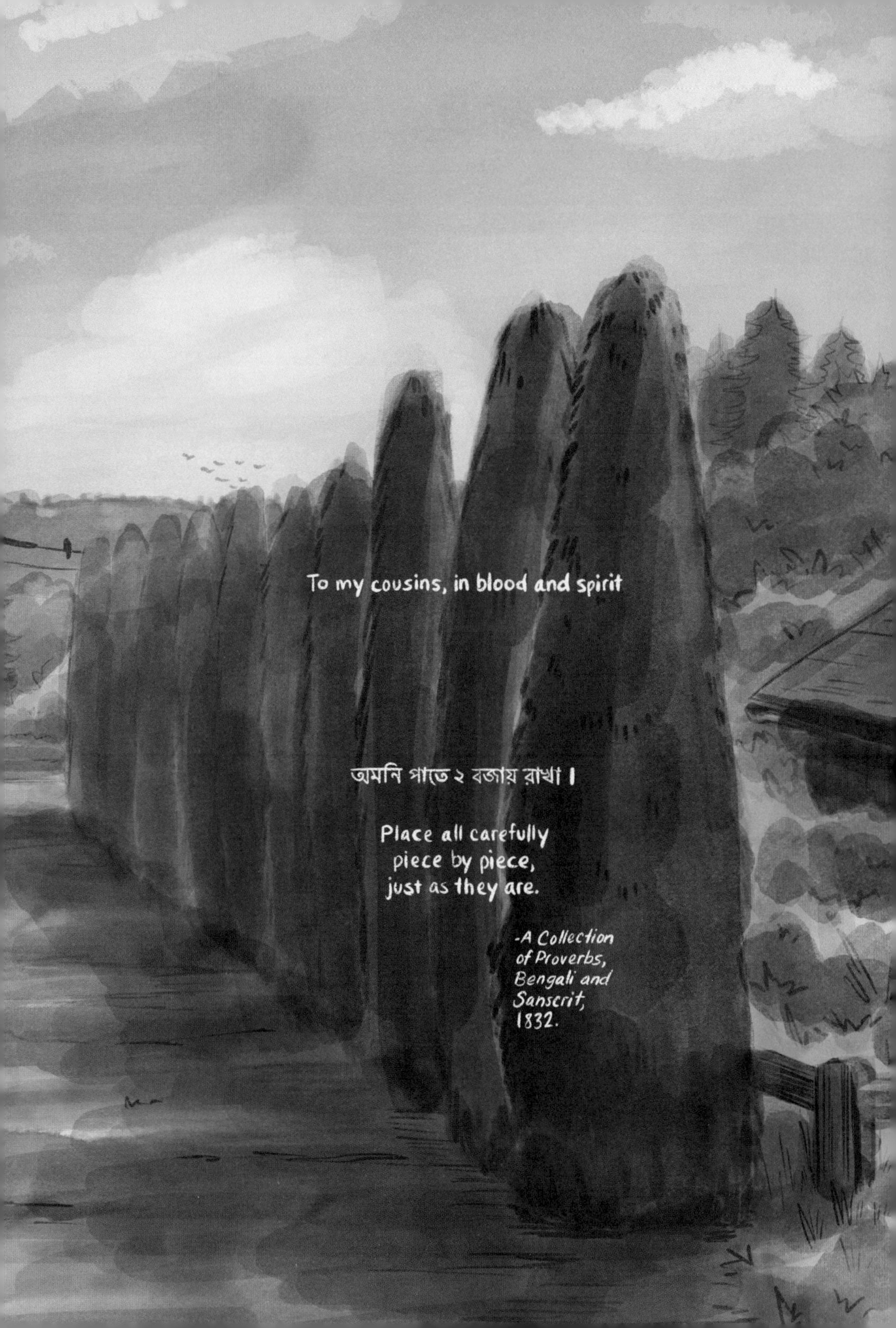

To my cousins, in blood and spirit

অমনি পাতে ২ বজায় রাখা ।

Place all carefully
piece by piece,
just as they are.

*-A Collection
of Proverbs,
Bengali and
Sanscrit,
1832.*

Portland, Oregon. 2002

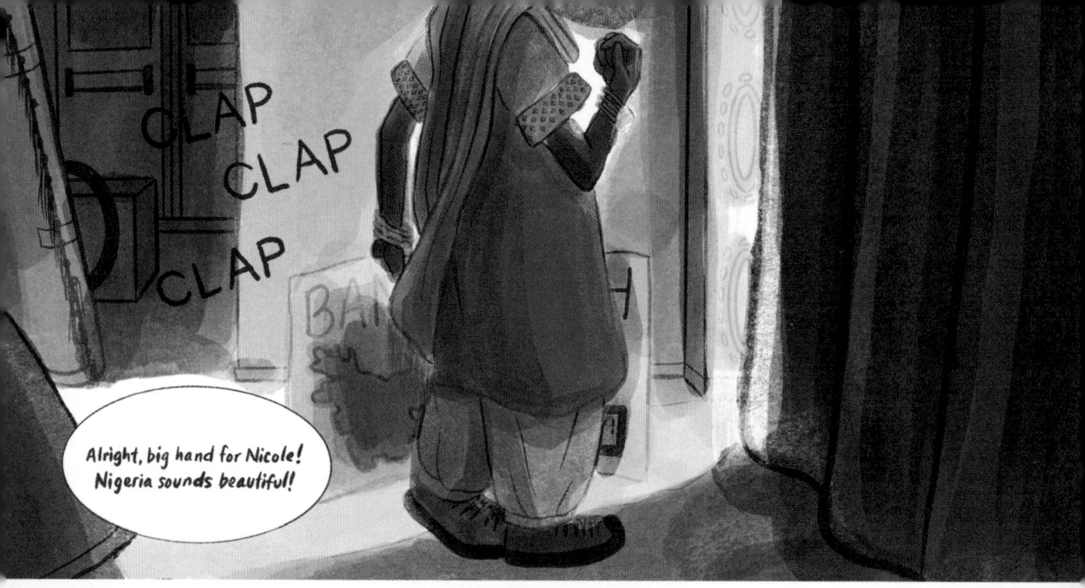
CLAP
CLAP
CLAP
Alright, big hand for Nicole! Nigeria sounds beautiful!

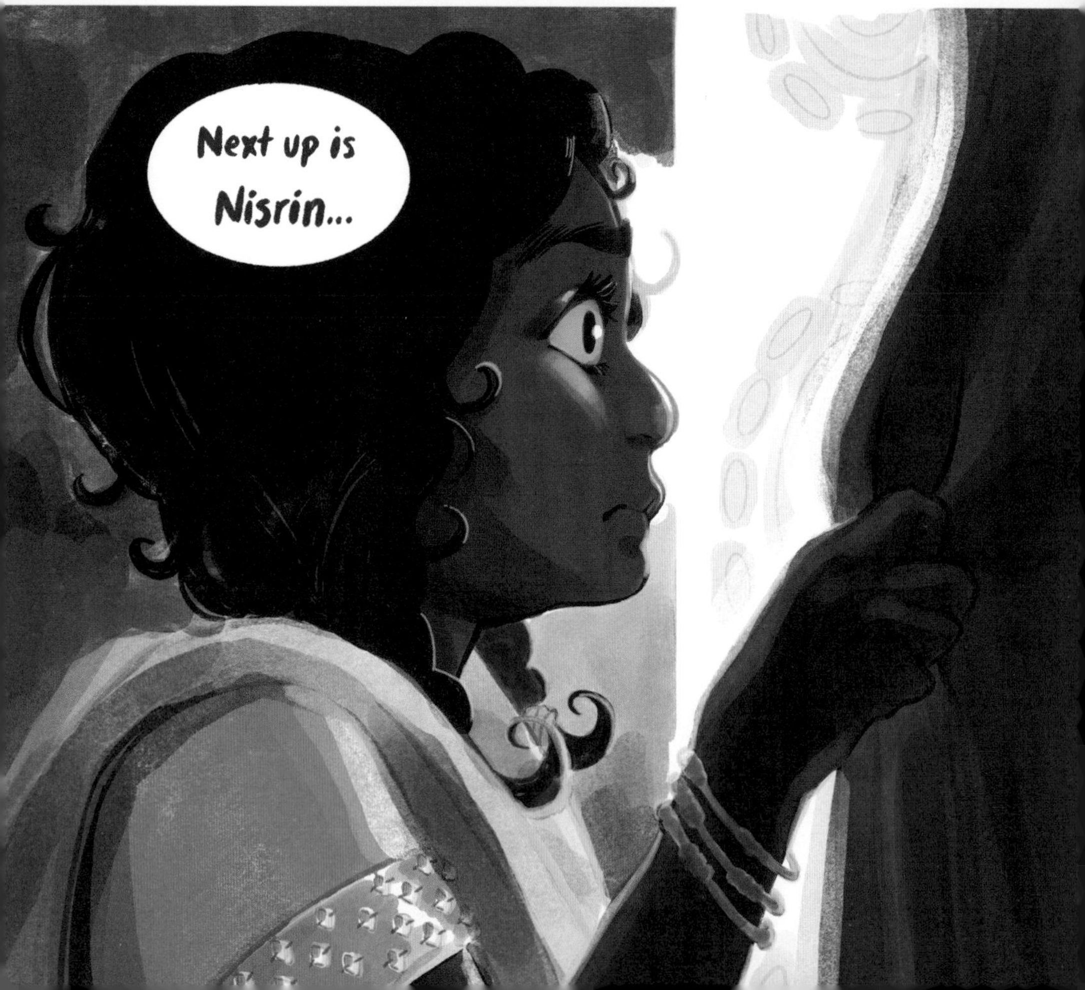
Next up is Nisrin...

BANGLADESH!

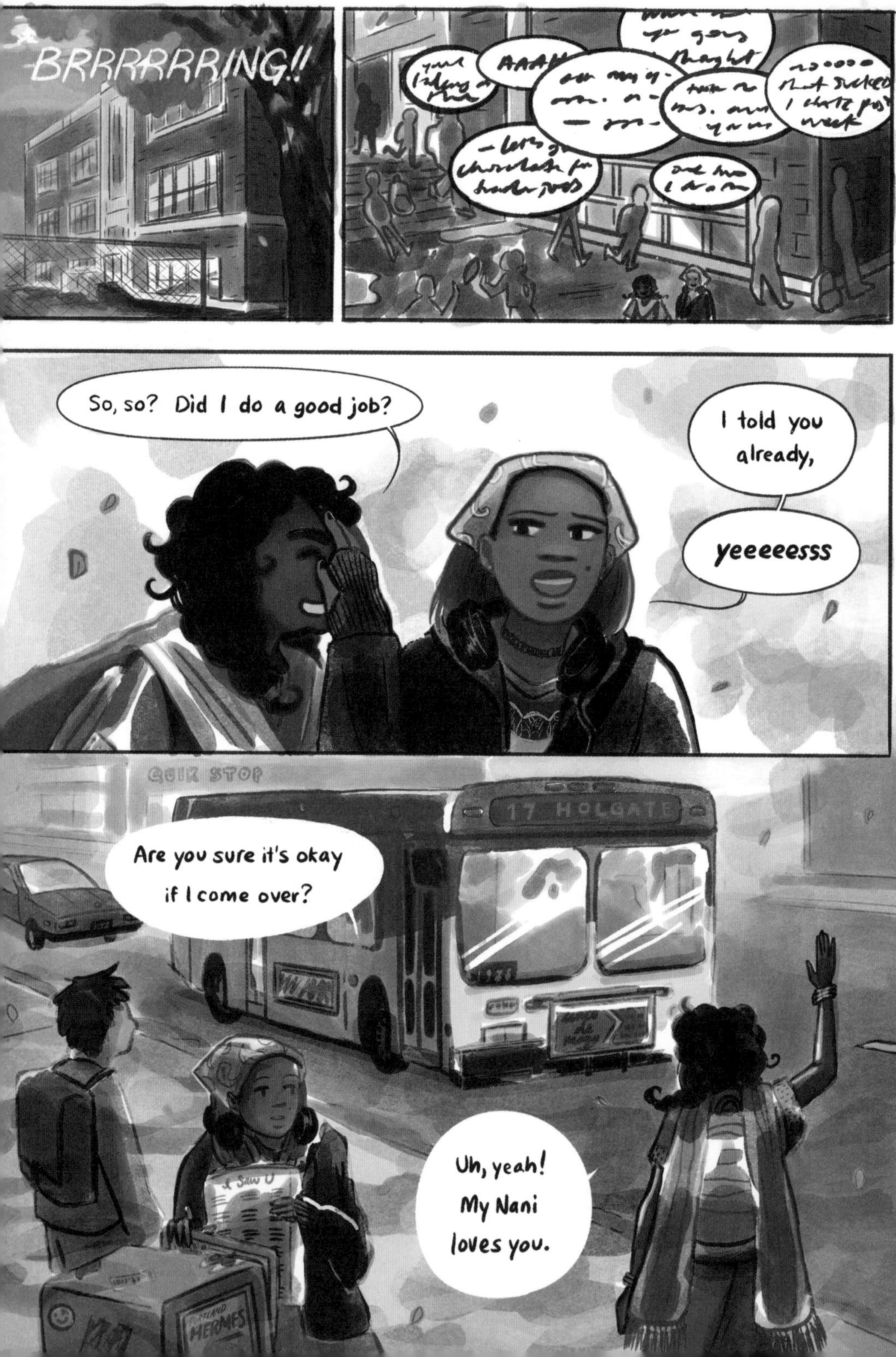
BRRRRRRRING!!
So, so? Did I do a good job?
I told you already,
yeeeeesss
QUIK STOP
17 HOLGATE
Are you sure it's okay if I come over?
Uh, yeah! My Nani loves you.

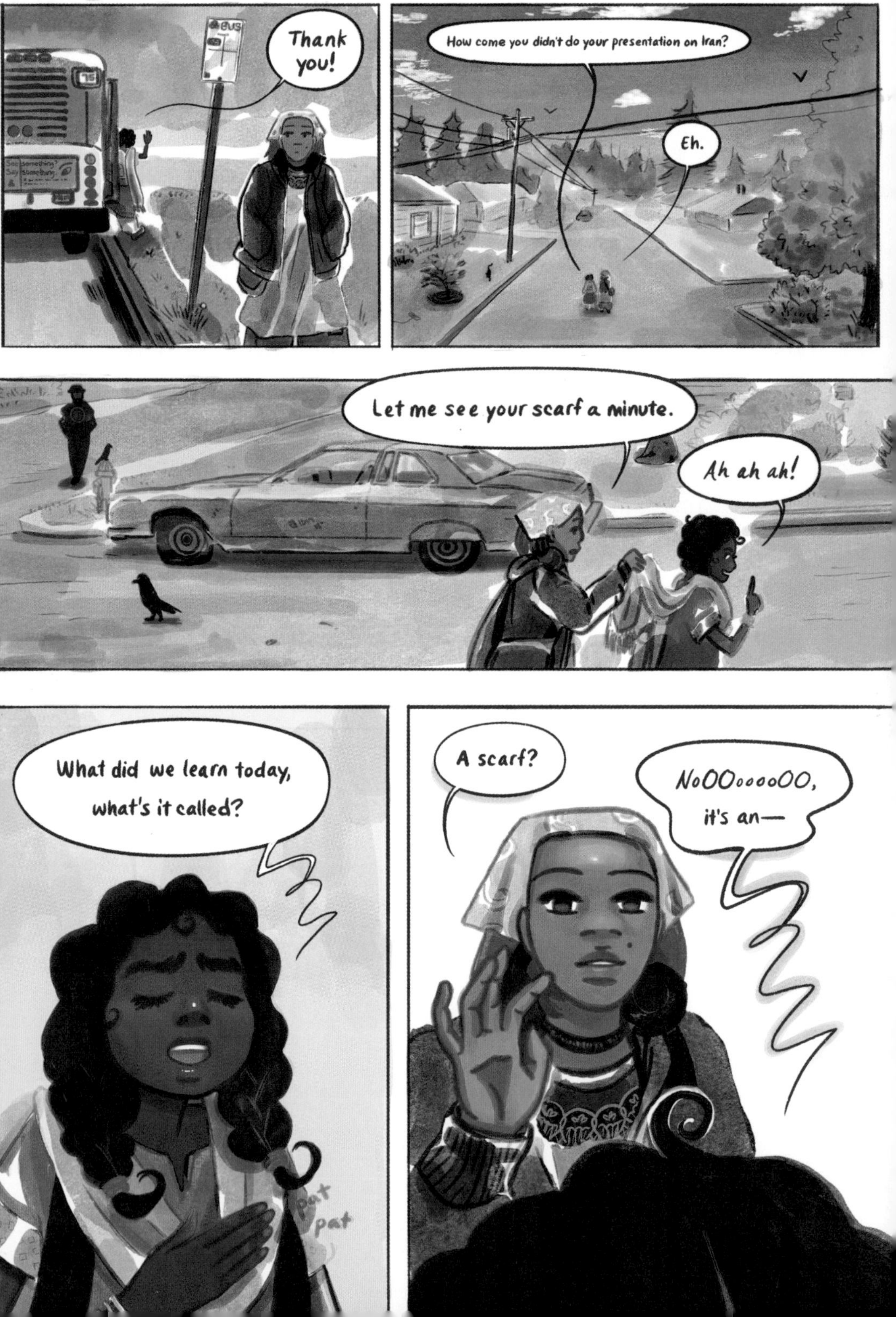
Thank you!
How come you didn't do your presentation on Iran?
Eh.
Let me see your scarf a minute.
Ah ah ah!
What did we learn today, what's it called?
pat pat
A scarf?
NoOOooooOO, it's an—

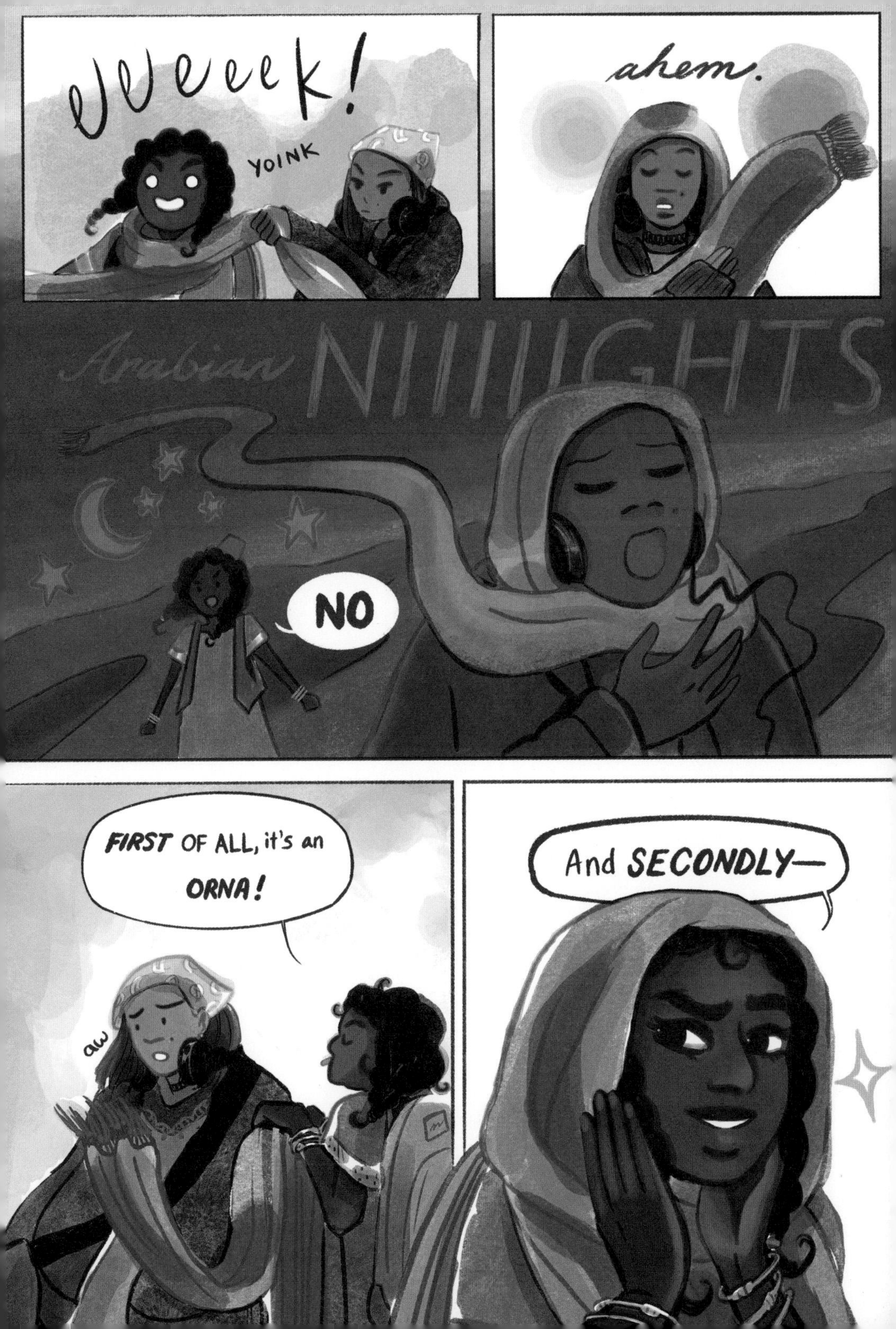
Uueeek!
YOINK
ahem.
Arabian NIIIIGHTS
NO
FIRST OF ALL, it's an ORNA!
aw
And SECONDLY—

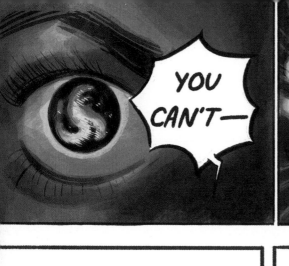

YOU CAN'T—

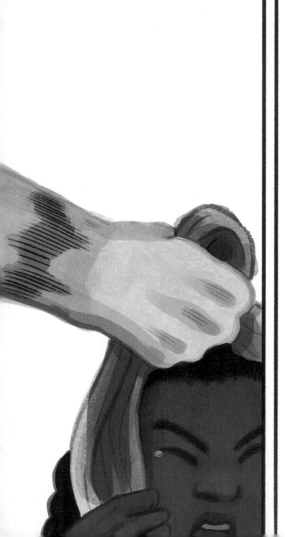

RRIP

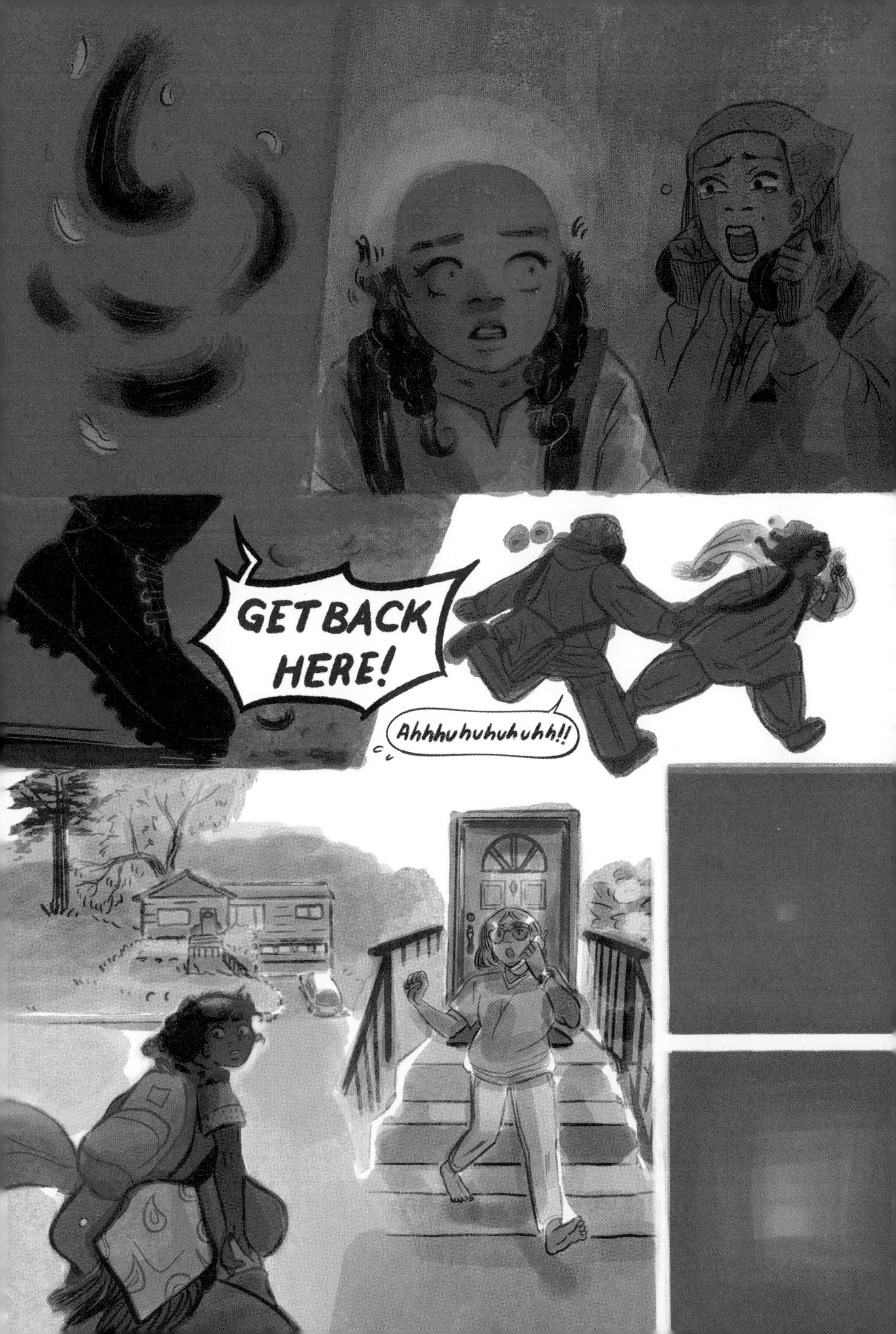
GET BACK HERE!
Ahhhuhuhuhuhh!!

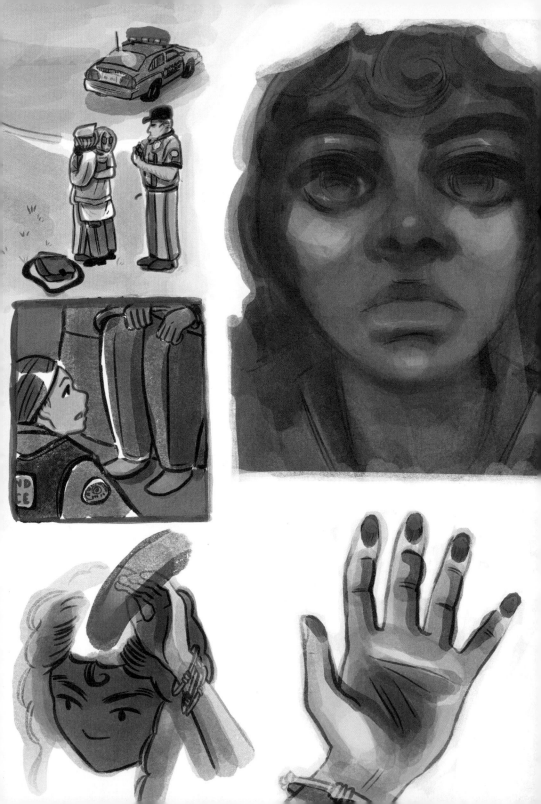

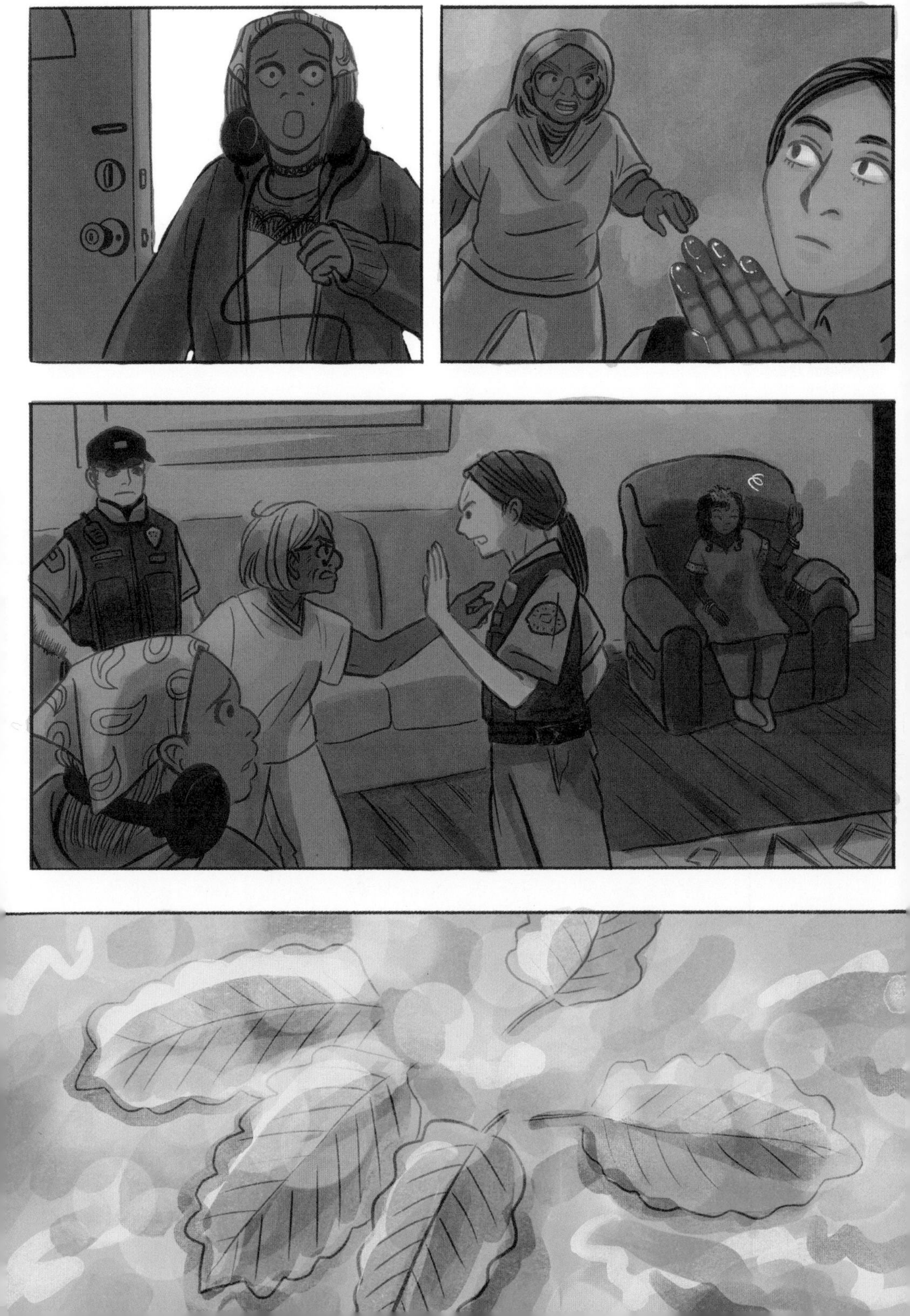

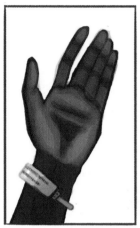

It's going to be very important moving forward that they both receive therapy ... otherwise they will start to exhibit trauma symptoms and may develop PTSD ...

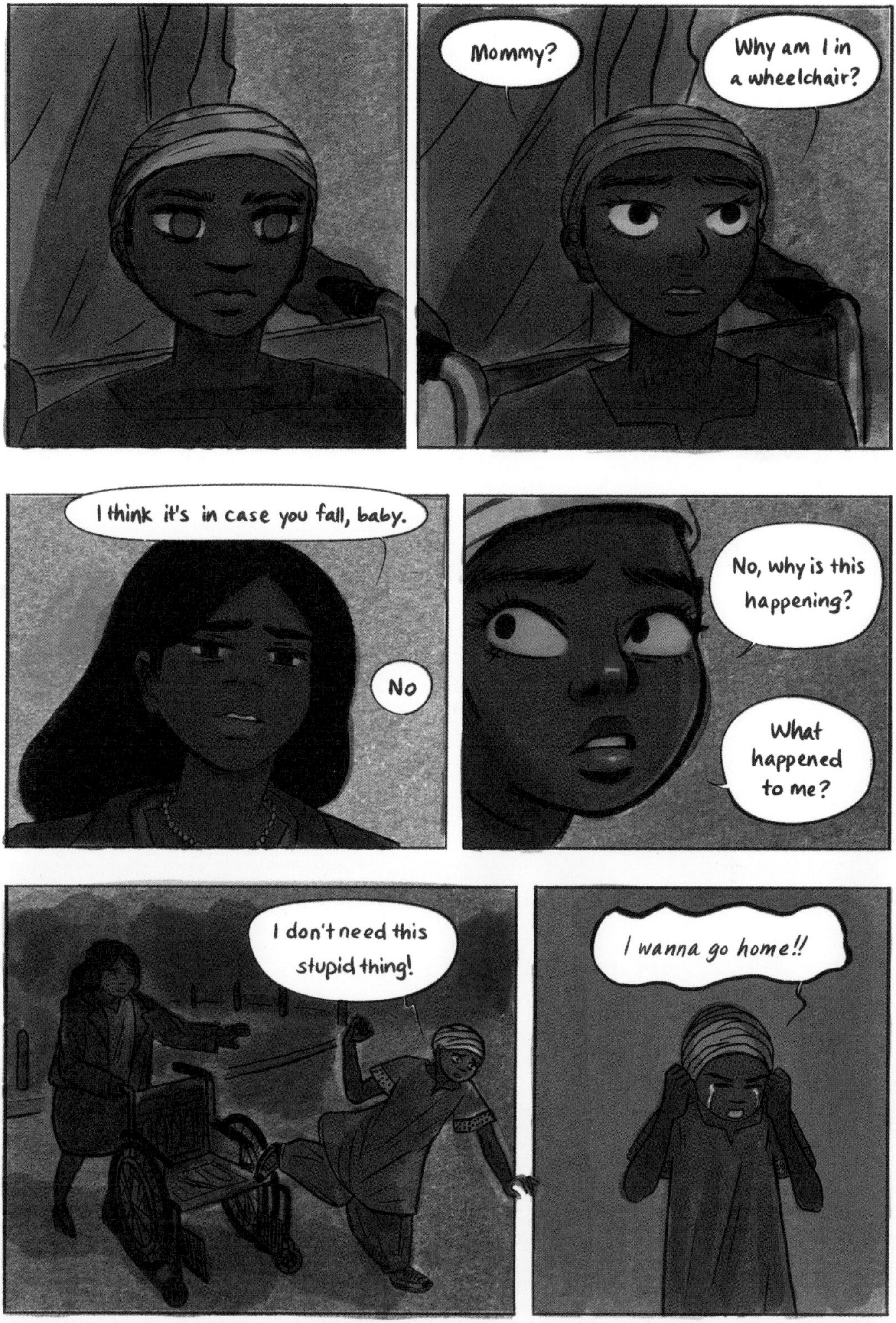
Mommy?
Why am I in a wheelchair?
I think it's in case you fall, baby.
No
No, why is this happening?
What happened to me?
I don't need this stupid thing!
I wanna go home!!

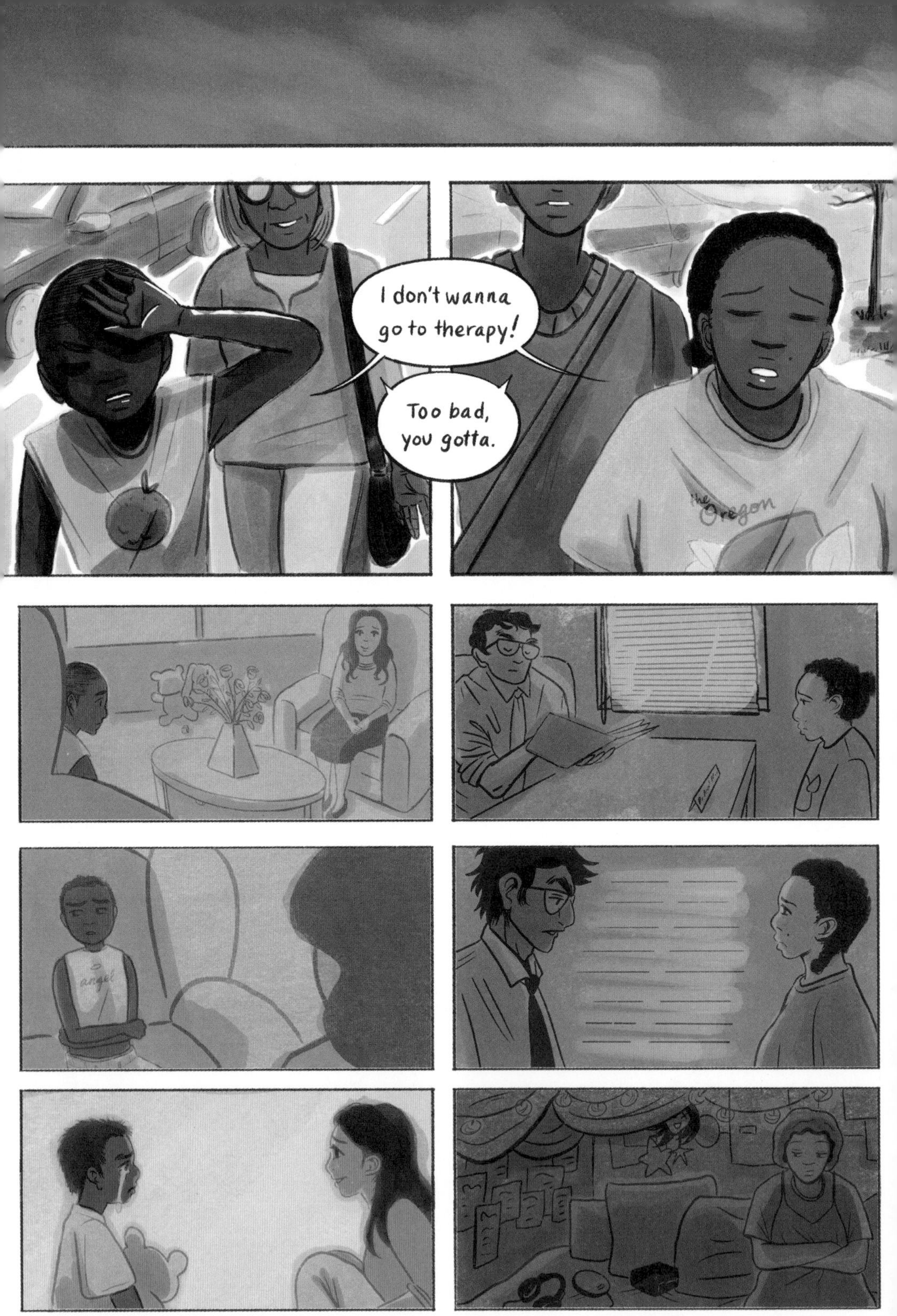
I don't wanna go to therapy!
Too bad, you gotta.

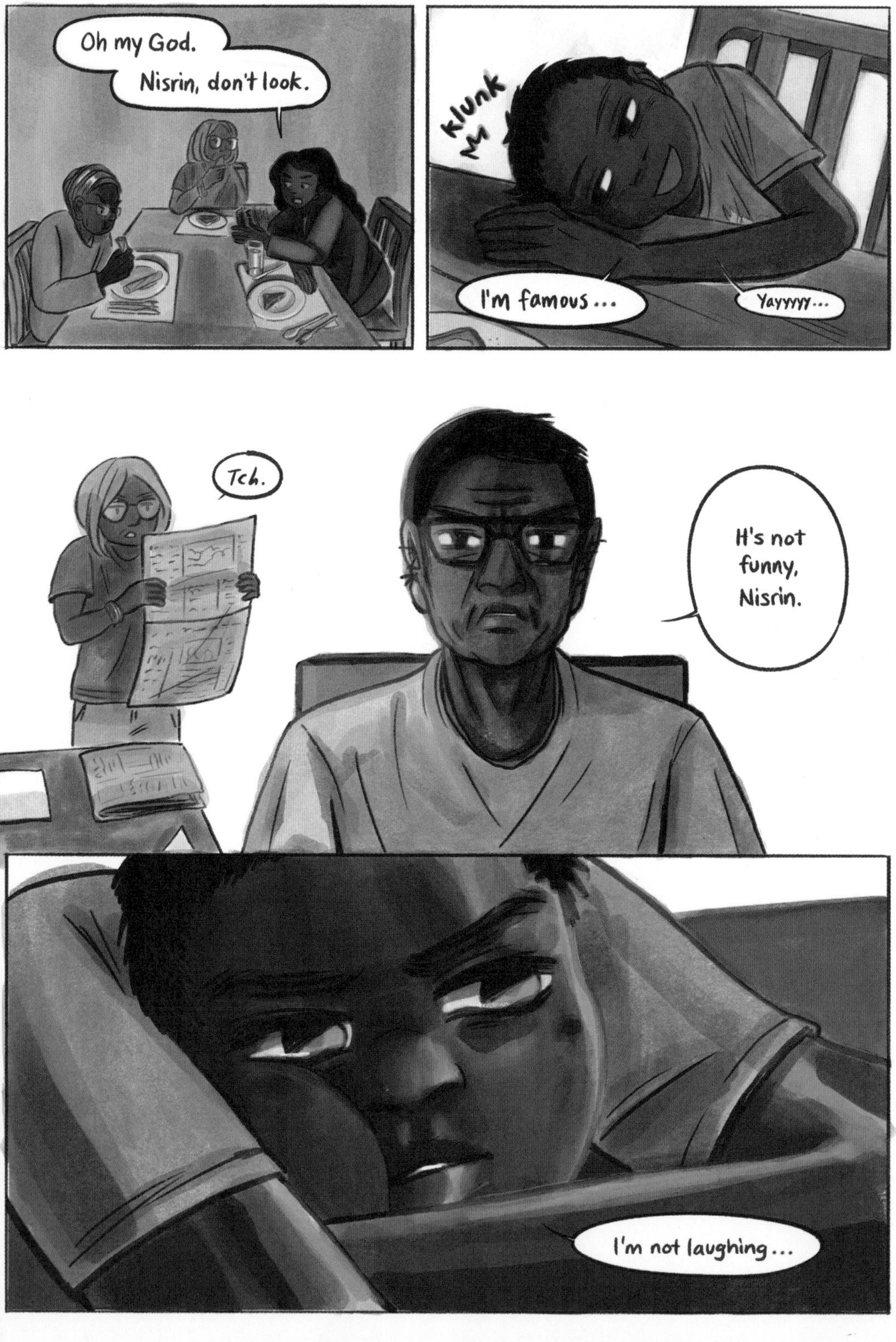
Oh my God.
Nisrin, don't look.
klunk
I'm famous...
Yayyyyy...
Tch.
It's not funny, Nisrin.
I'm not laughing...

You've made a lot of progress! I think we should focus on lowering your agoraphobia symptoms, so you can start the new school year on time.

Okay.

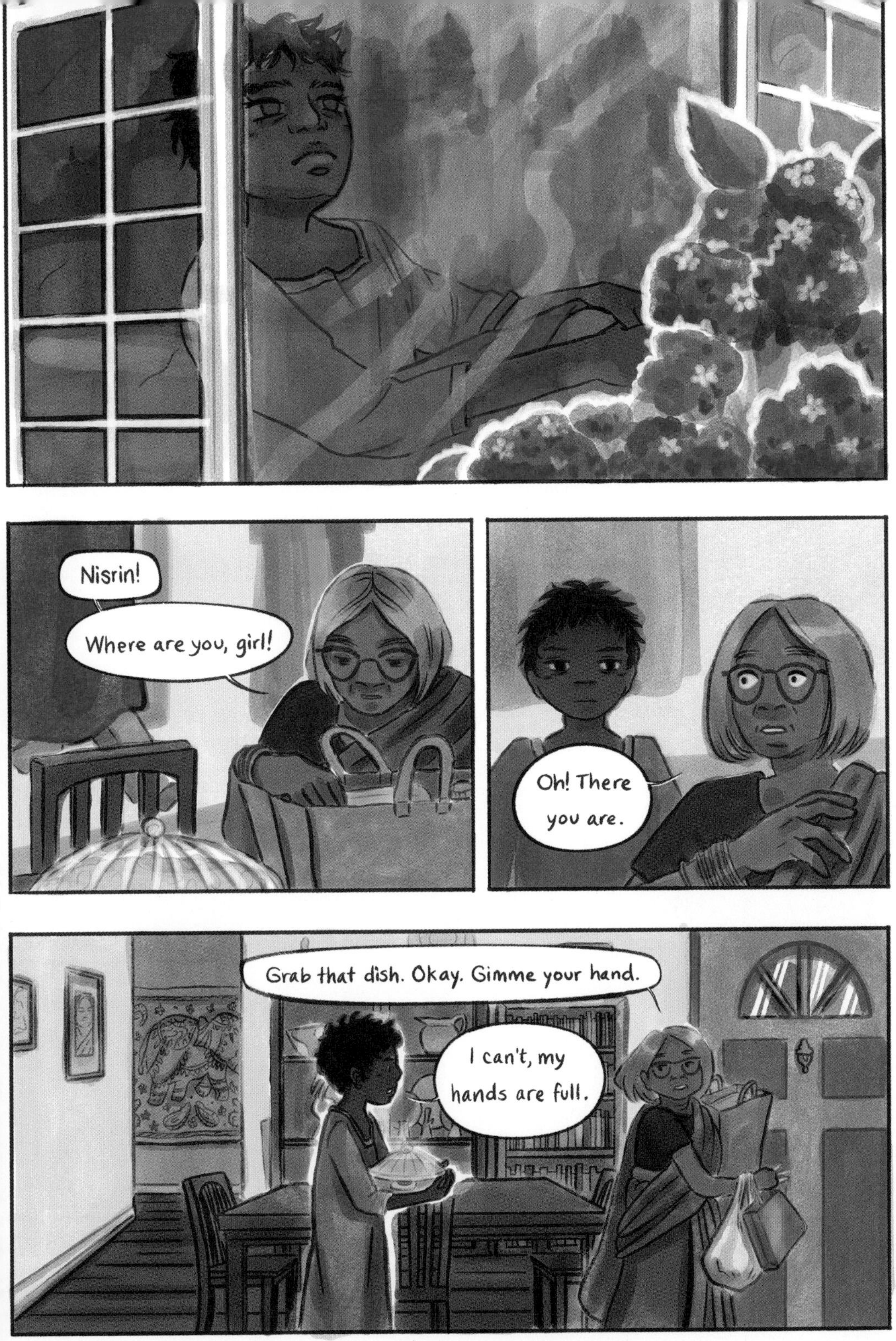
Nisrin!
Where are you, girl!
Oh! There you are.
Grab that dish. Okay. Gimme your hand.
I can't, my hands are full.

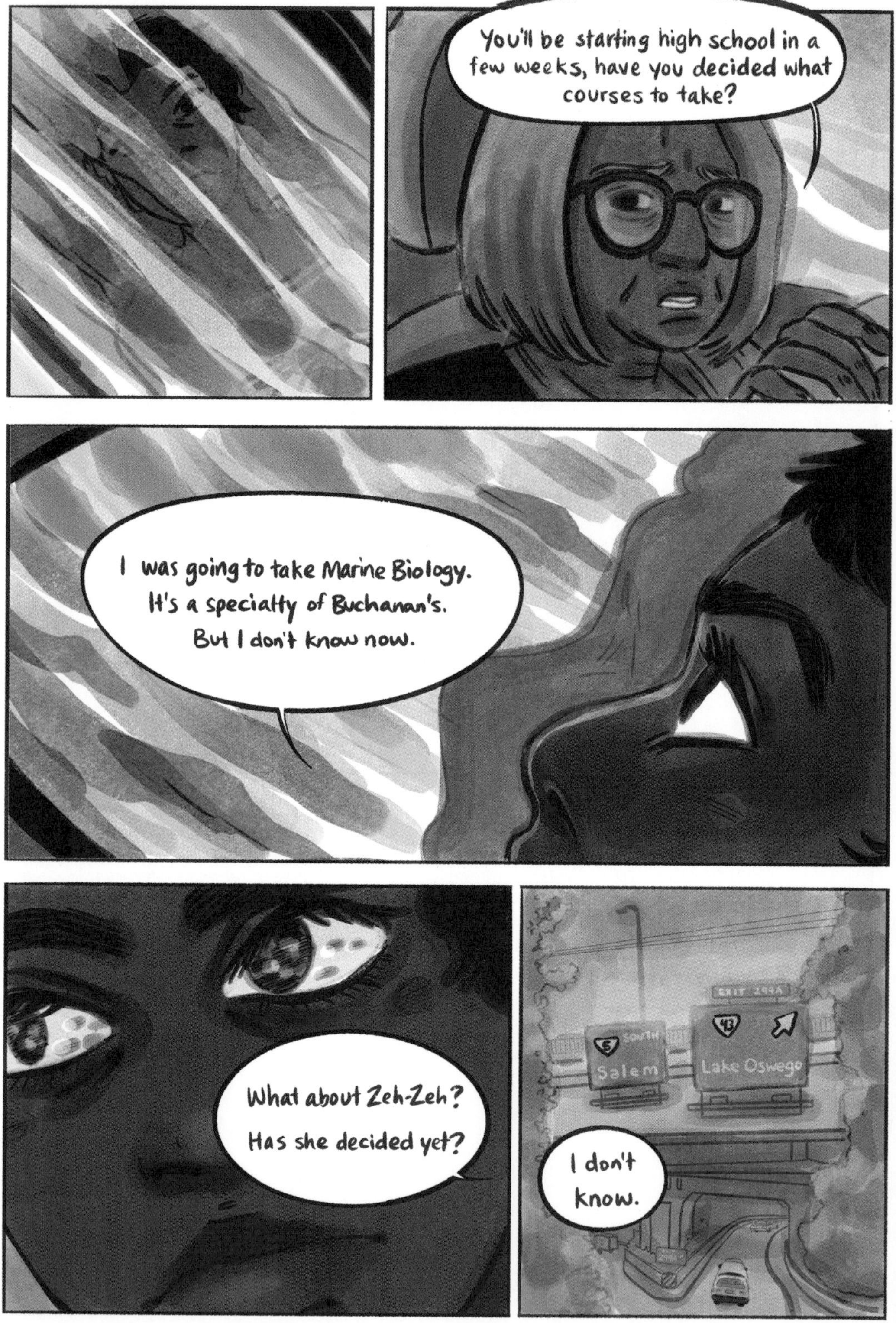
You'll be starting high school in a few weeks, have you decided what courses to take?
I was going to take Marine Biology. It's a specialty of Buchanan's. But I don't know now.
What about Zeh-Zeh? Has she decided yet?
EXIT 299A
5 SOUTH
Salem
43
Lake Oswego
I don't know.

*Poroma, grab that dish from Nisrin quickly please, so she can help me.

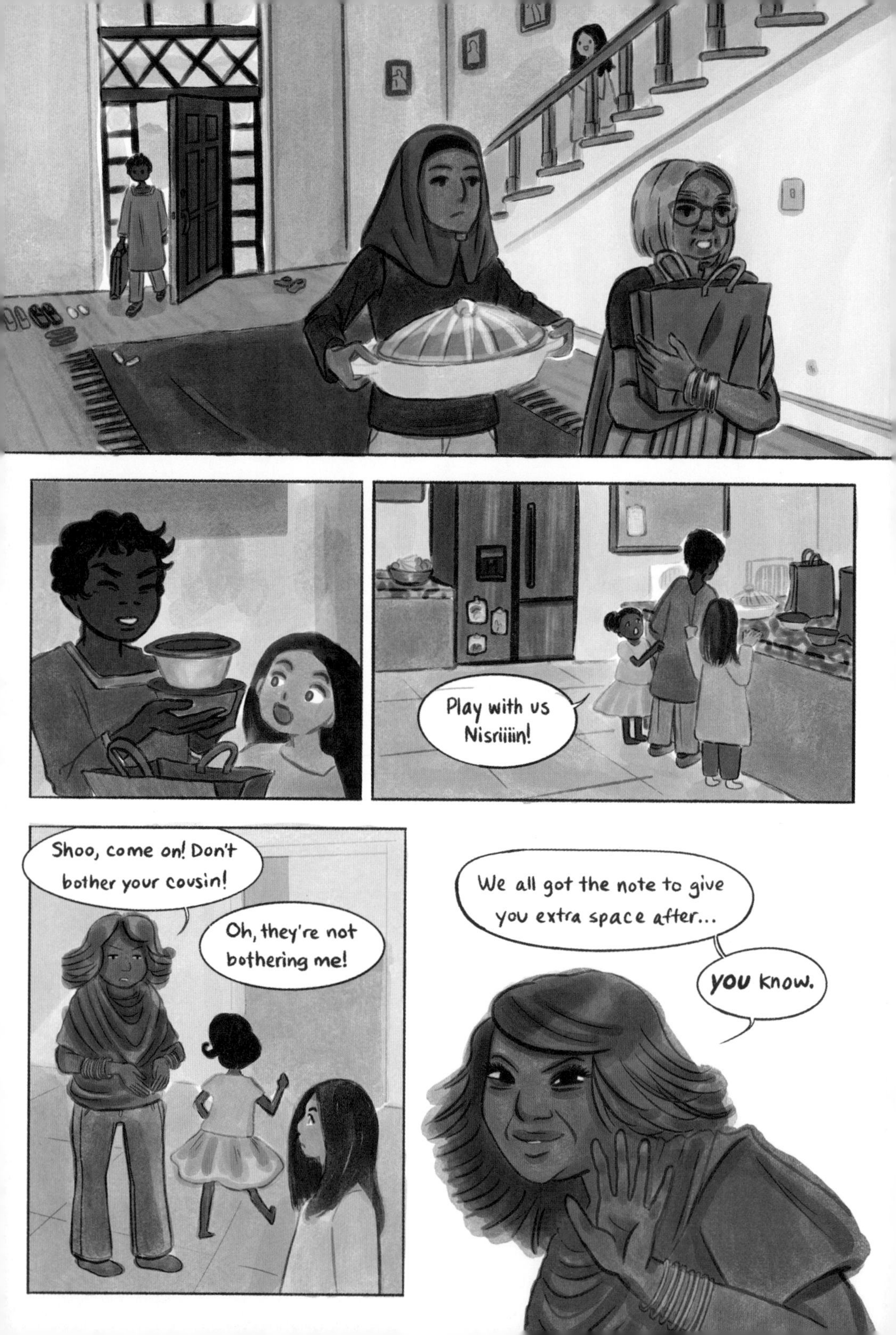
Play with us Nisriiiin!
Shoo, come on! Don't bother your cousin!
Oh, they're not bothering me!
We all got the note to give you extra space after...
YOU know.

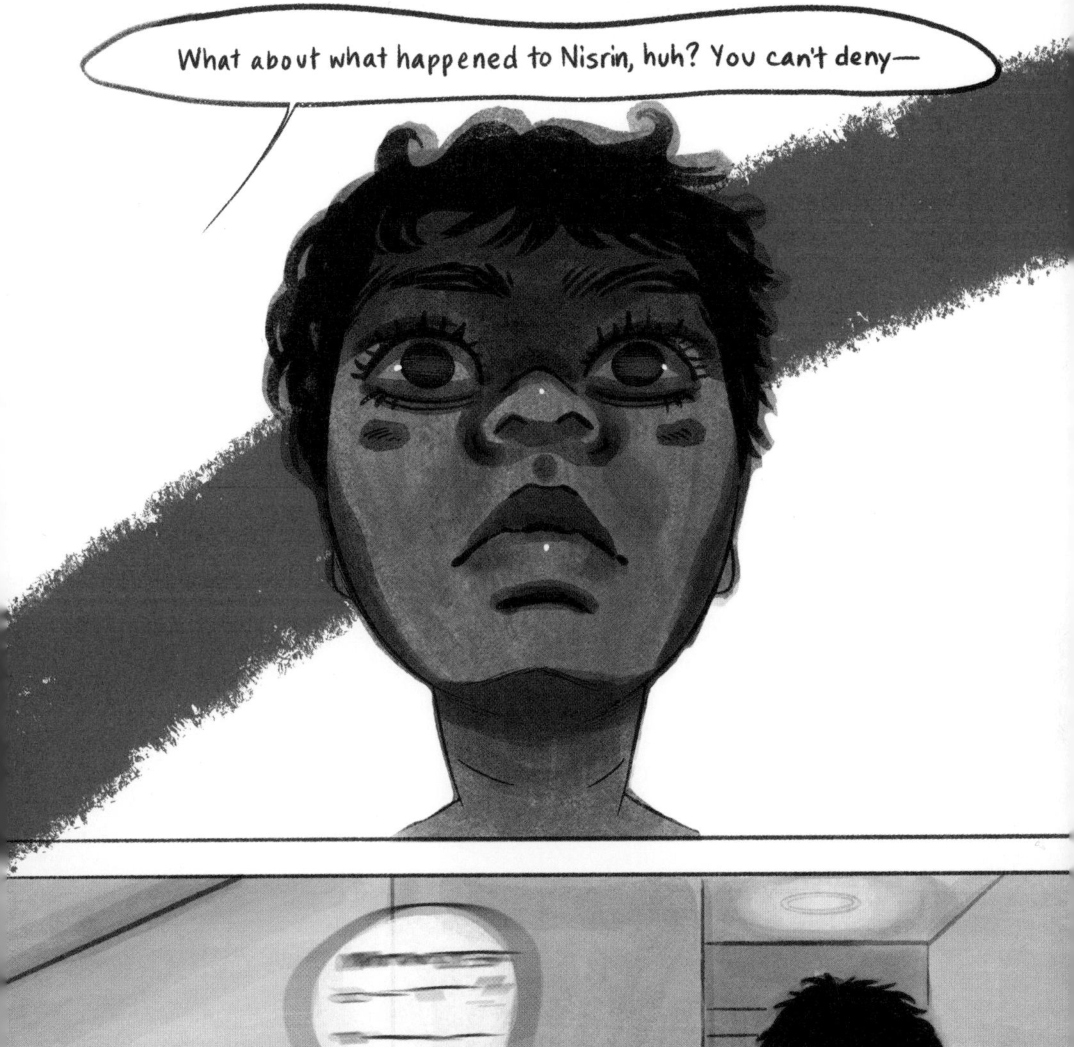
What about what happened to Nisrin, huh? You can't deny—

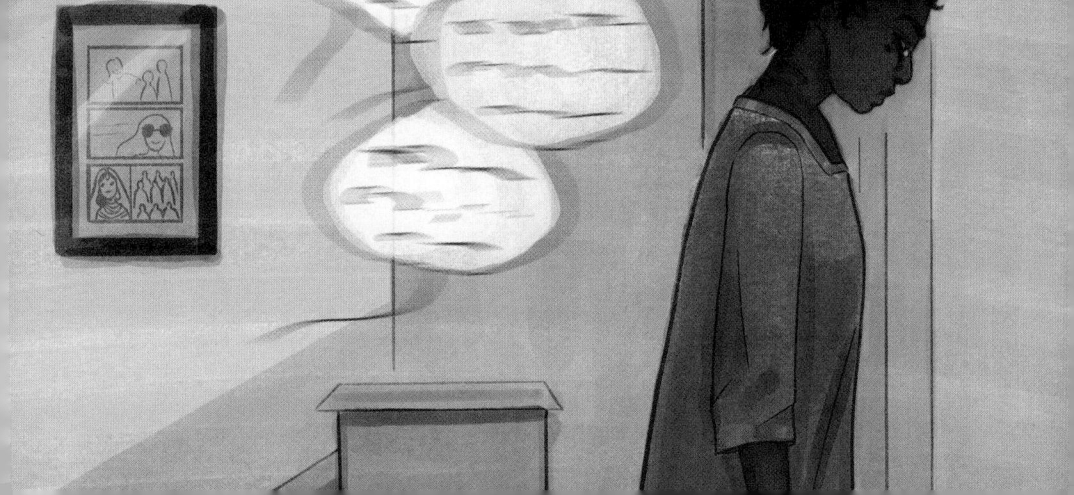

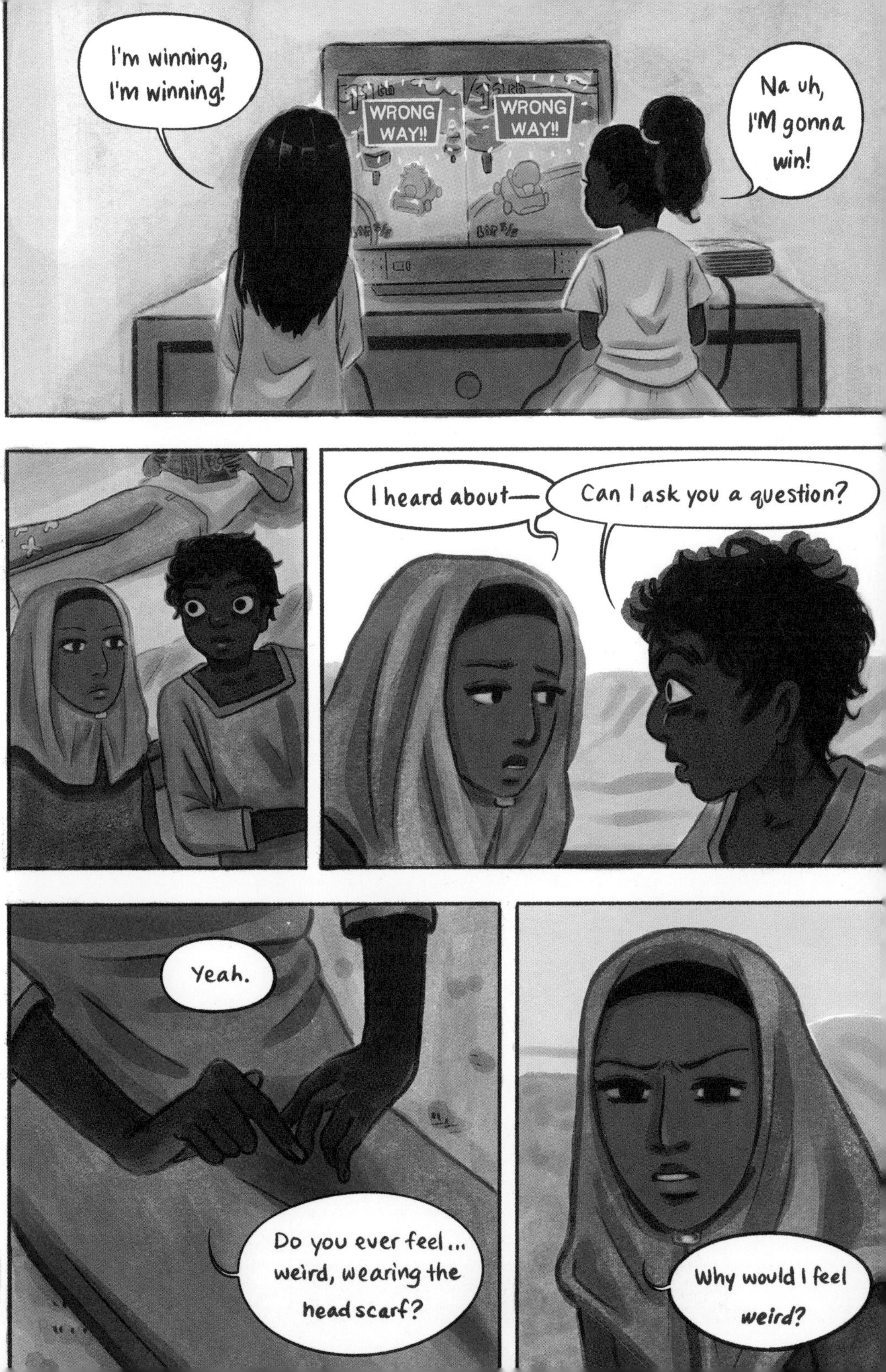
I'm winning, I'm winning!
WRONG WAY!!
WRONG WAY!!
Na uh, I'M gonna win!
I heard about—
Can I ask you a question?
Yeah.
Do you ever feel... weird, wearing the headscarf?
Why would I feel weird?

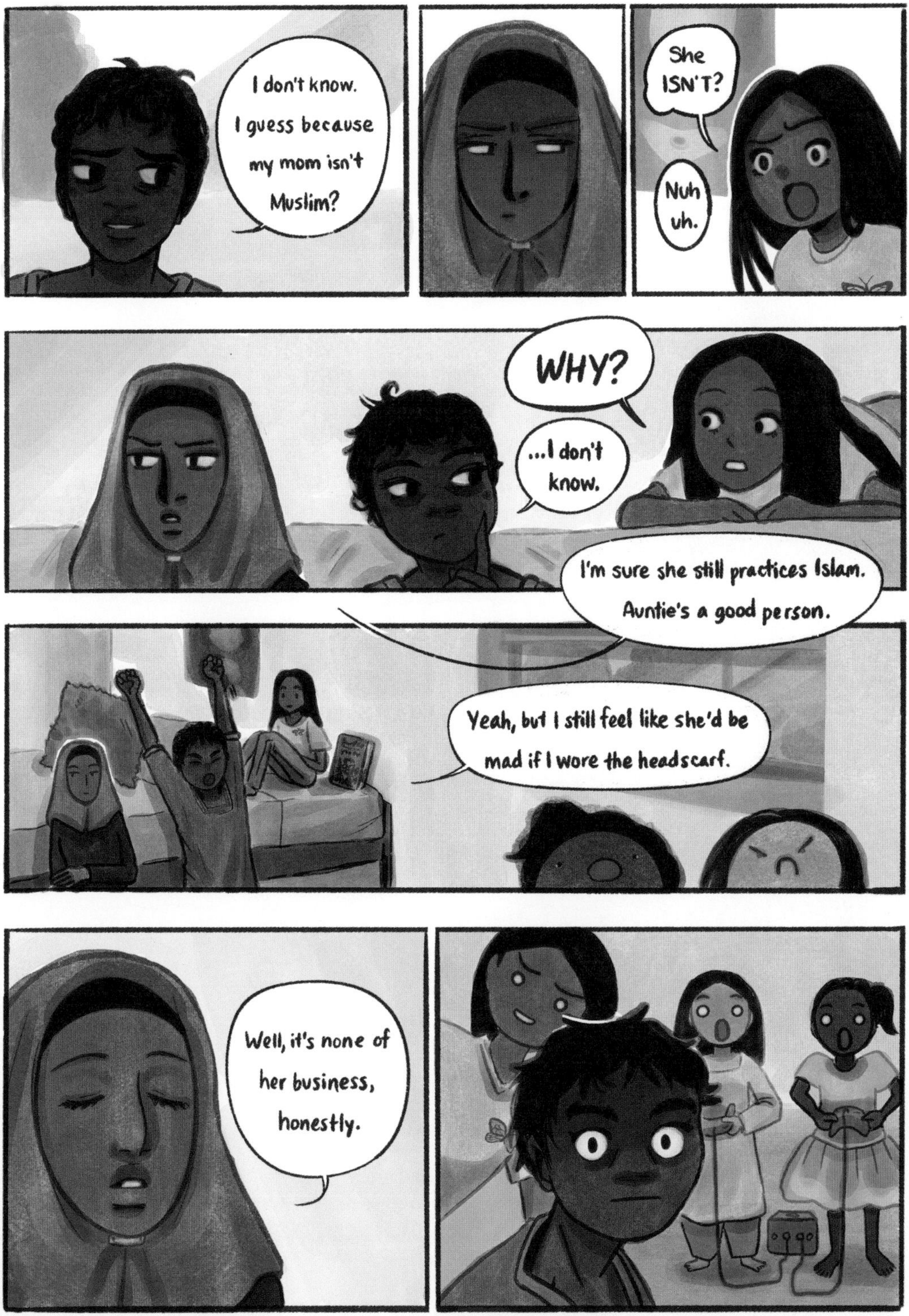
I don't know. I guess because my mom isn't Muslim?
She ISN'T?
Nuh uh.
WHY?
...I don't know.
I'm sure she still practices Islam. Auntie's a good person.
Yeah, but I still feel like she'd be mad if I wore the headscarf.
Well, it's none of her business, honestly.

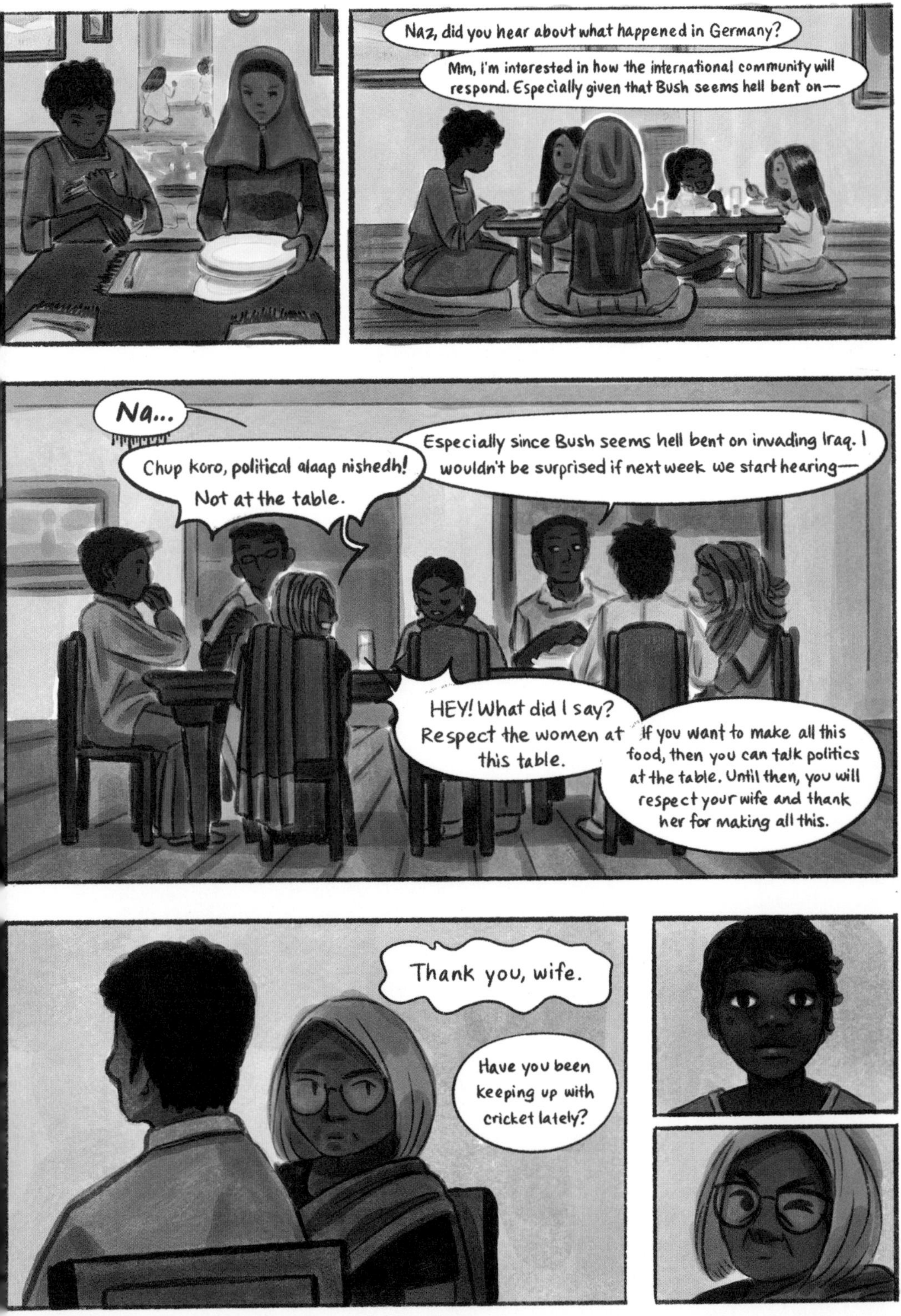
Naz, did you hear about what happened in Germany?
Mm, I'm interested in how the international community will respond. Especially given that Bush seems hell bent on—
Na...
Chup koro, political alaap nishedh! Not at the table.
Especially since Bush seems hell bent on invading Iraq. I wouldn't be surprised if next week we start hearing—
HEY! What did I say? Respect the women at this table.
If you want to make all this food, then you can talk politics at the table. Until then, you will respect your wife and thank her for making all this.
Thank you, wife.
Have you been keeping up with cricket lately?

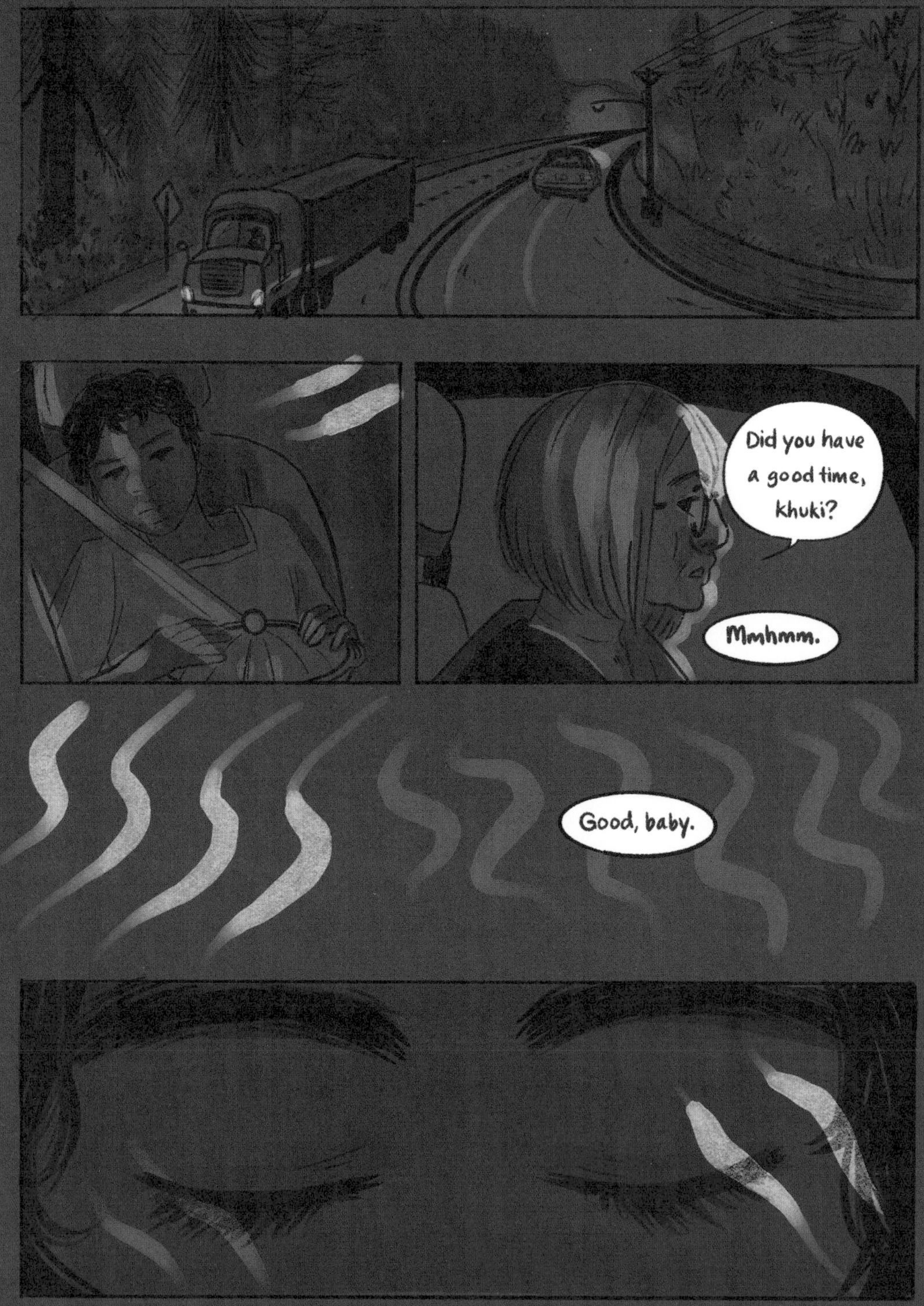
Did you have a good time, khuki?
Mmhmm.
Good, baby.

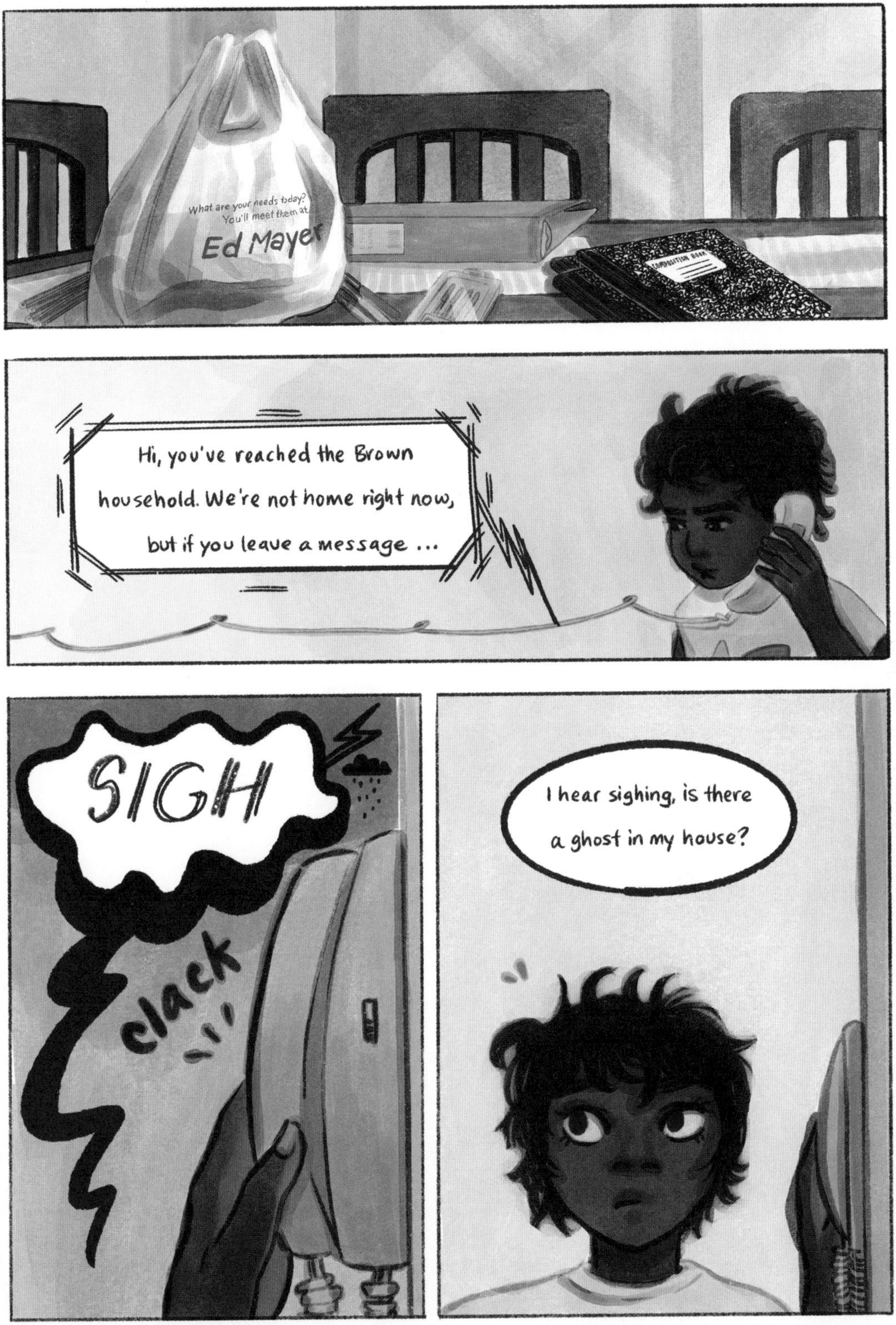
What are your needs today?
You'll meet them at
Ed Mayer
COMPOSITION BOOK
Hi, you've reached the Brown household. We're not home right now, but if you leave a message ...
SIGH
clack
I hear sighing, is there a ghost in my house?

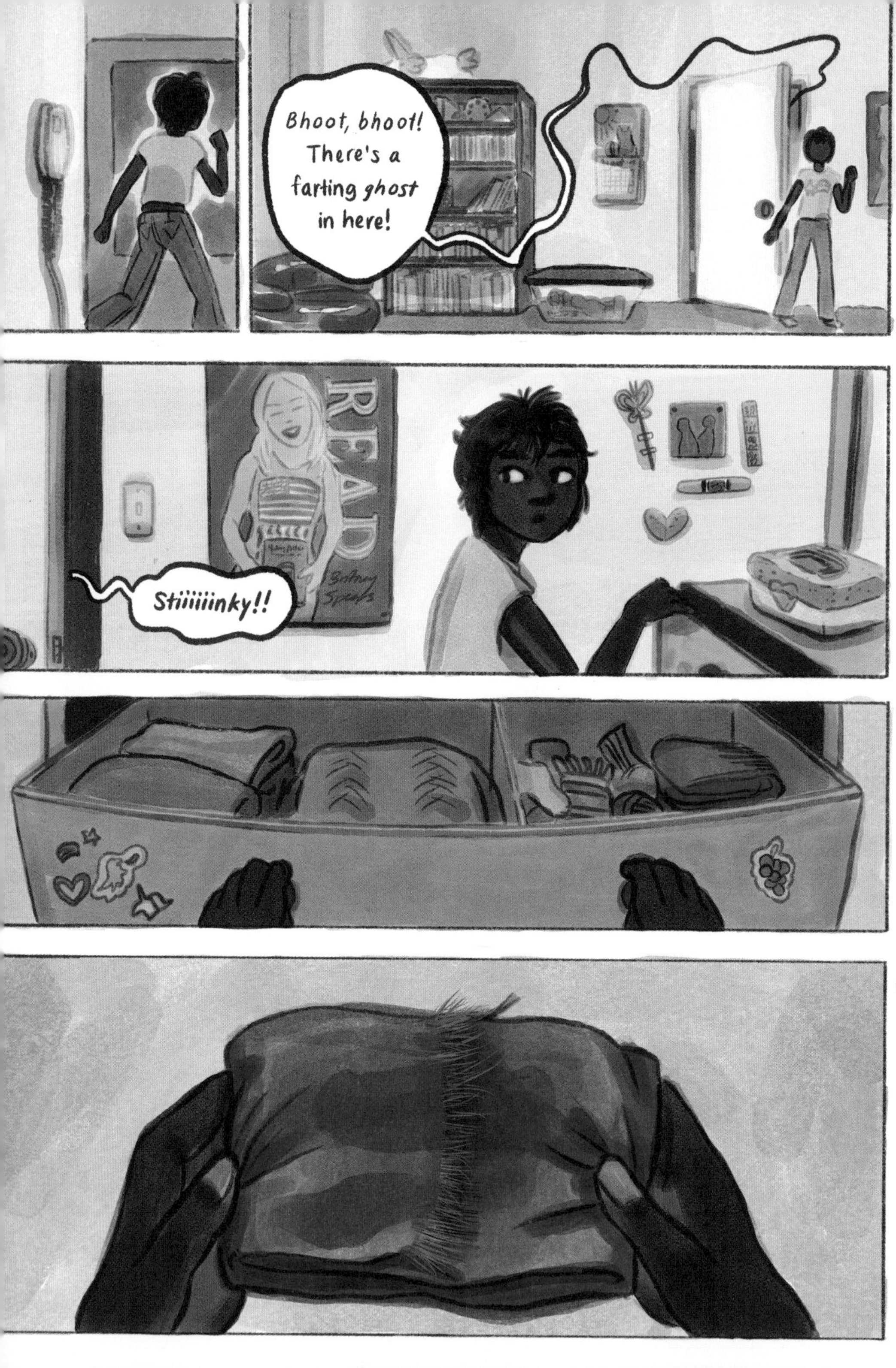
Bhoot, bhoot! There's a farting ghost in here!
READ
Britney Spears
Stiiiiiinky!!

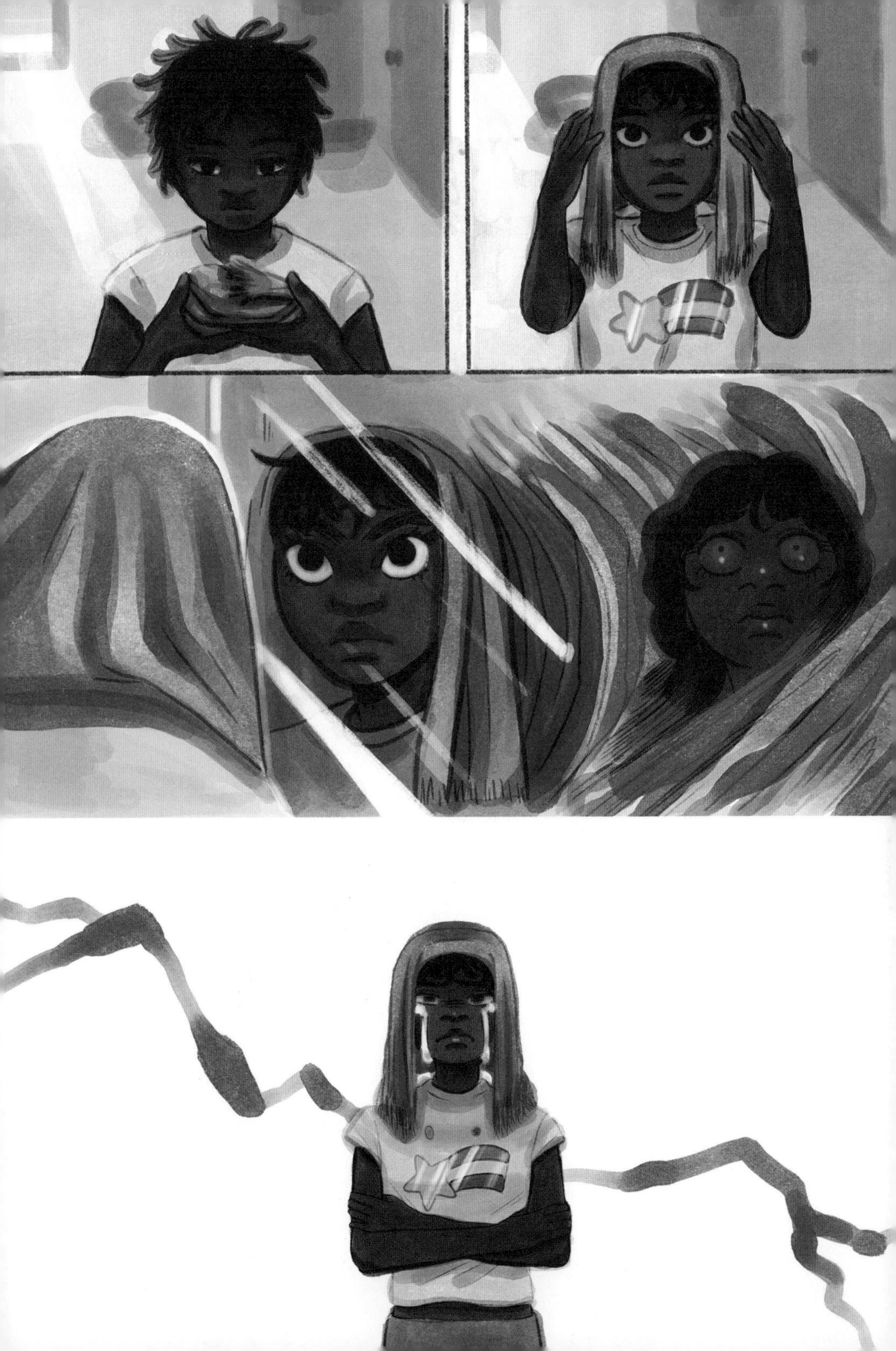

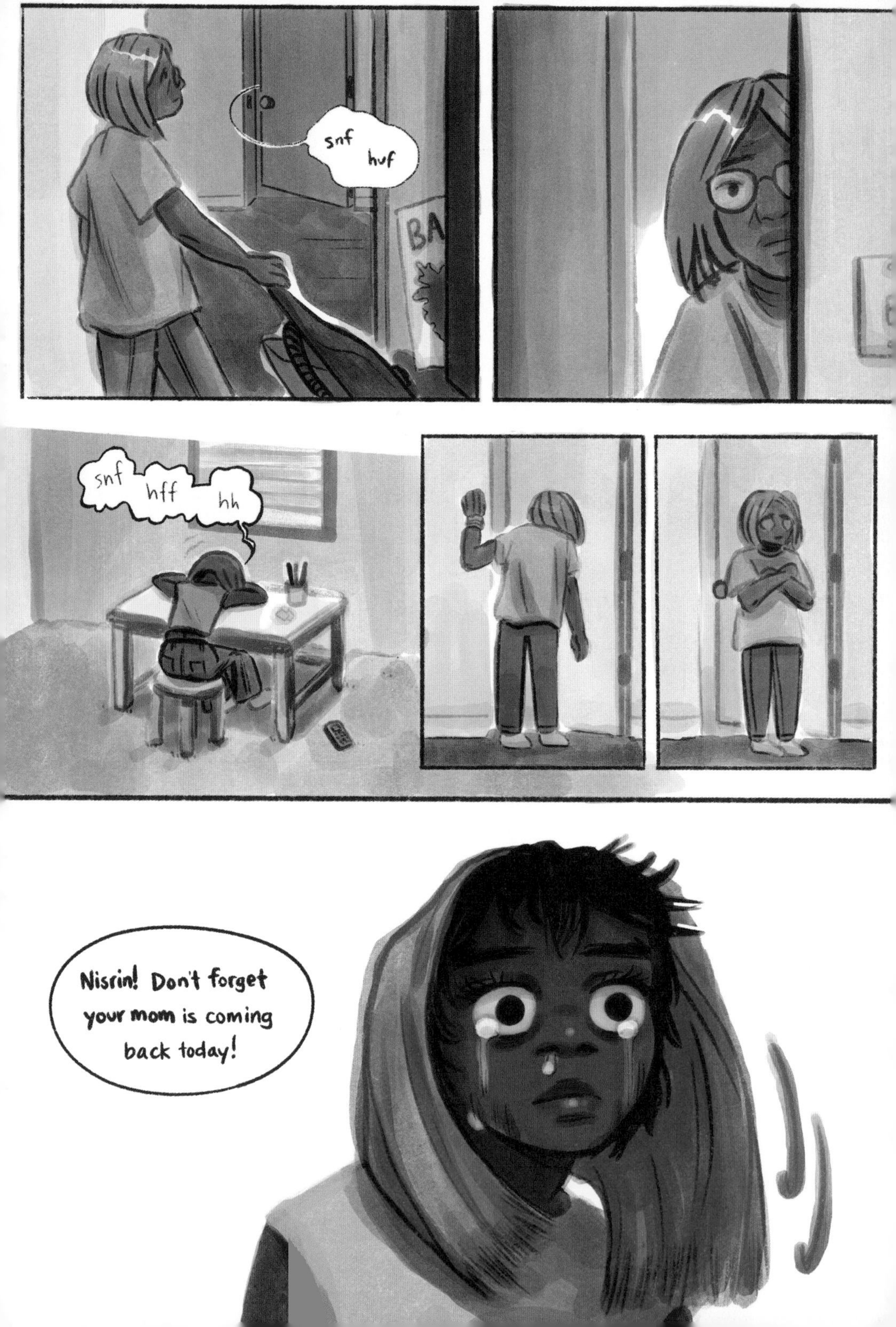
snf
huf
BA
snf
hff
hh
Nisrin! Don't forget your mom is coming back today!

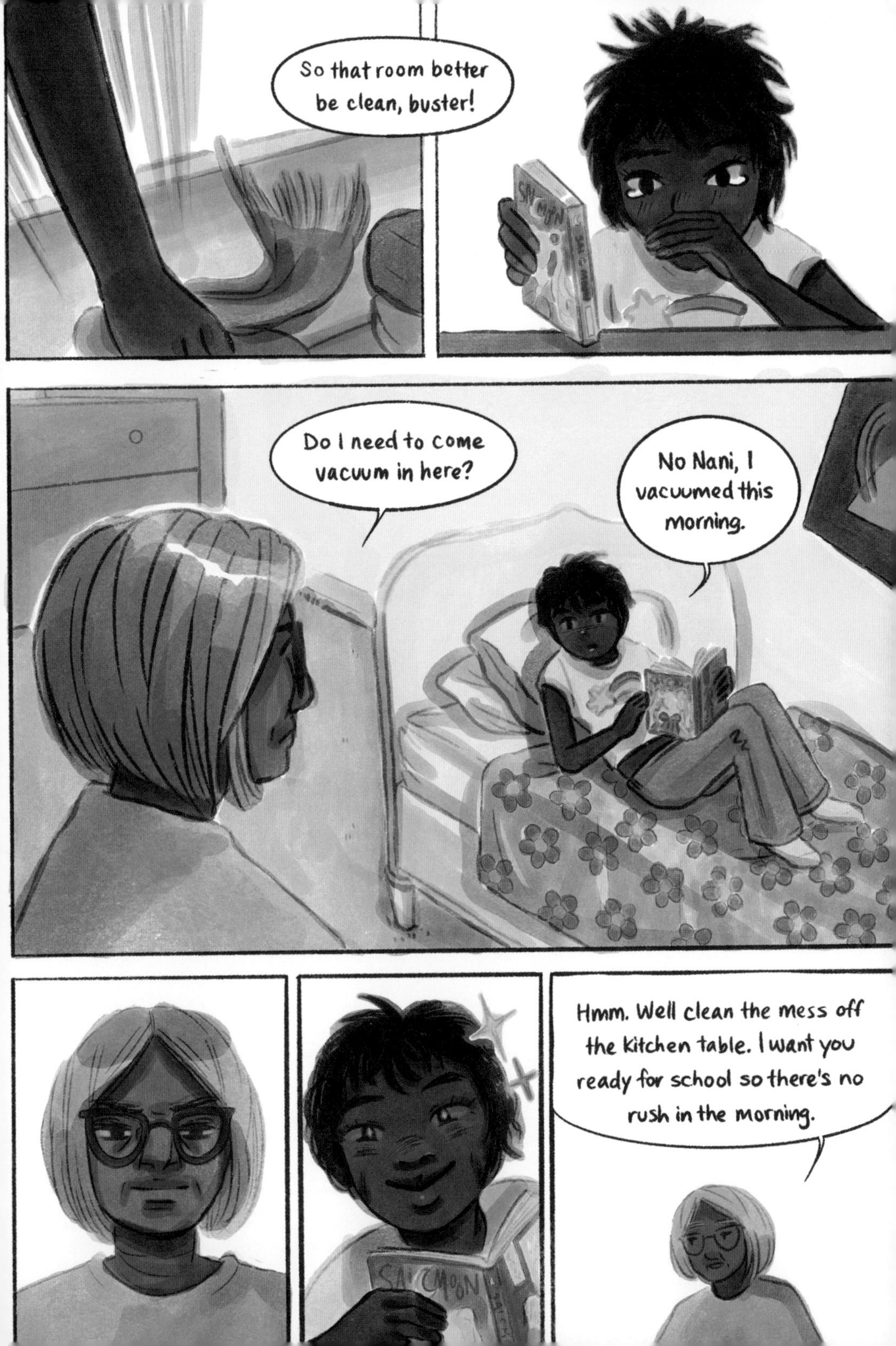
So that room better be clean, buster!
Do I need to come vacuum in here?
No Nani, I vacuumed this morning.
Hmm. Well clean the mess off the kitchen table. I want you ready for school so there's no rush in the morning.

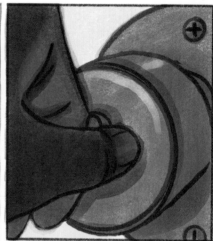

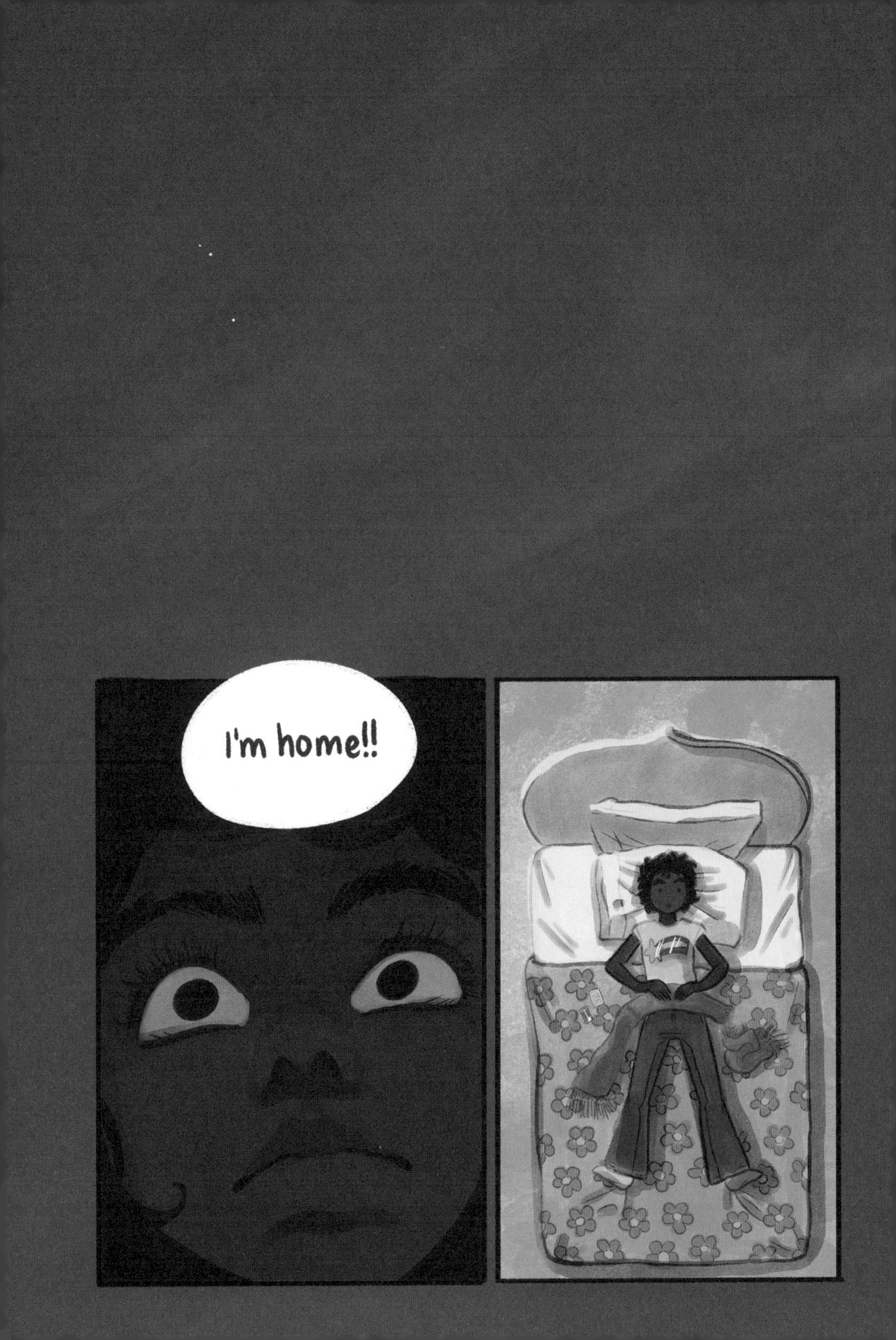
I'm home!!

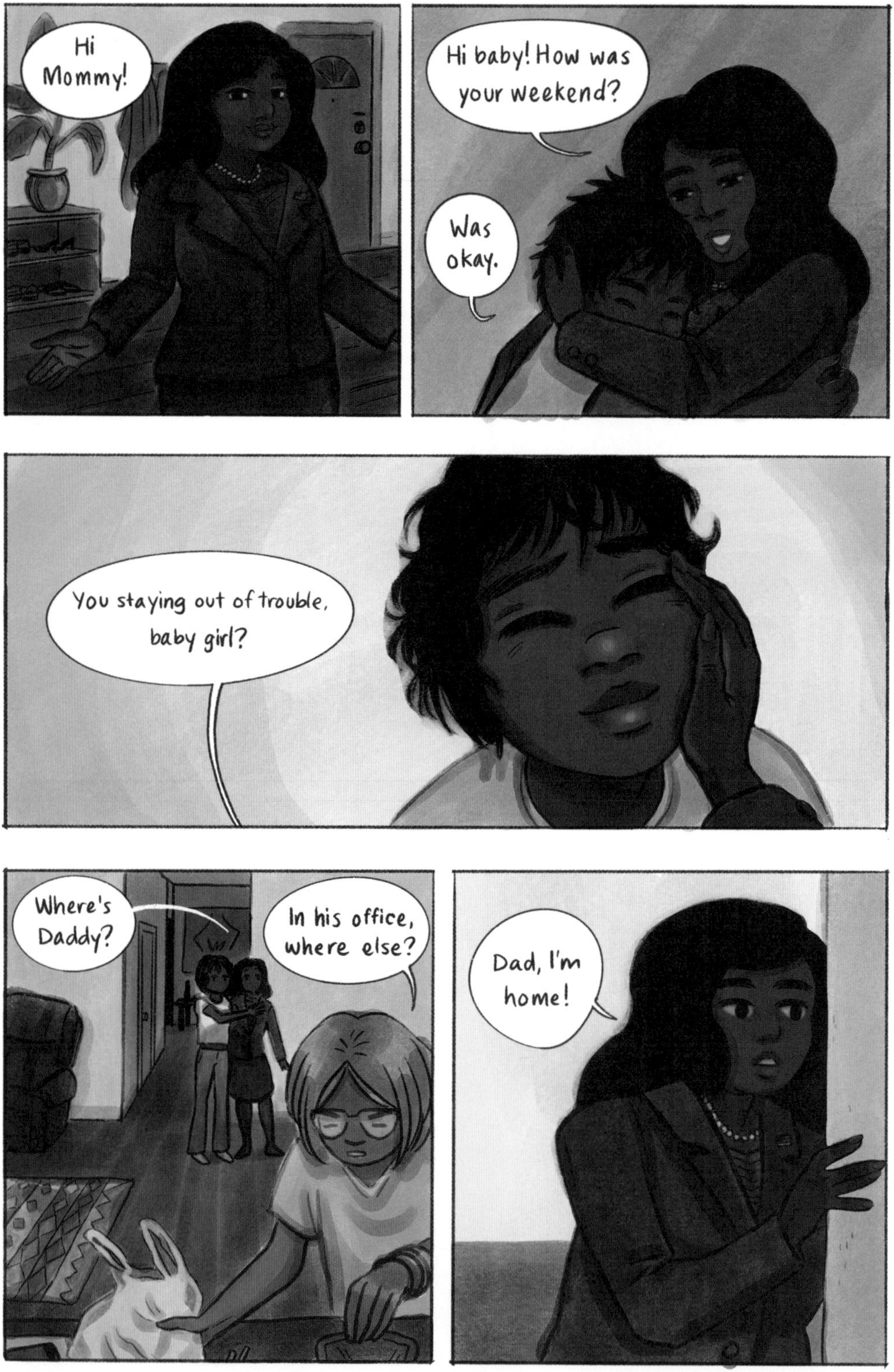
Hi Mommy!
Hi baby! How was your weekend?
Was okay.
You staying out of trouble, baby girl?
Where's Daddy?
In his office, where else?
Dad, I'm home!

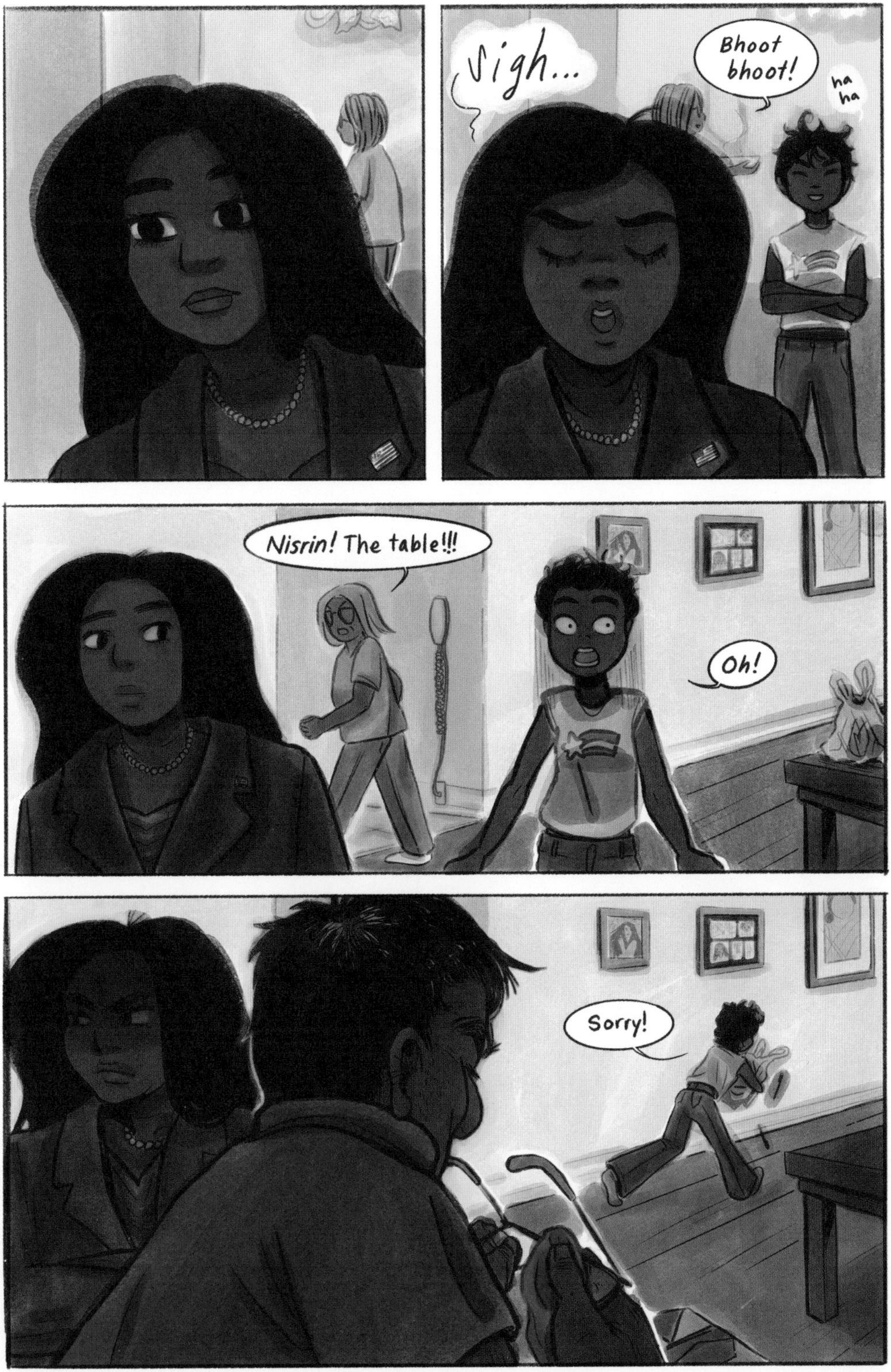
Sigh...
Bhoot bhoot!
ha ha
Nisrin! The table!!!
Oh!
Sorry!

*You were gone for too long. It's bad for Nisrin.

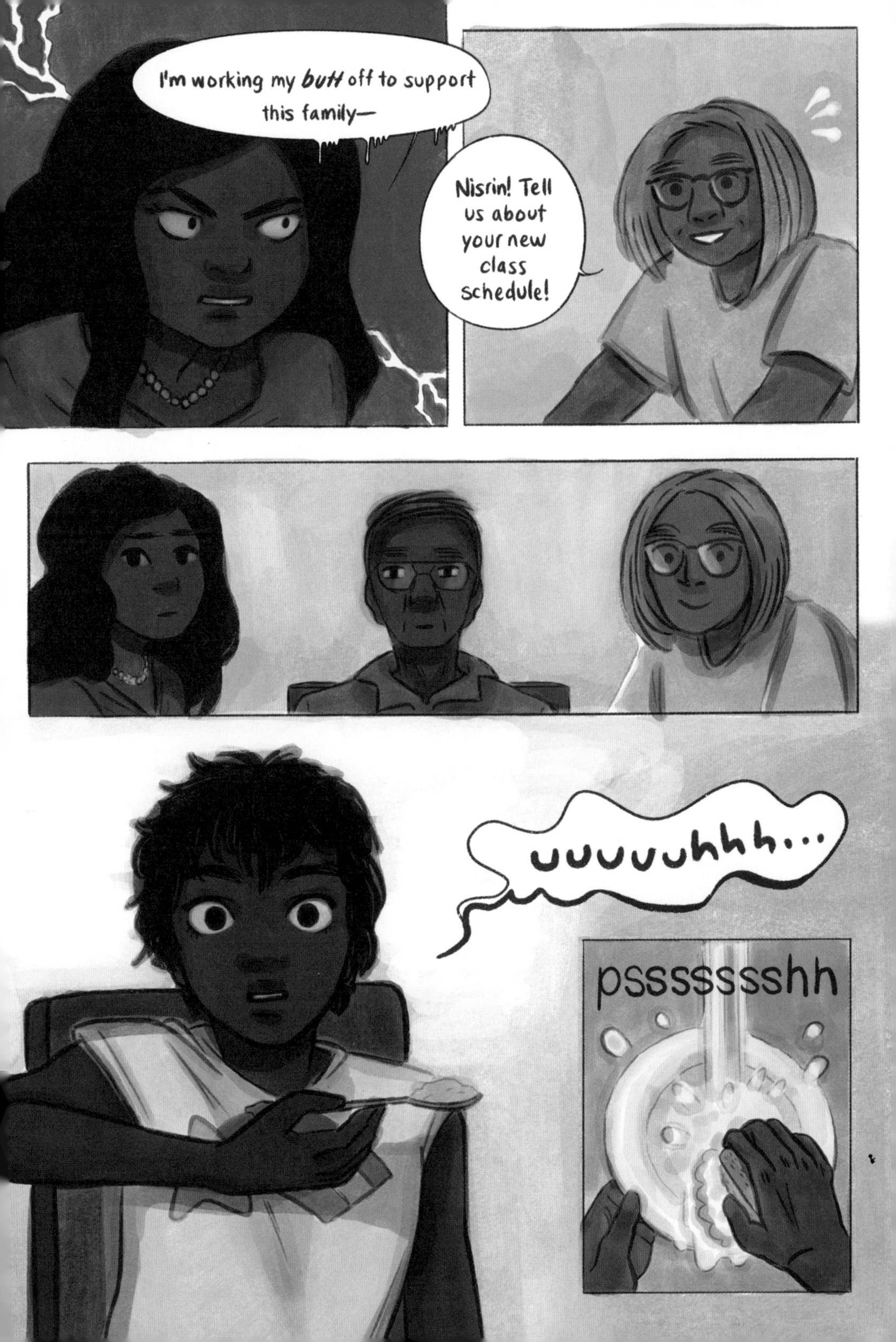
I'm working my *butt* off to support this family—
Nisrin! Tell us about your new class schedule!
uuuuuhhh...
psssssshh

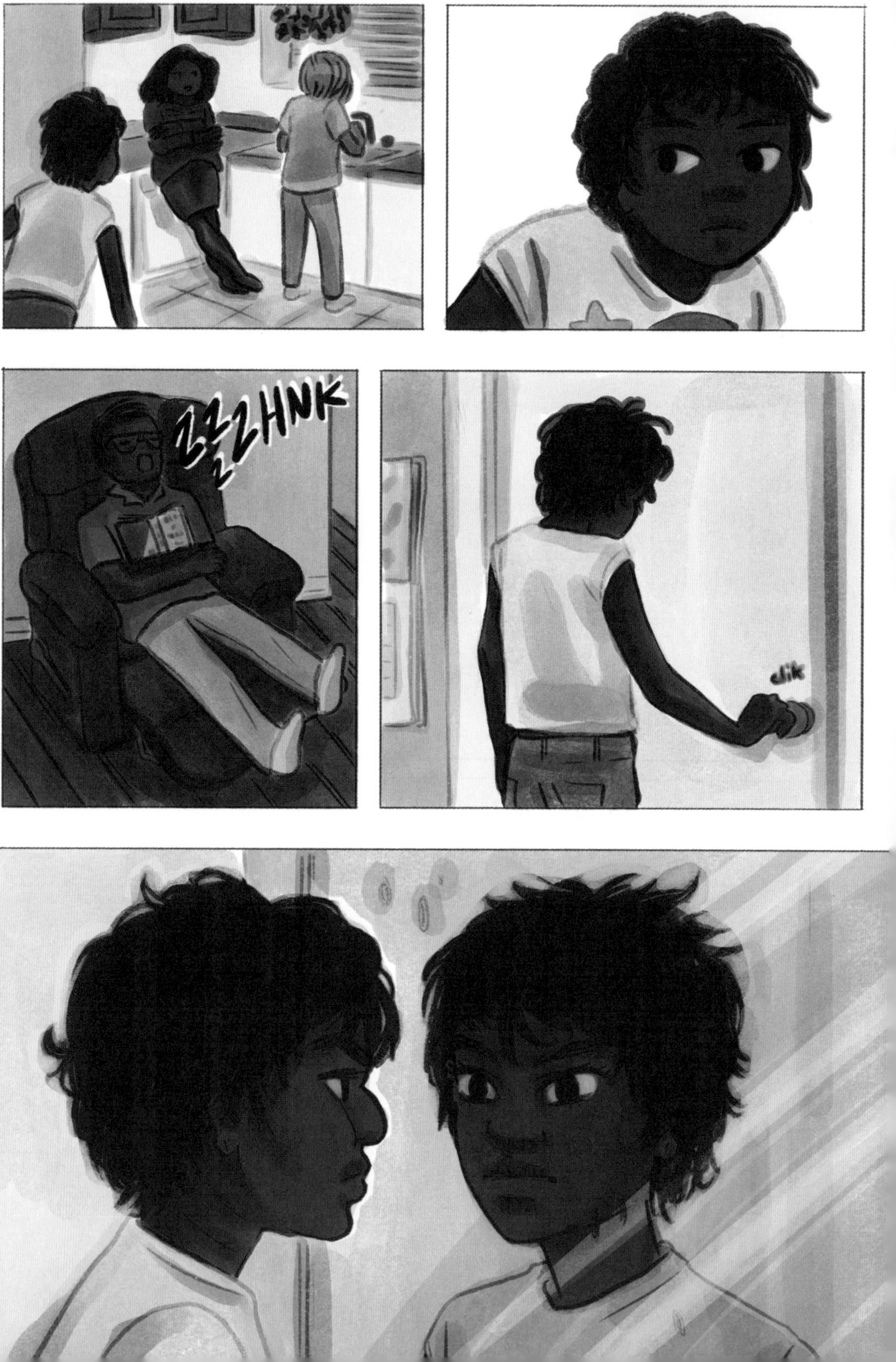
ZZZZHNK
clik

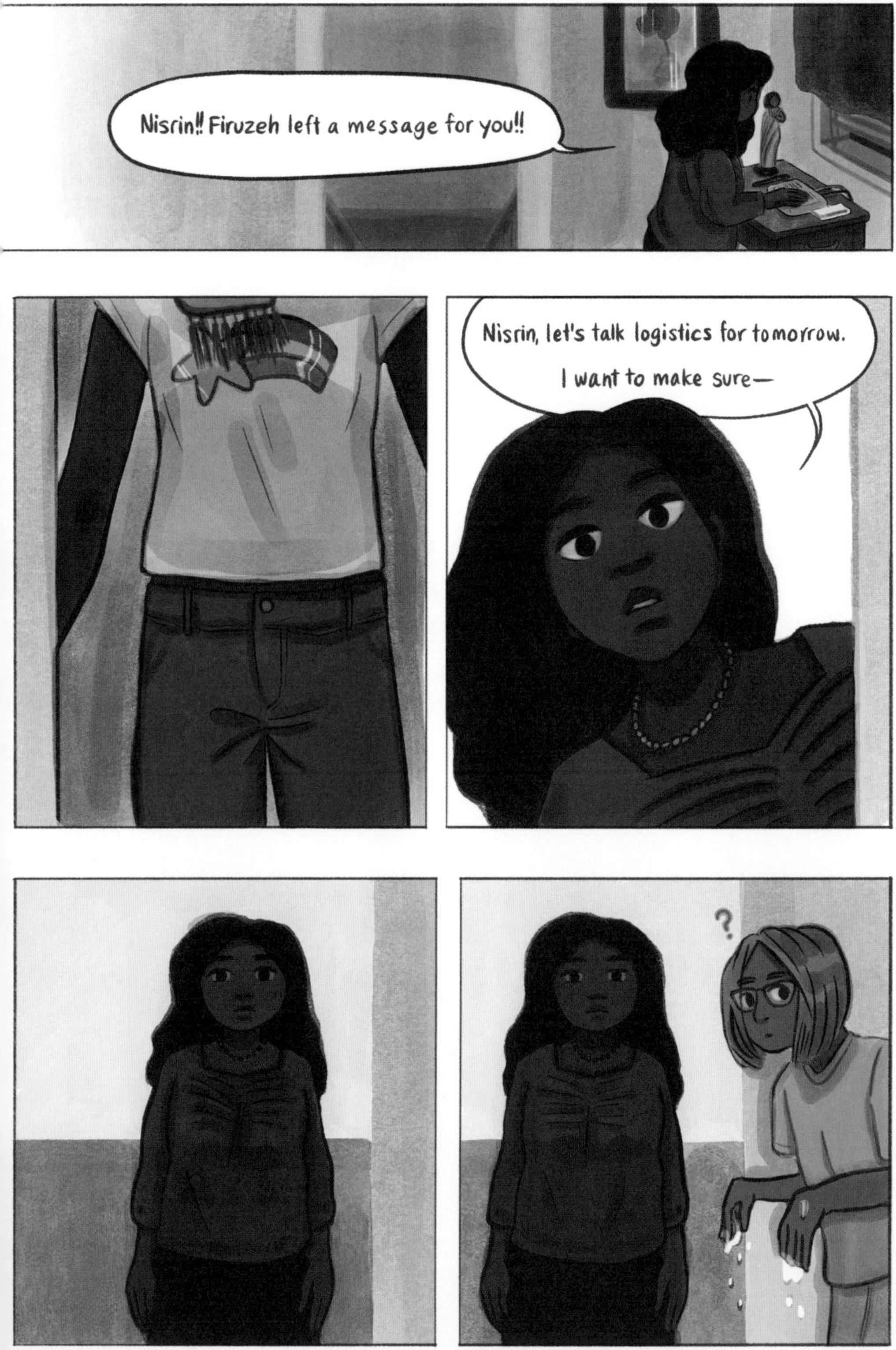
Nisrin!! Firuzeh left a message for you!!
Nisrin, let's talk logistics for tomorrow.
I want to make sure—
?

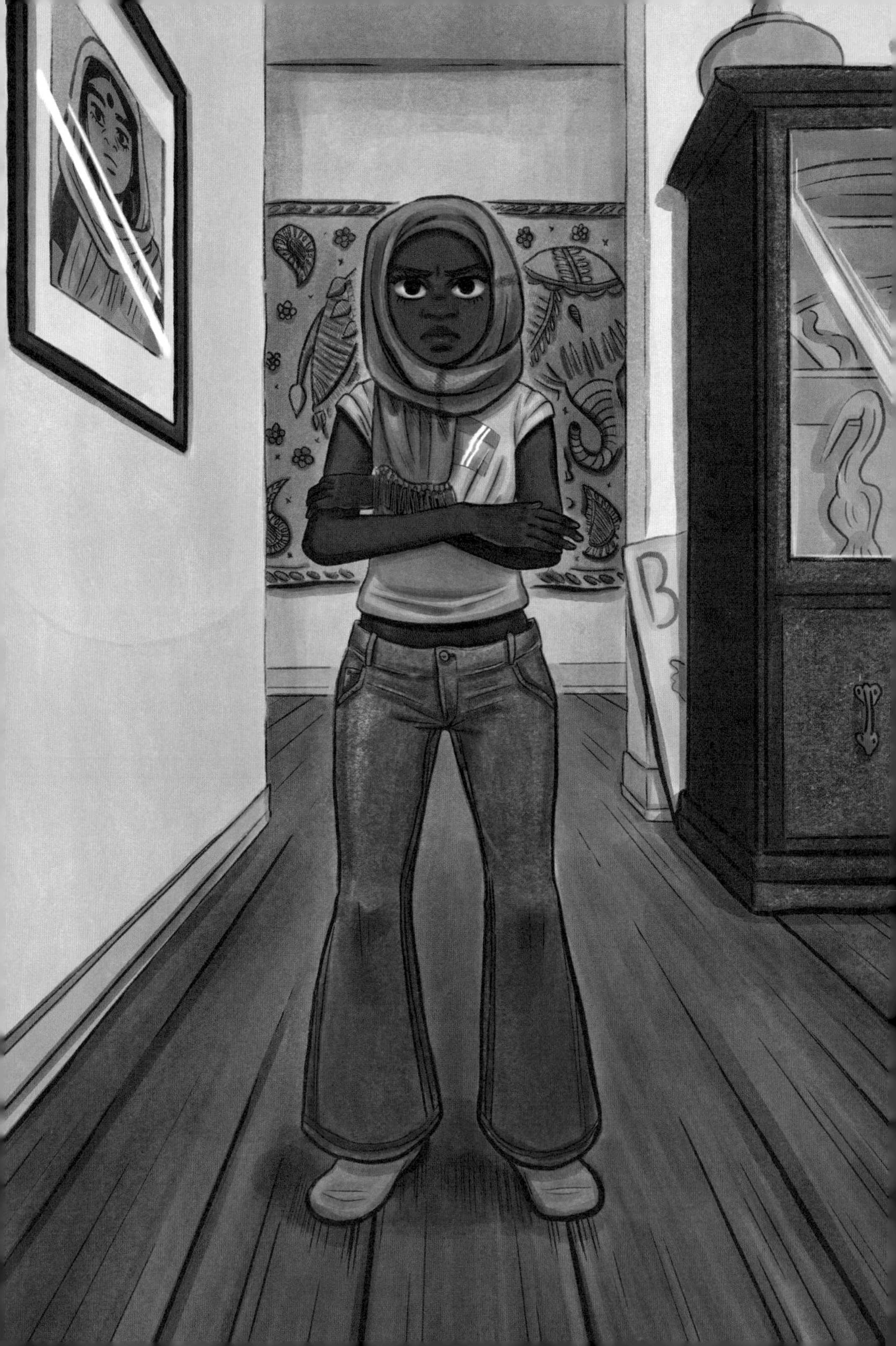
B

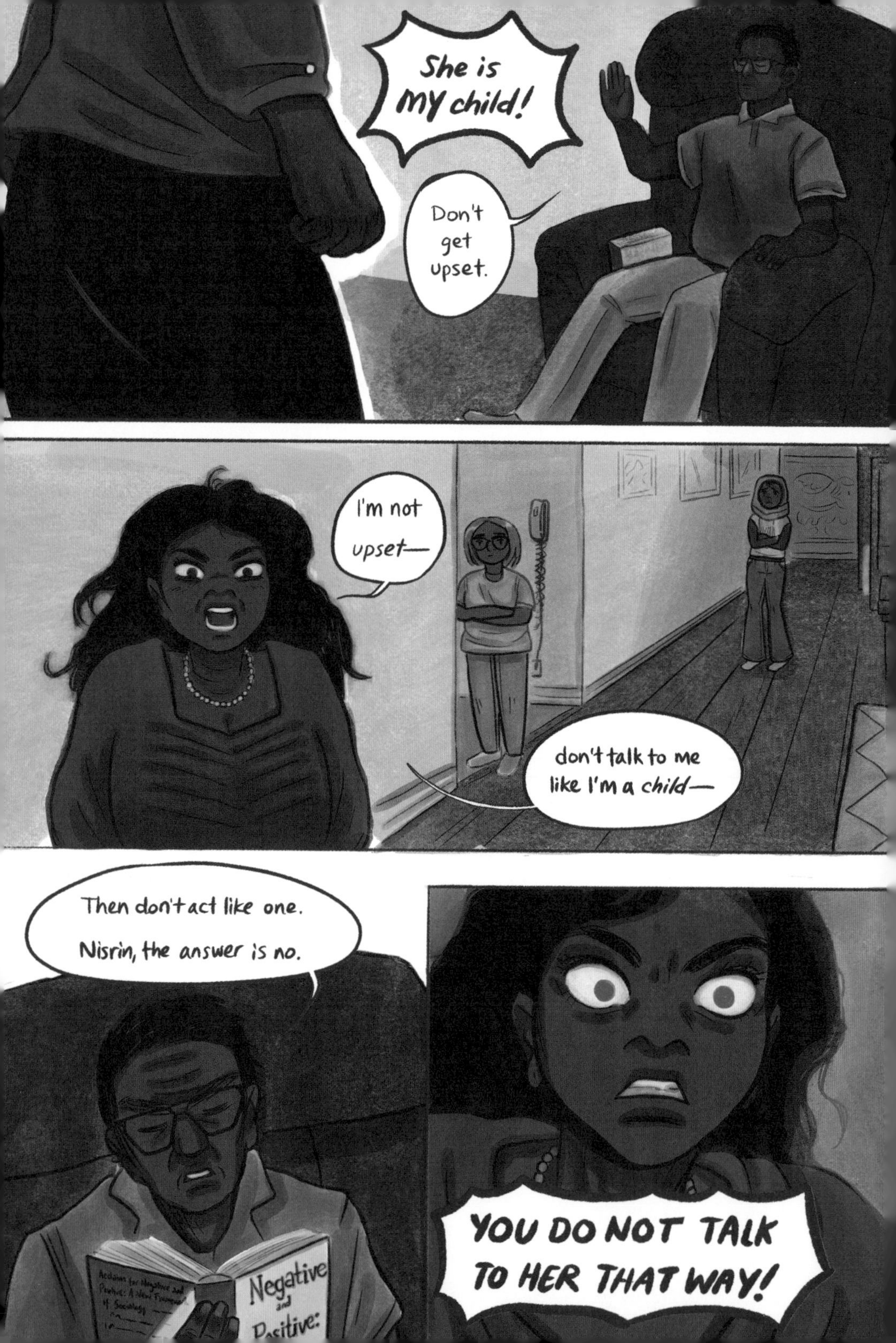
She is MY child!
Don't get upset.
I'm not upset—
don't talk to me like I'm a child—
Then don't act like one.
Nisrin, the answer is no.
YOU DO NOT TALK TO HER THAT WAY!
Negative and Positive:

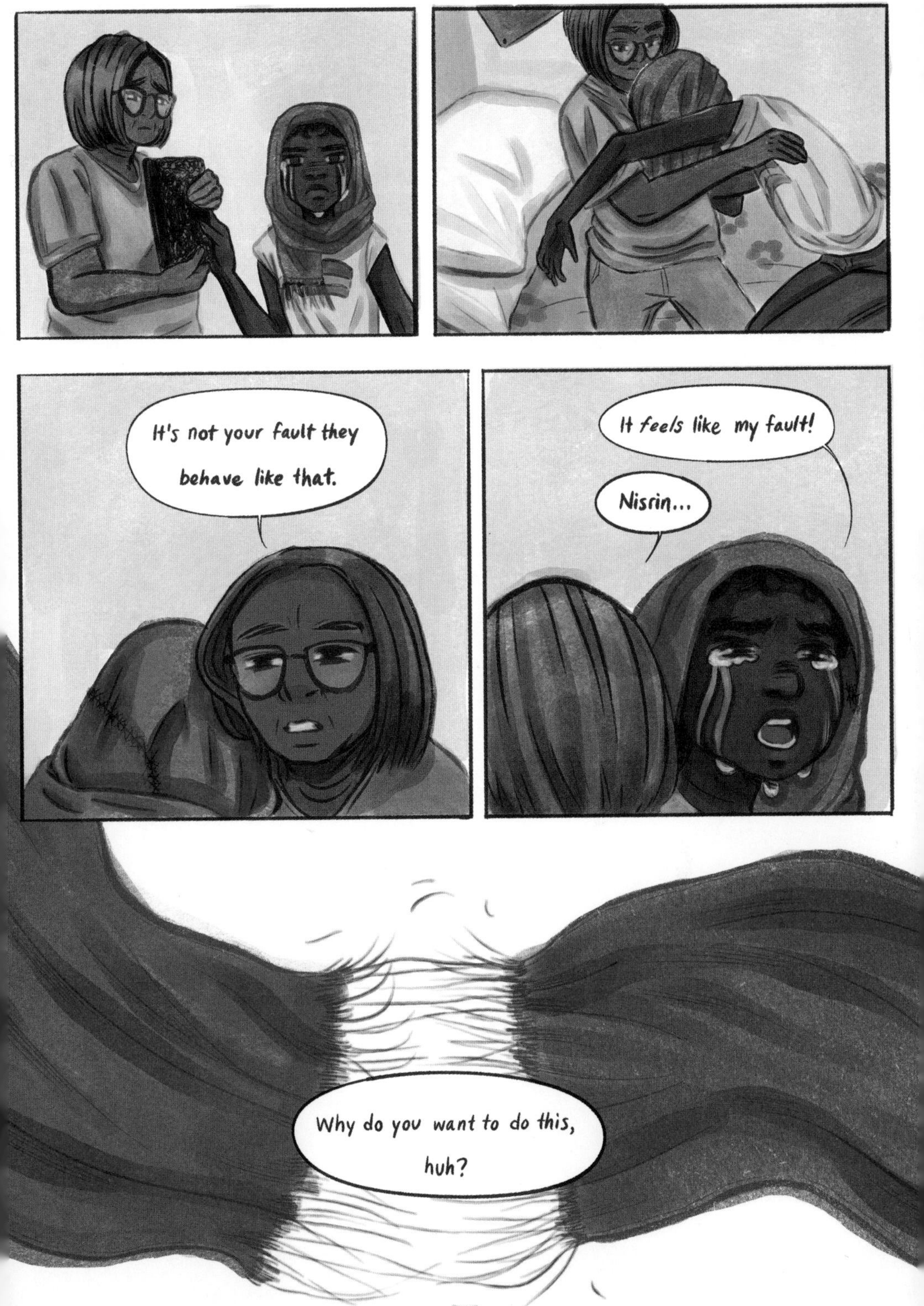
It's not your fault they behave like that.
It feels like my fault!
Nisrin...
Why do you want to do this, huh?

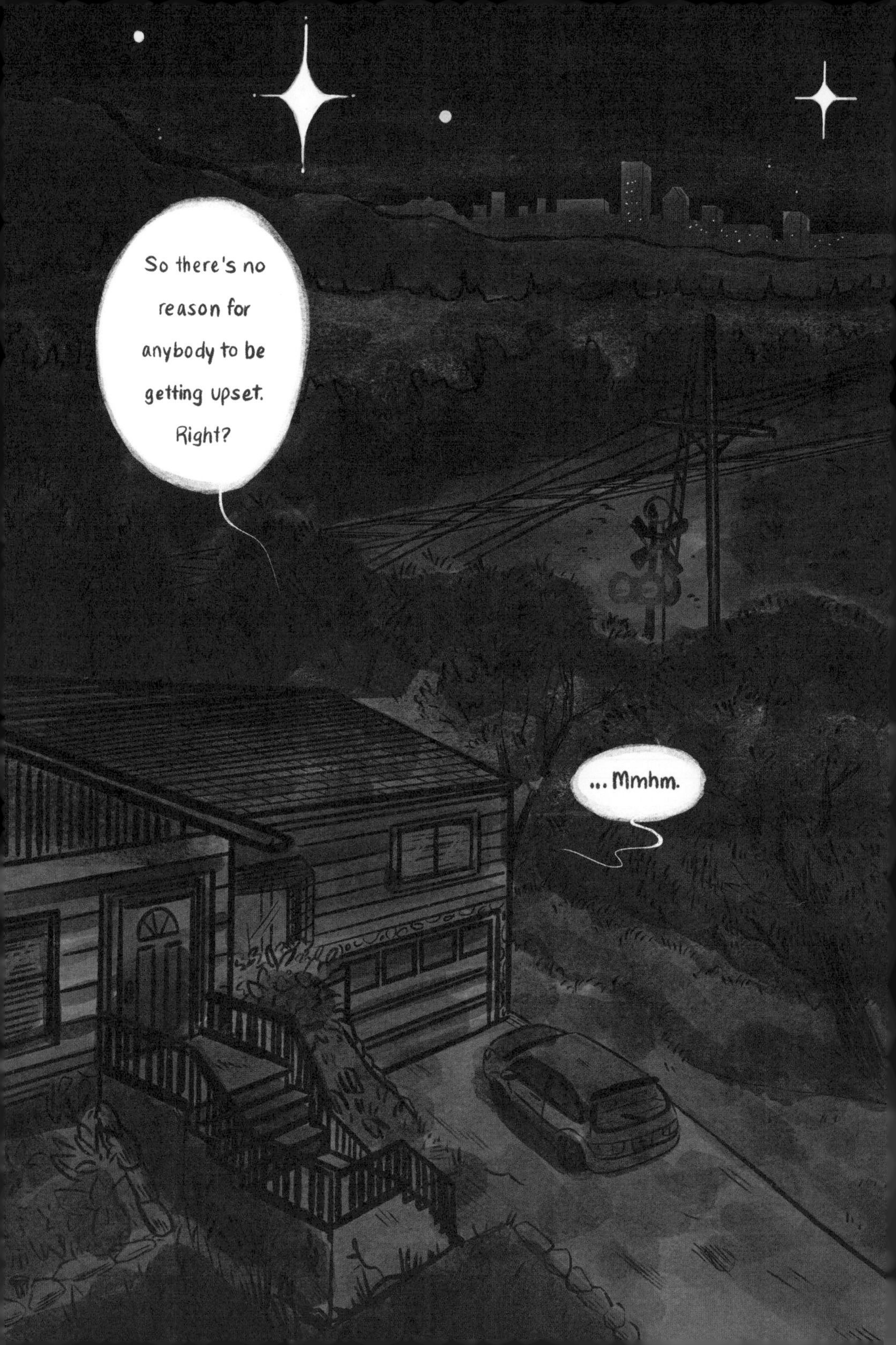
So there's no reason for anybody to be getting upset. Right?
...Mmhm.

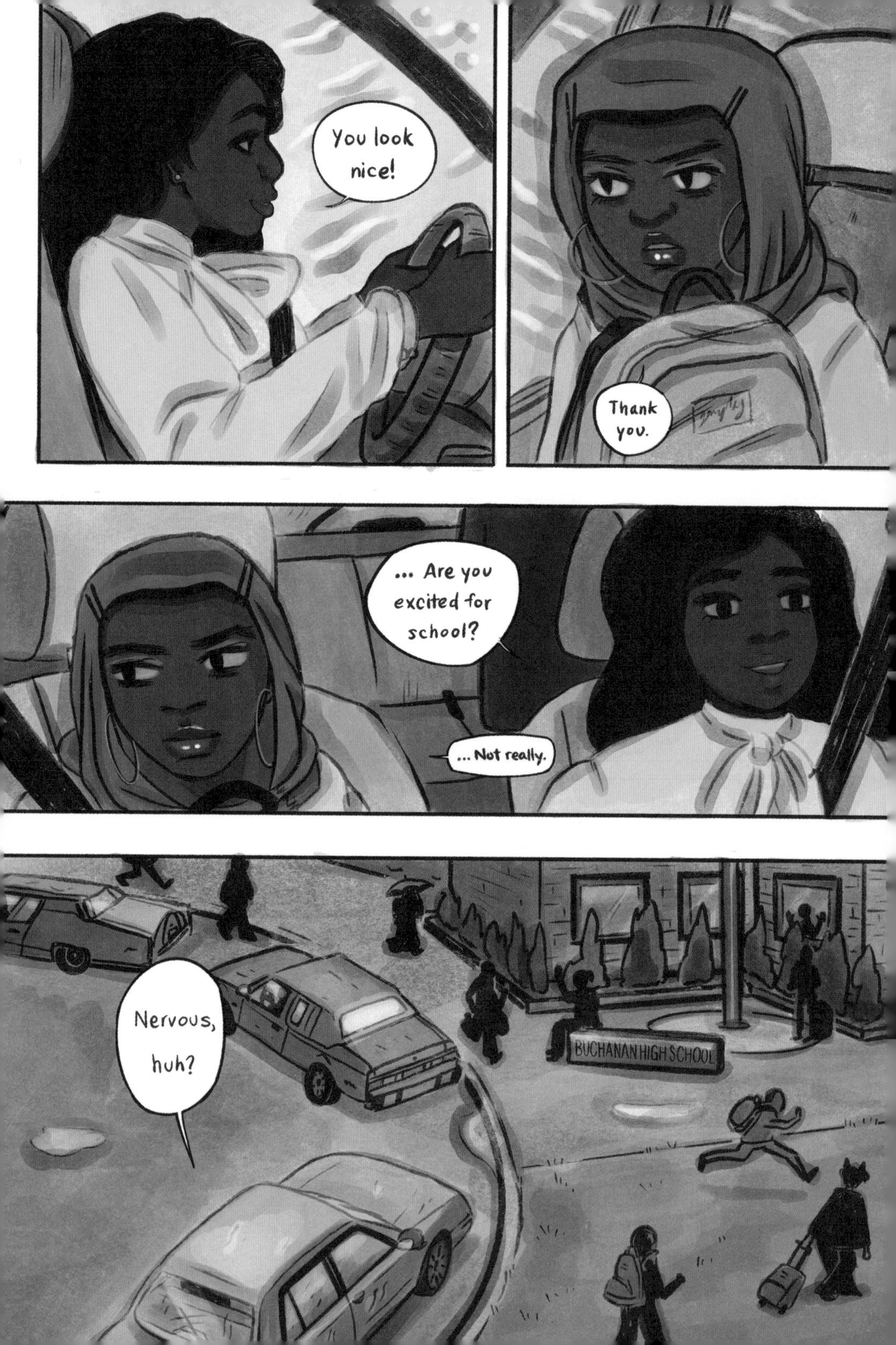
You look nice!
Thank you.
... Are you excited for school?
... Not really.
Nervous, huh?
BUCHANAN HIGH SCHOOL

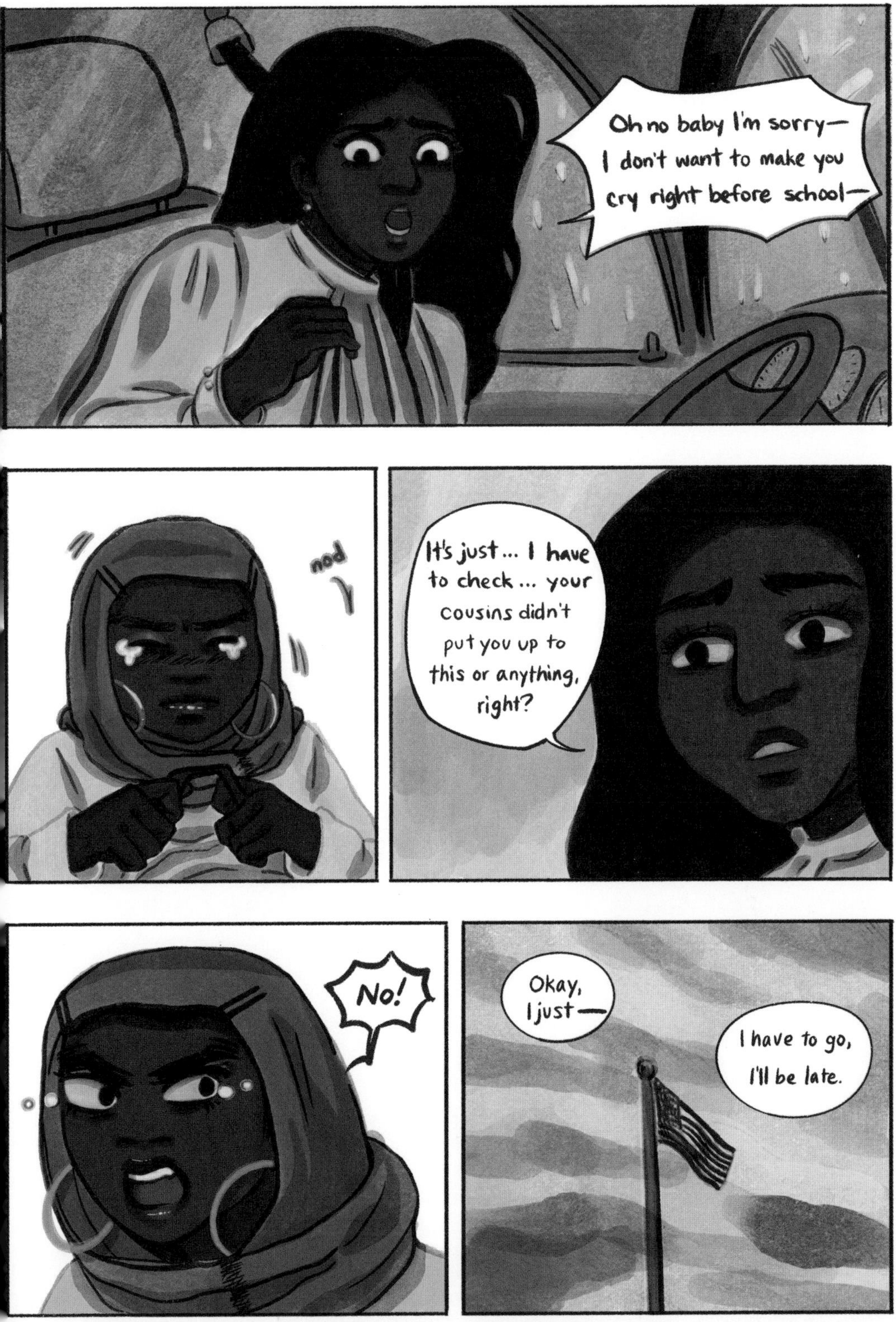
Oh no baby I'm sorry—
I don't want to make you
cry right before school—
nod
It's just... I have
to check... your
cousins didn't
put you up to
this or anything,
right?
No!
Okay,
I just—
I have to go,
I'll be late.

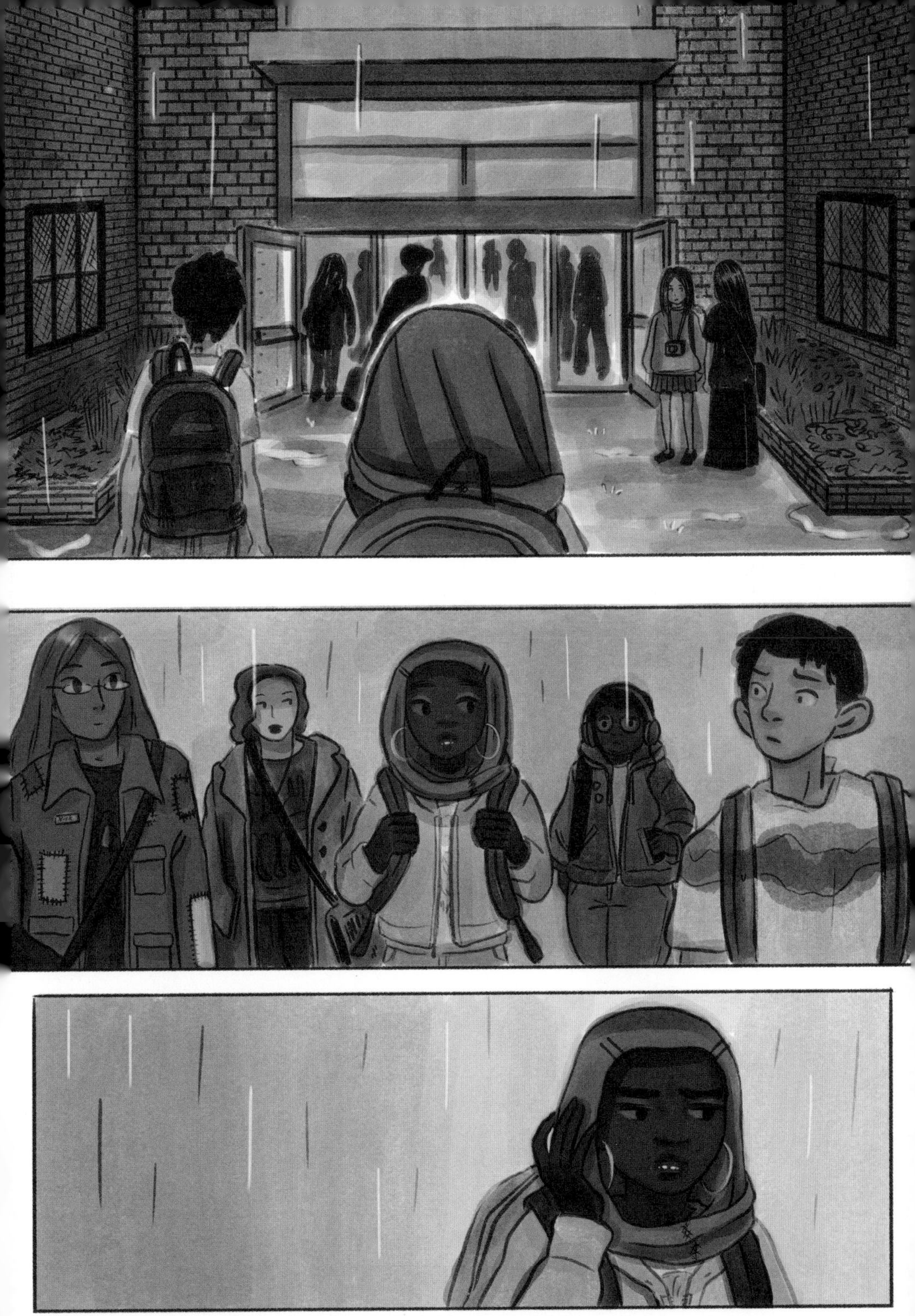

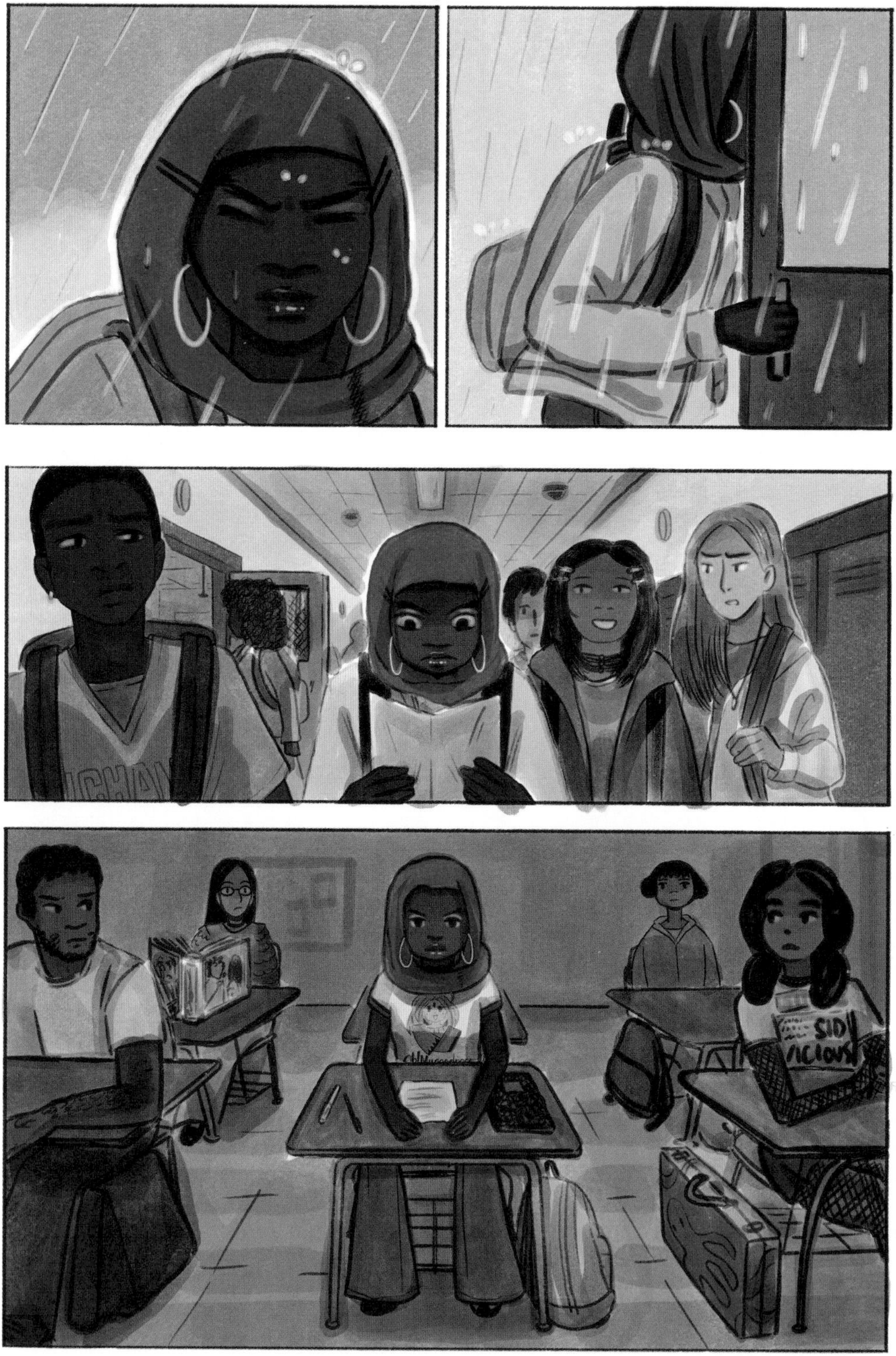
SID
VICIOUS

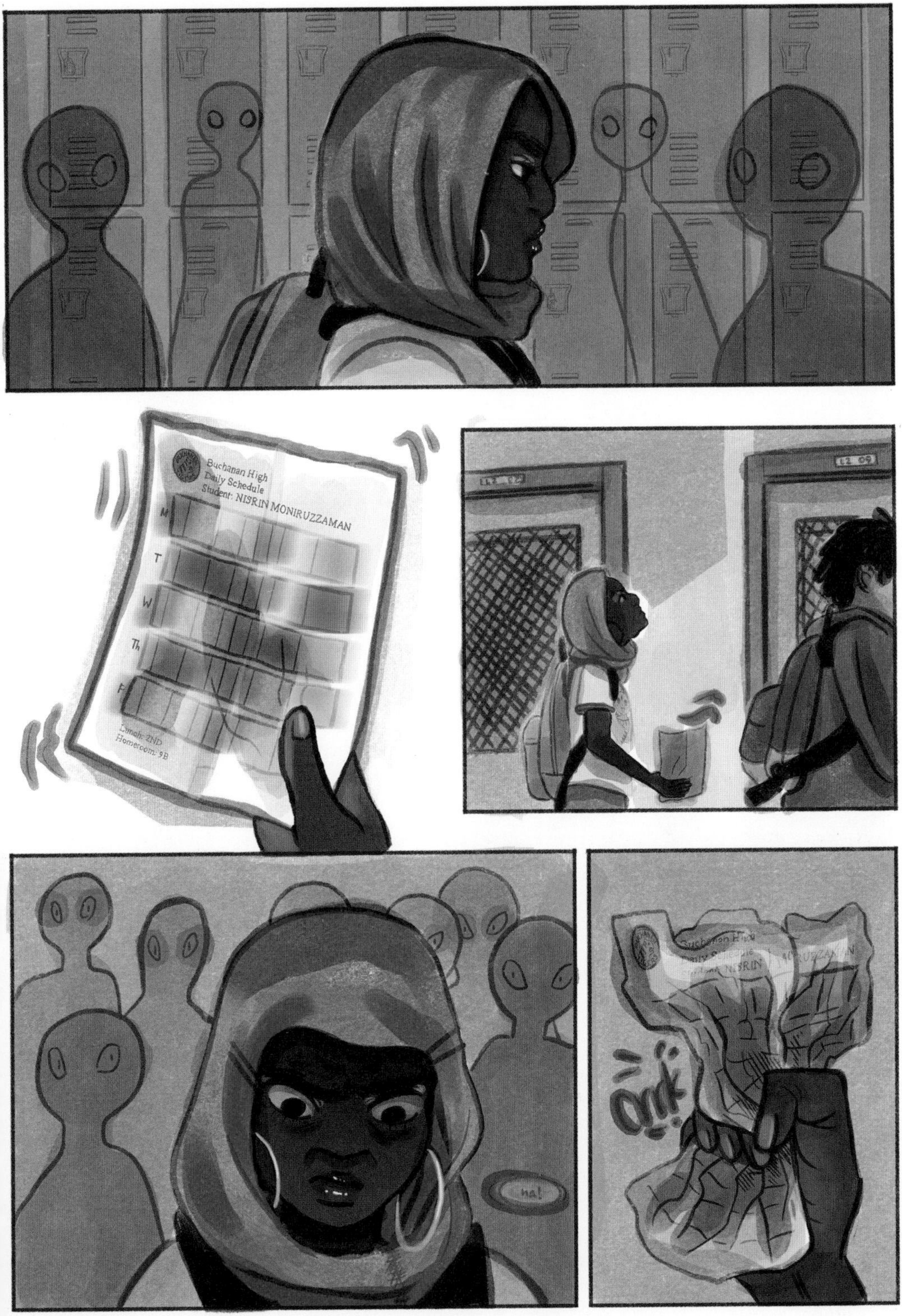
Buchanan High
Daily Schedule
Student: NISRIN MONIRUZZAMAN
M
T
W
Th
F
Lunch: 2ND
Homeroom: 9B
ha!
Crik

Excuse me, Ma'am...

Um...

LATE WORK

Oh! My goodness

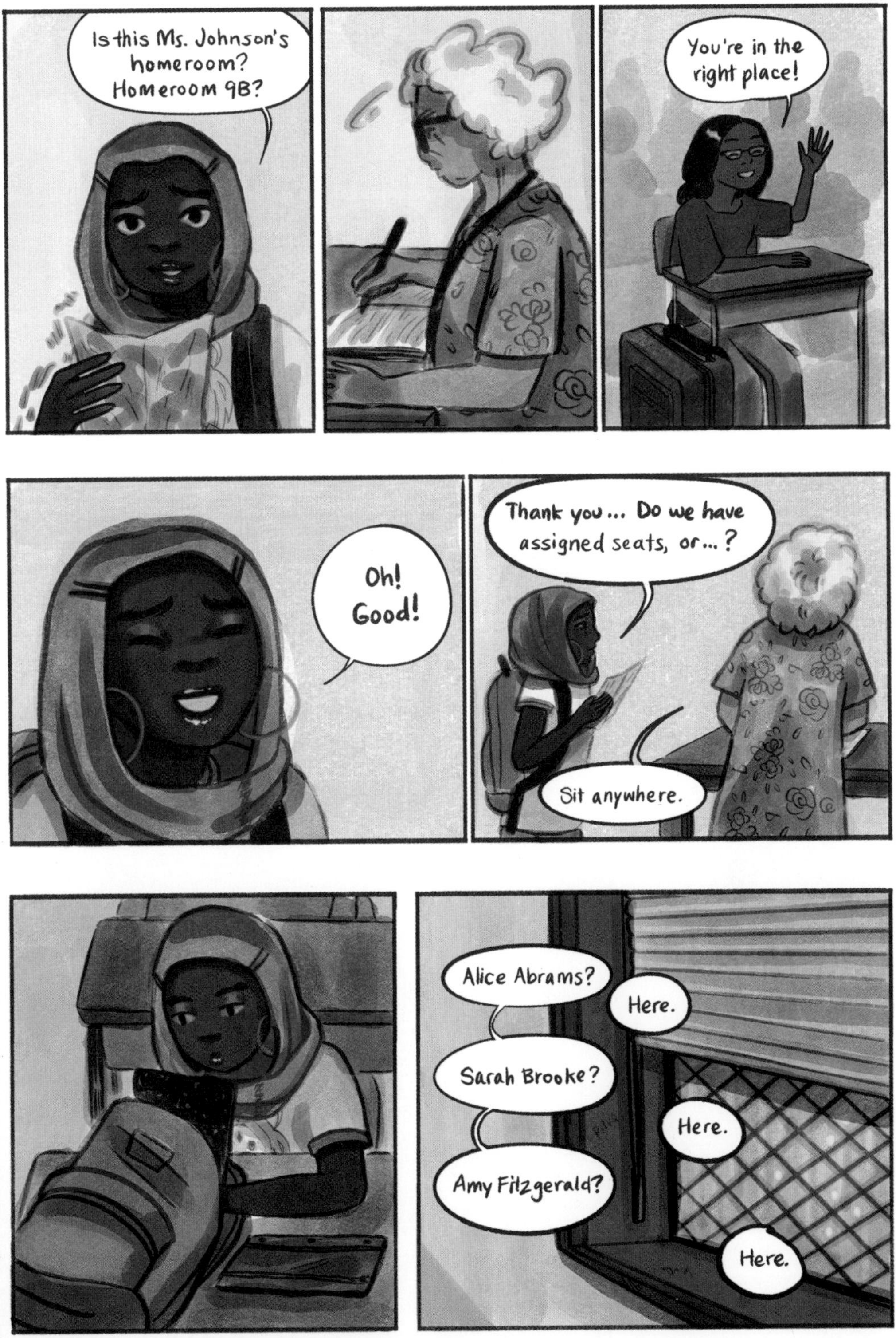
Is this Ms. Johnson's homeroom? Homeroom 9B?
You're in the right place!
Oh! Good!
Thank you... Do we have assigned seats, or...?
Sit anywhere.
Alice Abrams?
Here.
Sarah Brooke?
Here.
Amy Fitzgerald?
Here.

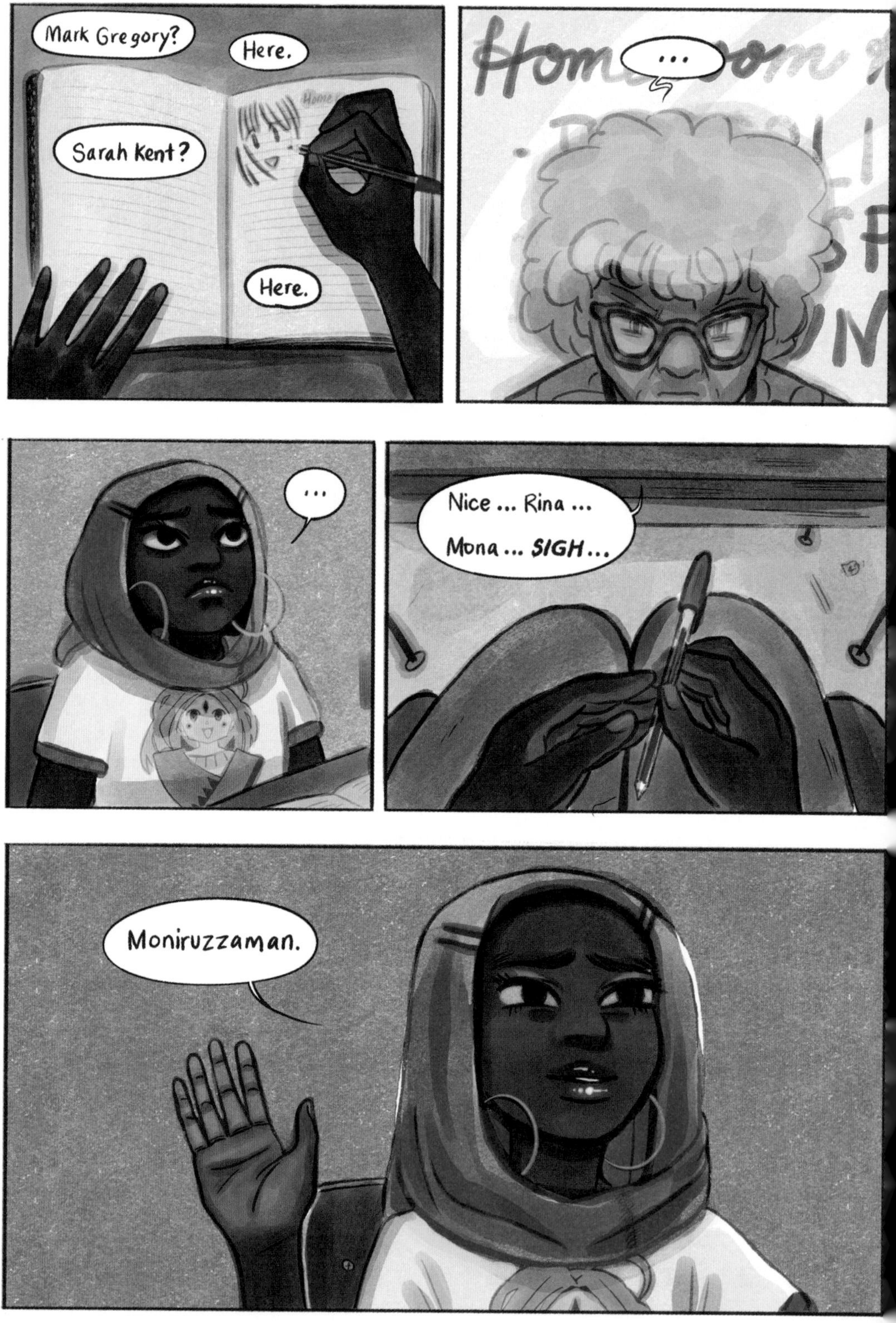
Mark Gregory?
Here.
Sarah Kent?
Here.
...
...
Nice ... Rina ...
Mona ... SIGH ...
Moniruzzaman.

Did I ask for your opinion?

I ... no?

There's no reason to make things difficult. I said it fine the first time.

Okay...

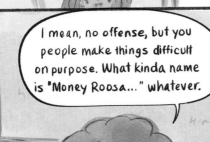
I mean, no offense, but you people make things difficult on purpose. What kinda name is "Money Roosa..." whatever.

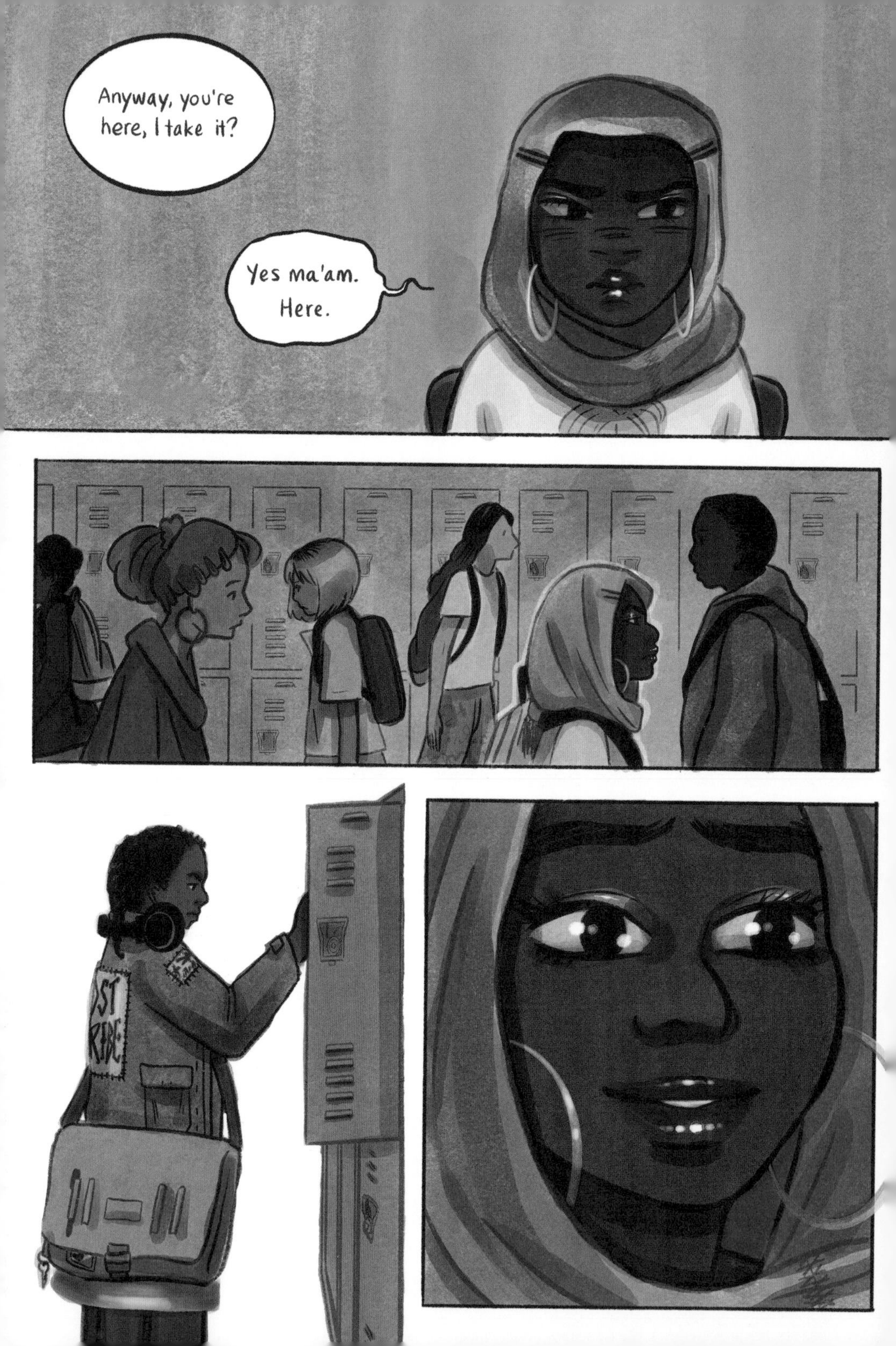
Anyway, you're here, I take it?
Yes ma'am. Here.

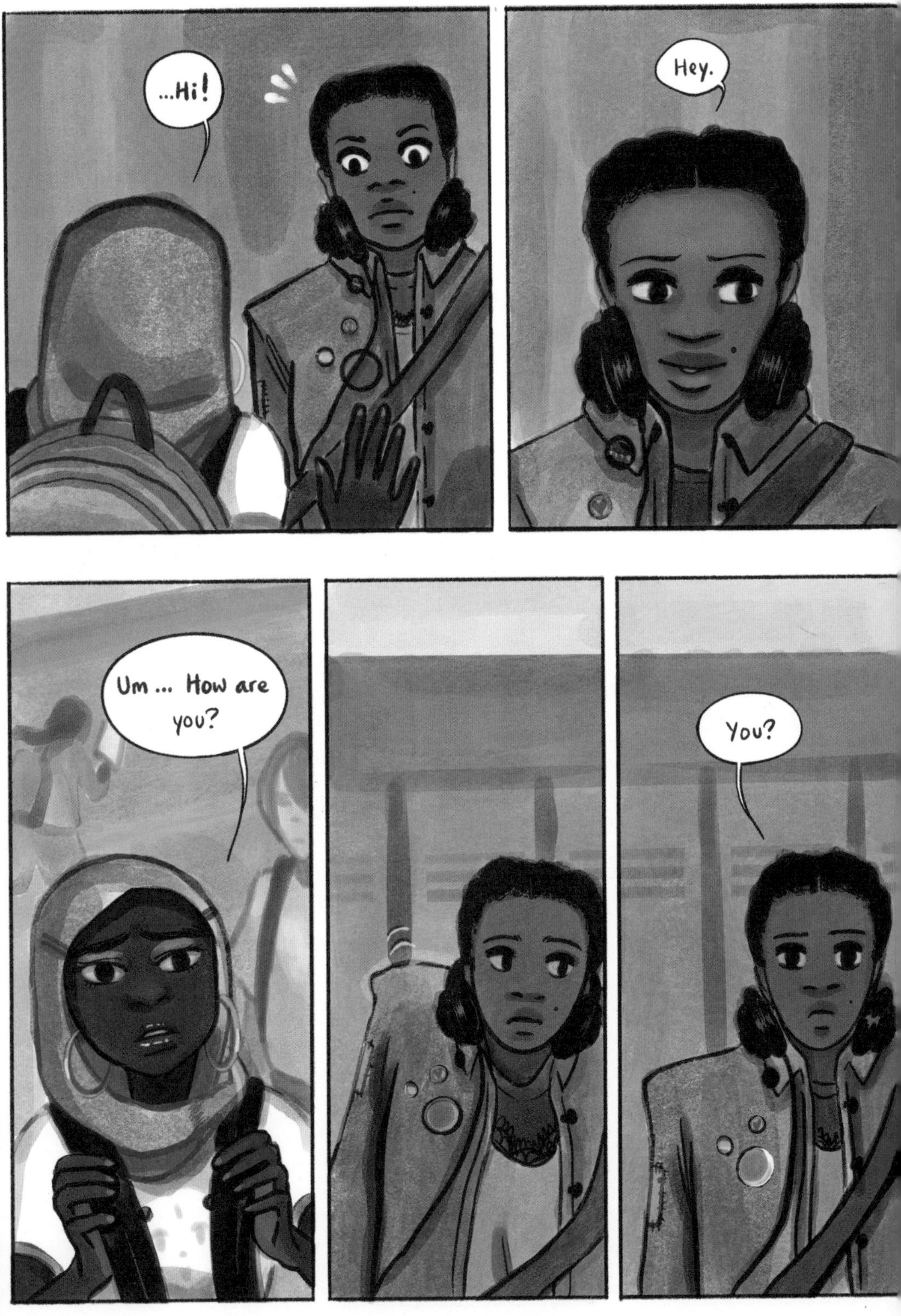
...Hi!
Hey.
Um ... How are you?
You?

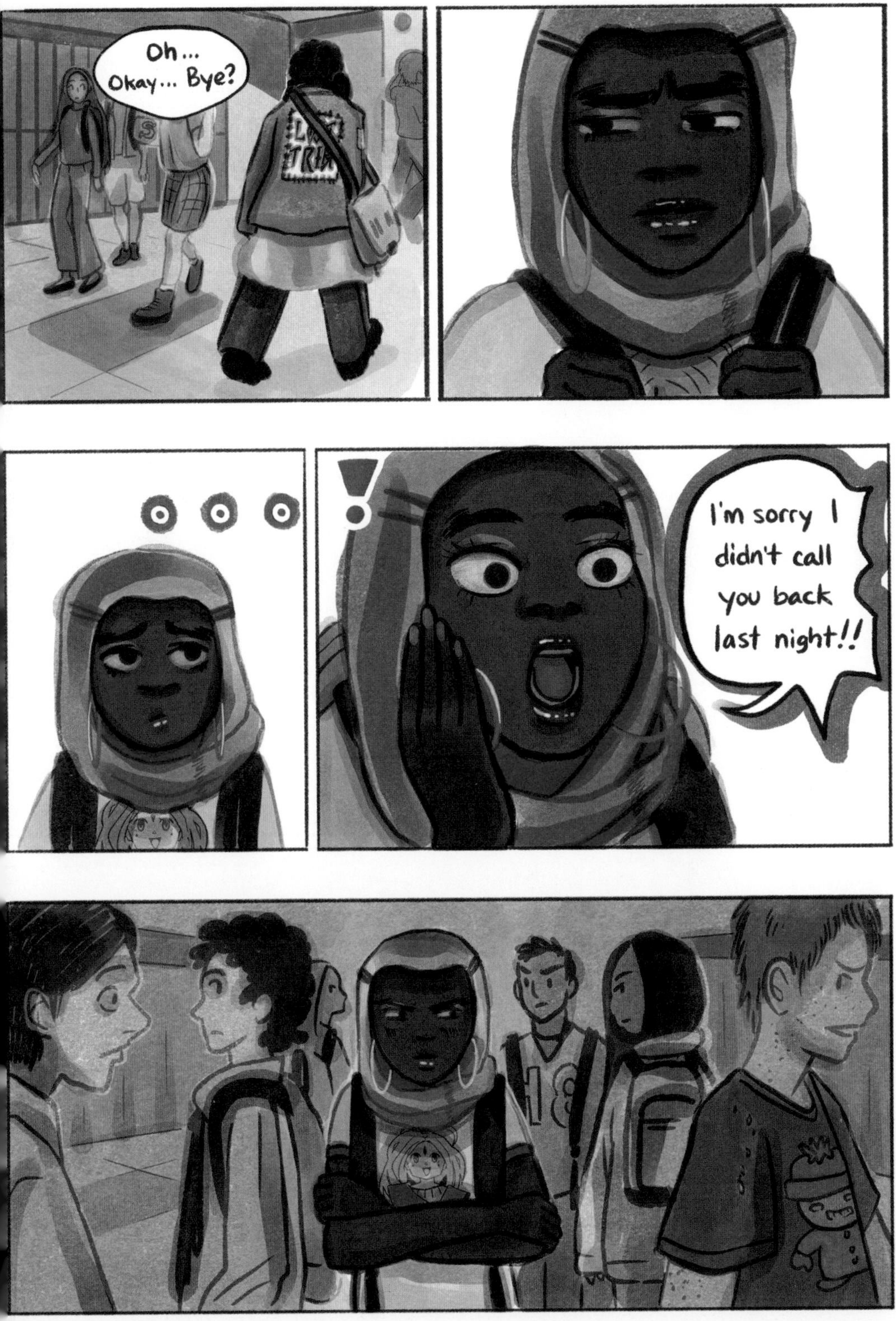
Oh... Okay... Bye?
I'm sorry I didn't call you back last night!!

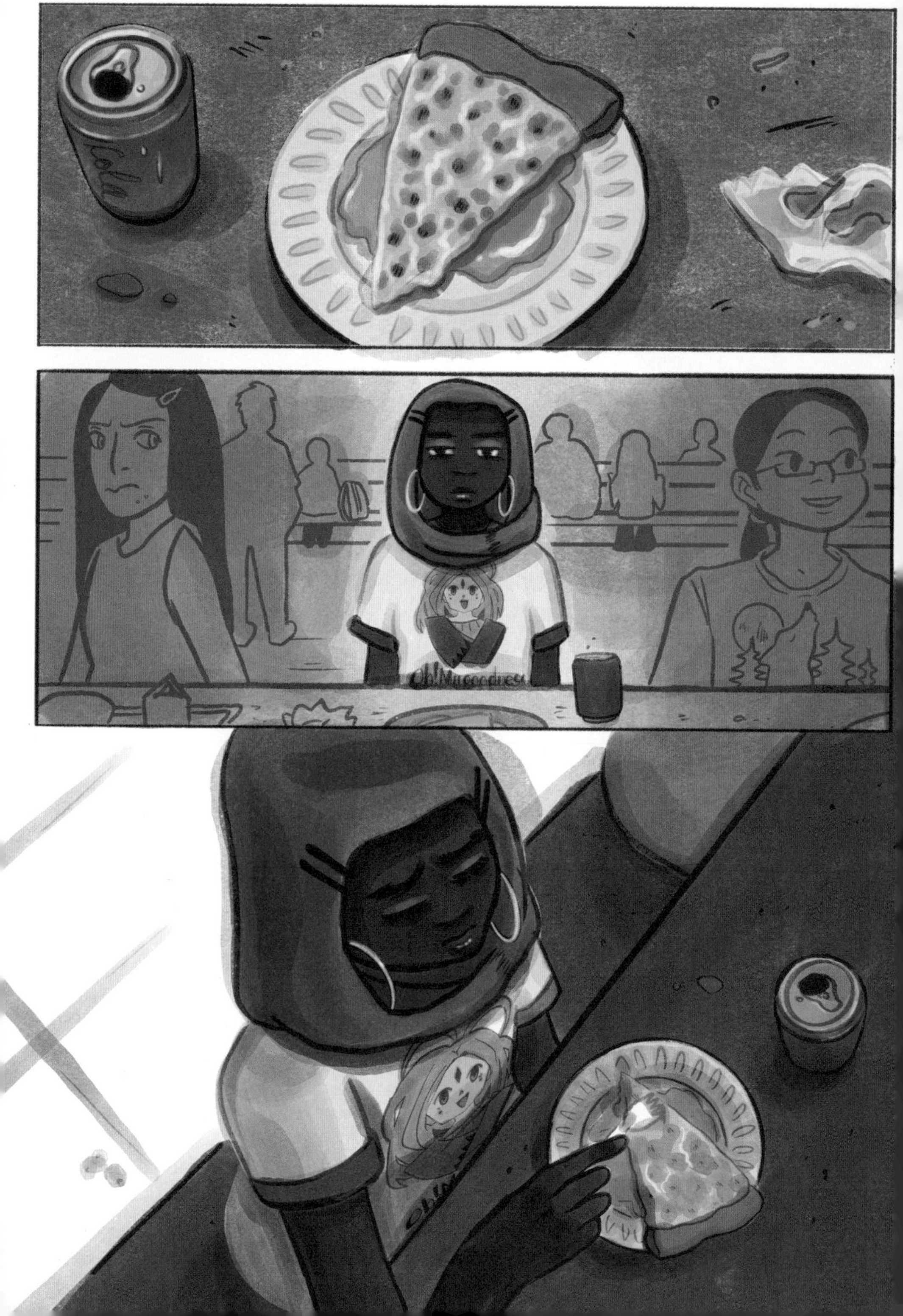

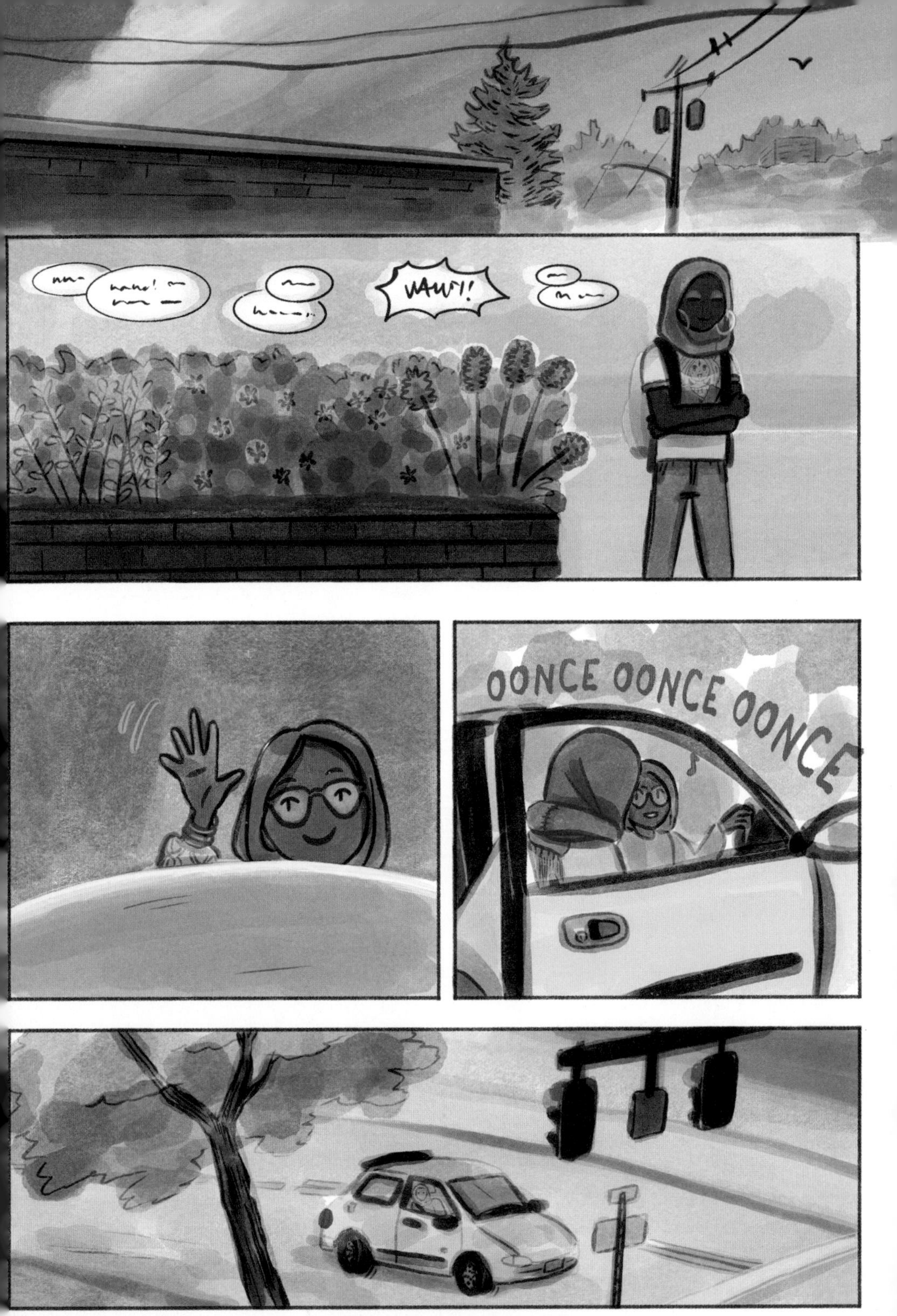

OONCE OONCE OONCE OONCE

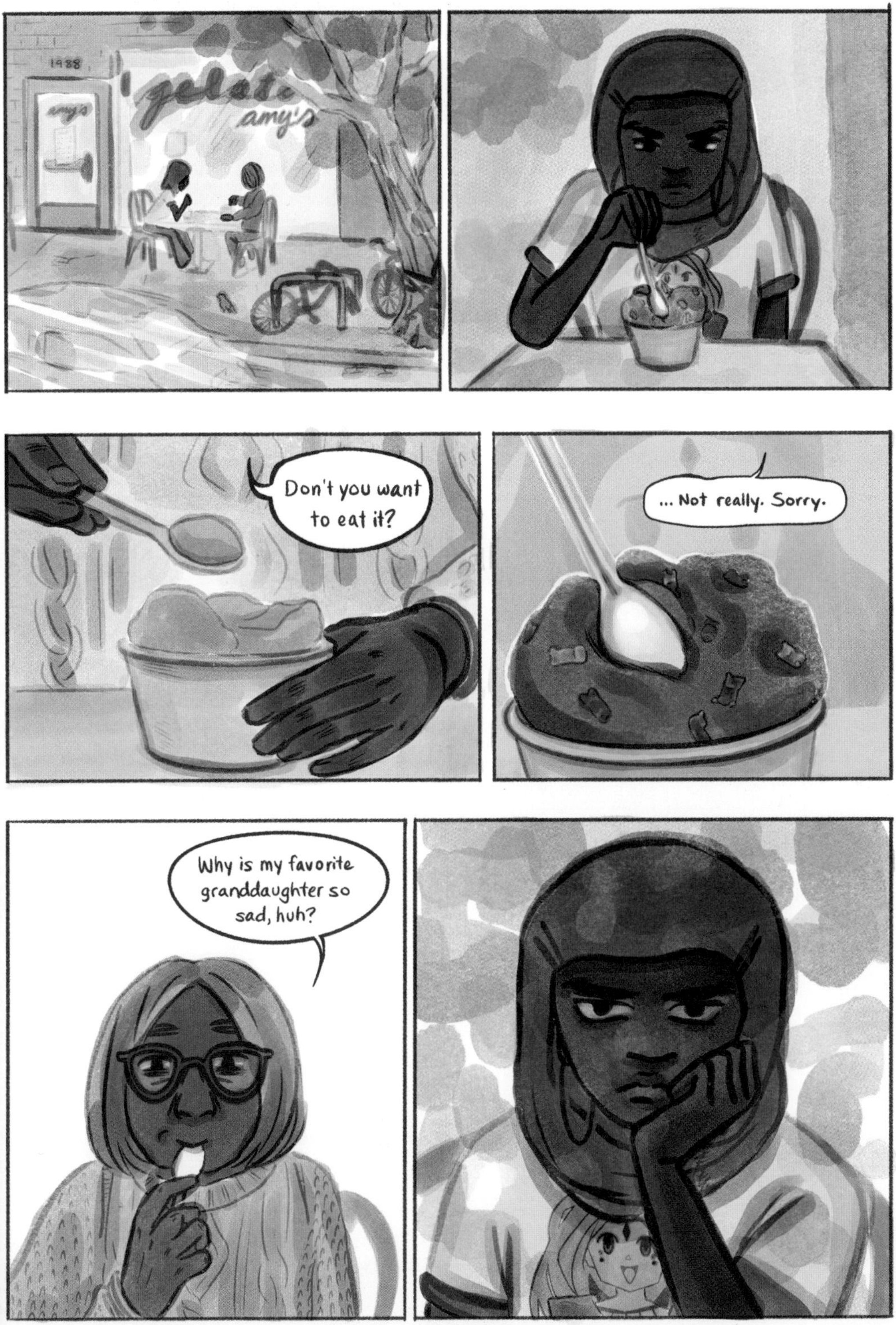
1988
amy's
Don't you want to eat it?
... Not really. Sorry.
Why is my favorite granddaughter so sad, huh?

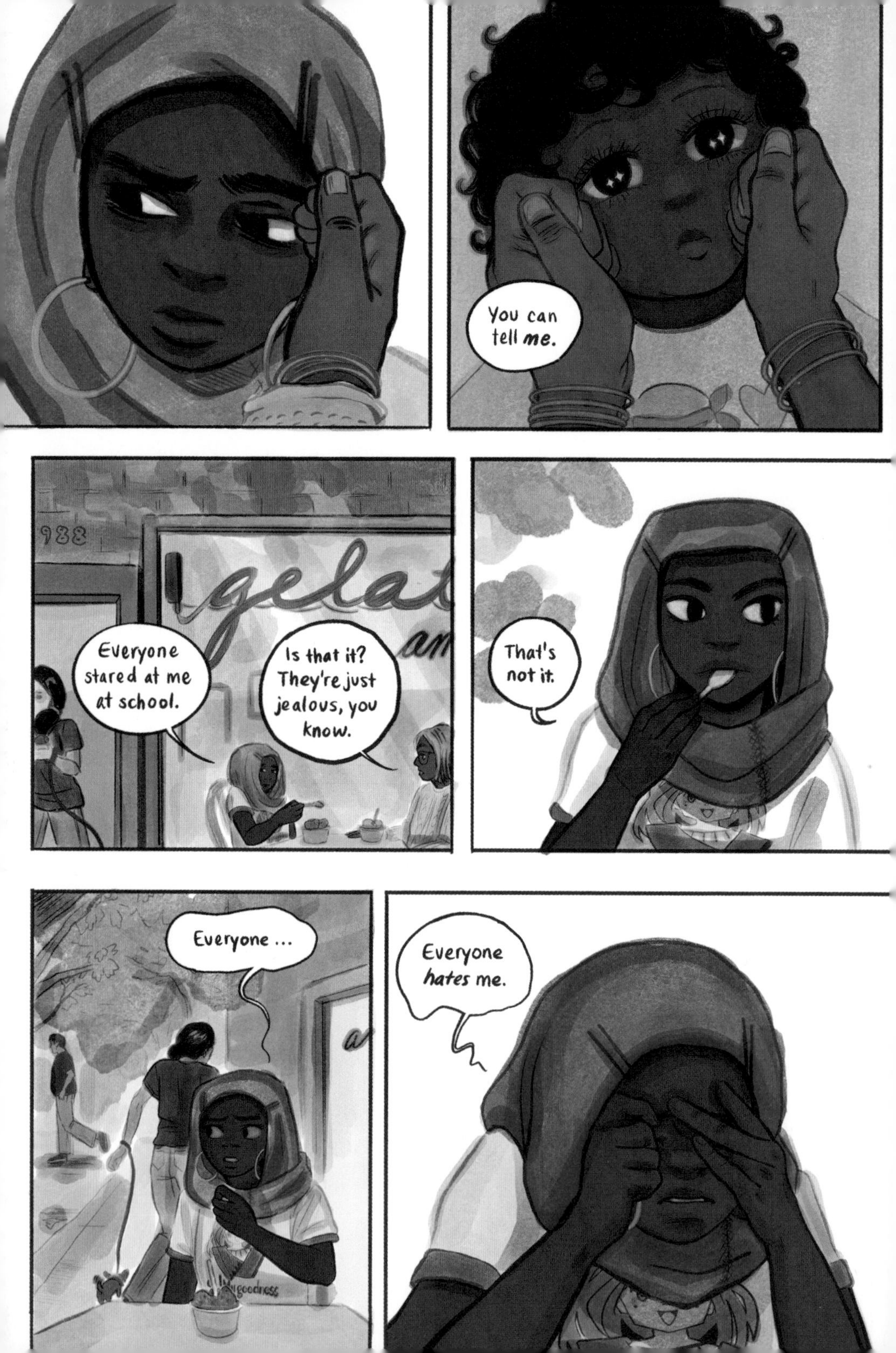
You can tell me.
988
gelat
Everyone stared at me at school.
Is that it? They're just jealous, you know.
That's not it.
Everyone ...
Everyone hates me.

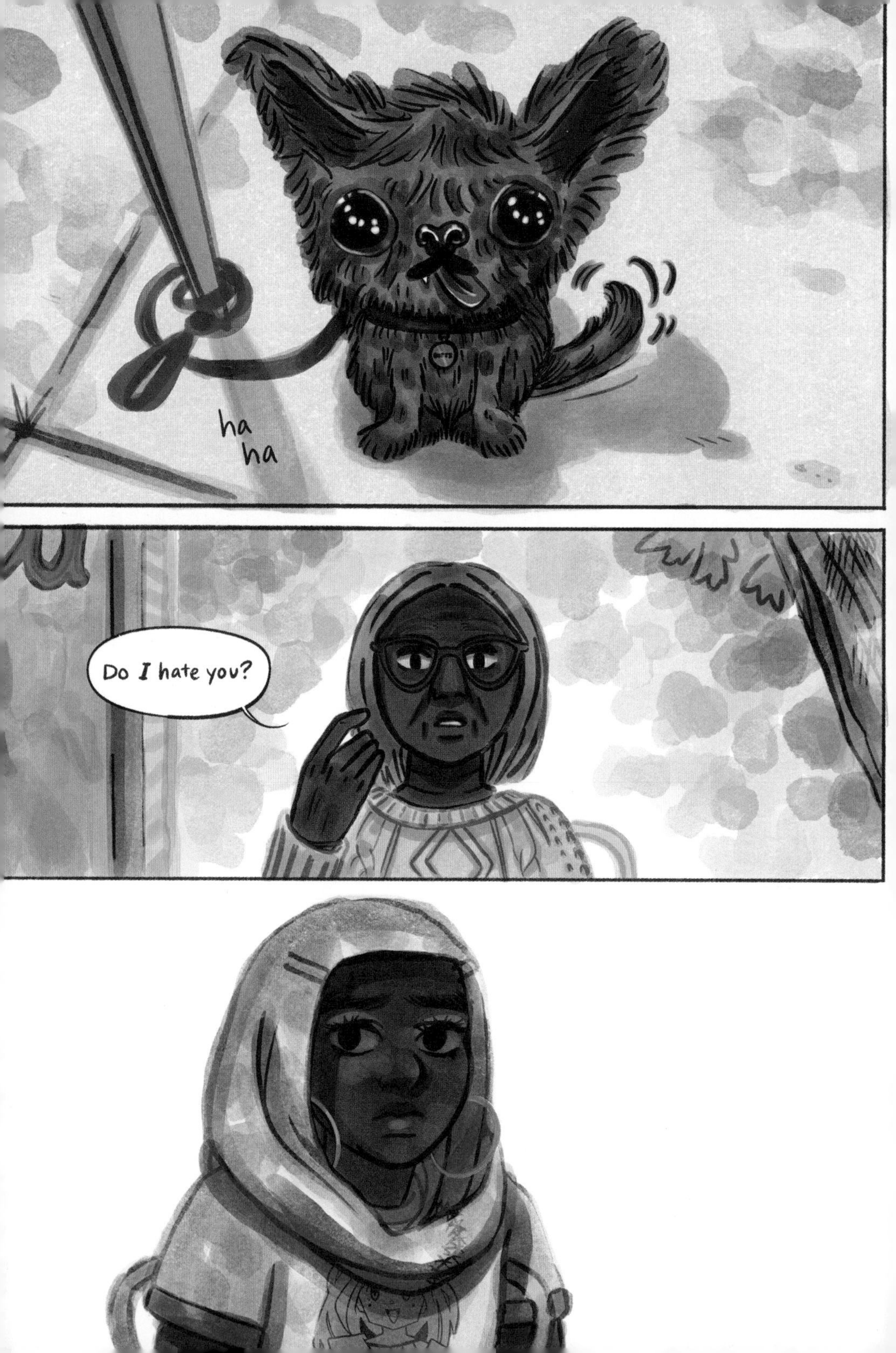
ha
ha
Do I hate you?

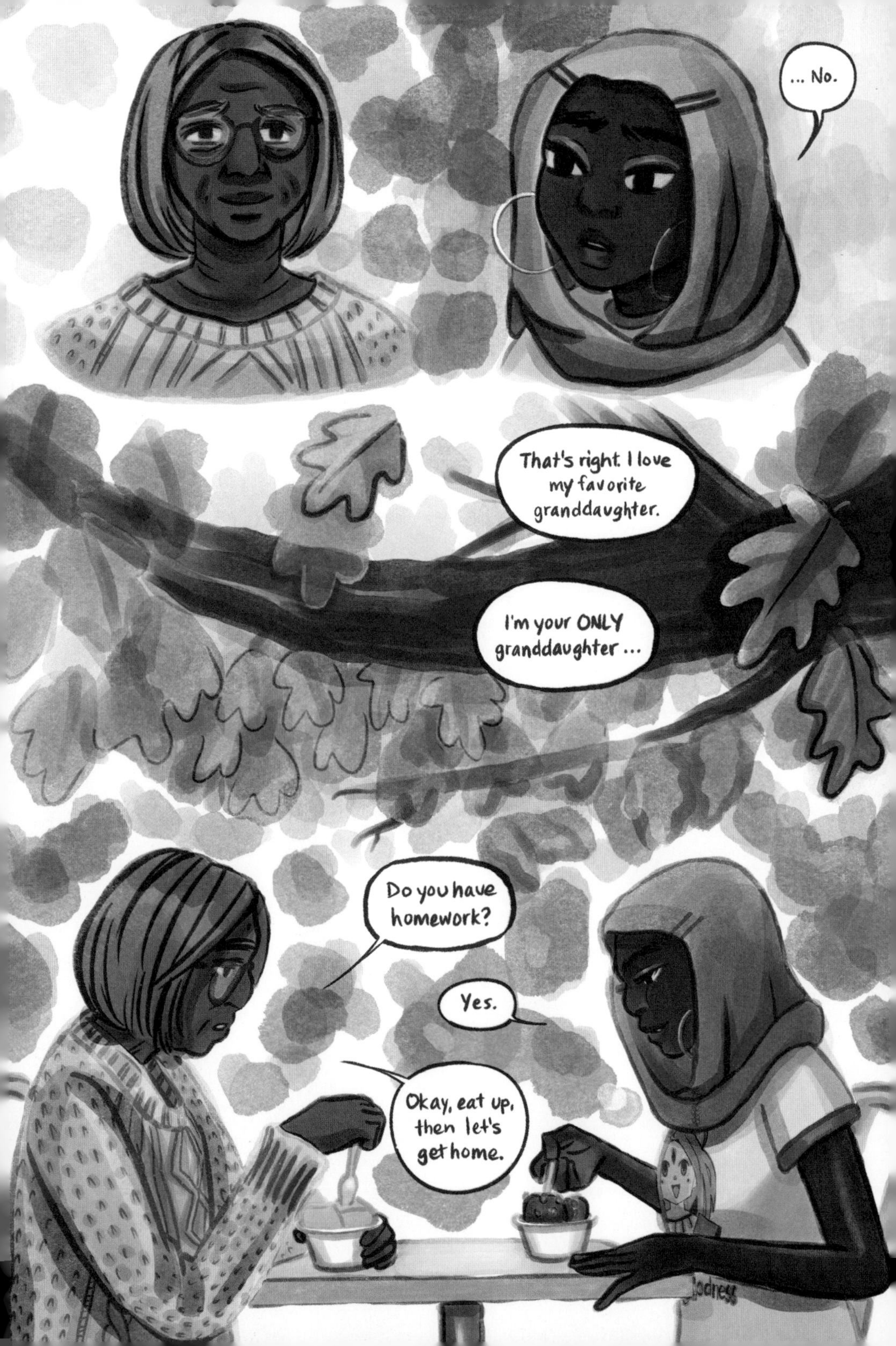
... No.
That's right. I love my favorite granddaughter.
I'm your ONLY granddaughter ...
Do you have homework?
Yes.
Okay, eat up, then let's get home.

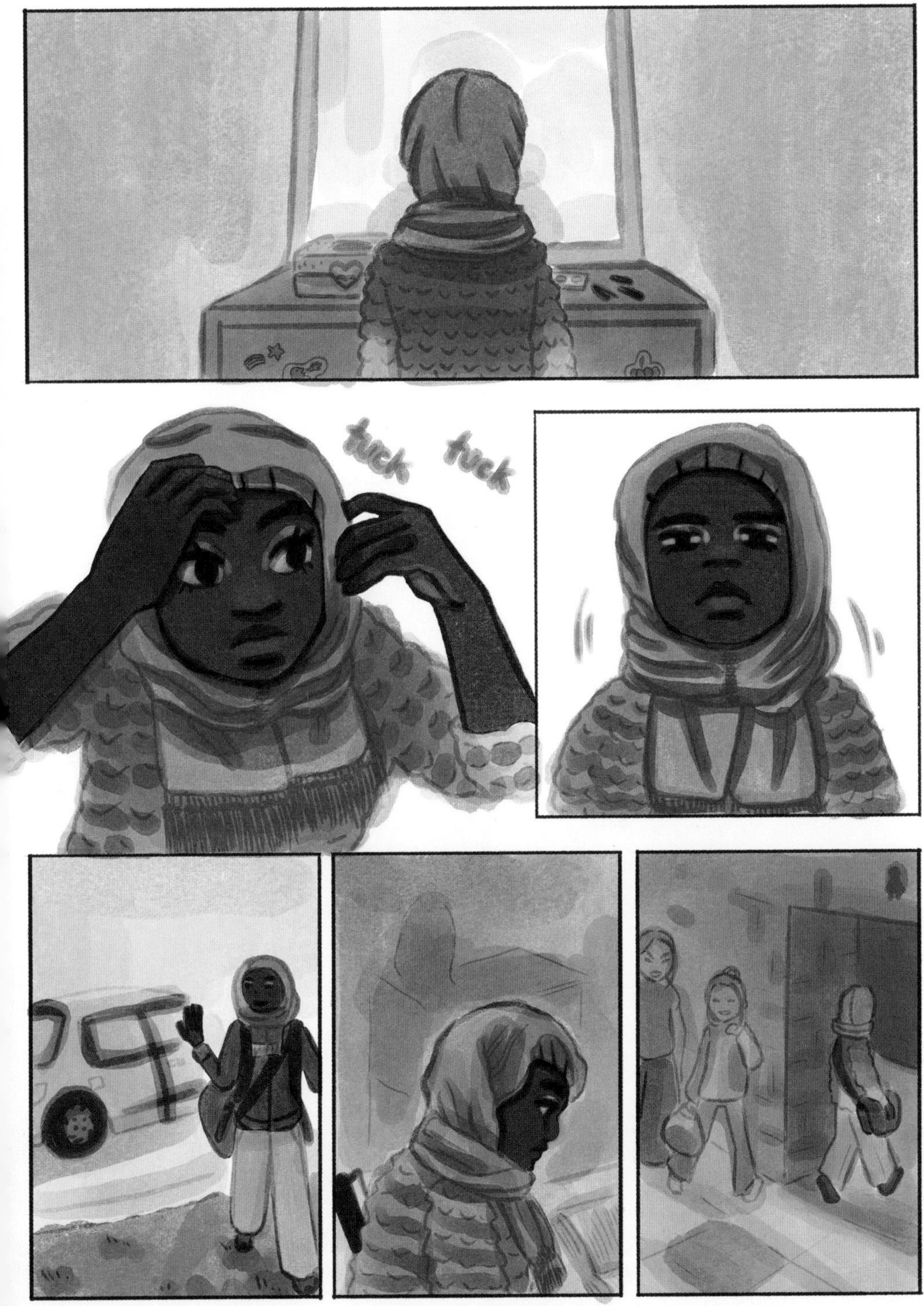
tuck
tuck

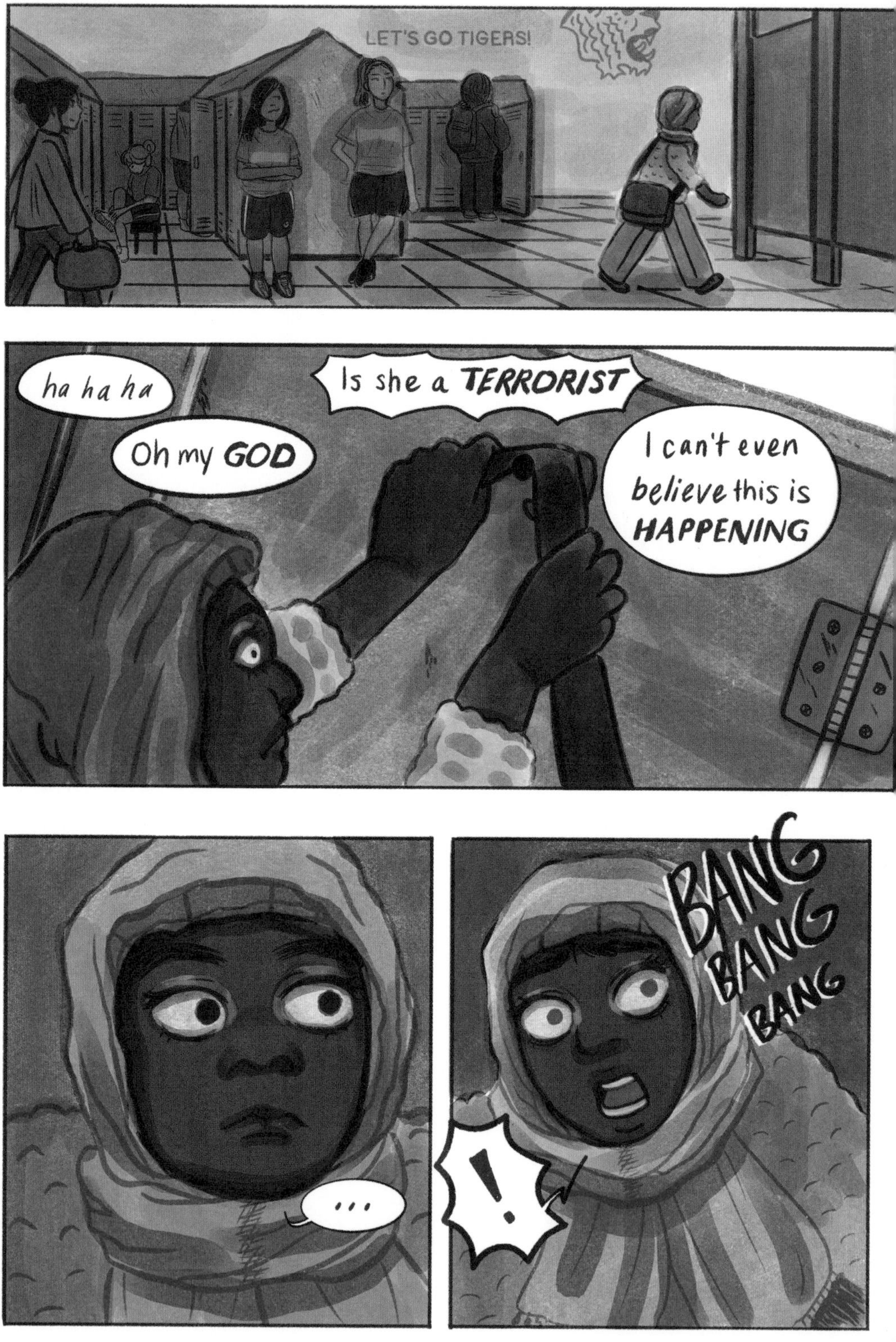
LET'S GO TIGERS!
ha ha ha
Is she a TERRORIST
Oh my GOD
I can't even believe this is HAPPENING
...
BANG
BANG
BANG
!

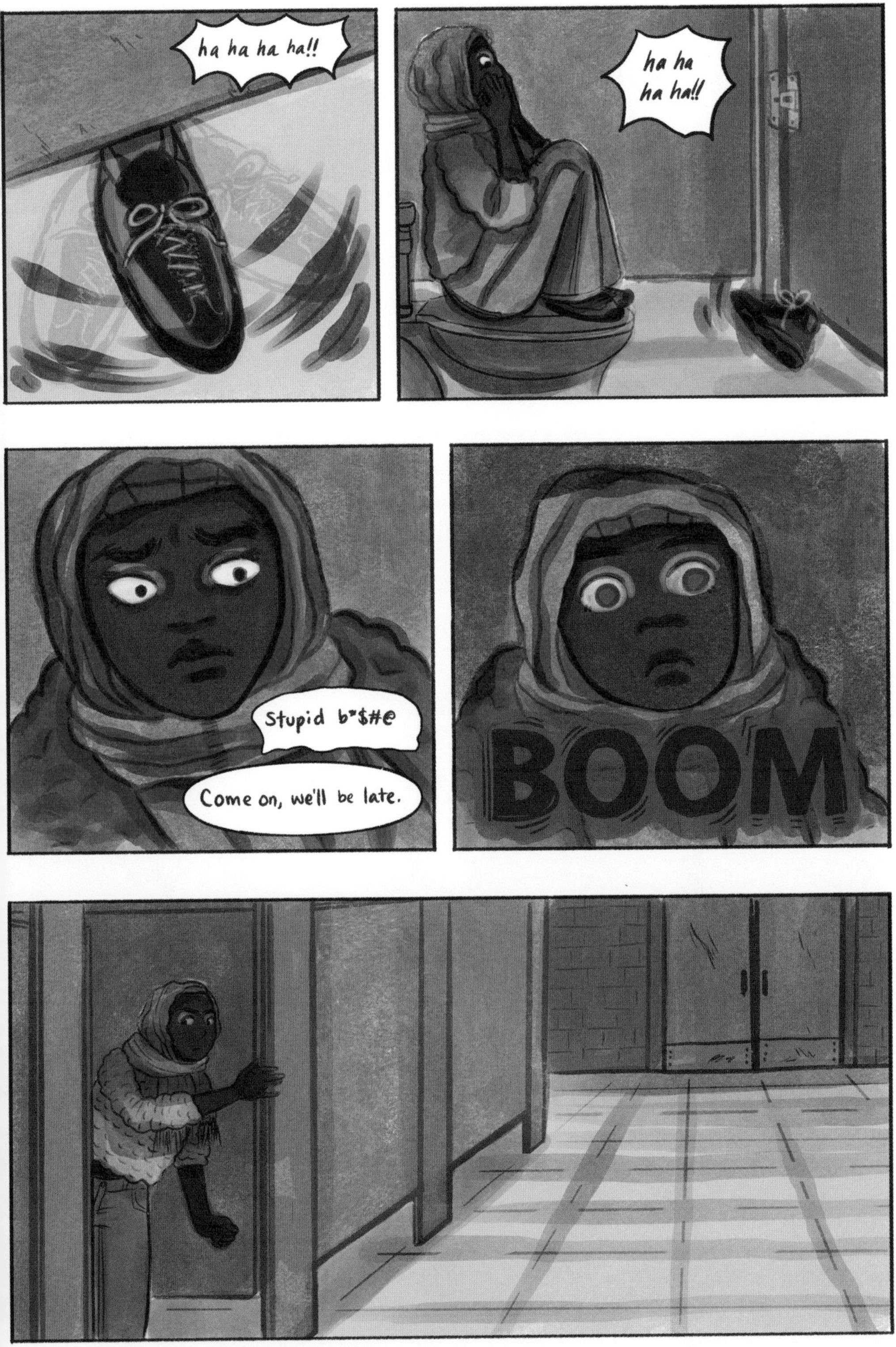
ha ha ha ha!!
ha ha ha ha!!
Stupid b*$#@
Come on, we'll be late.
BOOM

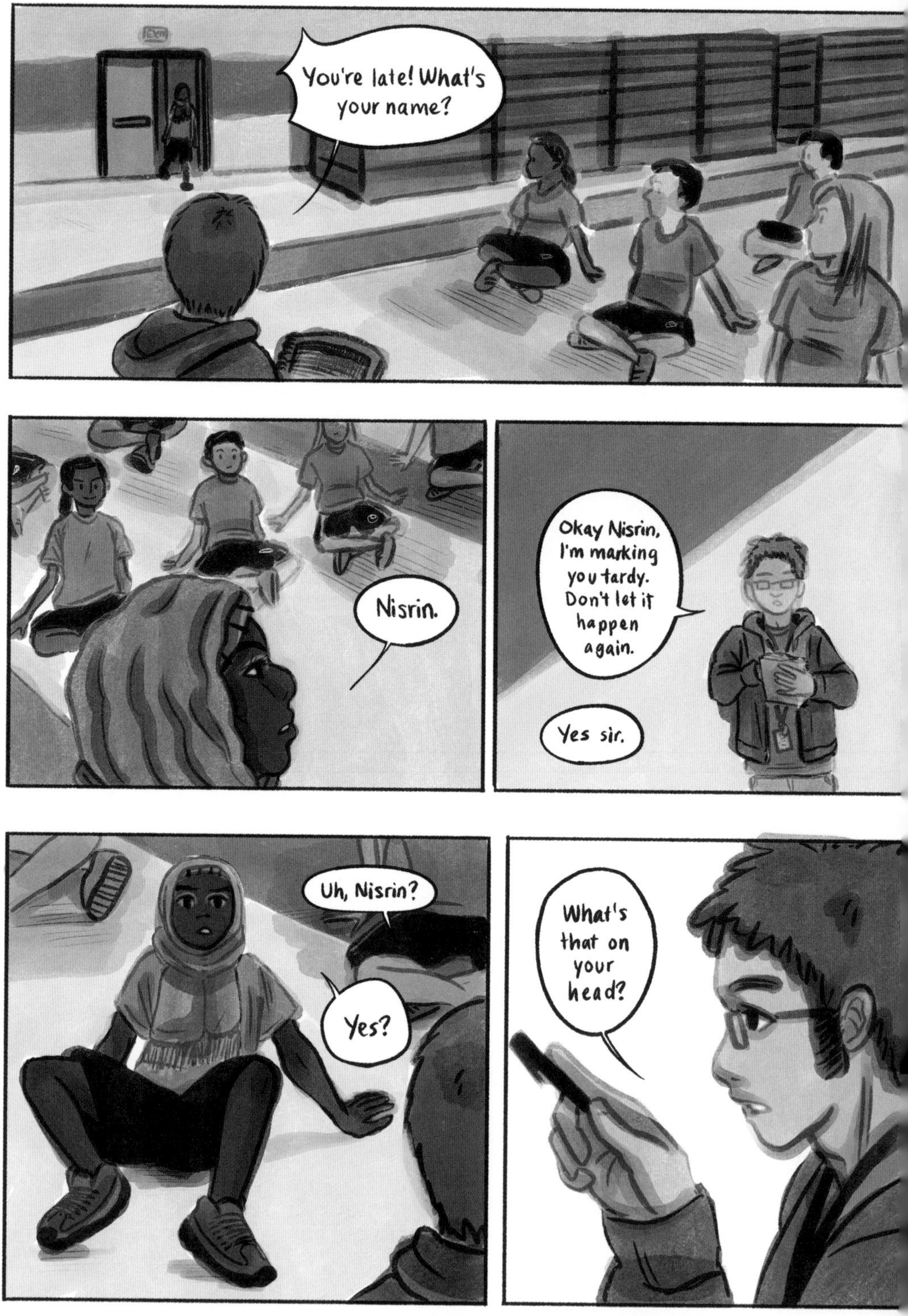
You're late! What's your name?
Nisrin.
Okay Nisrin, I'm marking you tardy. Don't let it happen again.
Yes sir.
Uh, Nisrin?
Yes?
What's that on your head?

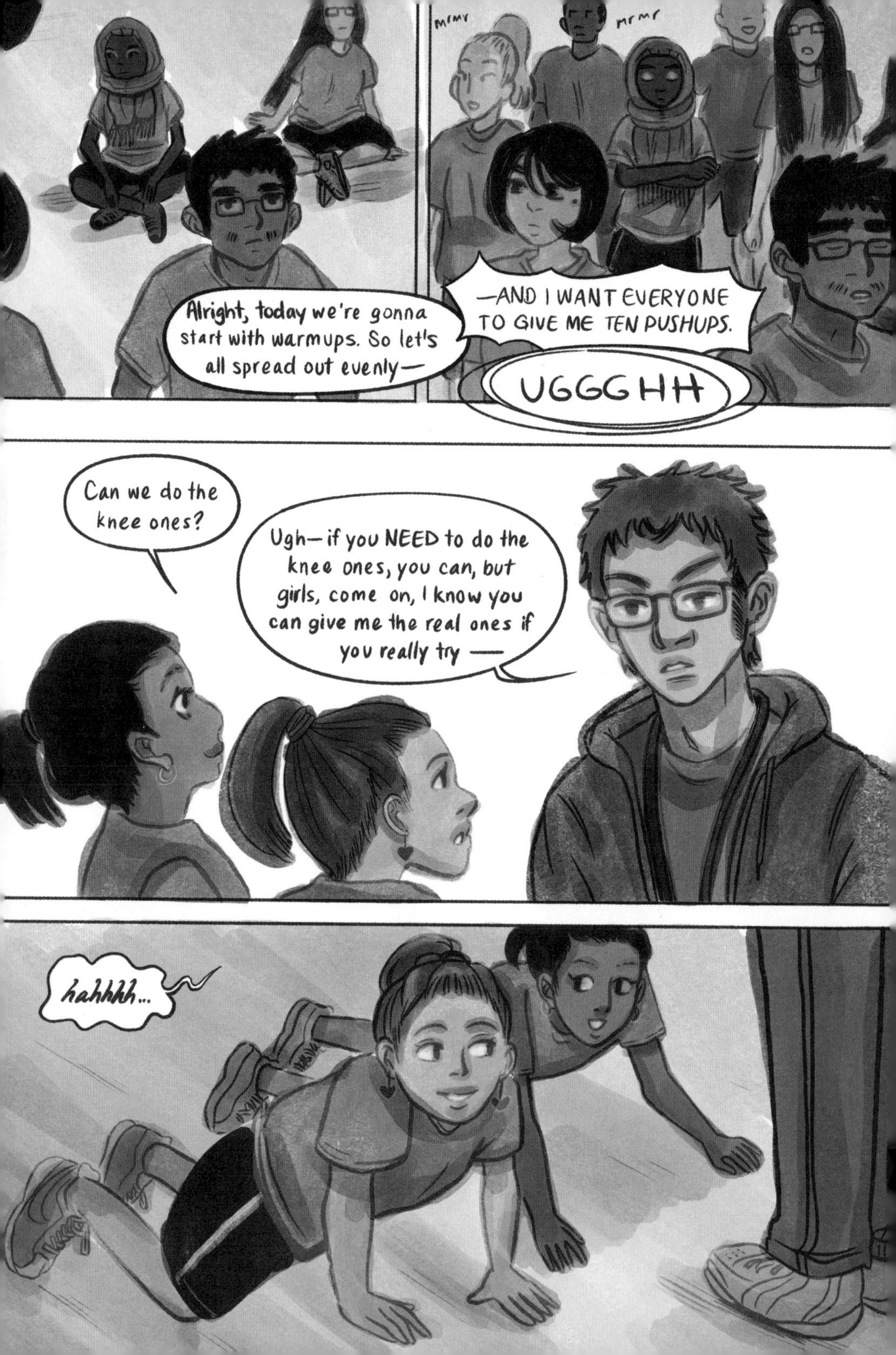
mrmr
mrmr
Alright, today we're gonna start with warmups. So let's all spread out evenly—
—AND I WANT EVERYONE TO GIVE ME TEN PUSHUPS.
UGGGHH
Can we do the knee ones?
Ugh— if you NEED to do the knee ones, you can, but girls, come on, I know you can give me the real ones if you really try —
hahhhh...

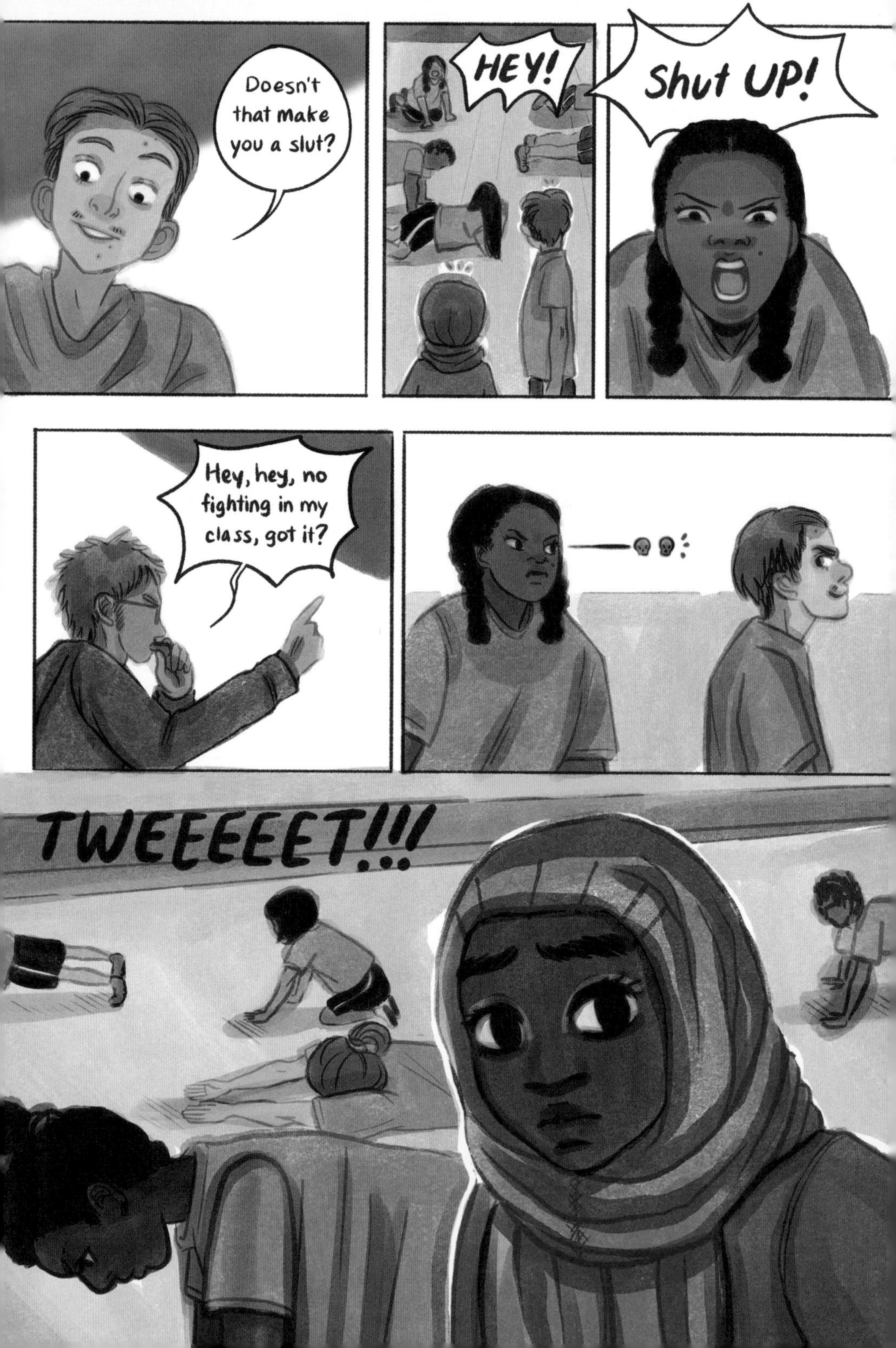
Doesn't that make you a slut?
HEY!
Shut UP!
Hey, hey, no fighting in my class, got it?
TWEEEEET!!!

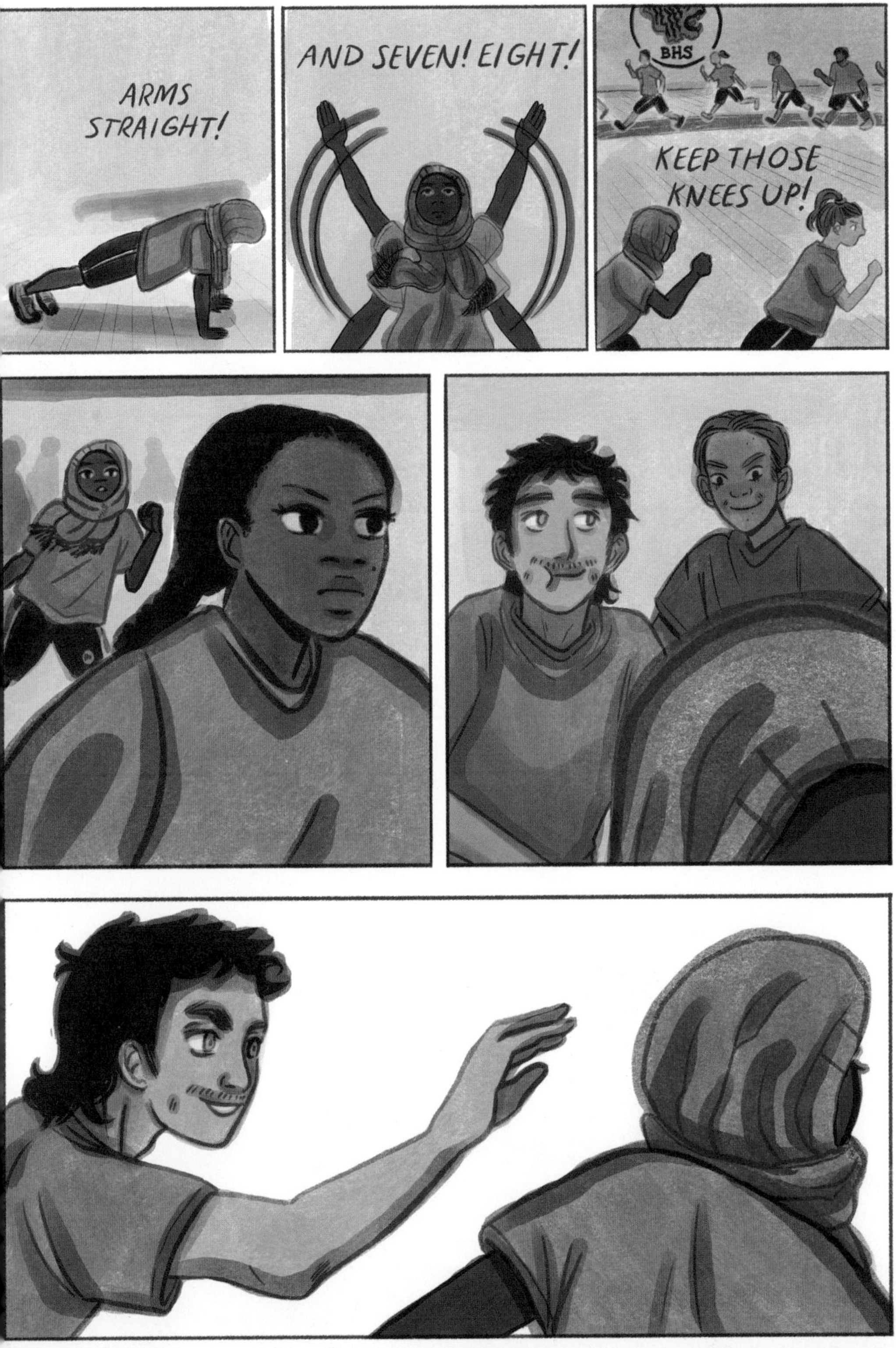
ARMS STRAIGHT!
AND SEVEN! EIGHT!
BHS
KEEP THOSE KNEES UP!

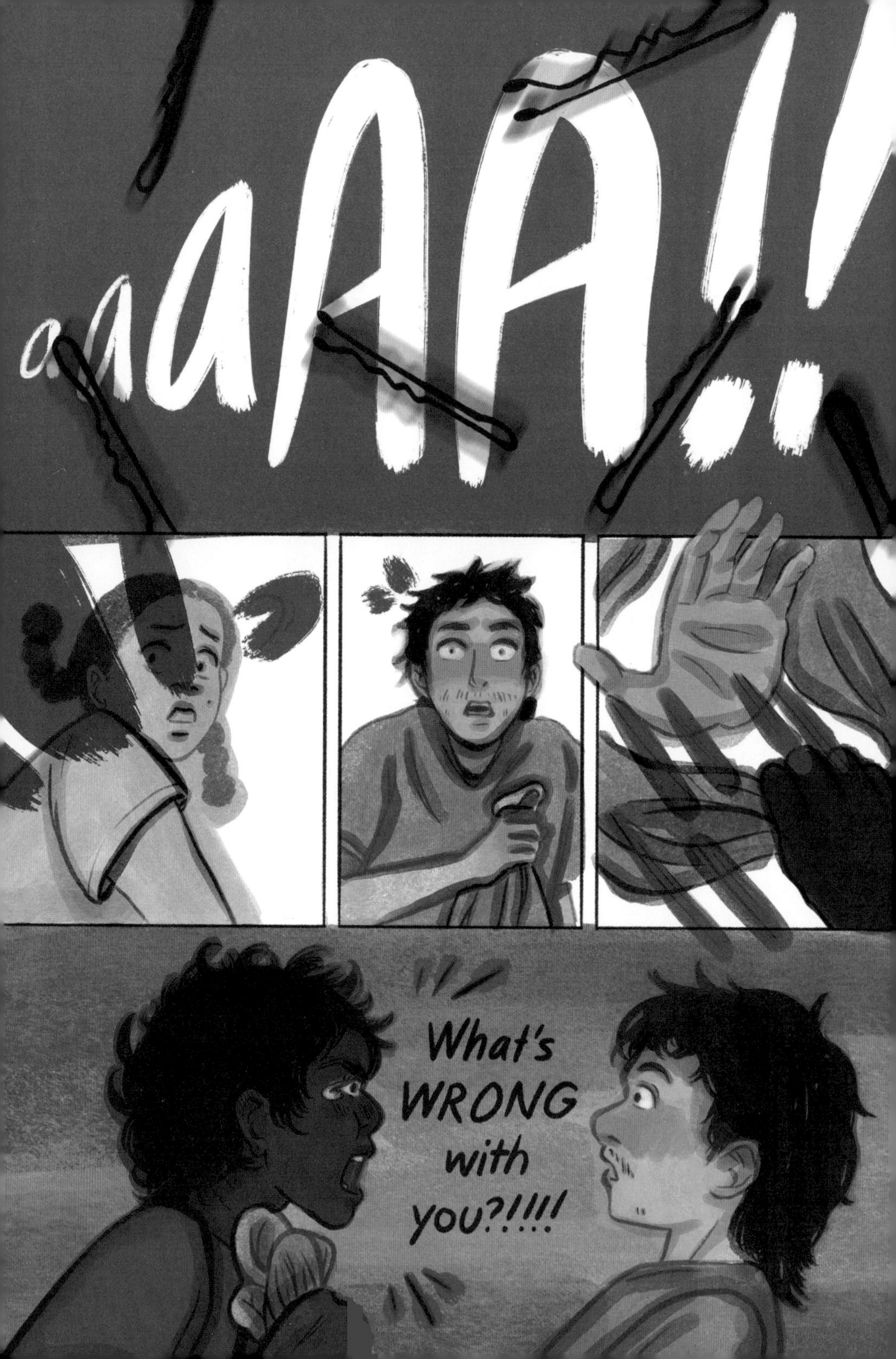
aaAAA!!
What's WRONG with you?!!!!

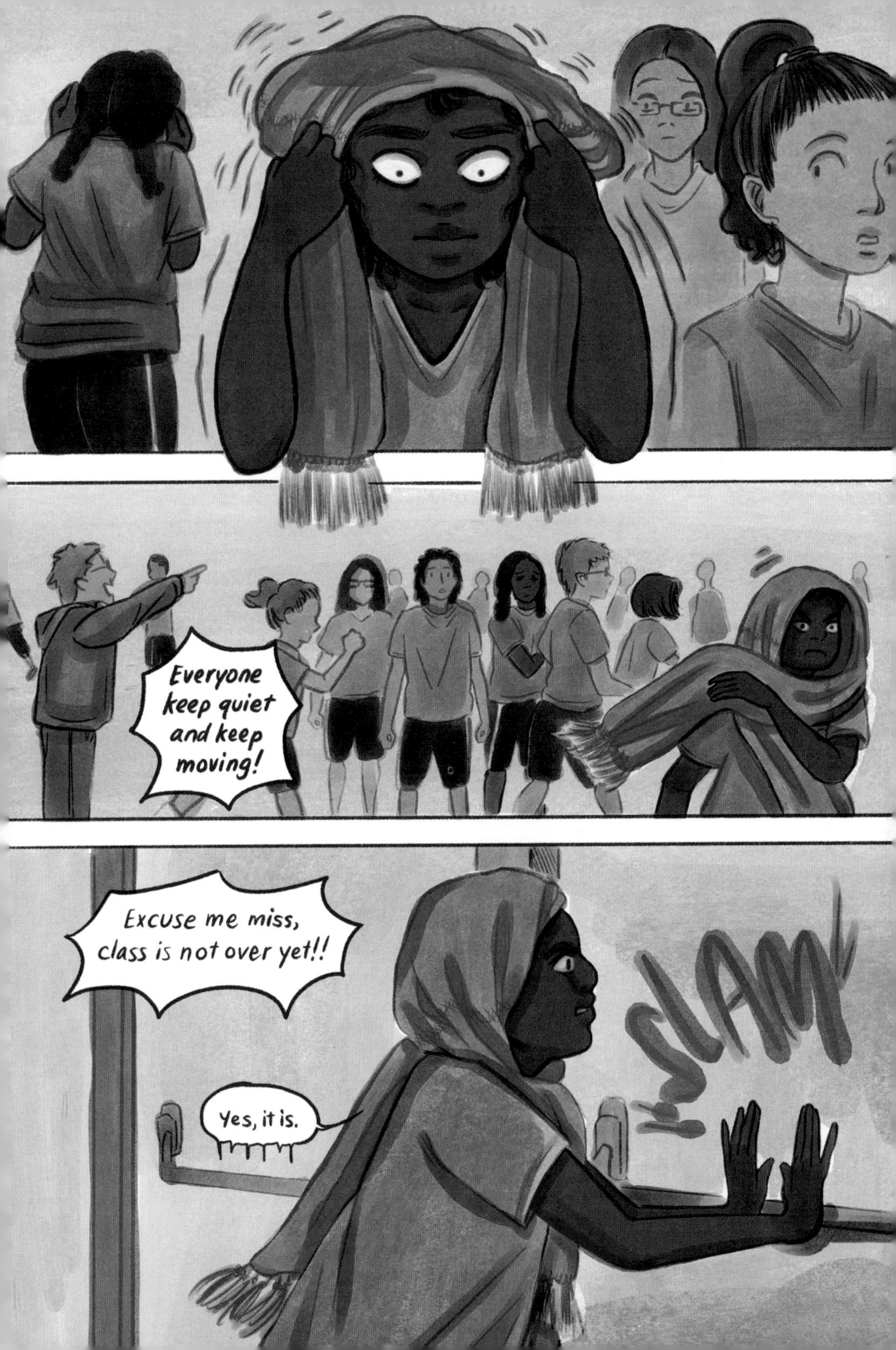
Everyone keep quiet and keep moving!
Excuse me miss, class is not over yet!!
Yes, it is.
SLAM

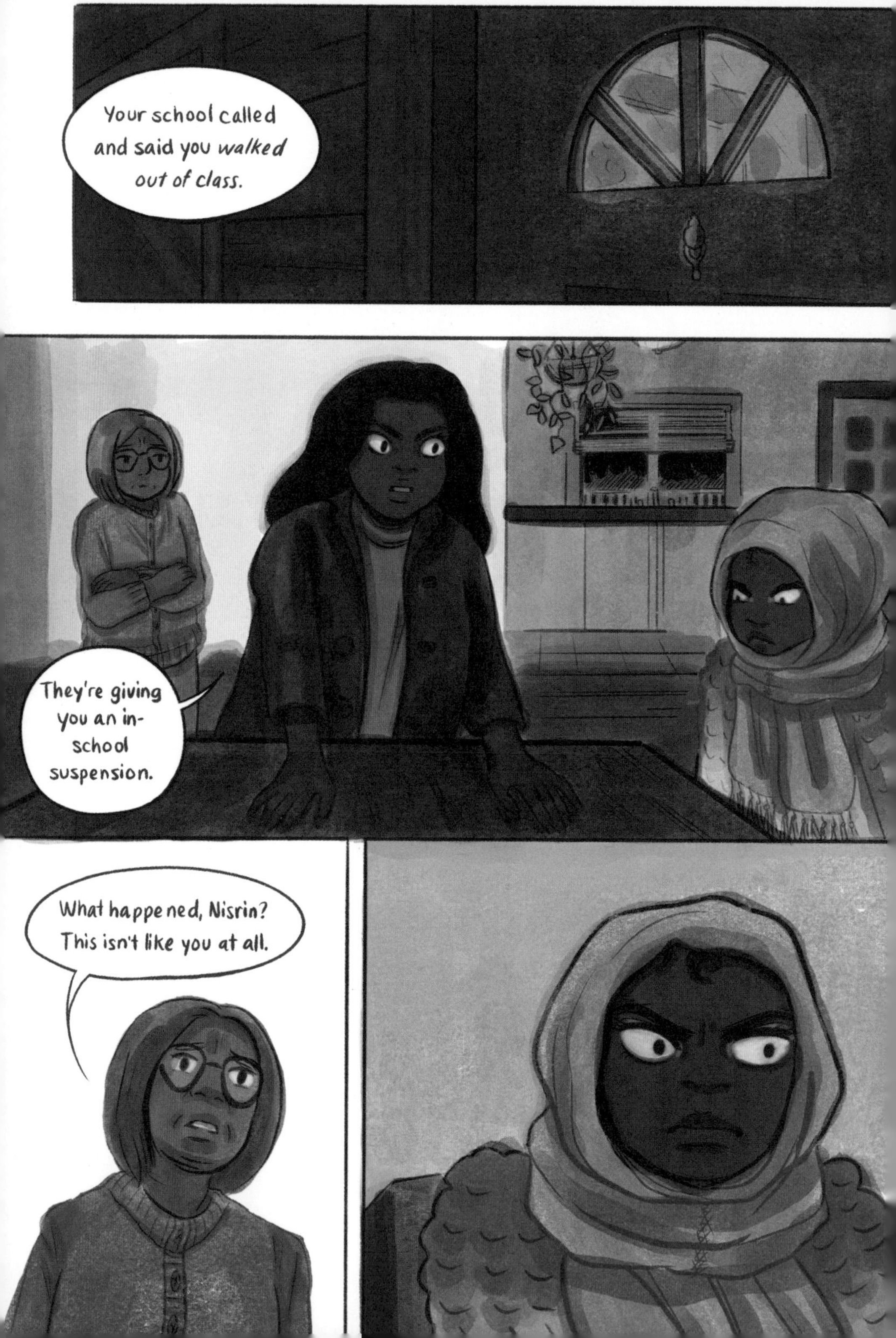
Your school called and said you *walked* out of class.
They're giving you an in-school suspension.
What happened, Nisrin? This isn't like you at all.

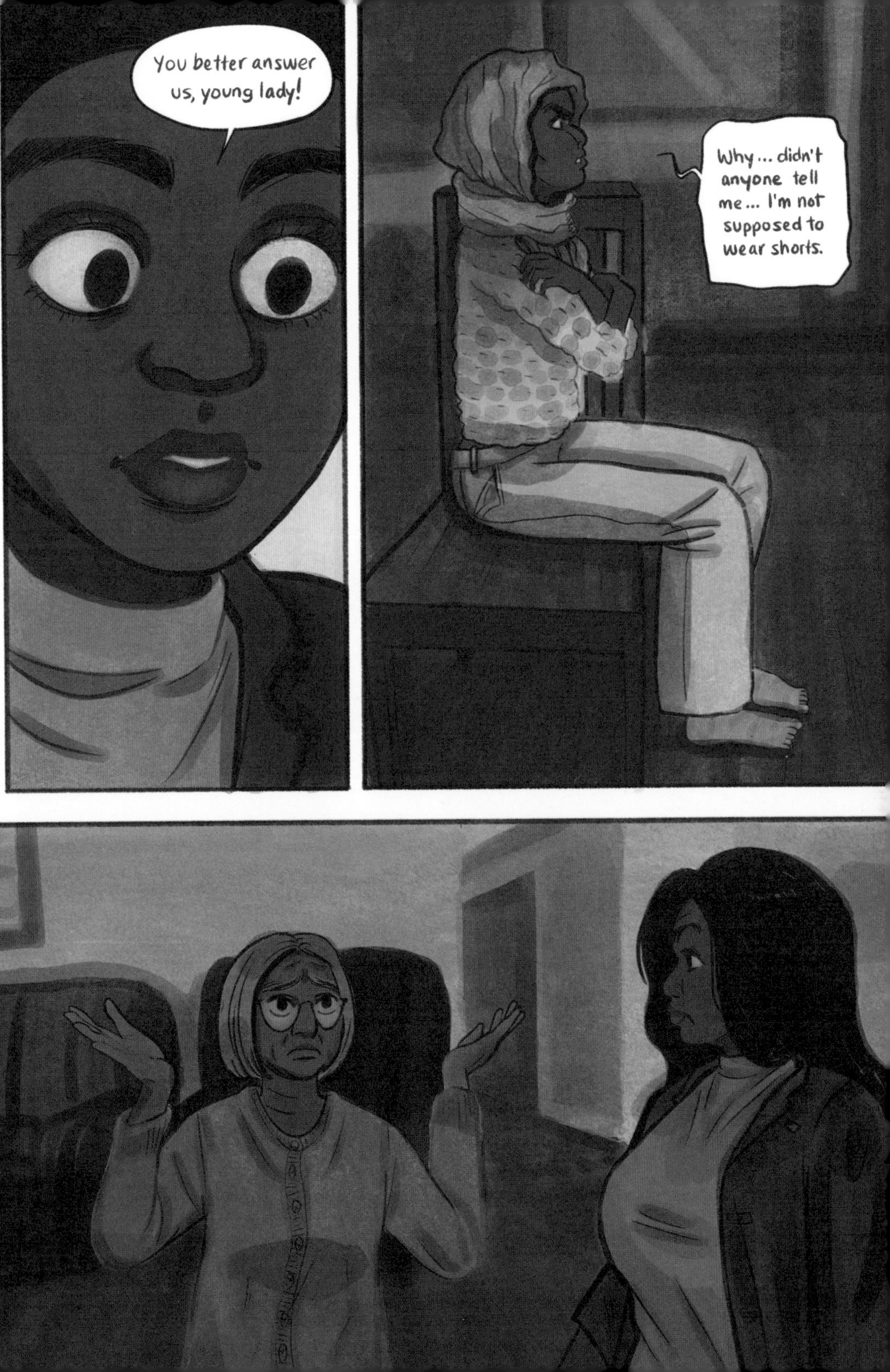
You better answer us, young lady!
Why... didn't anyone tell me... I'm not supposed to wear shorts.

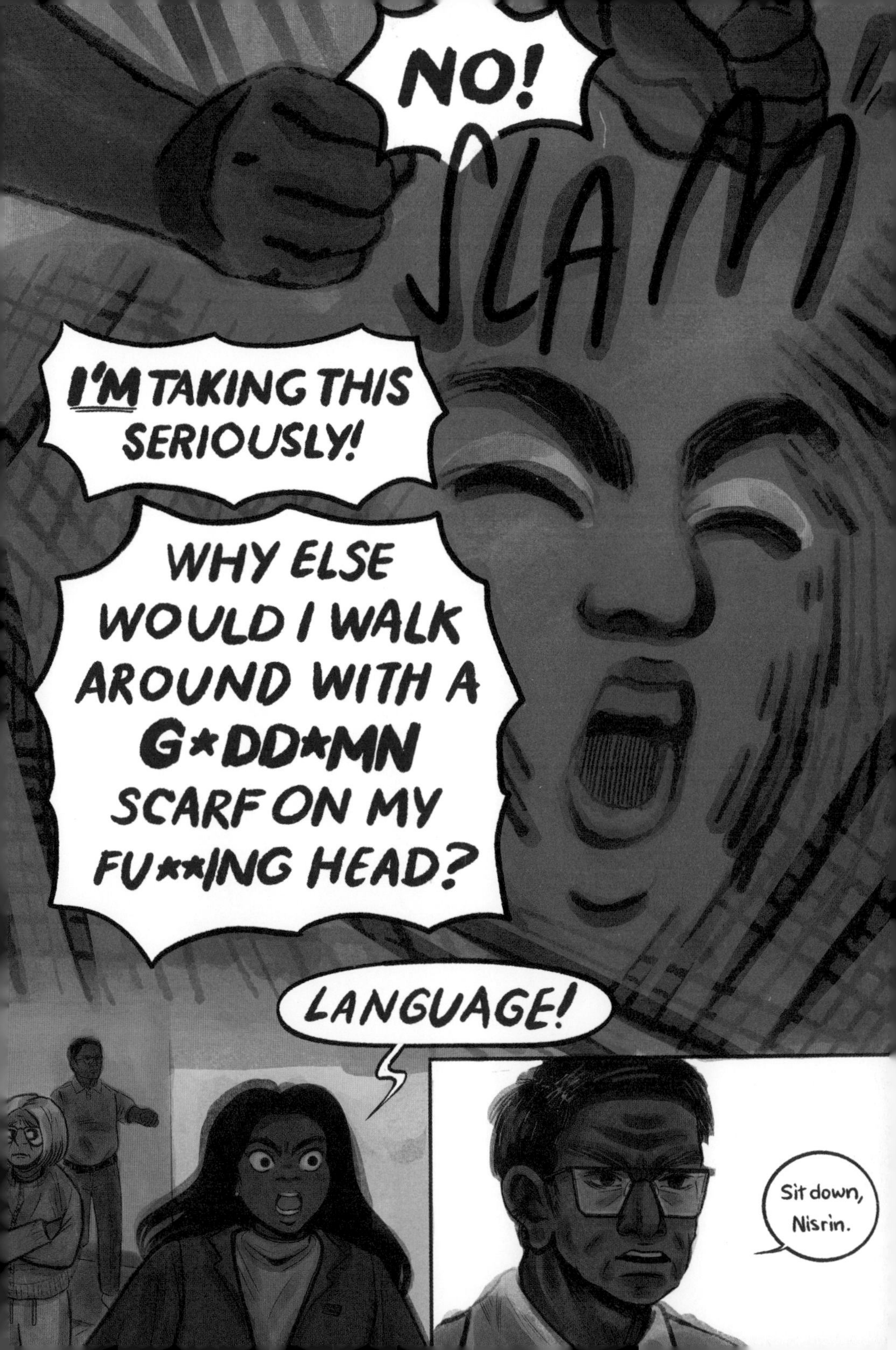
NO!
SLAM
I'M TAKING THIS SERIOUSLY!
WHY ELSE WOULD I WALK AROUND WITH A G*DD*MN SCARF ON MY FU**ING HEAD?
LANGUAGE!
Sit down, Nisrin.

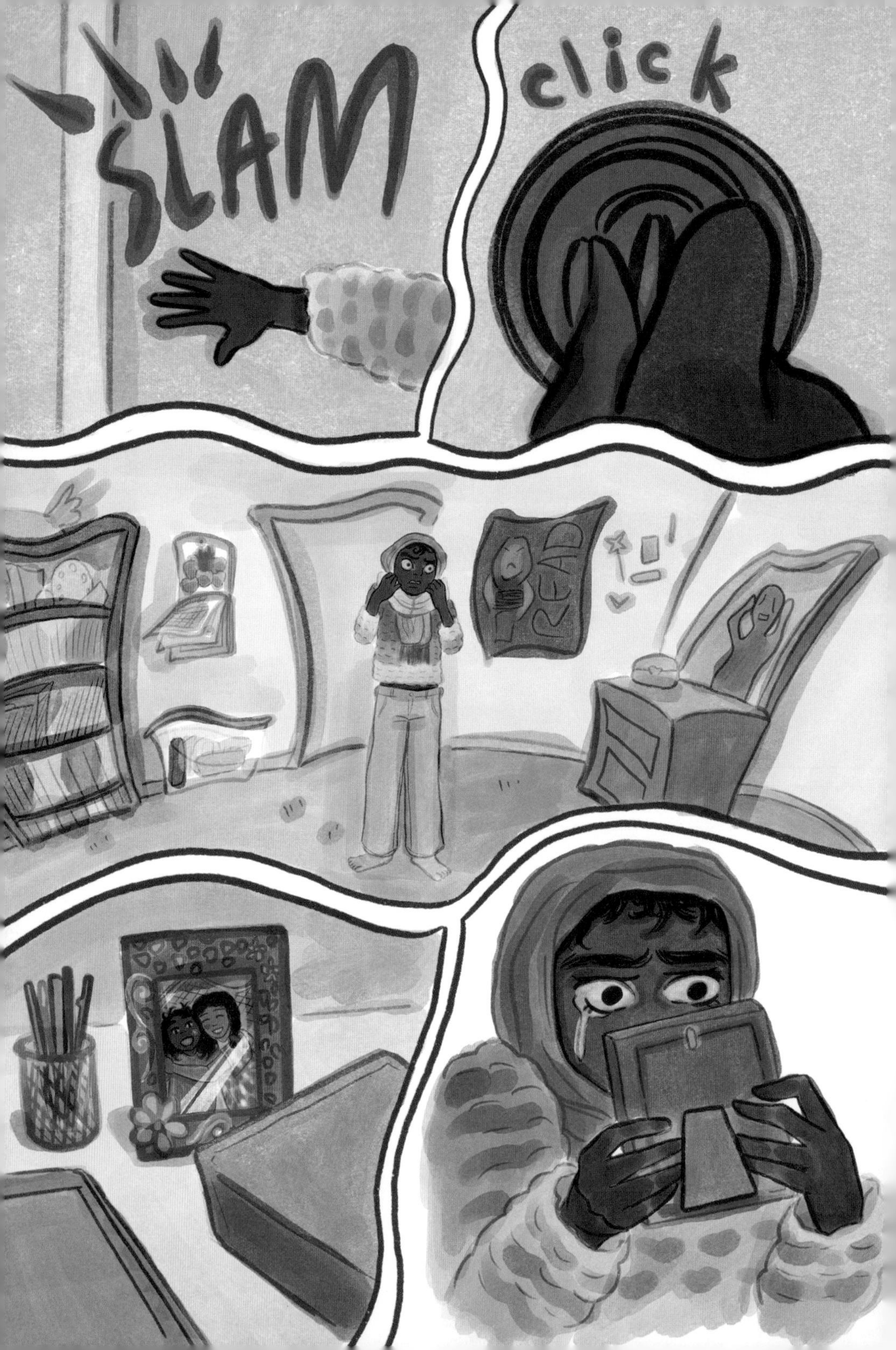
SLAM
click
READ

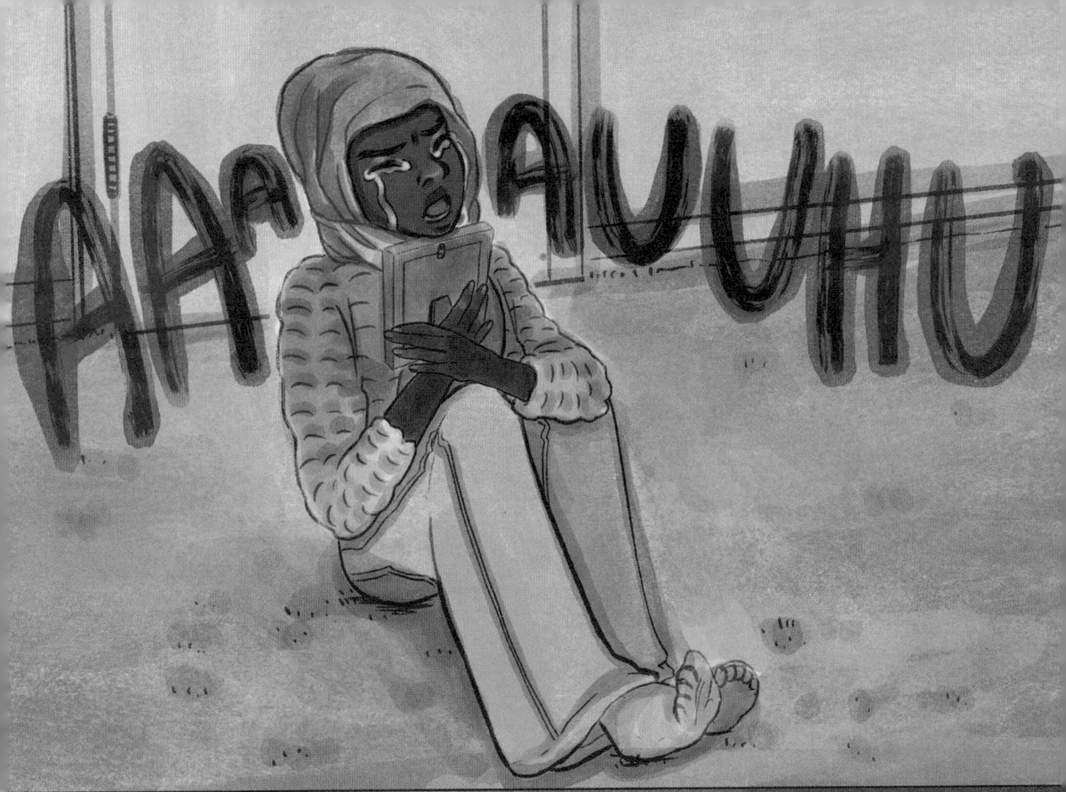
AAAAAUUHU

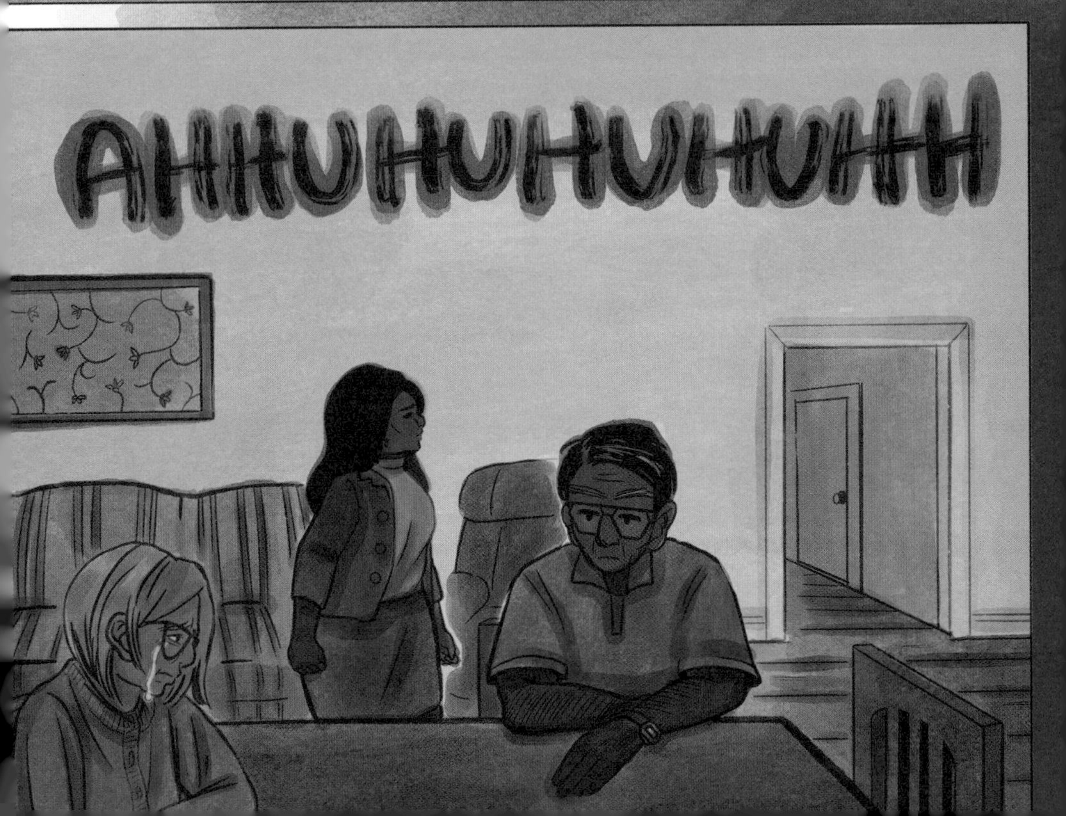
AHHUHUHUHUHH

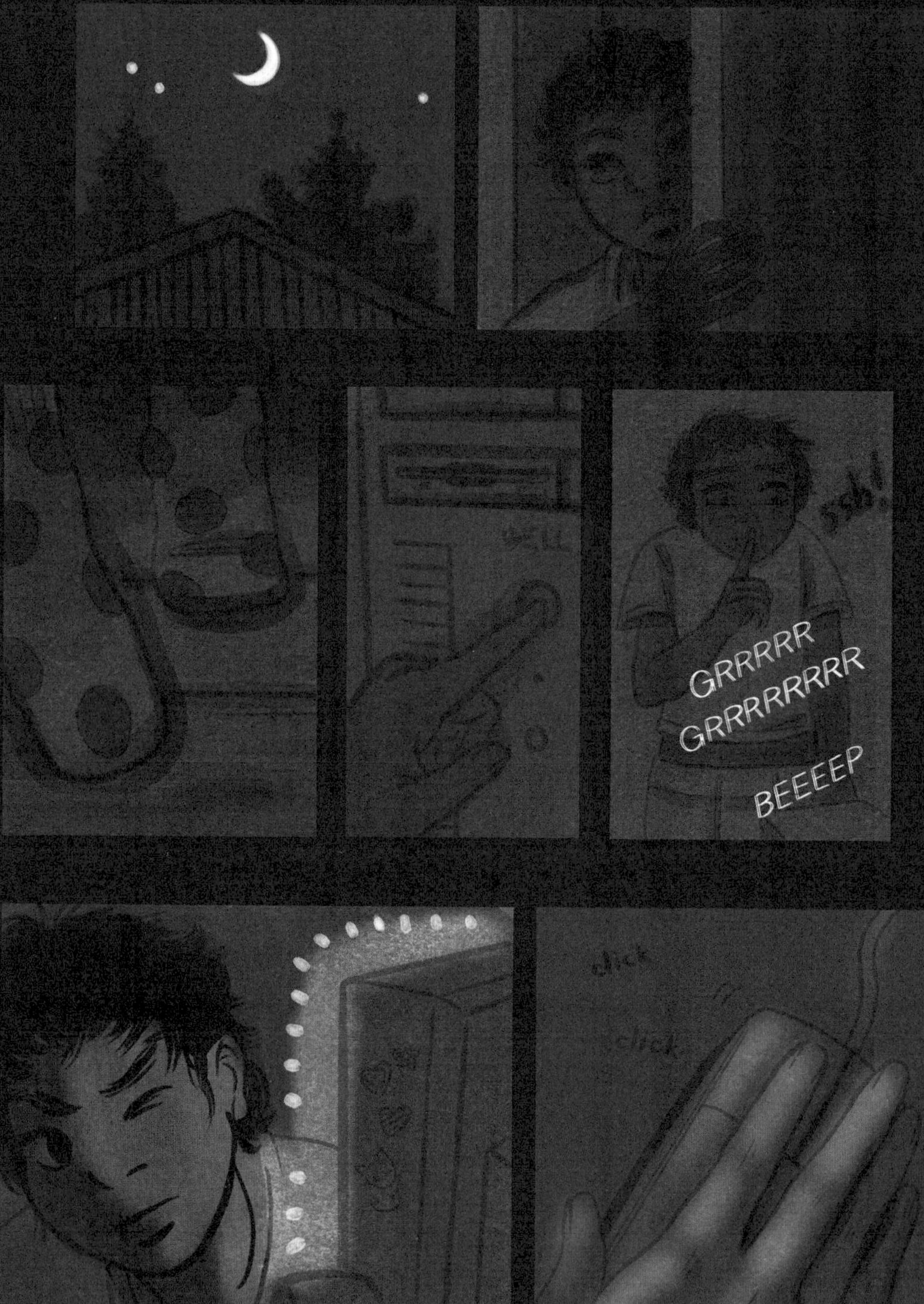
ssh!
GRRRRR
GRRRRRRRR
BEEEEP
click
click

Sturmforce

...WHAT IS BURQ
the lesser HIJAB
www.sturmforce.org/fo

they cover their hair to keep the men
from lusting after them
Their fathers make them do it...
keeps them pure for marriage

click

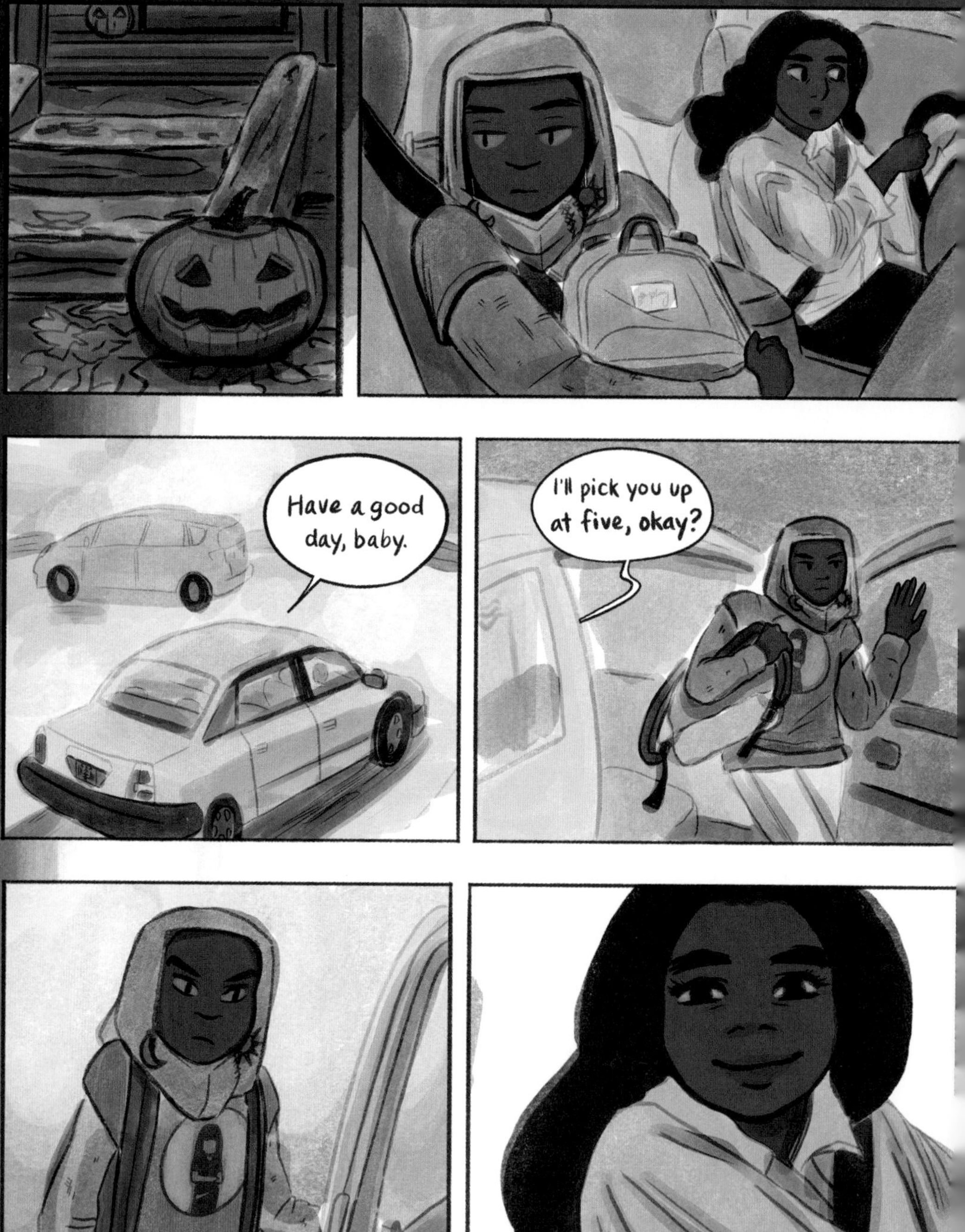
Have a good day, baby.
I'll pick you up at five, okay?

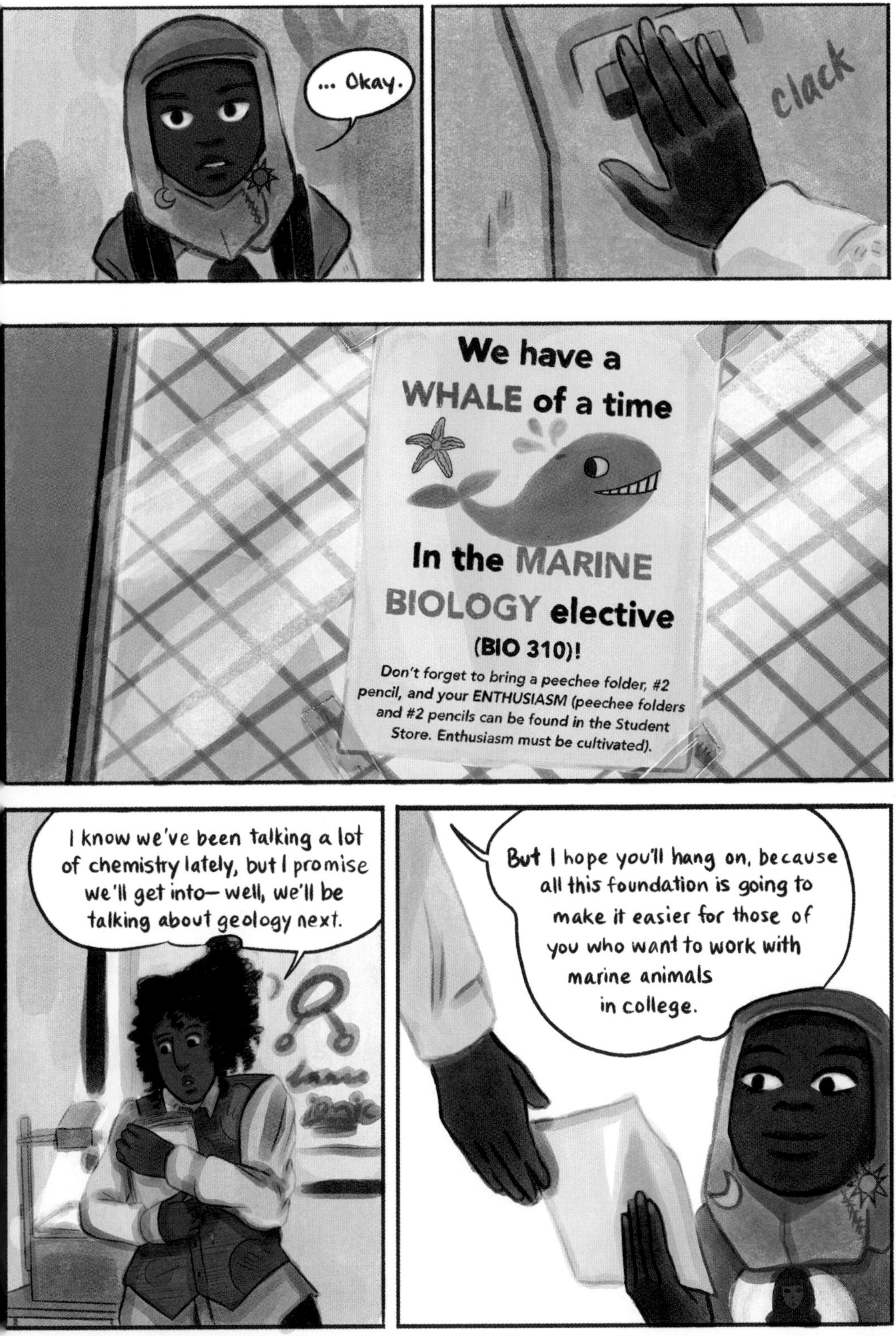
... Okay.
clack
We have a WHALE of a time
In the MARINE BIOLOGY elective
(BIO 310)!
Don't forget to bring a peechee folder, #2 pencil, and your ENTHUSIASM (peechee folders and #2 pencils can be found in the Student Store. Enthusiasm must be cultivated).
I know we've been talking a lot of chemistry lately, but I promise we'll get into— well, we'll be talking about geology next.
But I hope you'll hang on, because all this foundation is going to make it easier for those of you who want to work with marine animals in college.

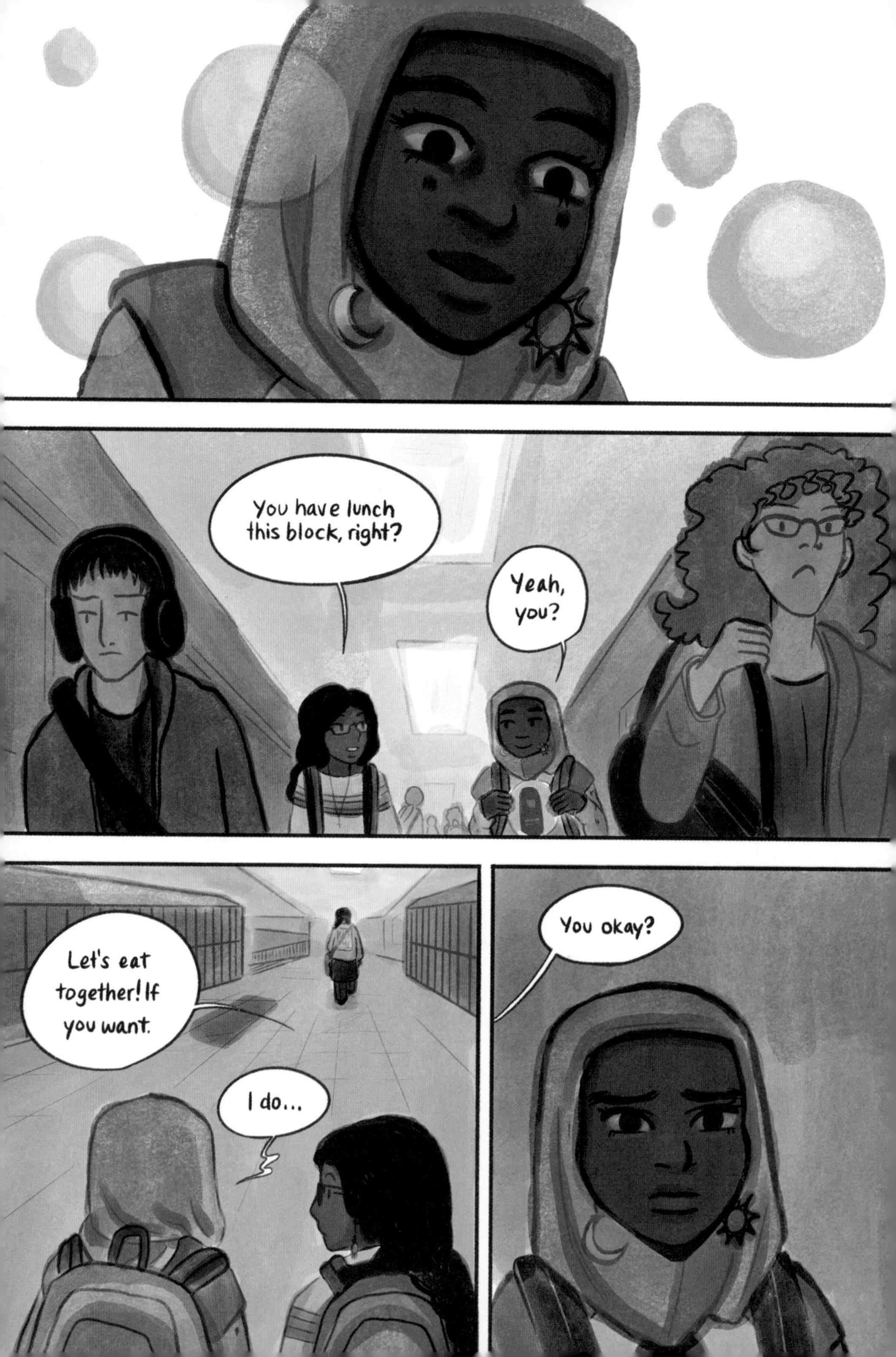

You have lunch this block, right?
Yeah, you?
Let's eat together! If you want.
I do...
You okay?

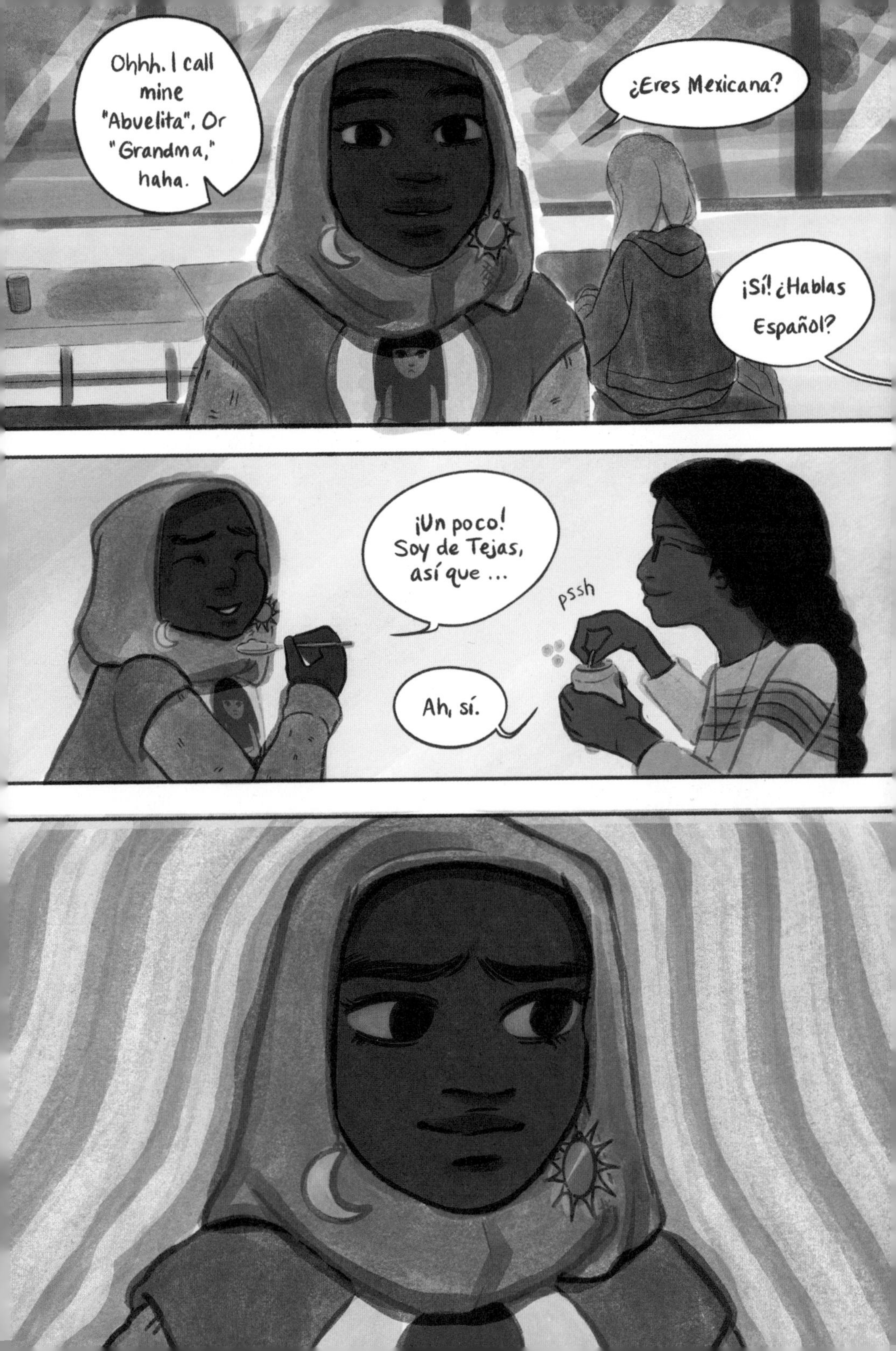
Ohhh. I call mine "Abuelita". Or "Grandma," haha.
¿Eres Mexicana?
¡Sí! ¿Hablas Español?
¡Un poco! Soy de Tejas, así que ...
pssh
Ah, sí.

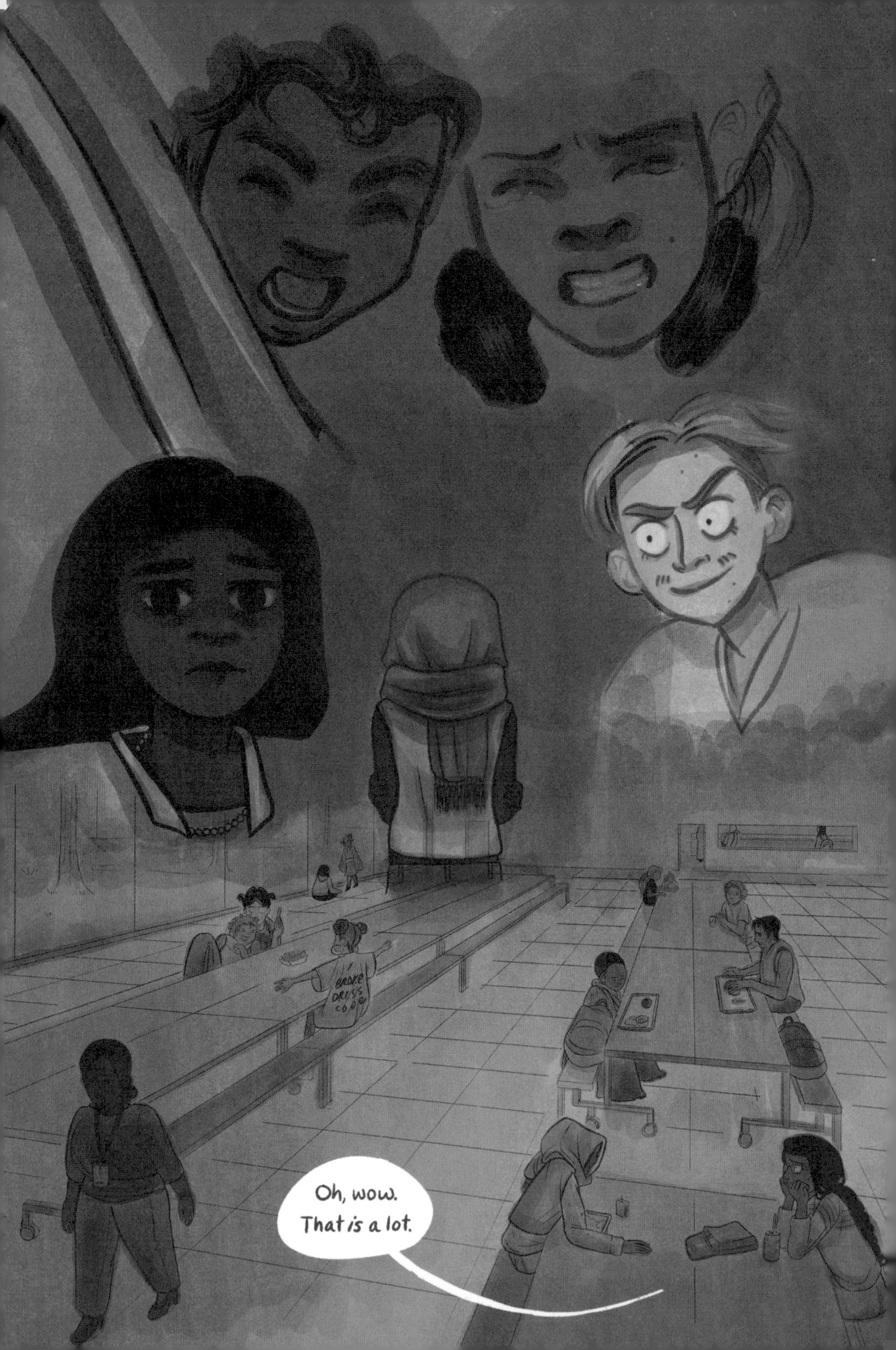
I BROKE DRESS CODE
Oh, wow. That is a lot.

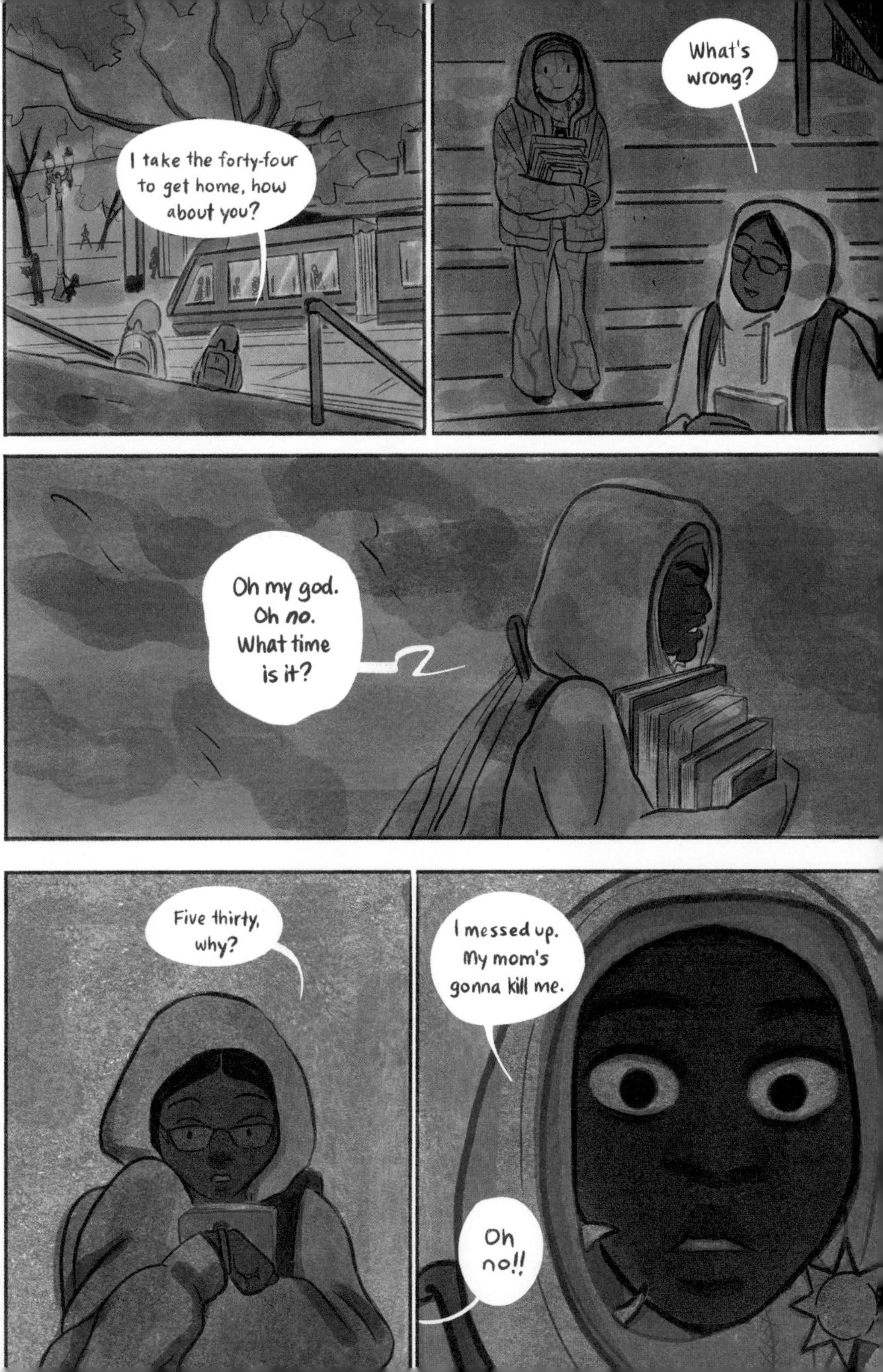
I take the forty-four to get home, how about you?
What's wrong?
Oh my god. Oh *no*. What time is it?
Five thirty, why?
I messed up. My mom's gonna kill me.
Oh no!!

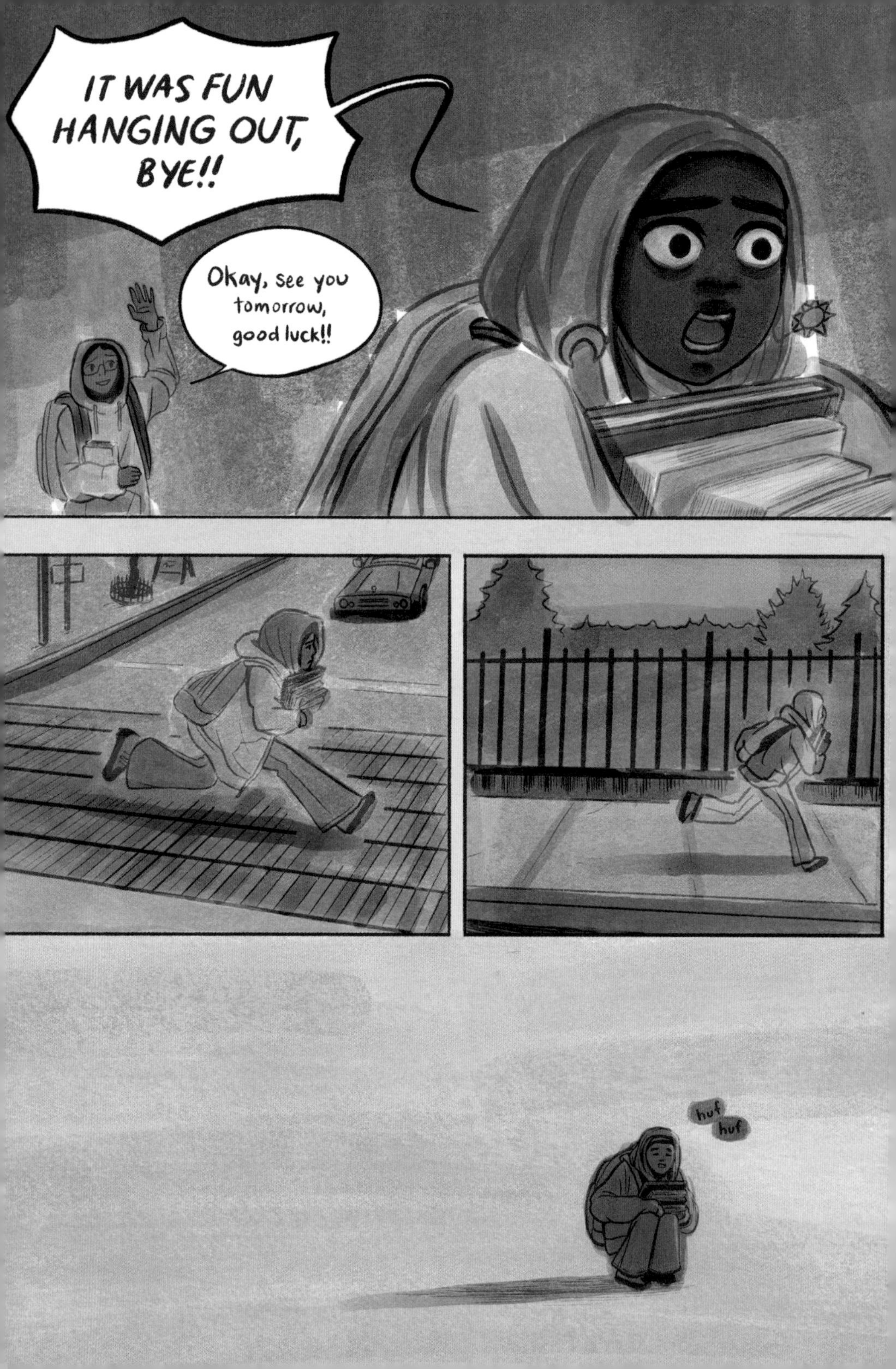
IT WAS FUN HANGING OUT, BYE!!
Okay, see you tomorrow, good luck!!
huf
huf

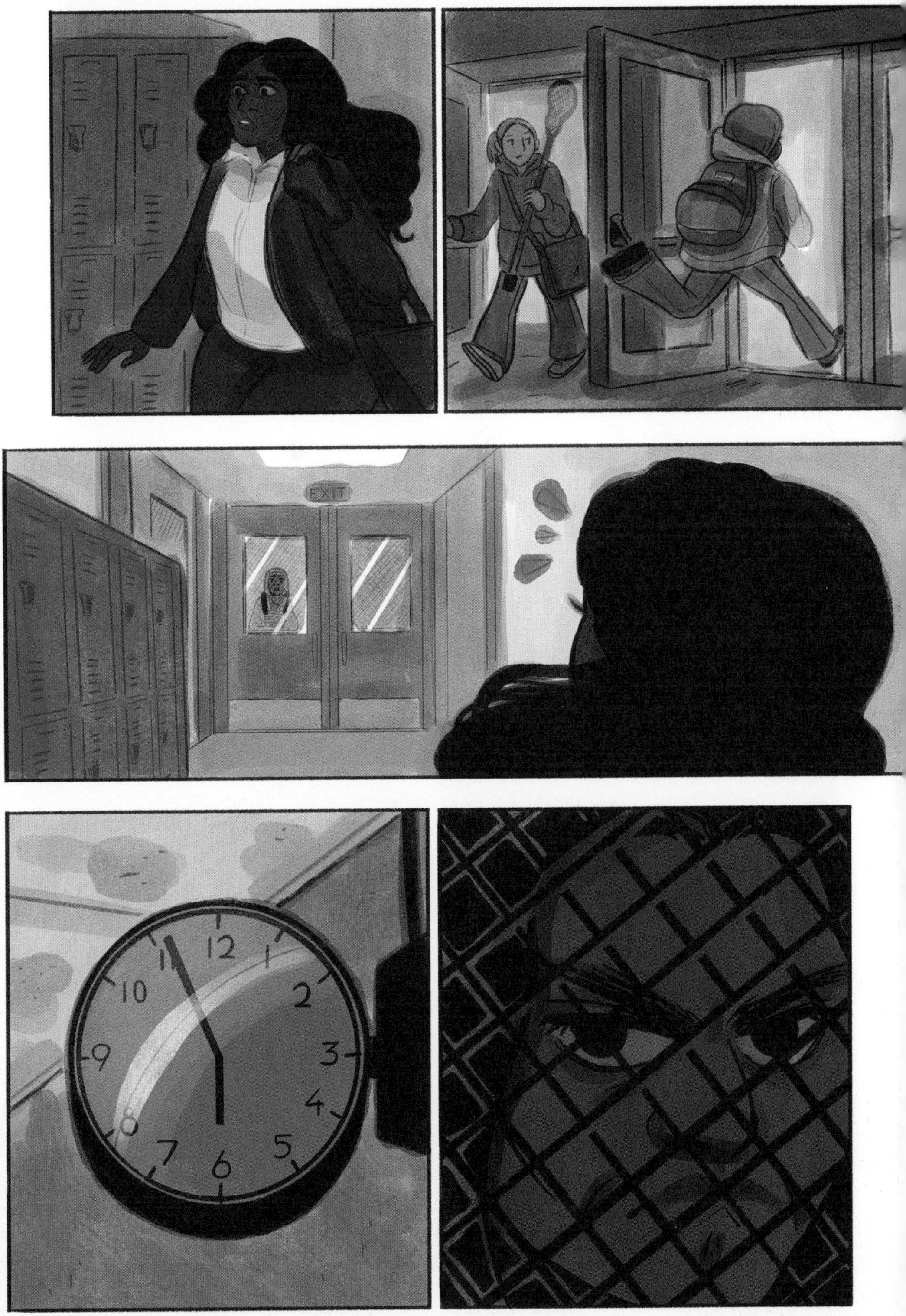
EXIT

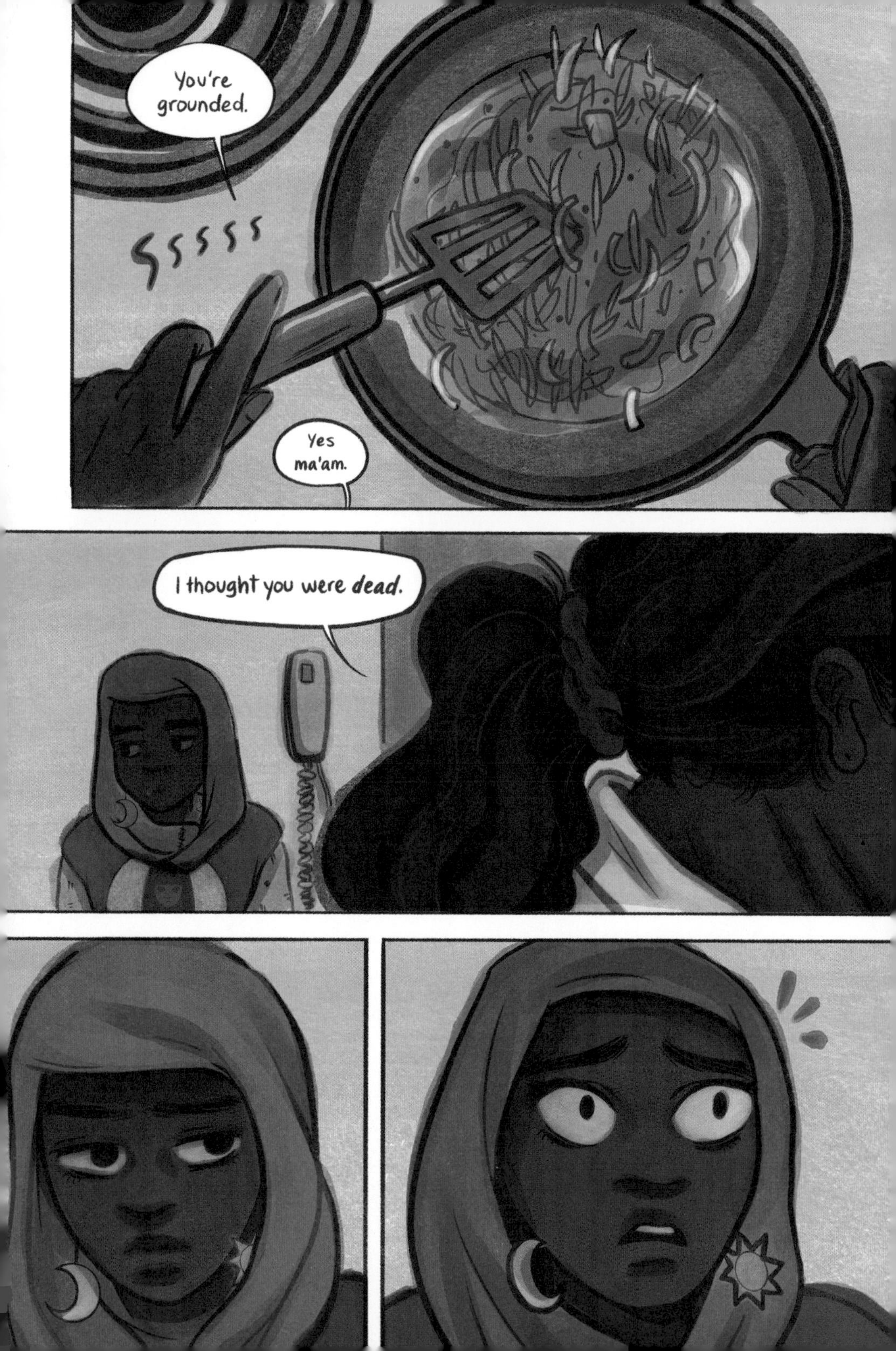
You're grounded.
SSSSS
Yes ma'am.
I thought you were *dead*.

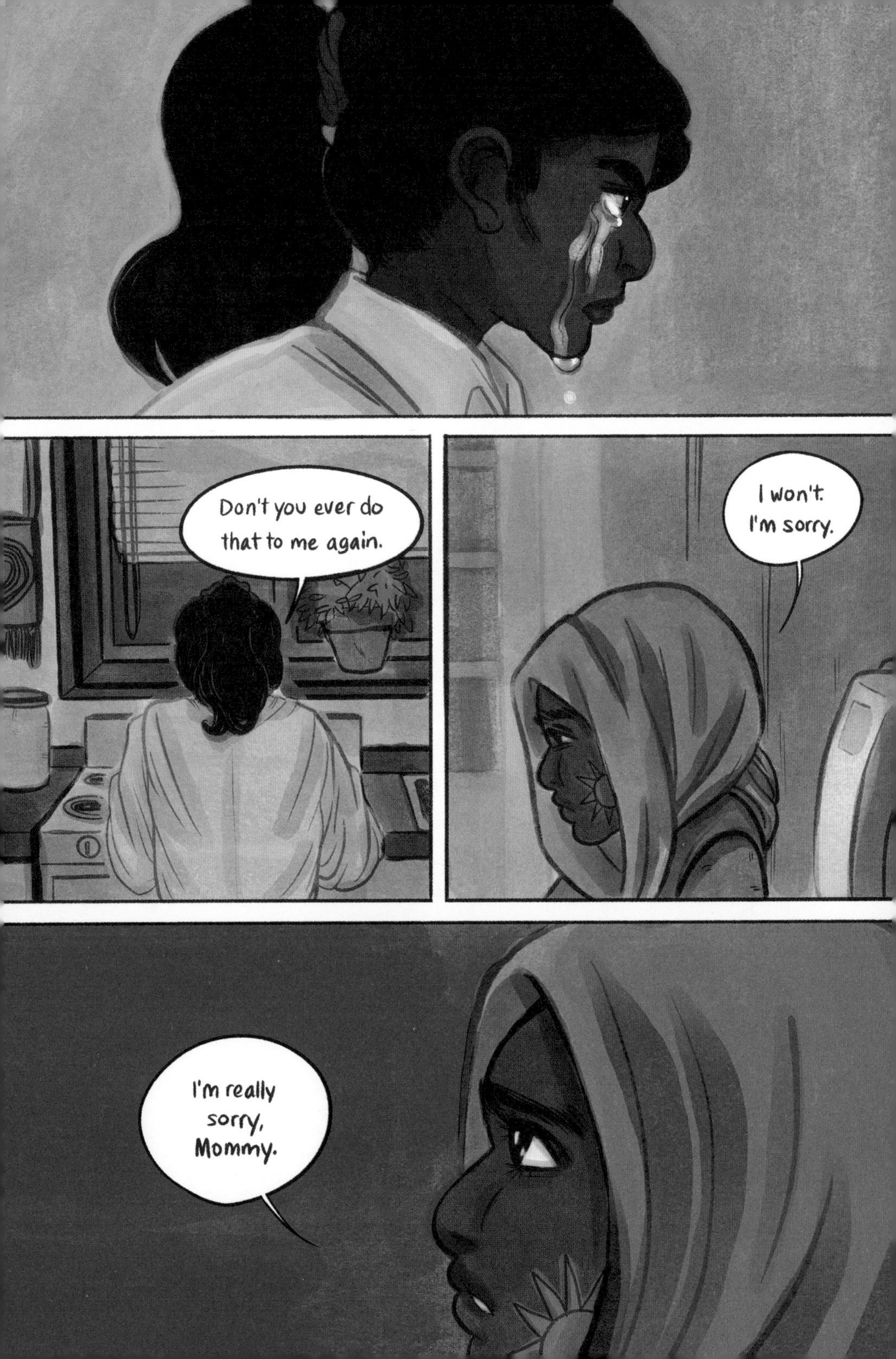
Don't you ever do that to me again.
I won't. I'm sorry.
I'm really sorry, Mommy.

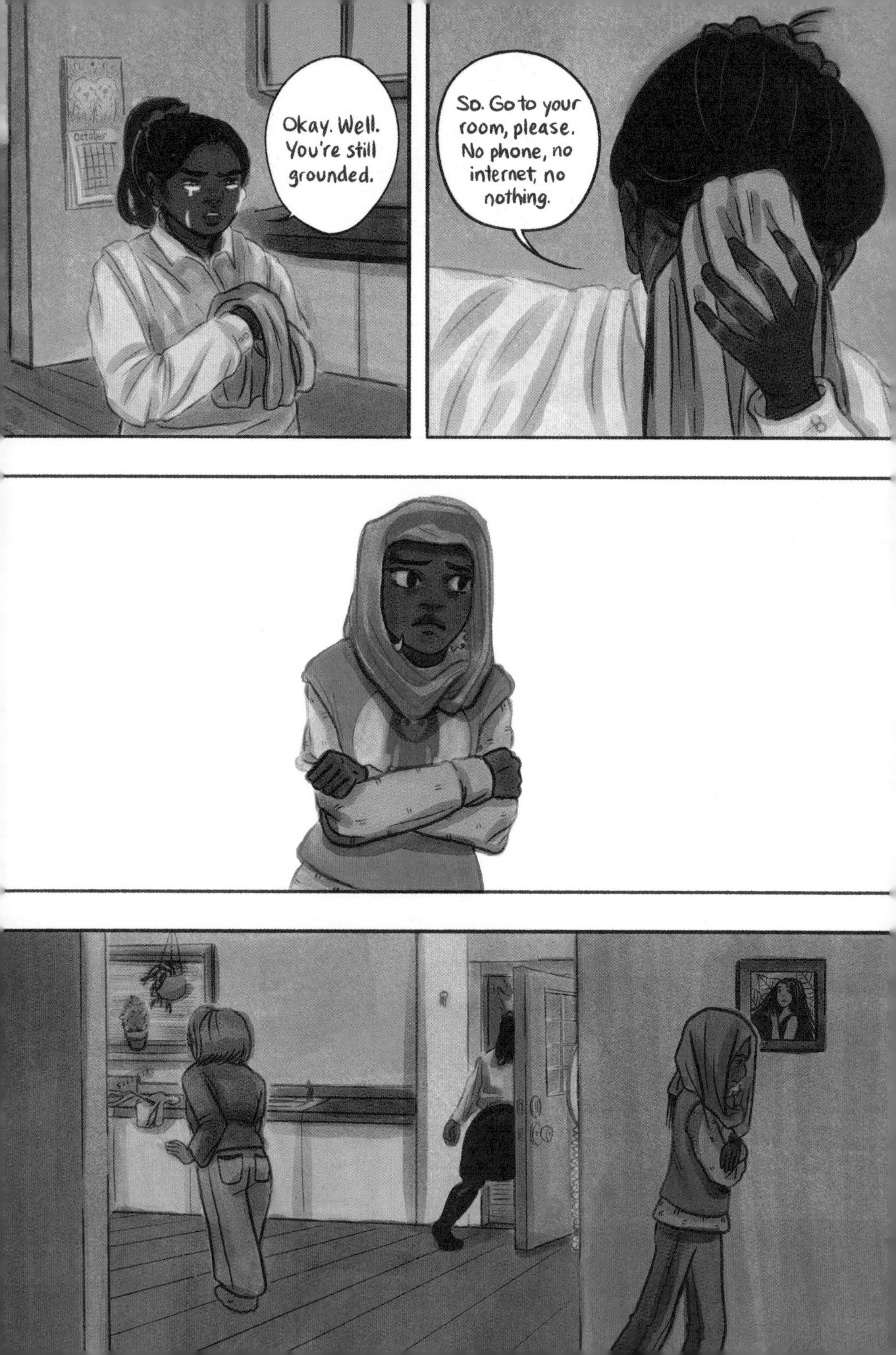
October
Okay. Well. You're still grounded.
So. Go to your room, please. No phone, no internet, no nothing.

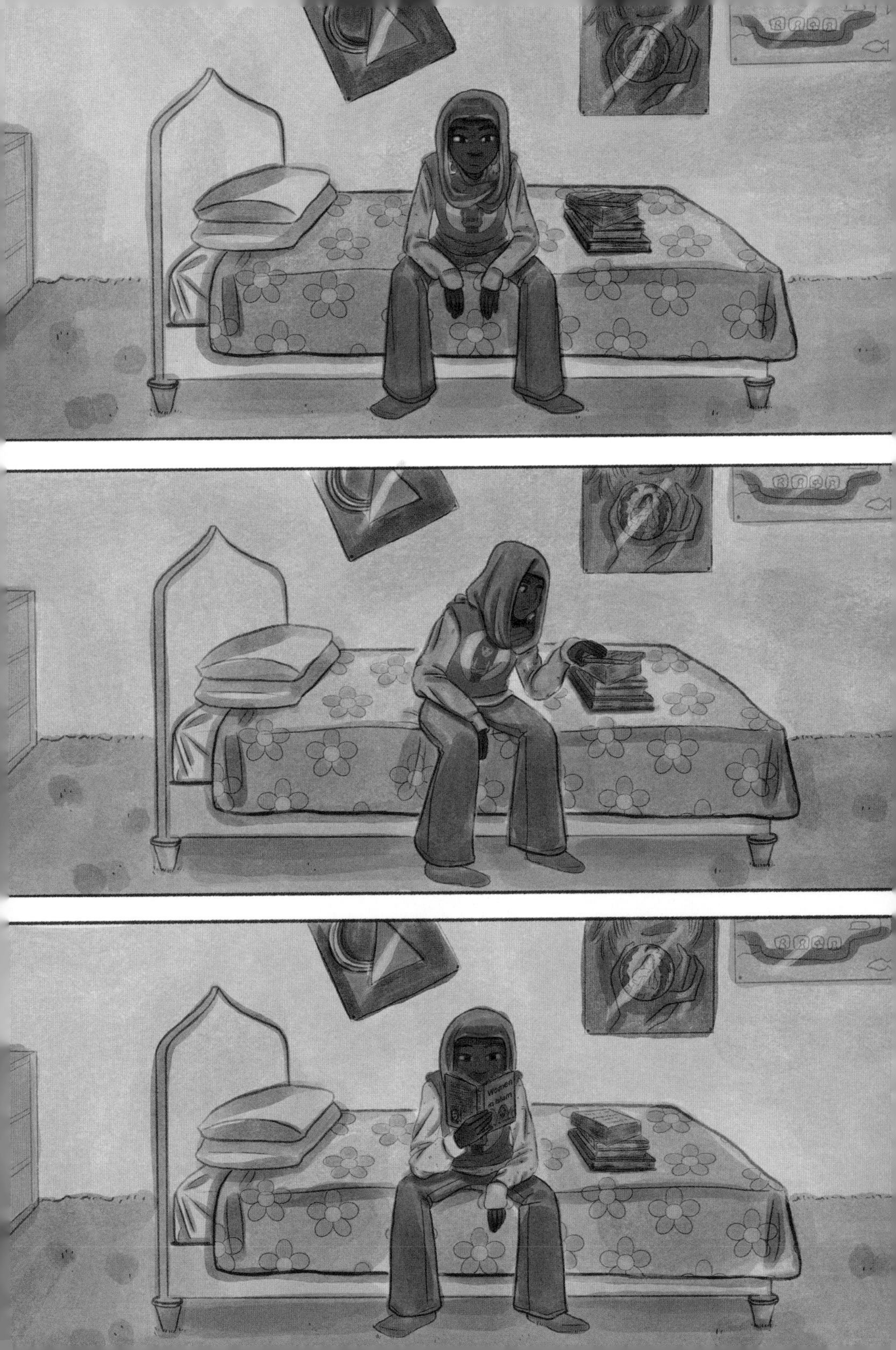
Women in Islam

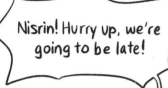

Nisrin! Hurry up, we're going to be late!

I'm ready!

Put on a coat!

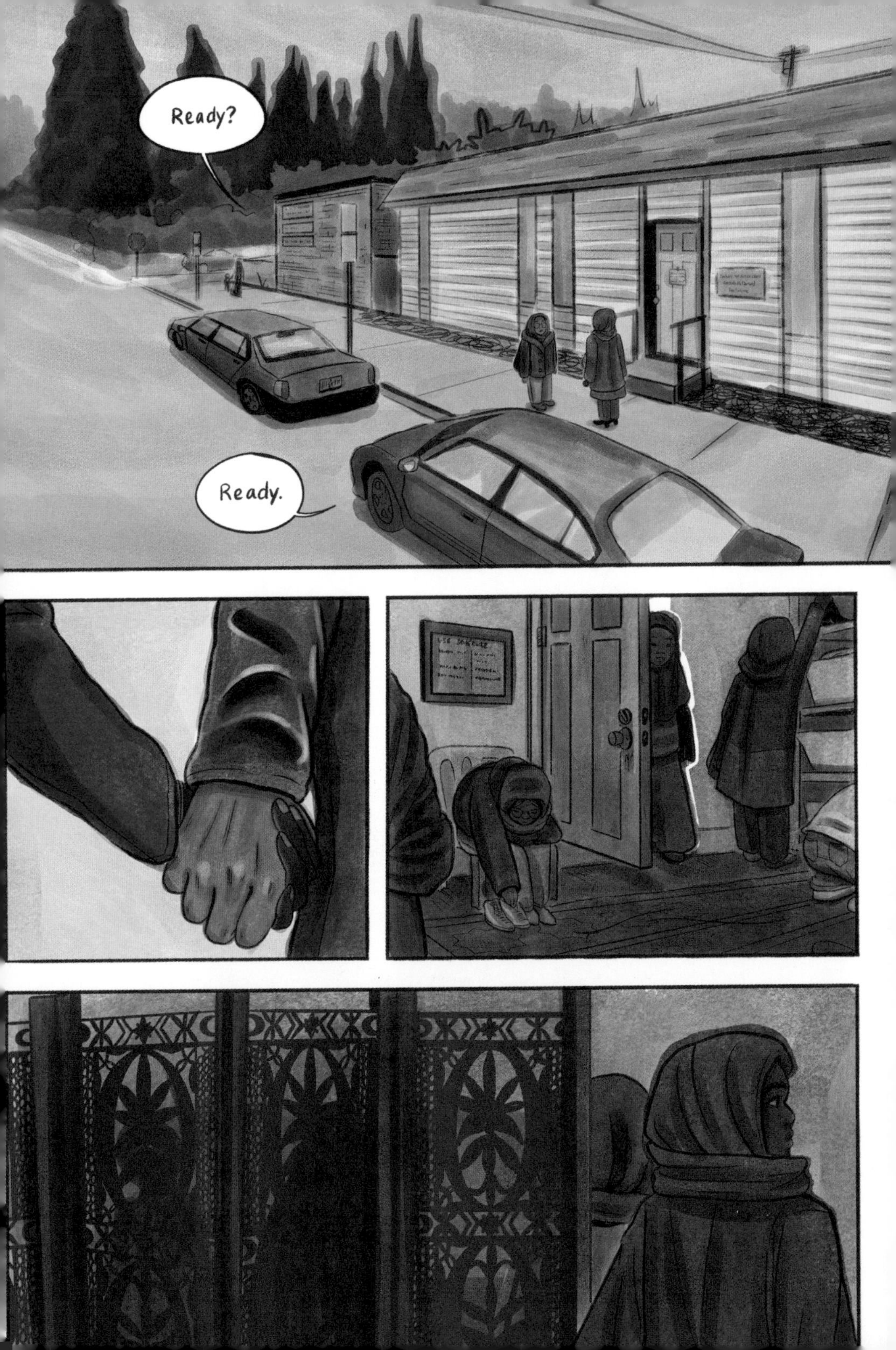
Ready?
Ready.

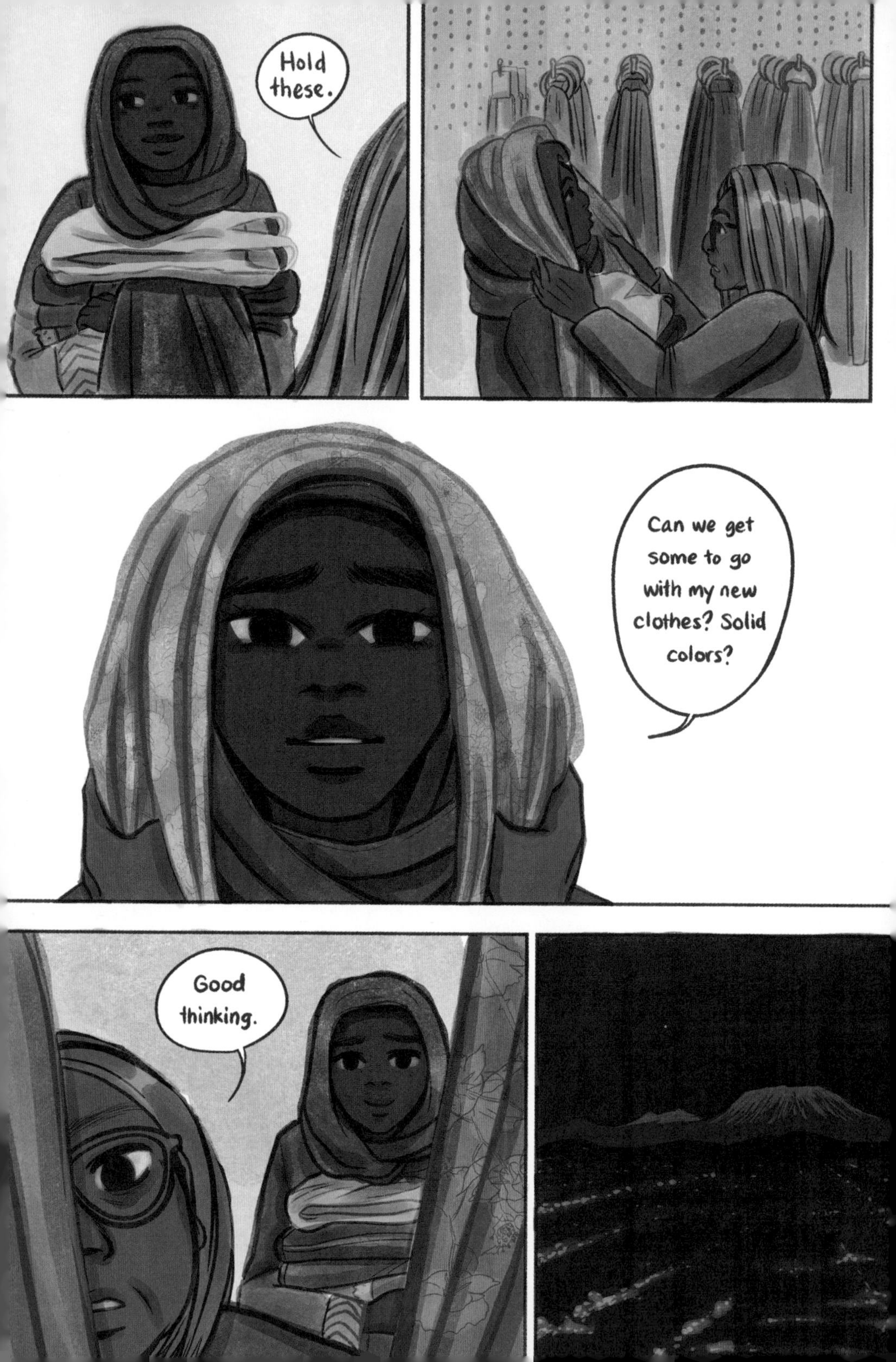
Hold these.
Can we get some to go with my new clothes? Solid colors?
Good thinking.

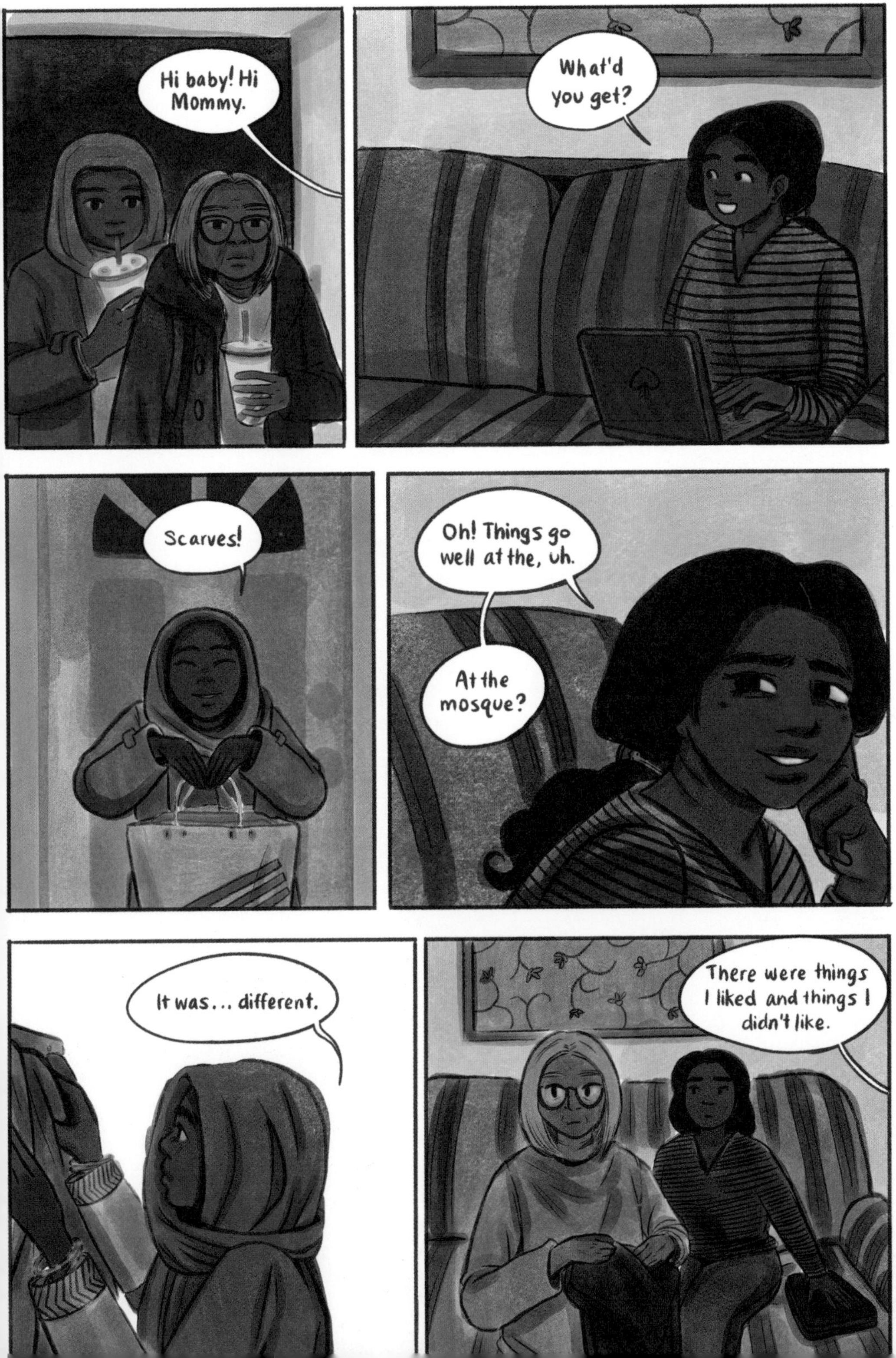
Hi baby! Hi Mommy.
What'd you get?
Scarves!
Oh! Things go well at the, uh.
At the mosque?
It was... different.
There were things I liked and things I didn't like.

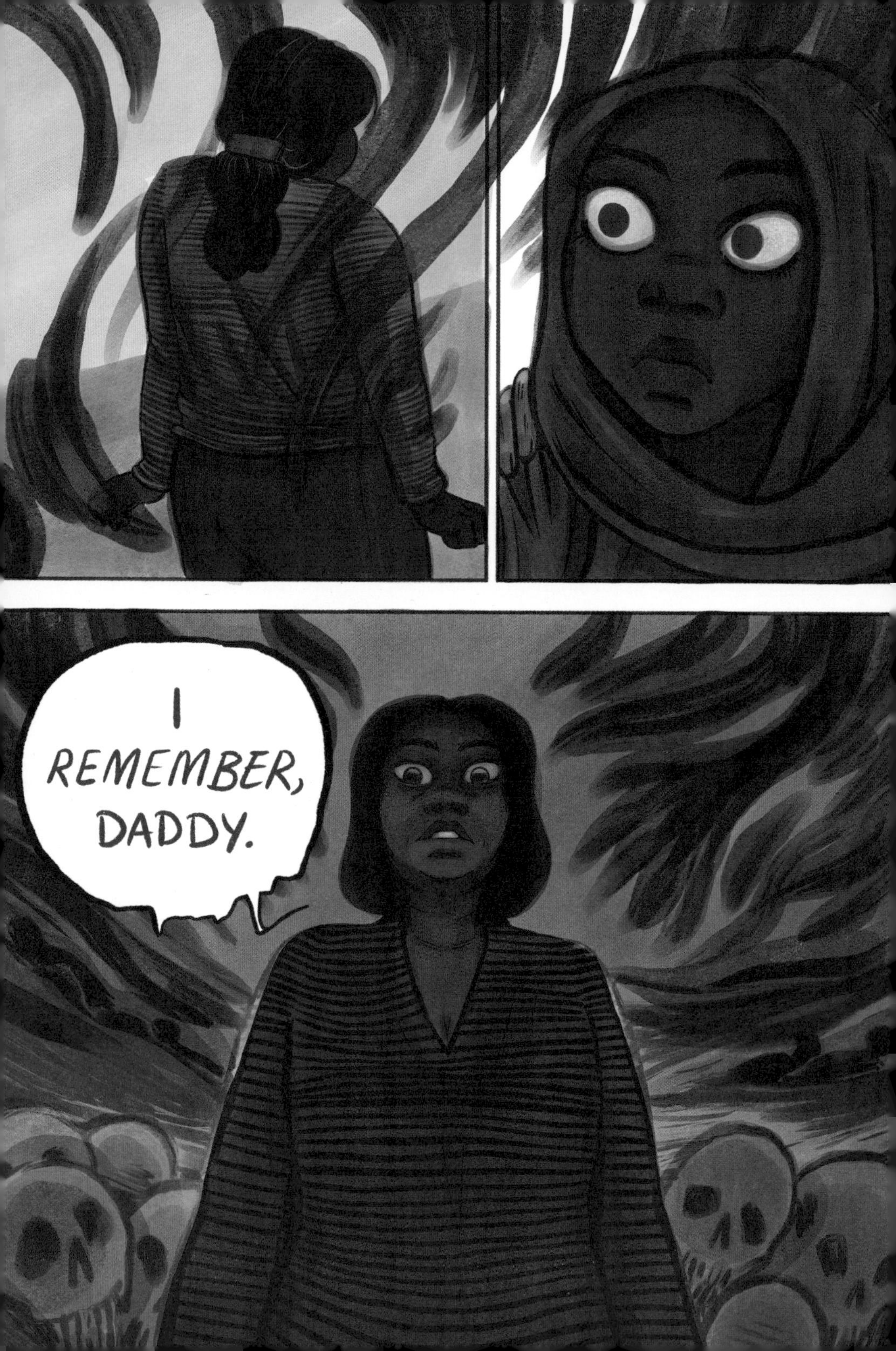
I REMEMBER, DADDY.

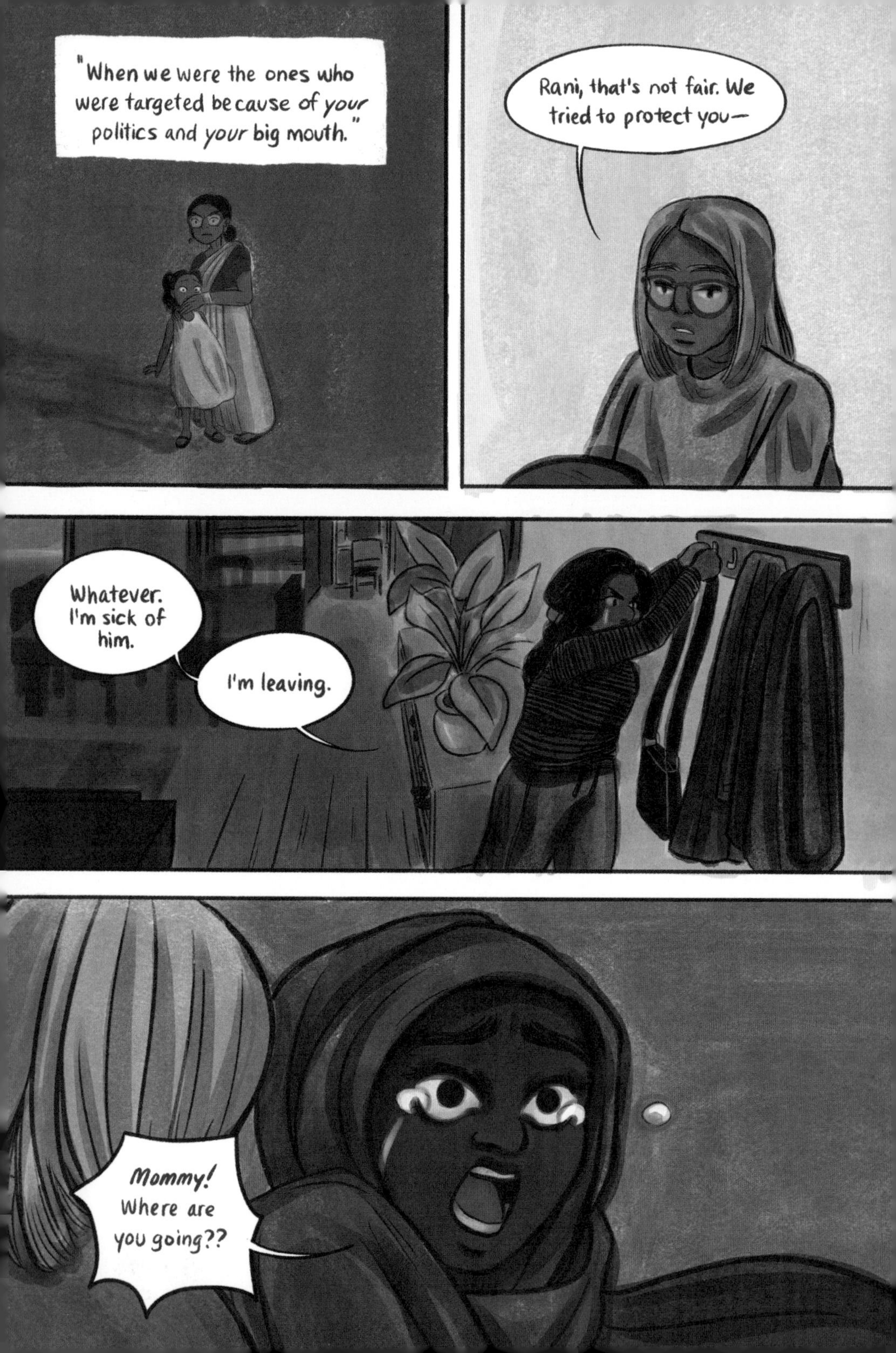
"When we were the ones who were targeted because of *your* politics and *your* big mouth."
Rani, that's not fair. We tried to protect you—
Whatever. I'm sick of him.
I'm leaving.
Mommy! Where are you going??

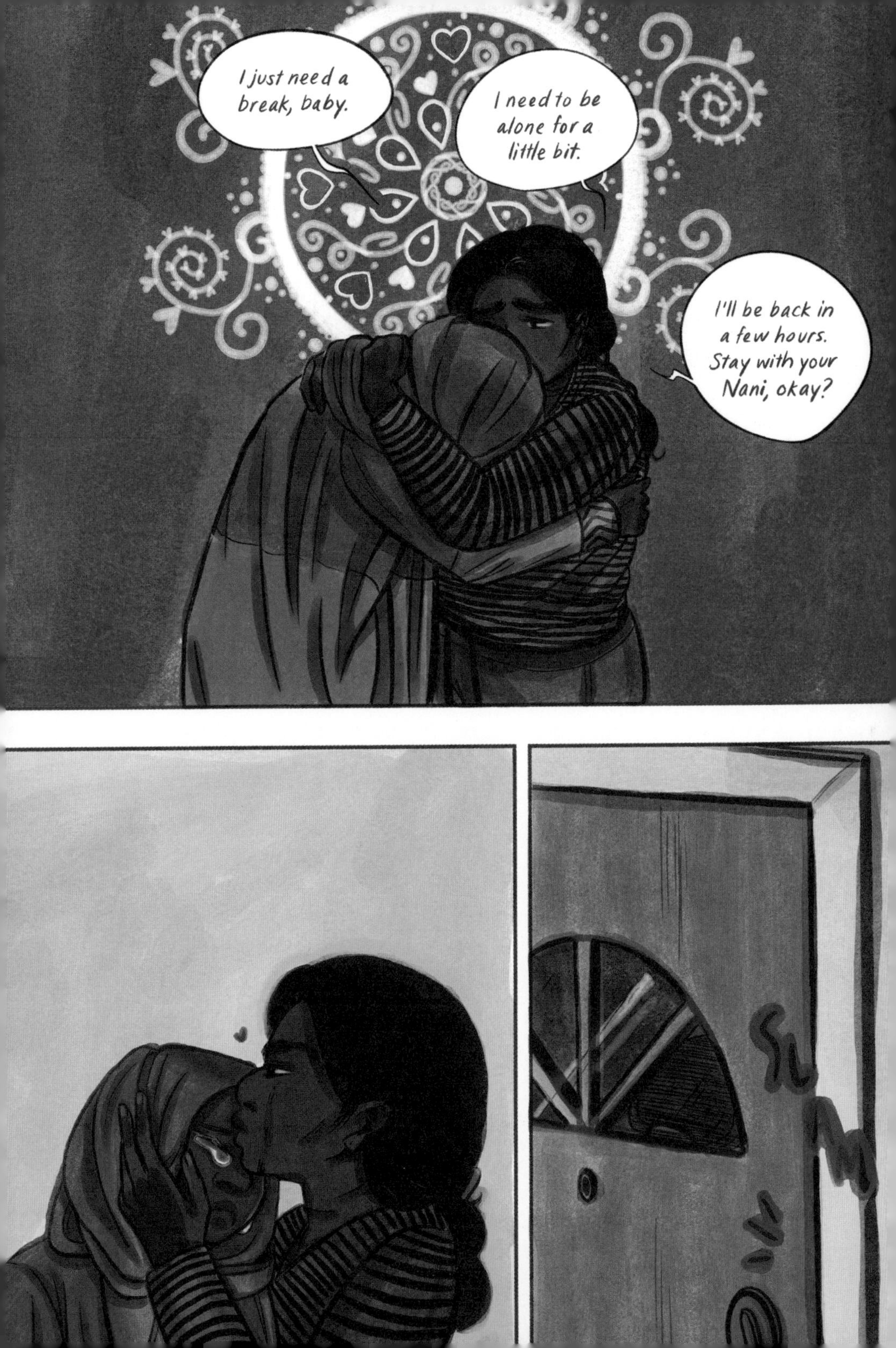
I just need a break, baby.
I need to be alone for a little bit.
I'll be back in a few hours. Stay with your Nani, okay?

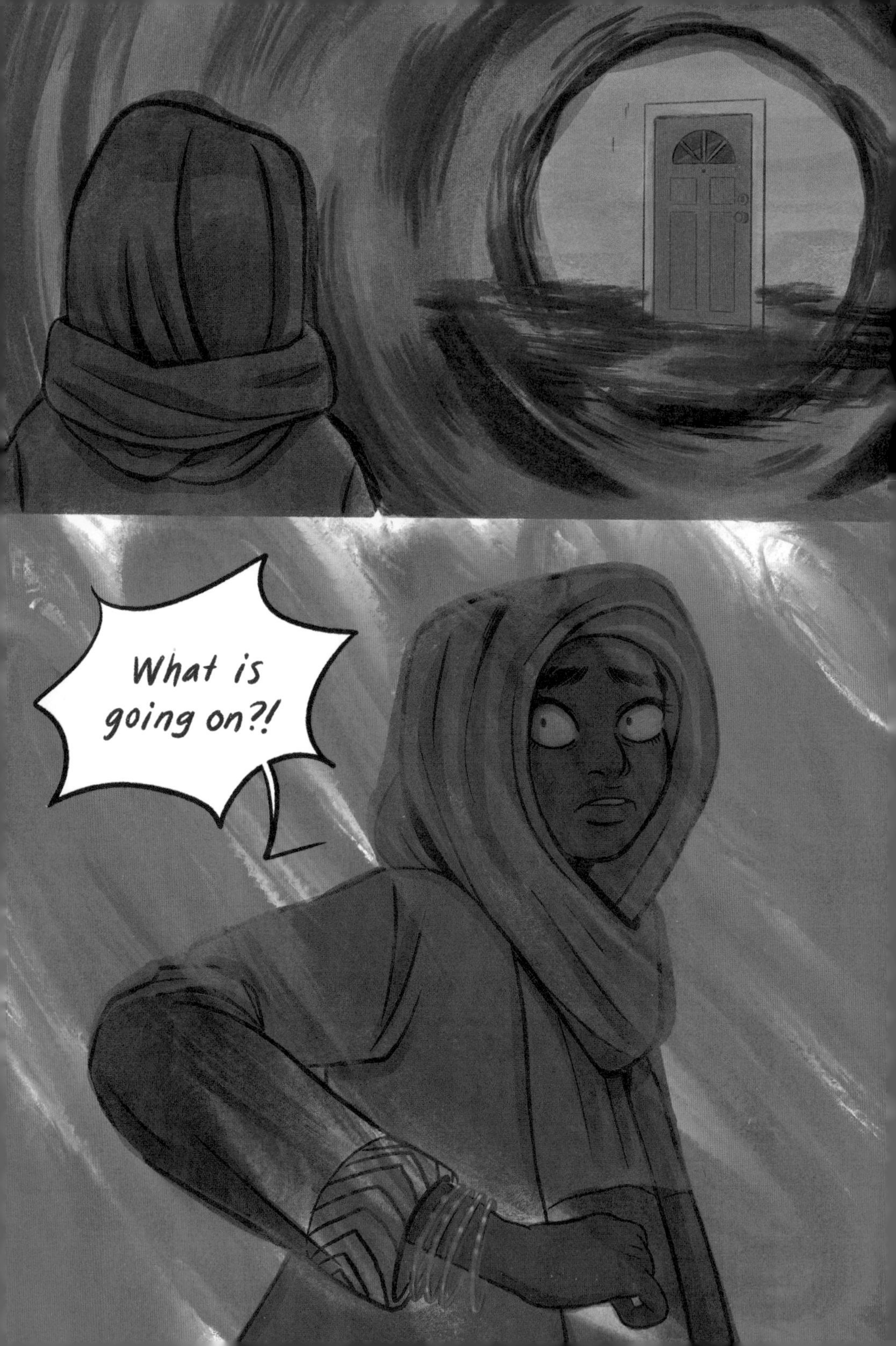
What is going on?!

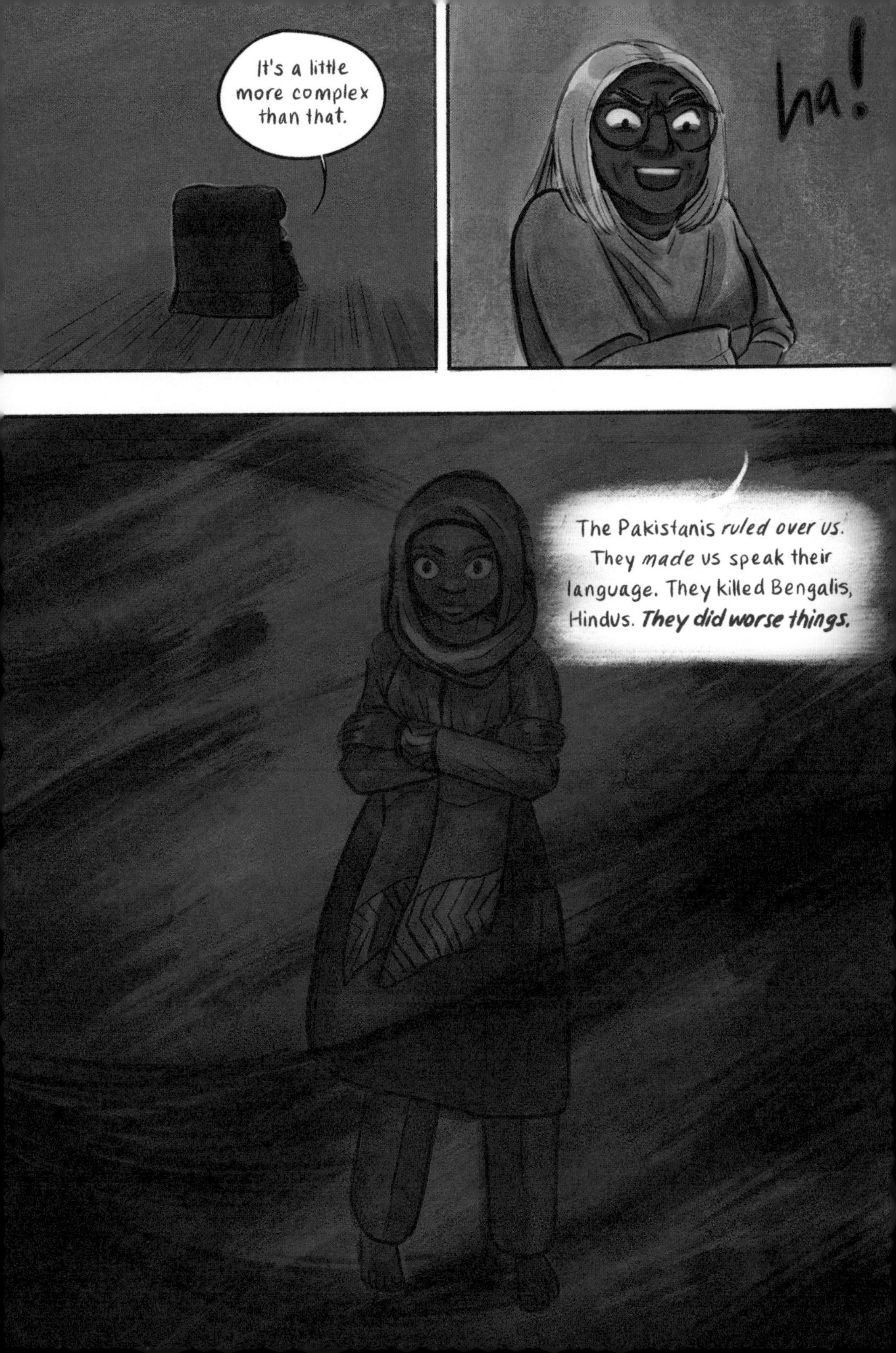
It's a little more complex than that.
ha!
The Pakistanis ruled over us. They made us speak their language. They killed Bengalis, Hindus. They did worse things.

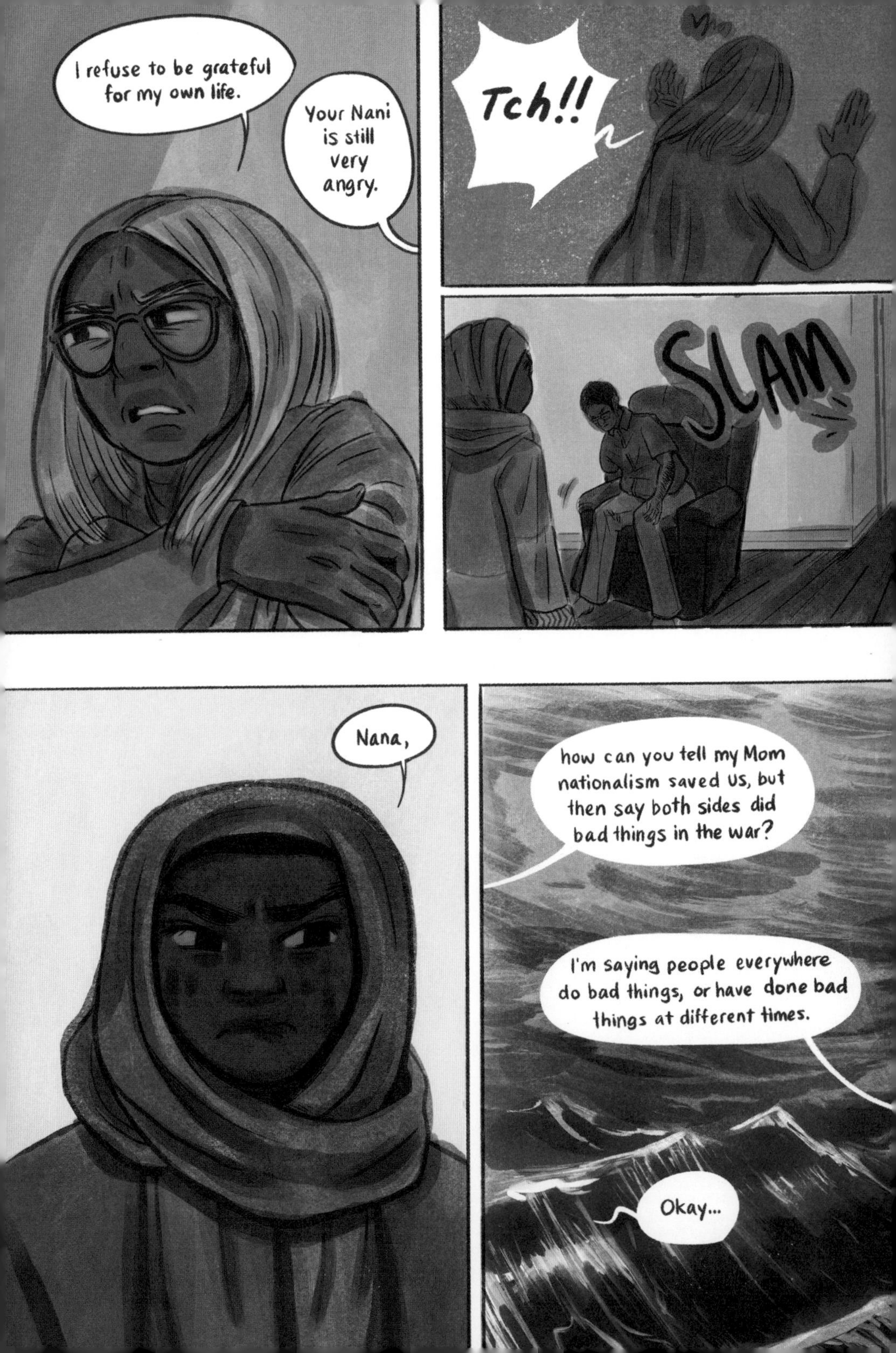
I refuse to be grateful for my own life.
Your Nani is still very angry.
Tch!!
SLAM
Nana,
how can you tell my Mom nationalism saved us, but then say both sides did bad things in the war?
I'm saying people everywhere do bad things, or have done bad things at different times.
Okay...

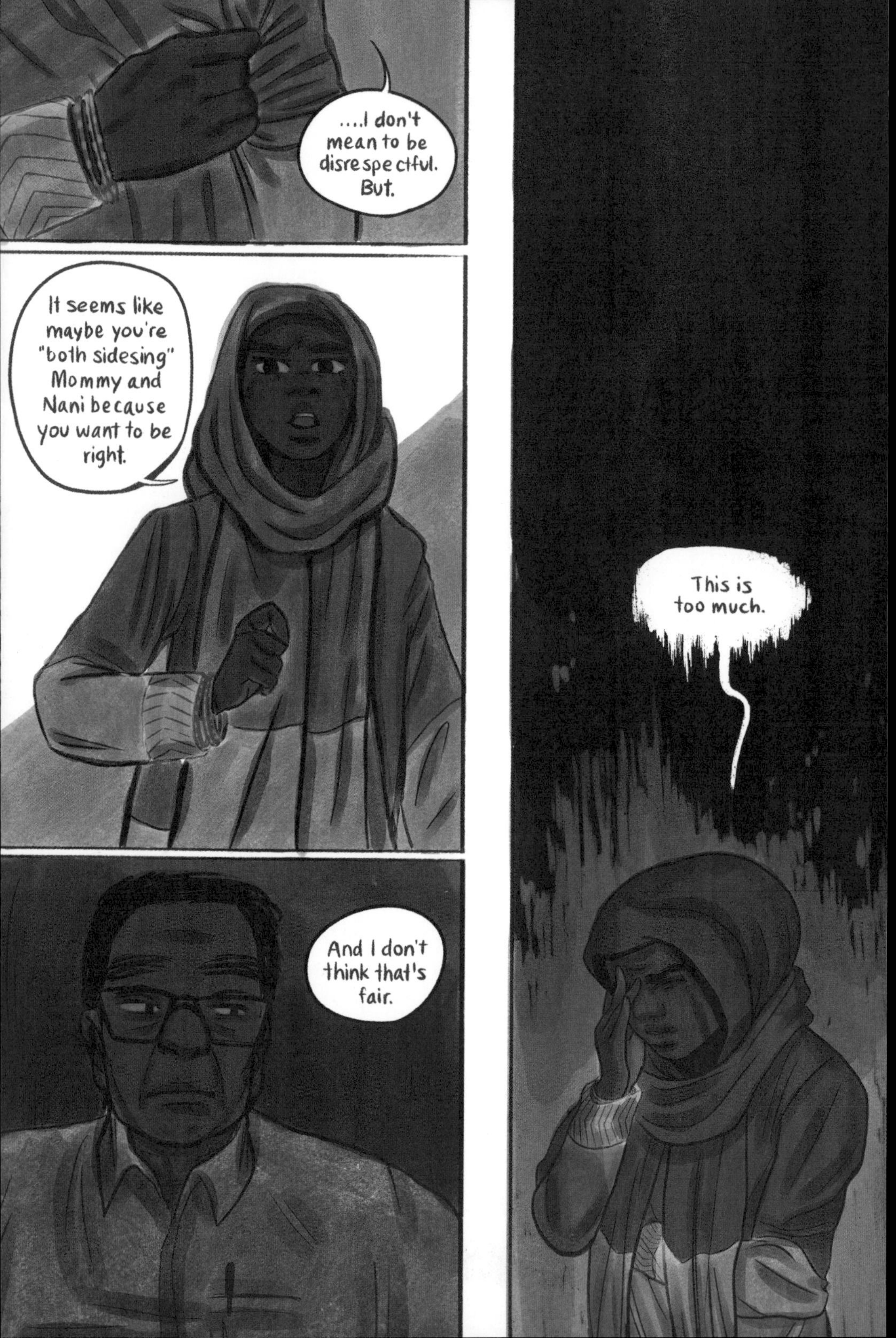

....I don't mean to be disrespectful. But.
It seems like maybe you're "both sidesing" Mommy and Nani because you want to be right.
And I don't think that's fair.
This is too much.

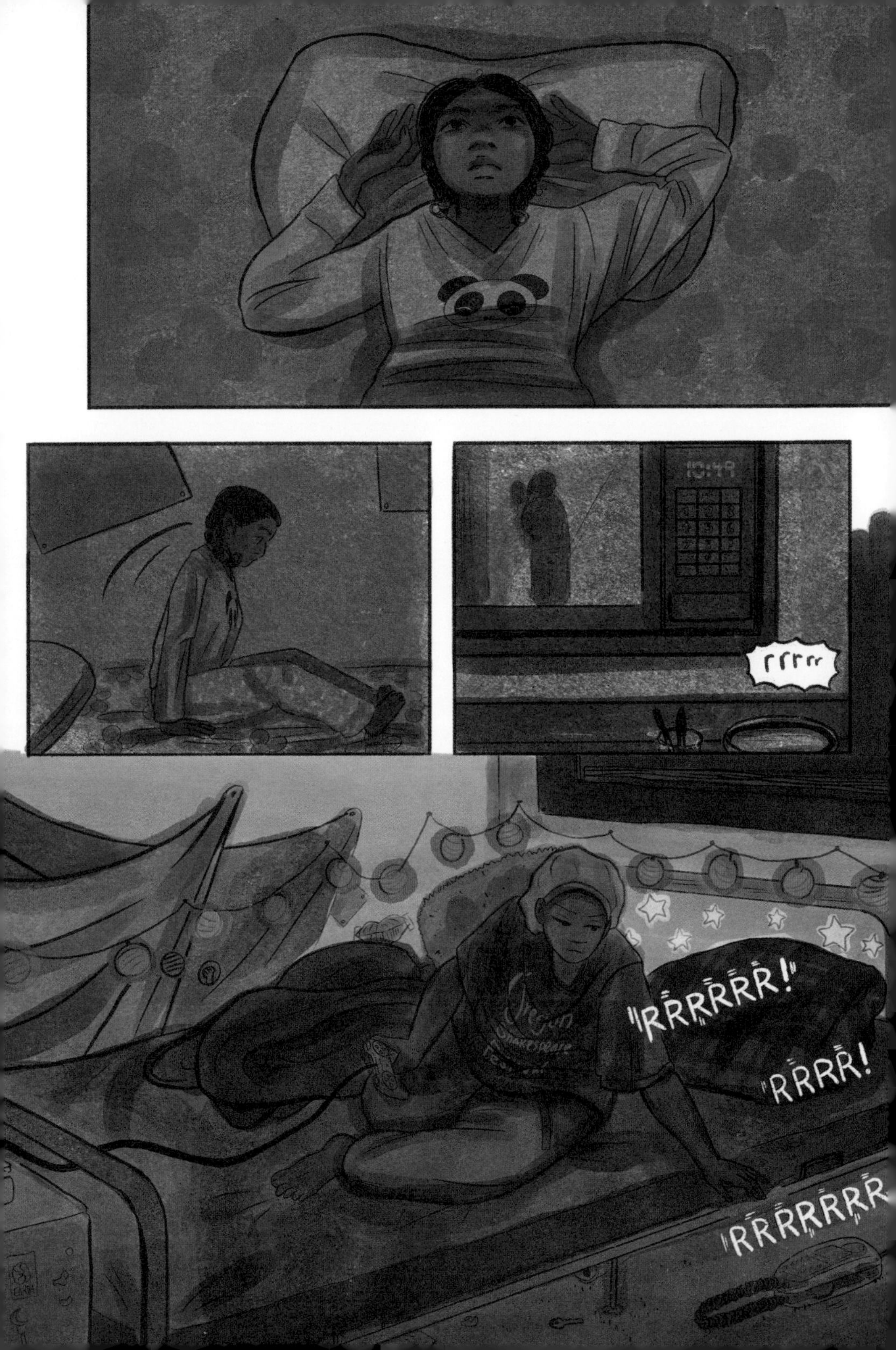

10:49
rrrrr
RRRRRR!
RRRR!
RRRRRRR

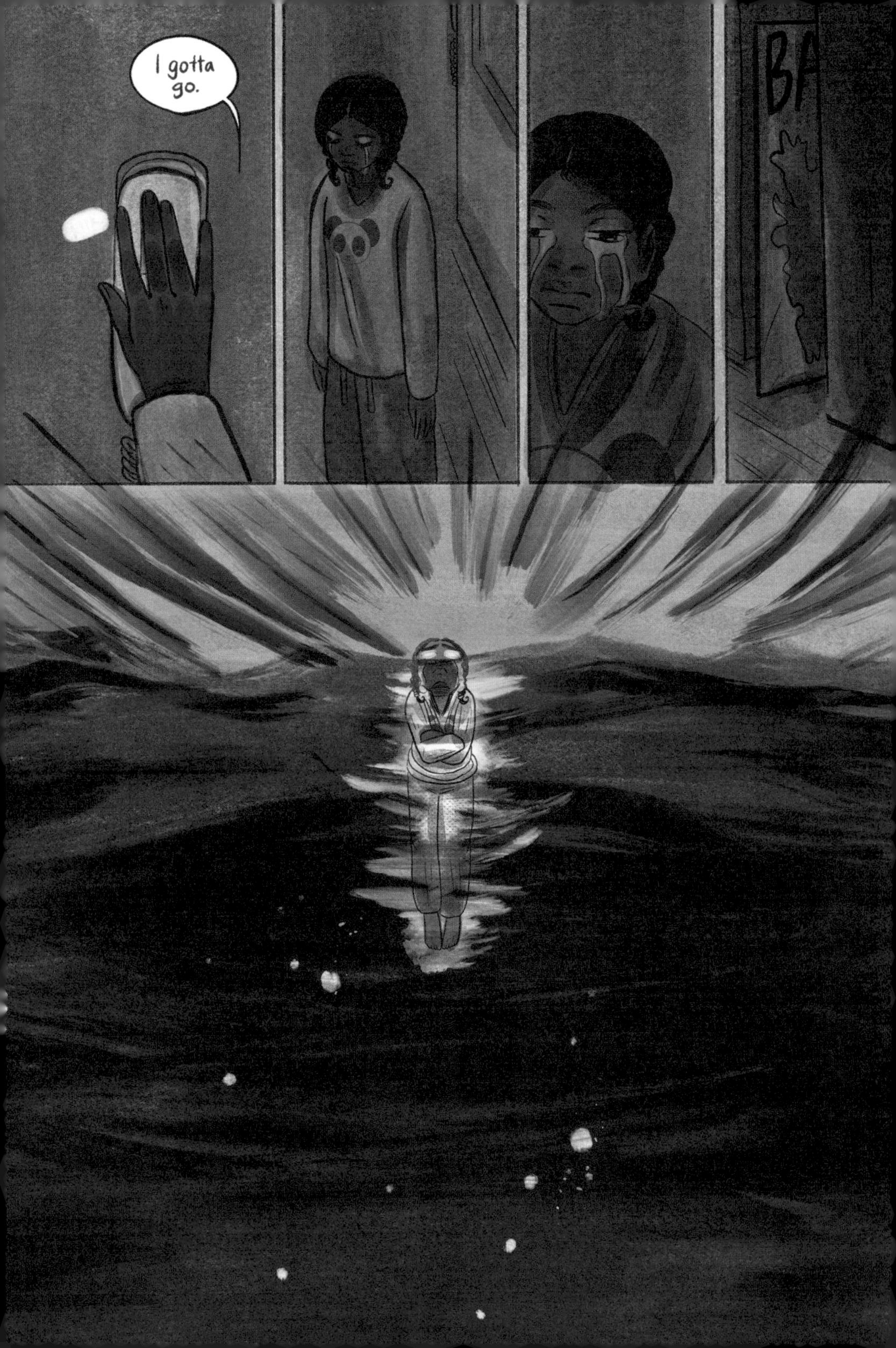
I gotta go.

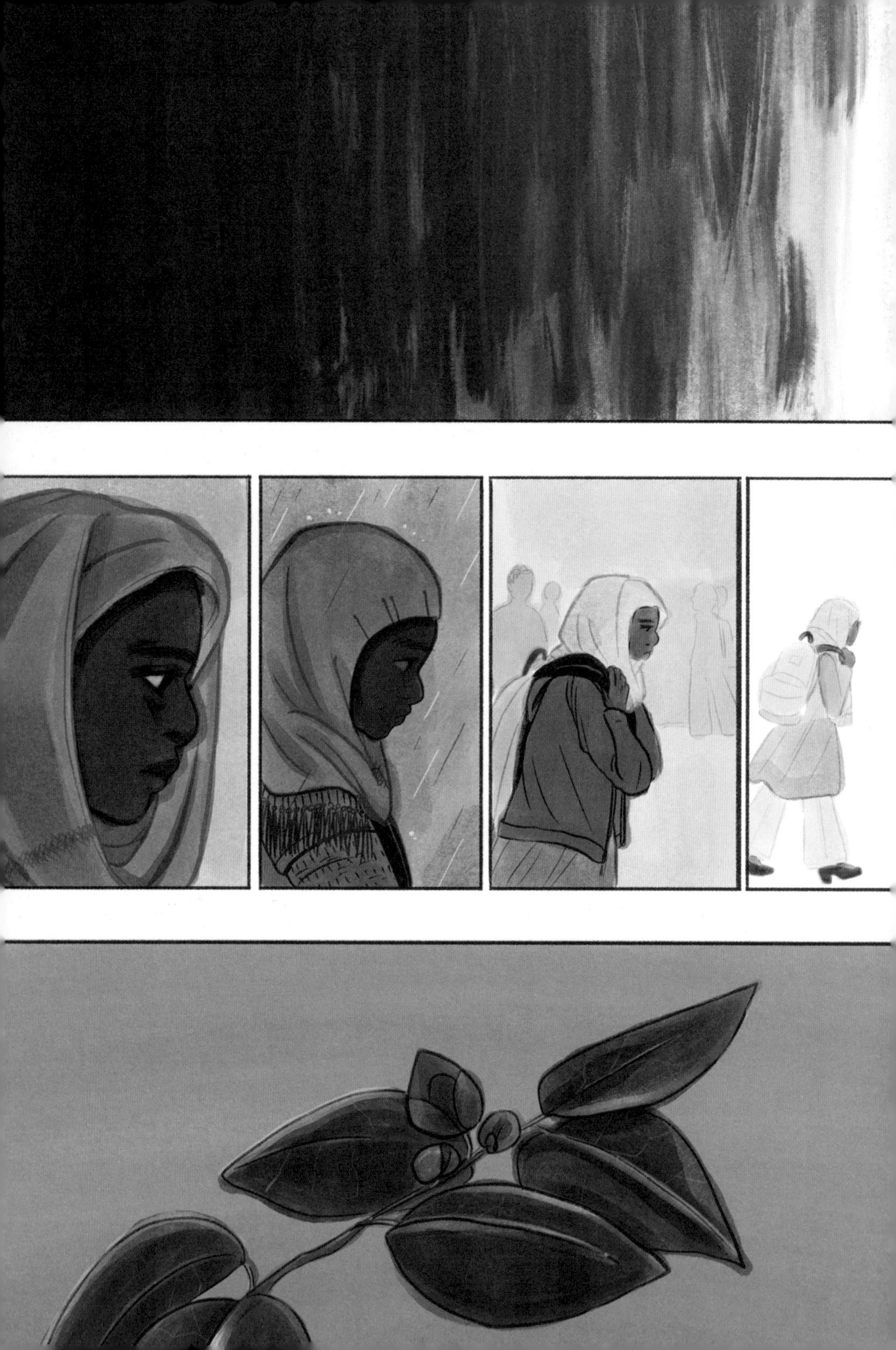

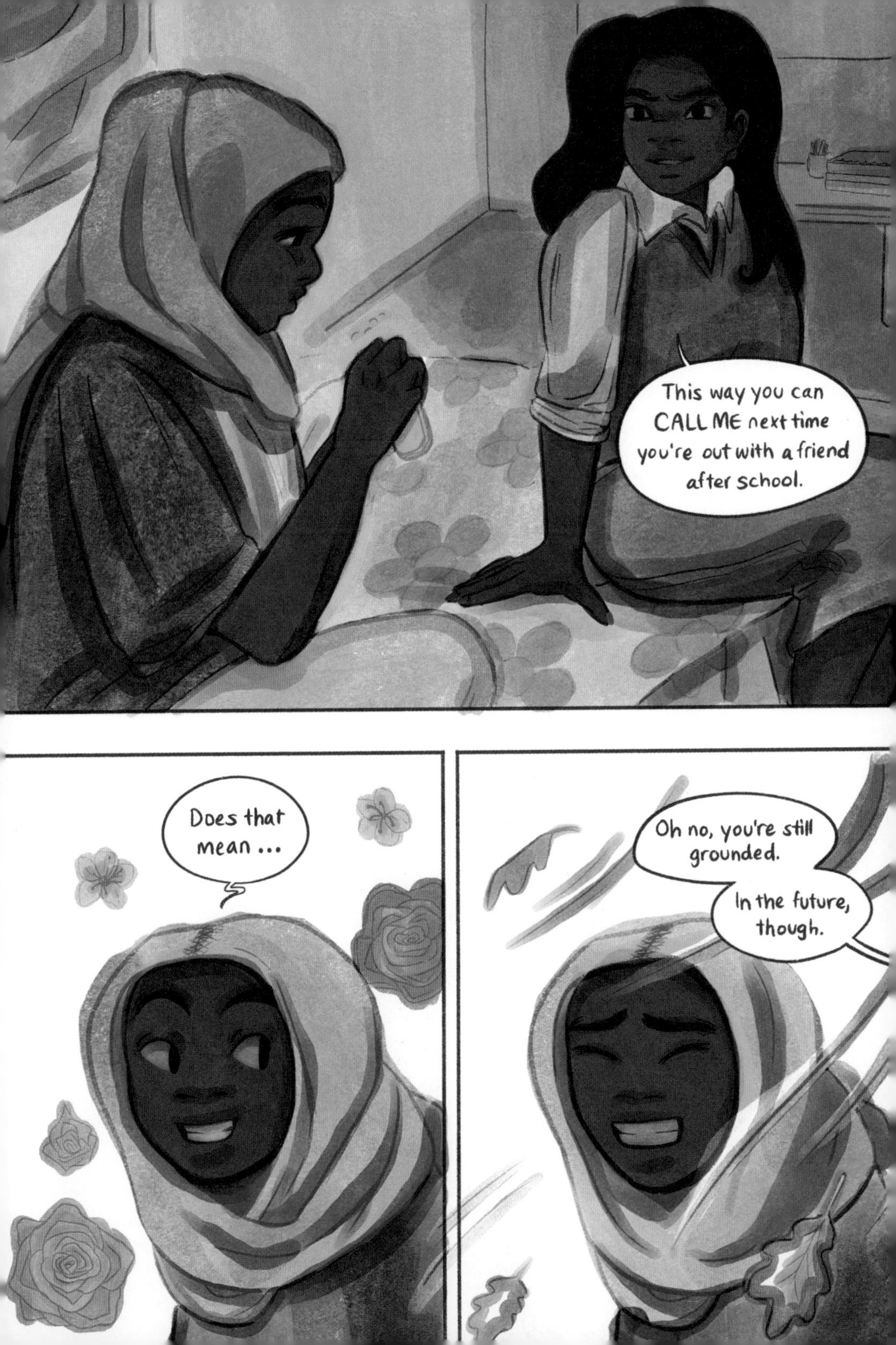
This way you can CALL ME next time you're out with a friend after school.
Does that mean ...
Oh no, you're still grounded.
In the future, though.

I think it has games, too.

It's really cool, Mommy, thank you.

... You don't have to wear the scarf inside the house, you know.

KEEP AUSTIN WEIRD

ISLAM

The Koran

Kids Learn Islam!

... Yeah, I know. I've been reading.

Oh! That's good.

I guess I just feel, like ... safer with it on.

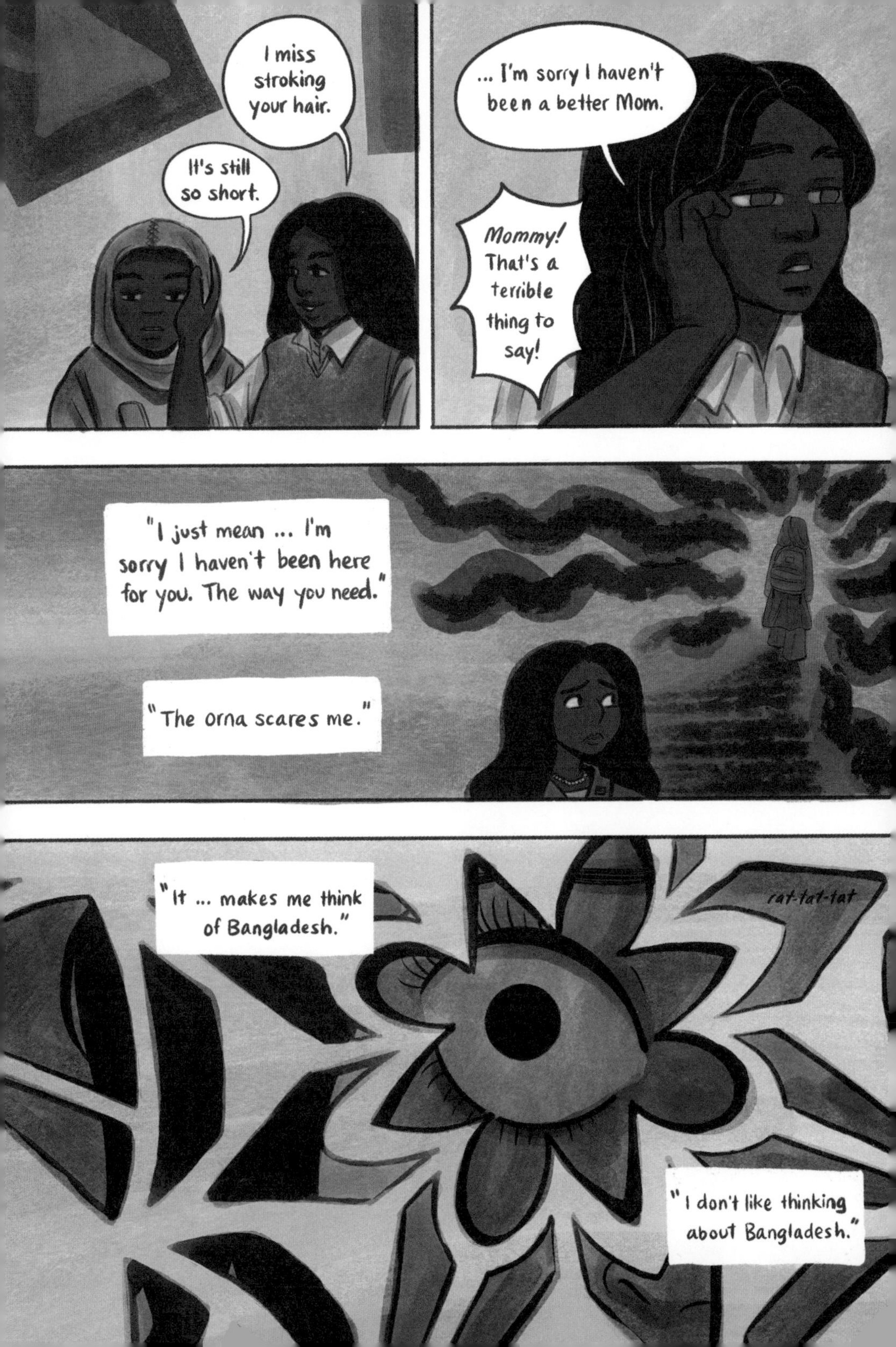
I miss stroking your hair.
It's still so short.
... I'm sorry I haven't been a better Mom.
Mommy! That's a terrible thing to say!
"I just mean ... I'm sorry I haven't been here for you. The way you need."
"The orna scares me."
"It ... makes me think of Bangladesh."
rat-tat-tat
"I don't like thinking about Bangladesh."

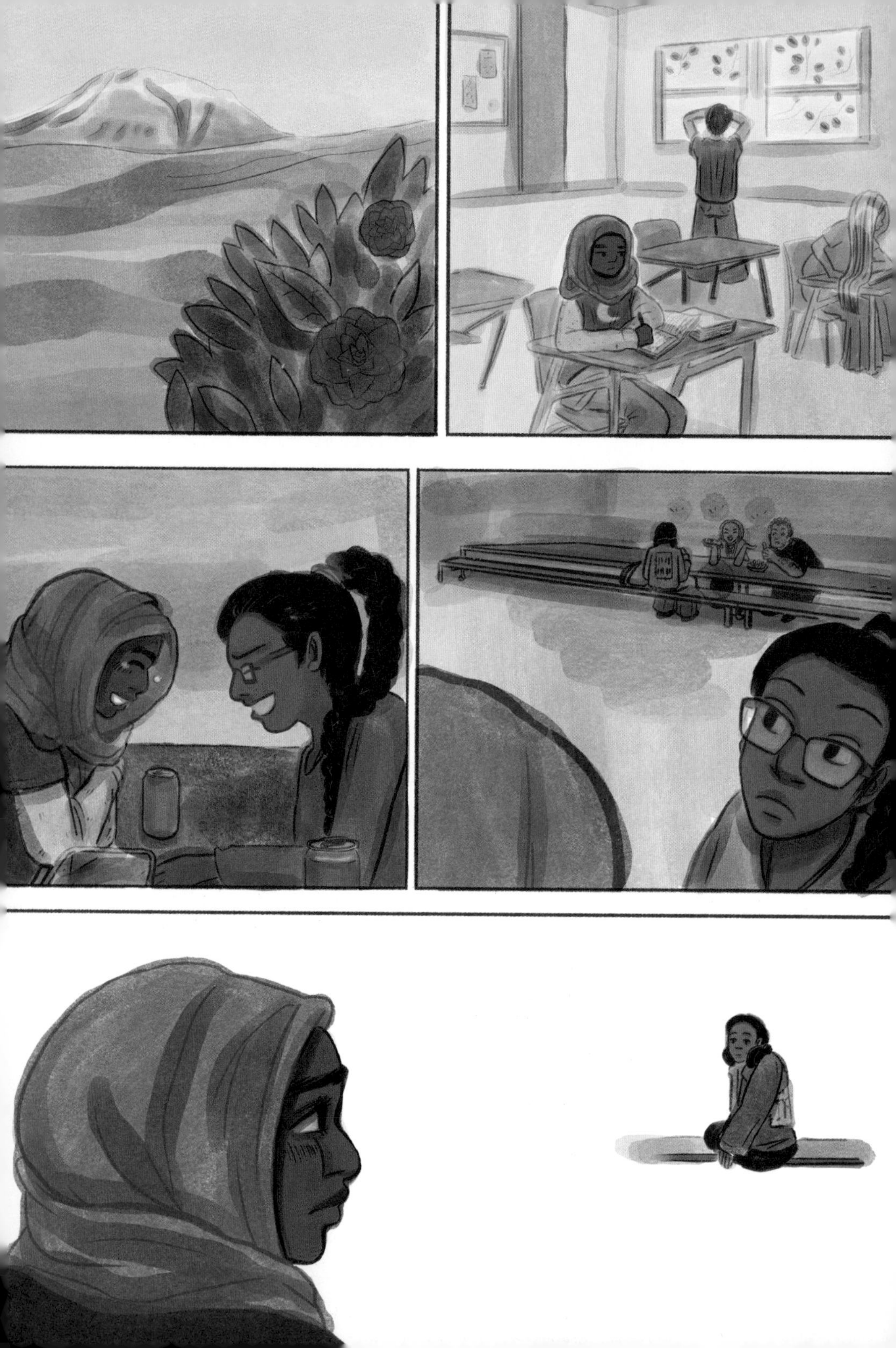

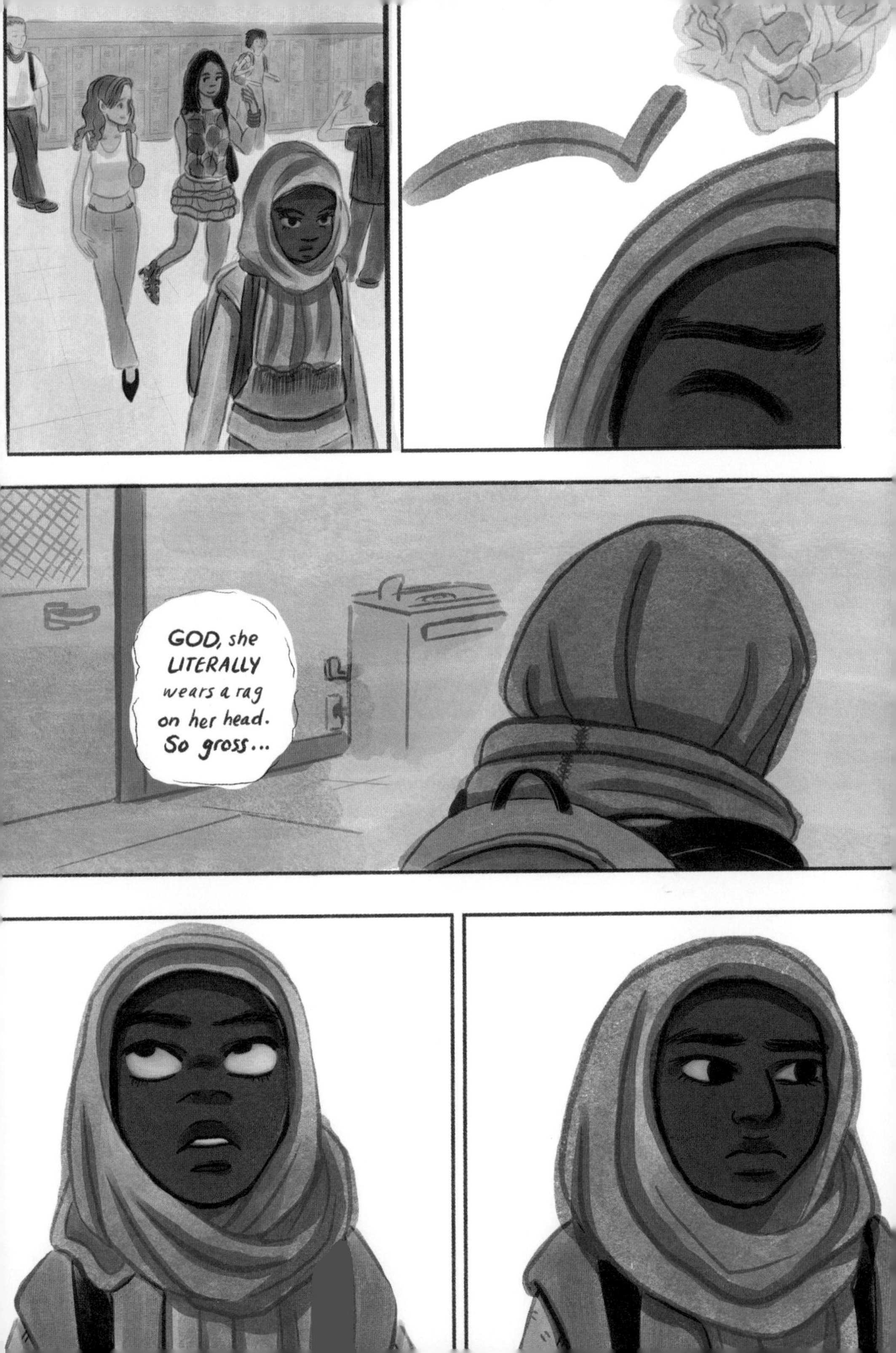
GOD, she LITERALLY wears a rag on her head. So gross...

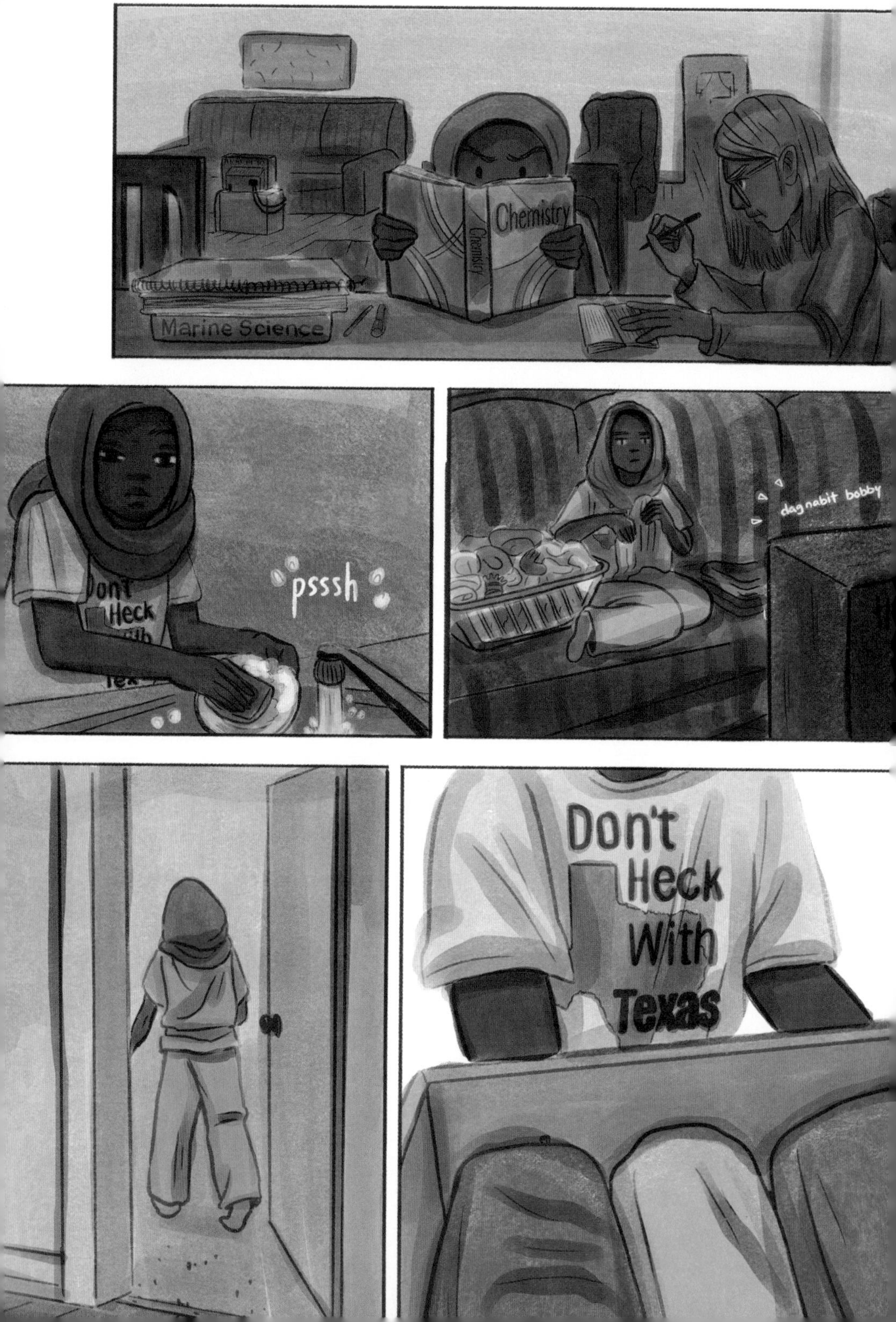

Chemistry
Chemistry
Marine Science
Don't Heck With Tex
psssh
dagnabit bobby
Don't Heck With Texas

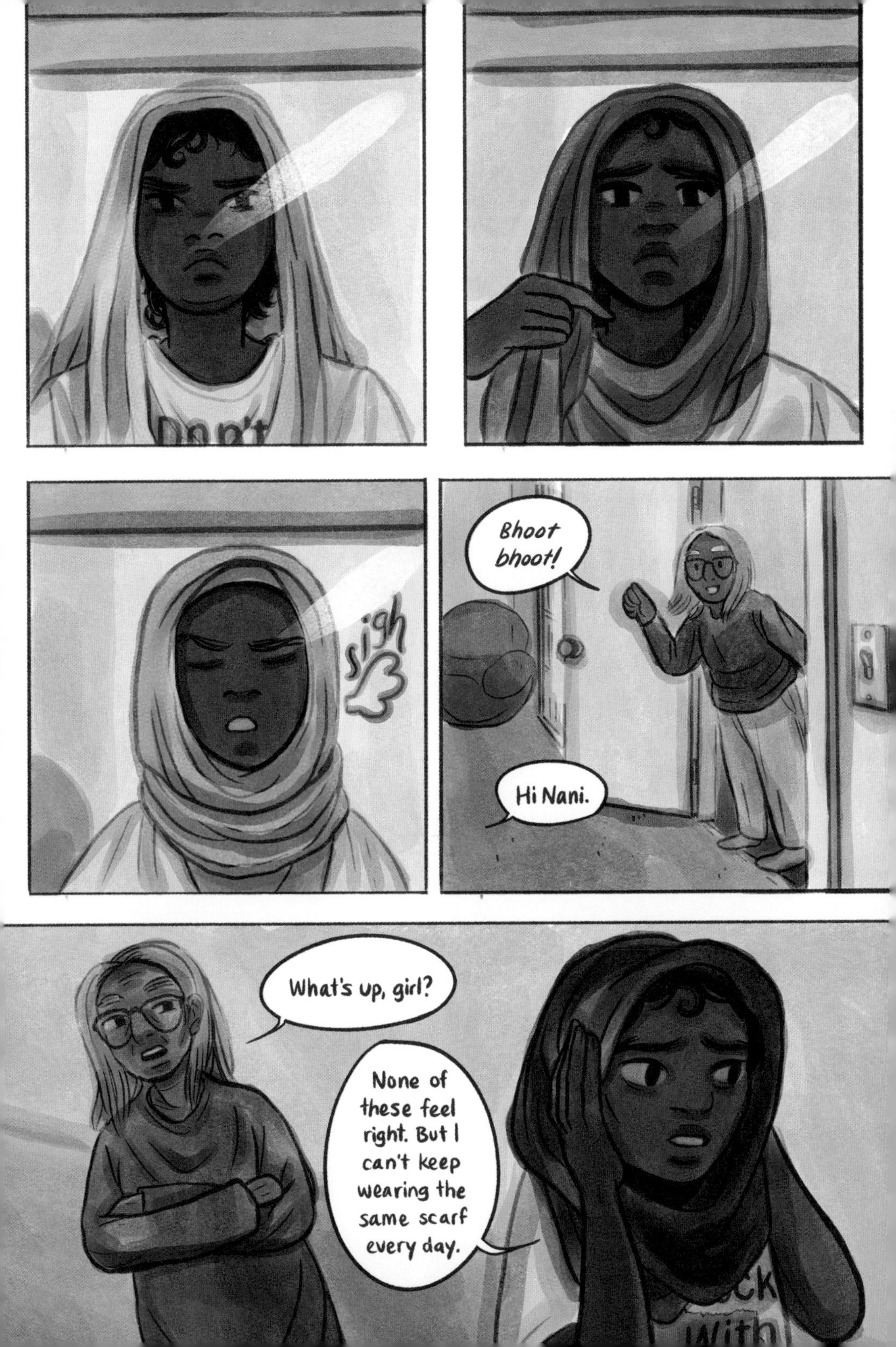
DON'T
sigh
Bhoot bhoot!
Hi Nani.
What's up, girl?
None of these feel right. But I can't keep wearing the same scarf every day.

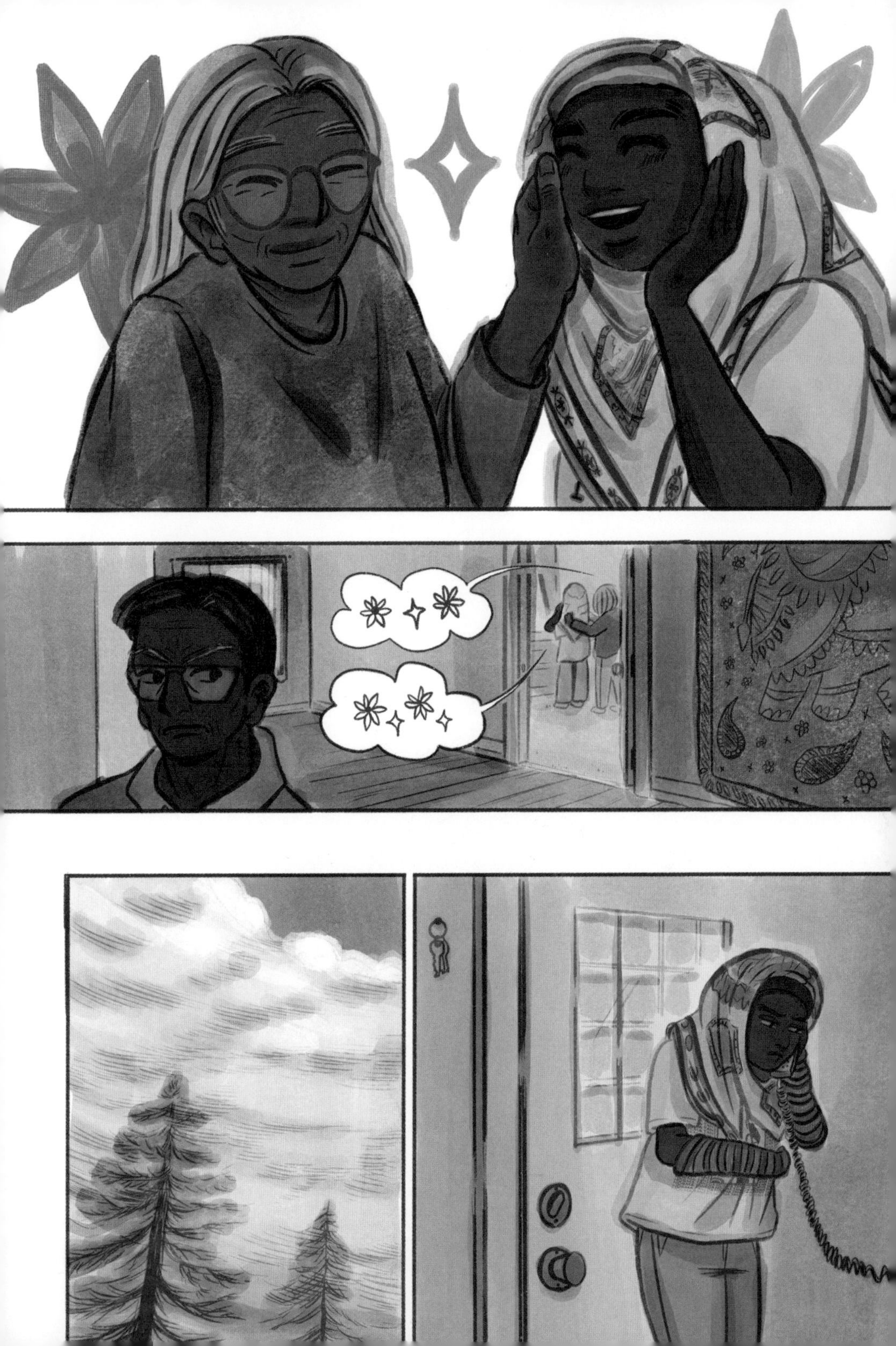

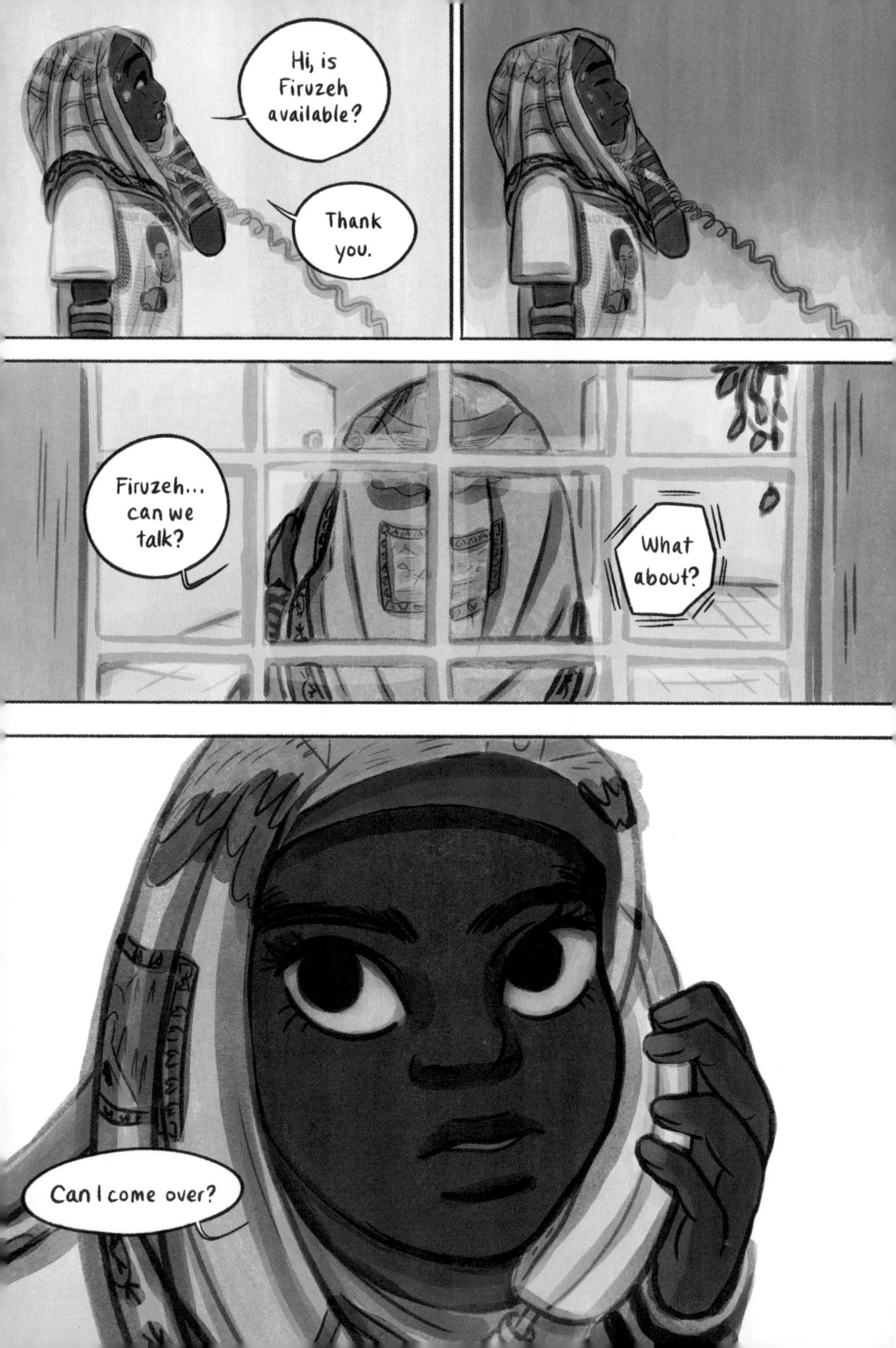
Hi, is Firuzeh available?
Thank you.
Firuzeh... can we talk?
What about?
Can I come over?

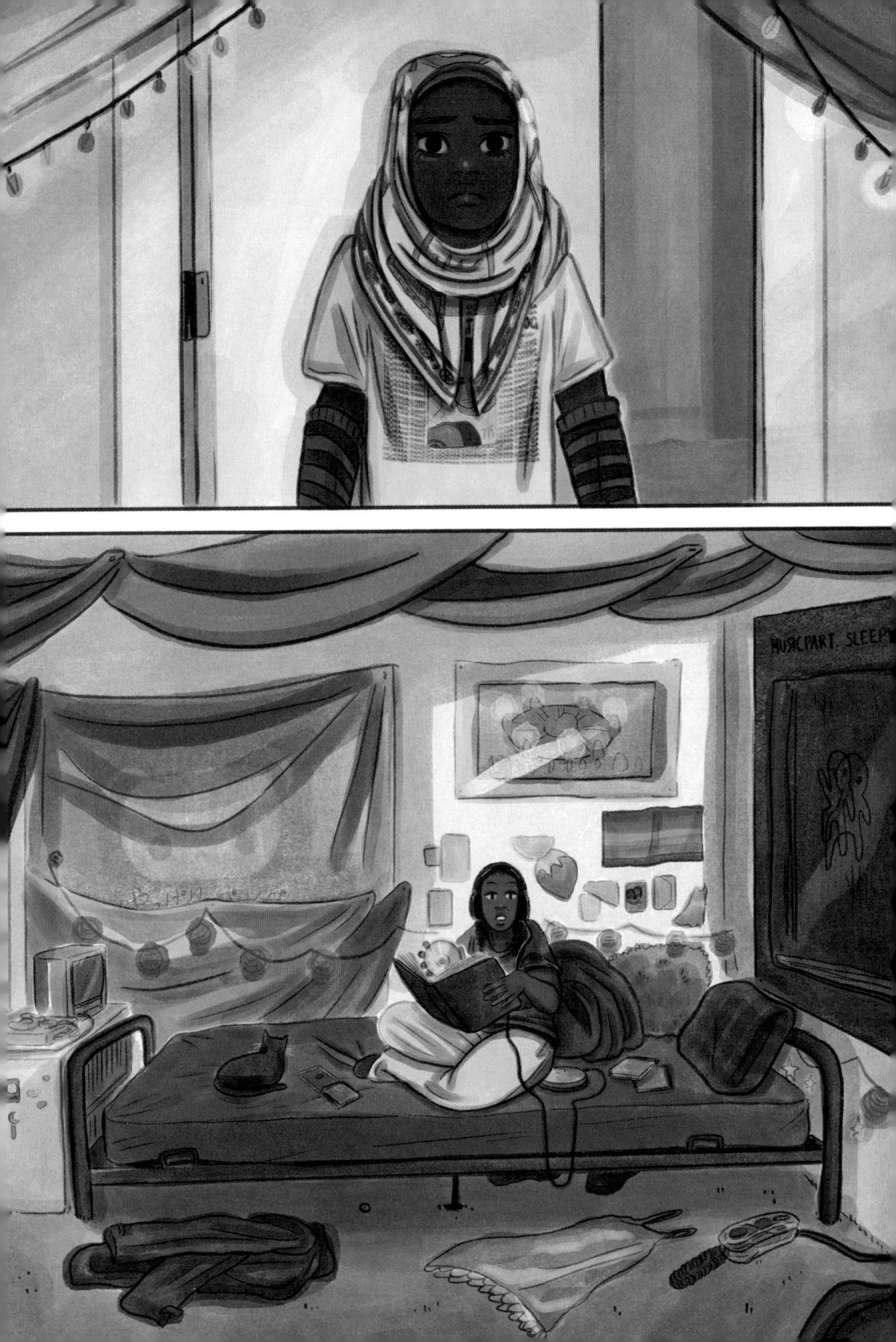

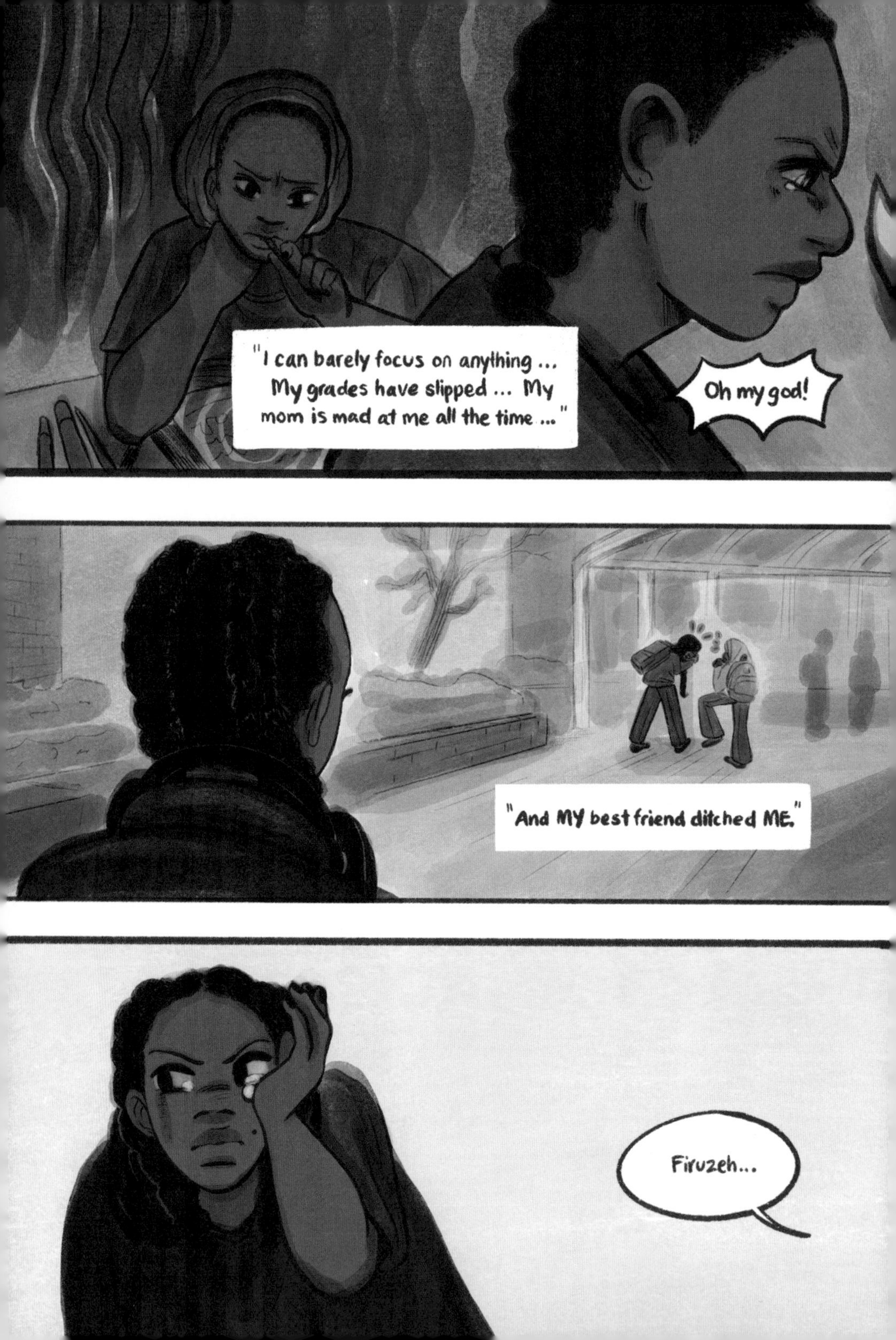
"I can barely focus on anything ... My grades have slipped ... My mom is mad at me all the time ..."
Oh my god!
"And MY best friend ditched ME."
Firuzeh...

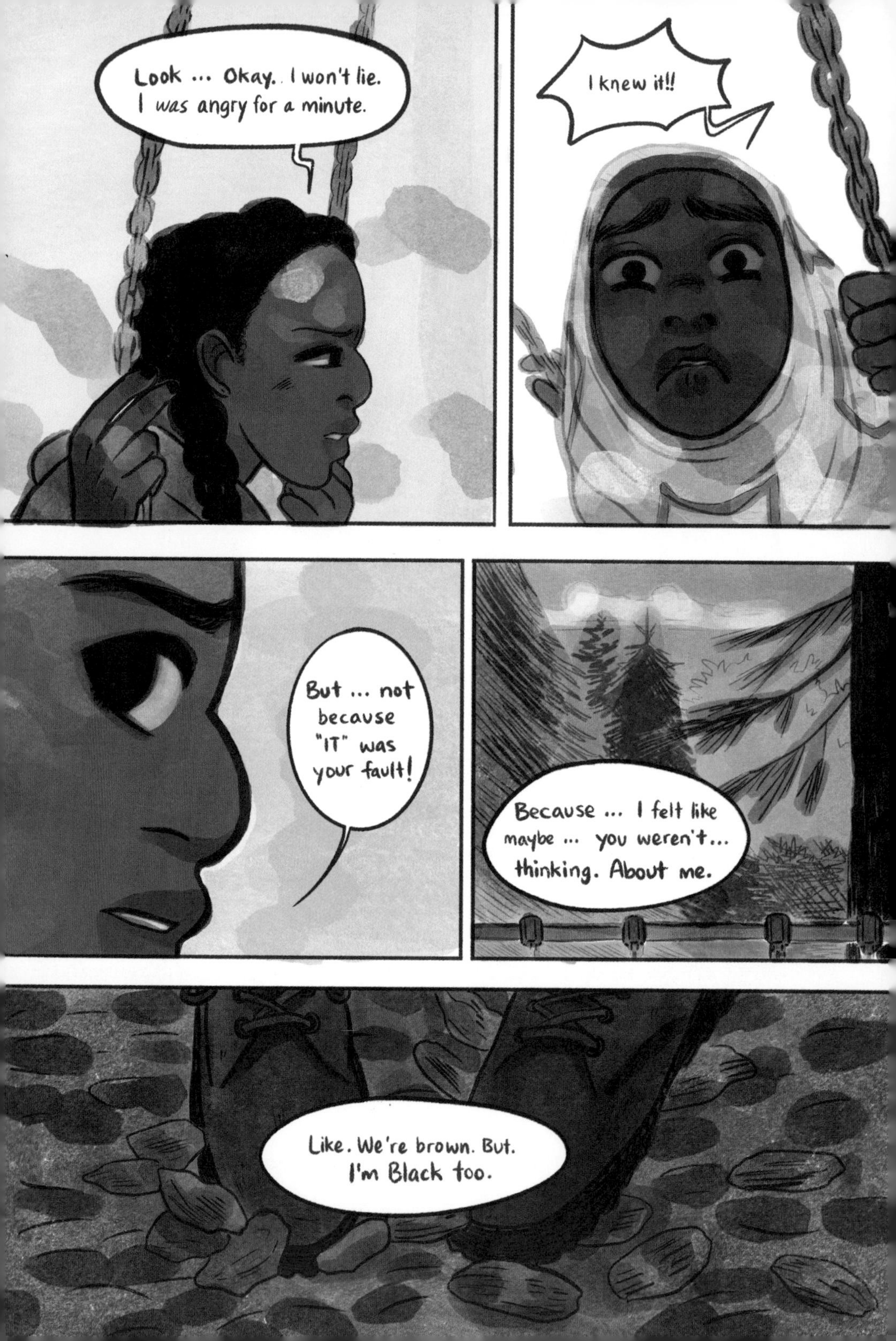
Look ... Okay. I won't lie. I was angry for a minute.
I knew it!!
But ... not because "IT" was your fault!
Because ... I felt like maybe ... you weren't... thinking. About me.
Like. We're brown. But. I'm Black too.

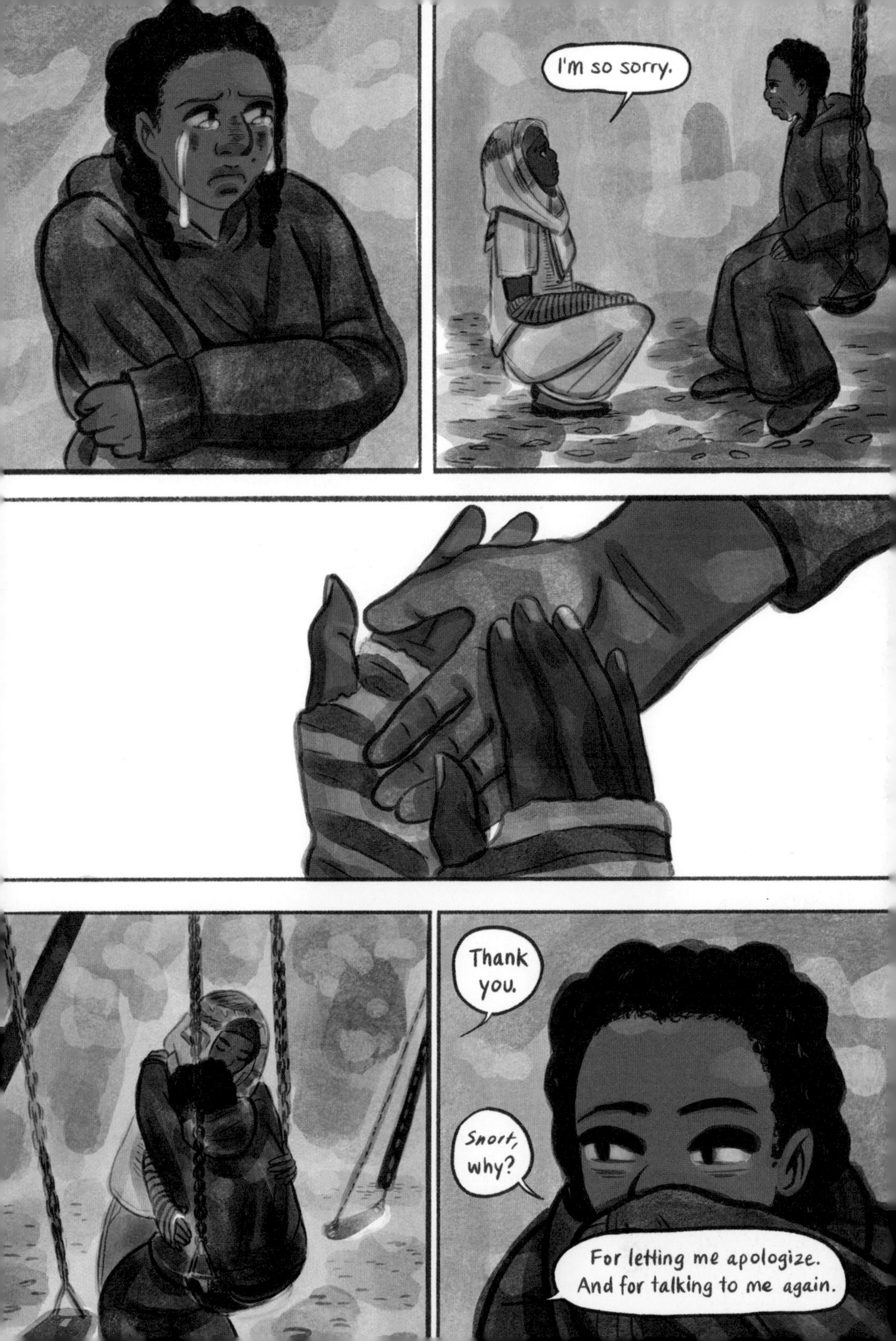
I'm so sorry.
Thank you.
Snort, why?
For letting me apologize. And for talking to me again.

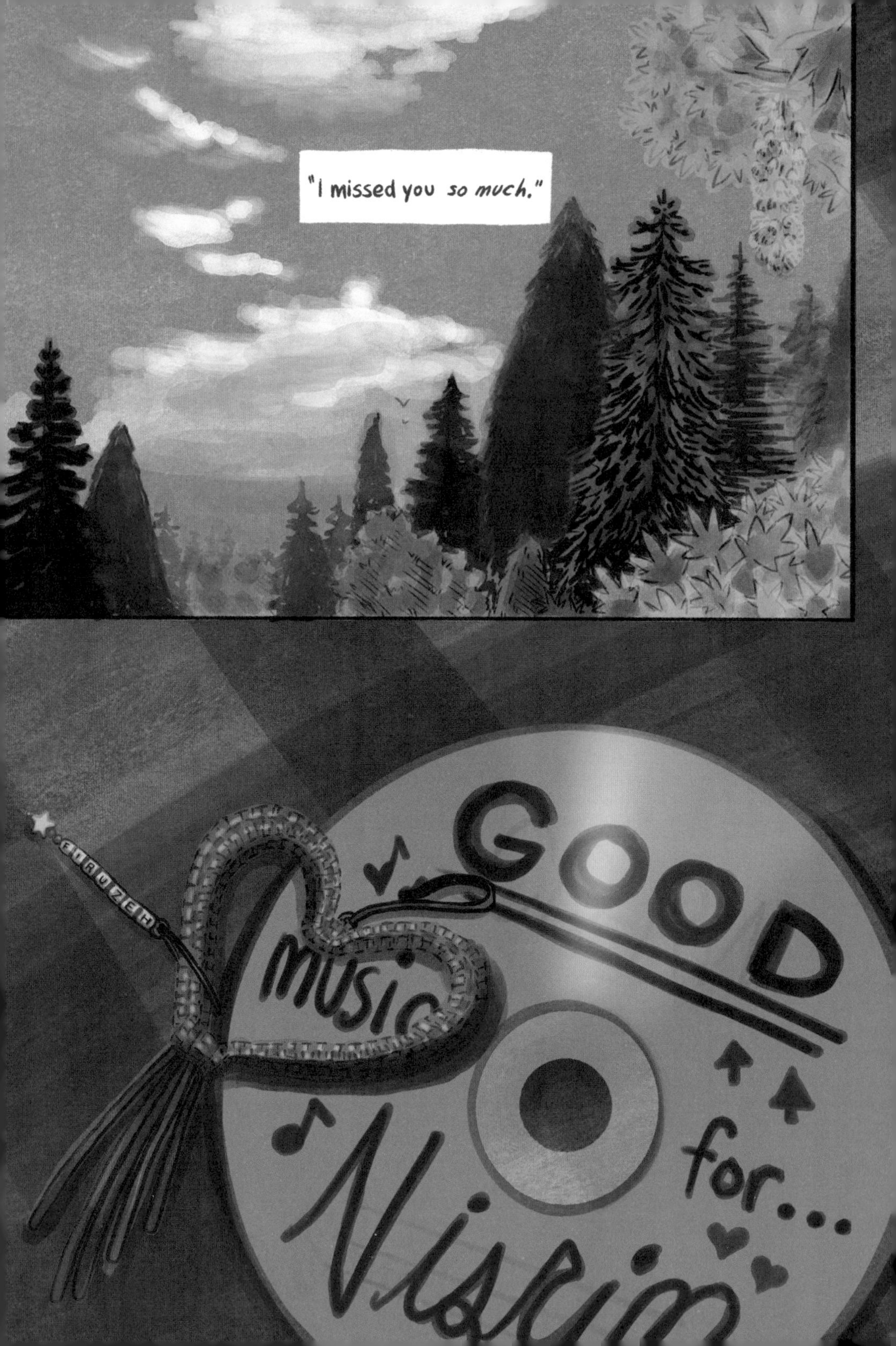
"I missed you so much."
GOOD
MUSIC
for...

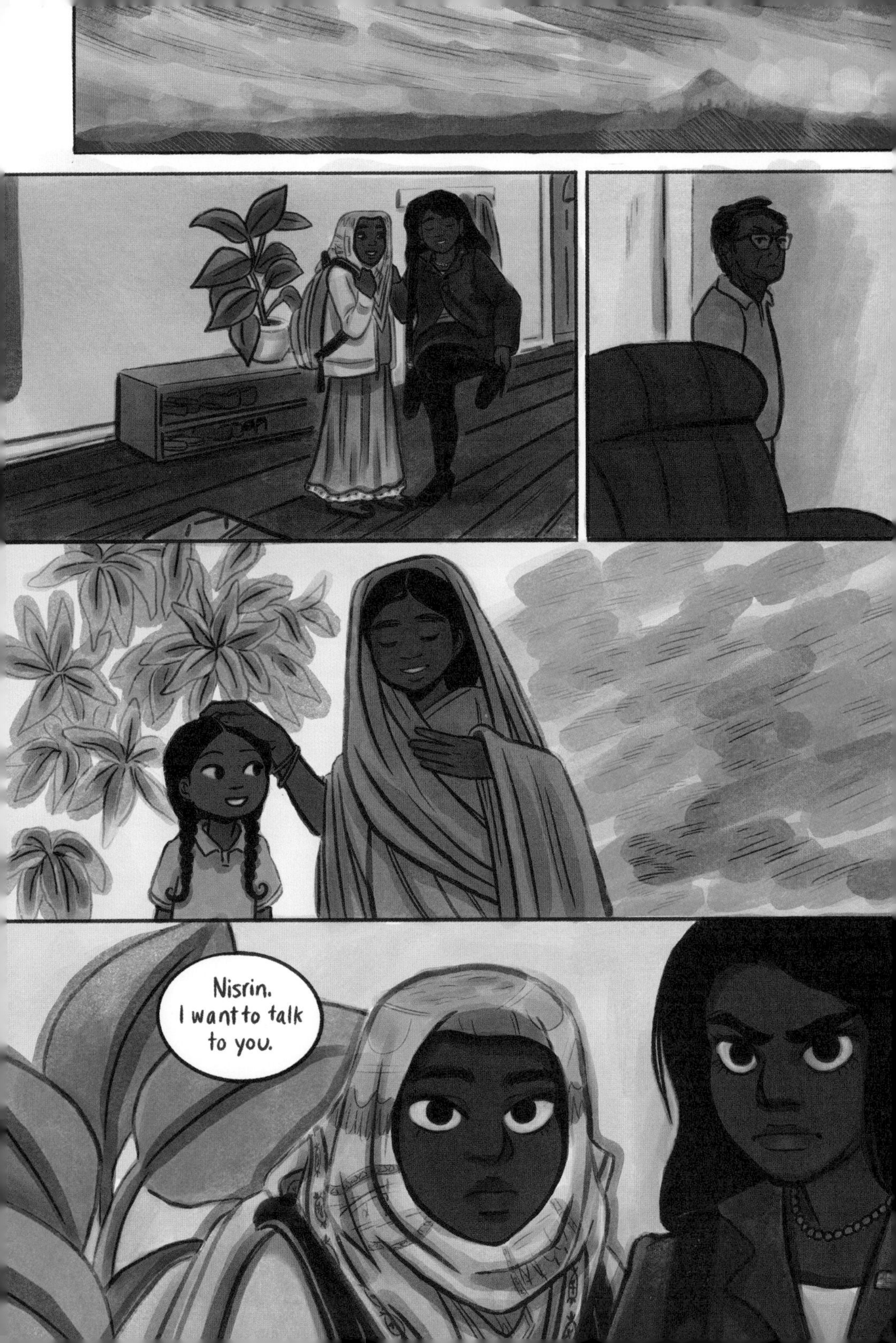
Nisrin. I want to talk to you.

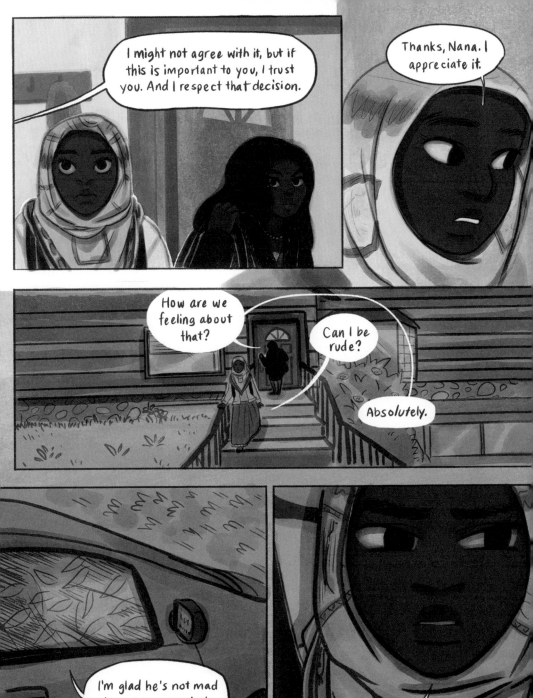

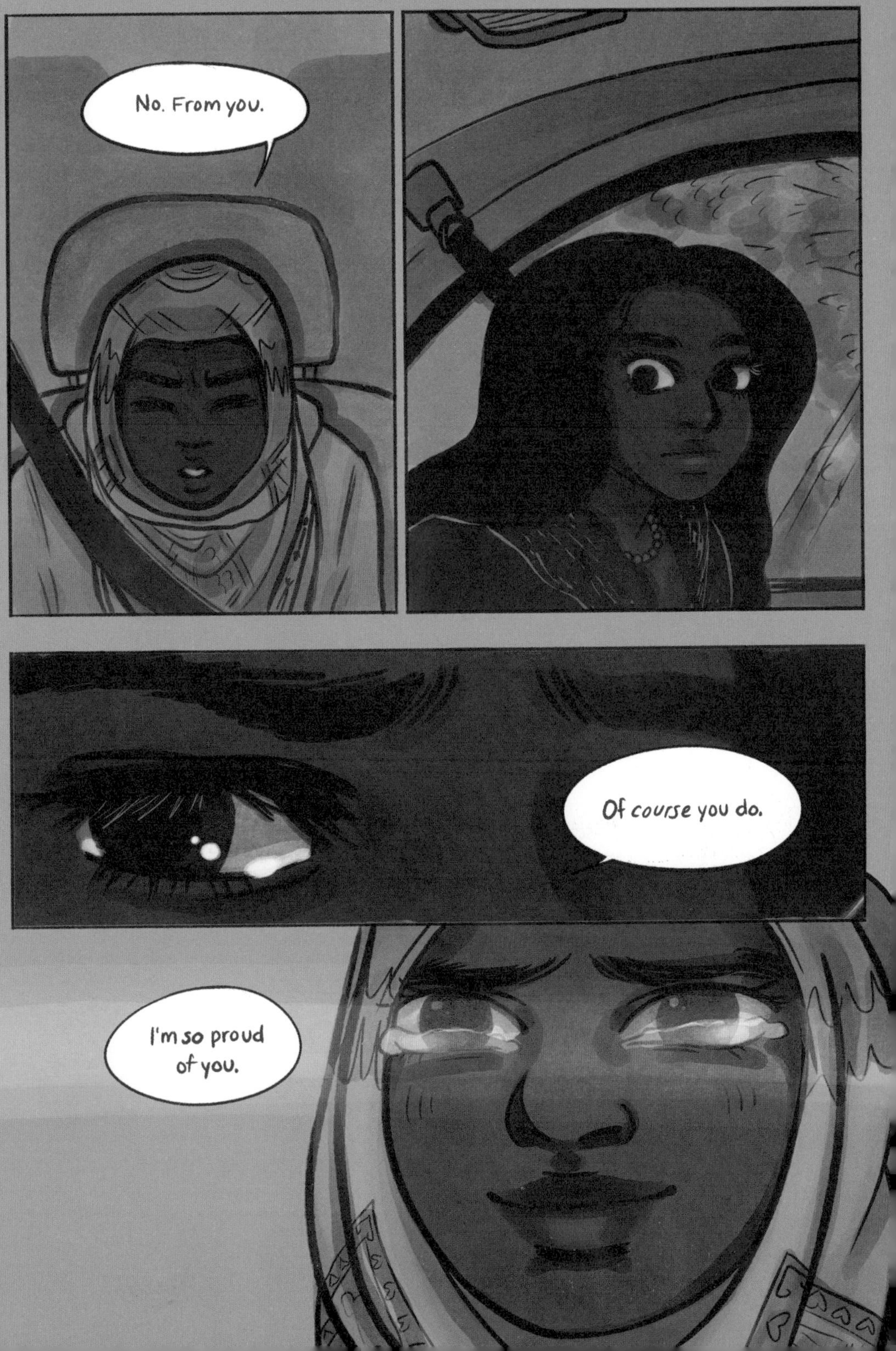
No. From you.
Of course you do.
I'm so proud of you.

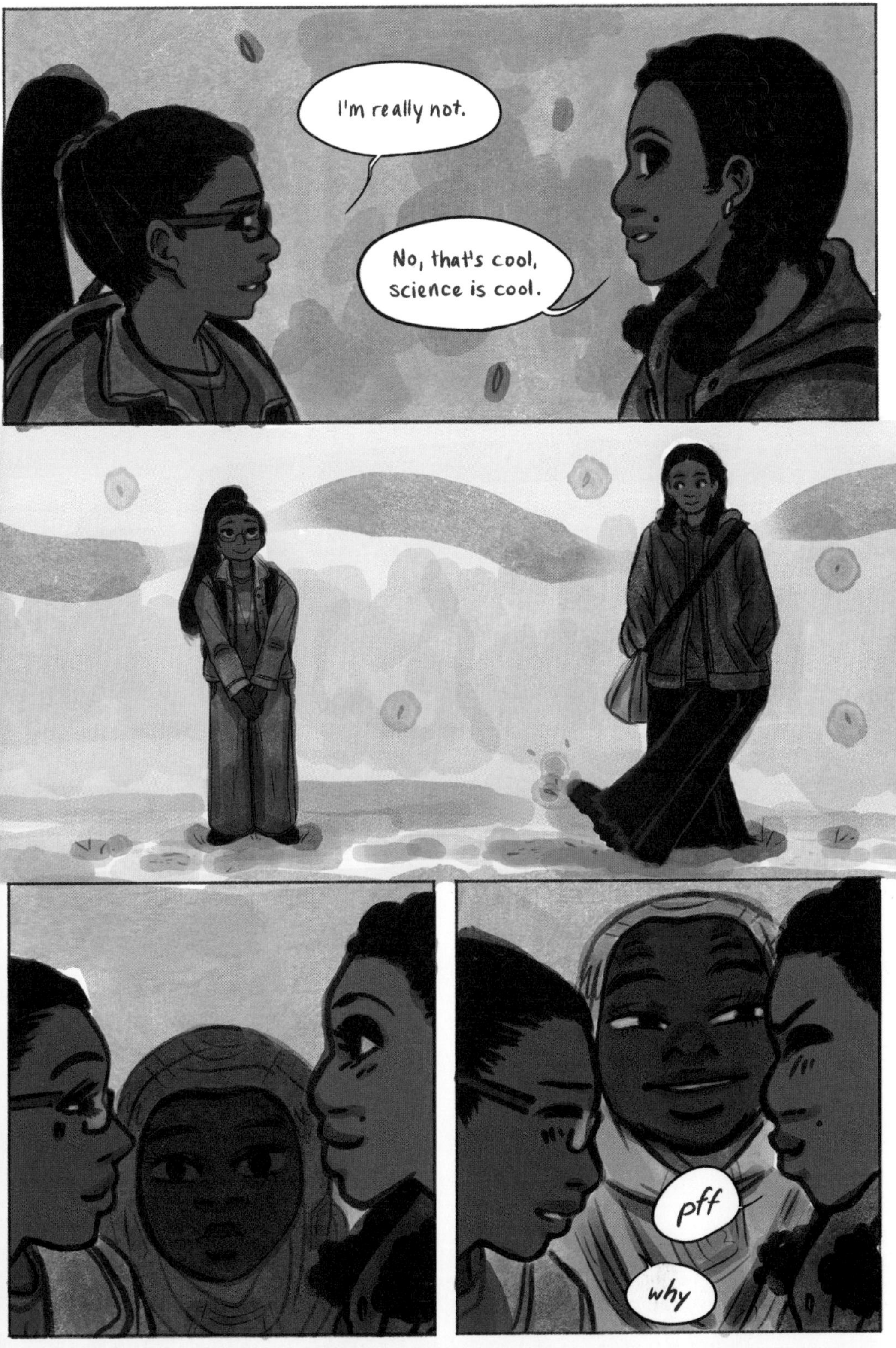
I'm really not.
No, that's cool, science is cool.
pff
why

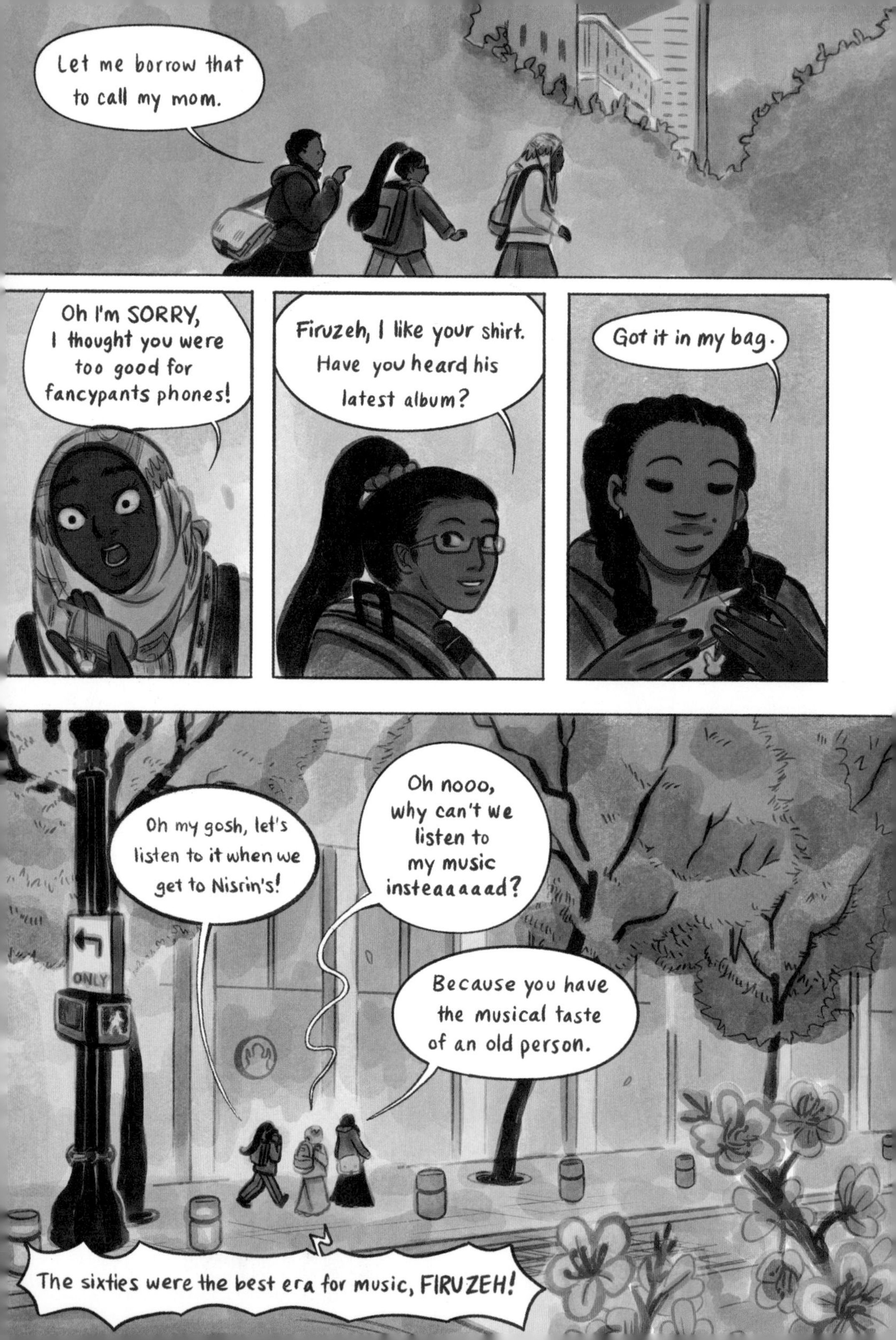
Let me borrow that to call my mom.
Oh I'm SORRY, I thought you were too good for fancypants phones!
Firuzeh, I like your shirt. Have you heard his latest album?
Got it in my bag.
Oh my gosh, let's listen to it when we get to Nisrin's!
Oh nooo, why can't we listen to my music insteaaaaad?
Because you have the musical taste of an old person.
The sixties were the best era for music, FIRUZEH!
ONLY

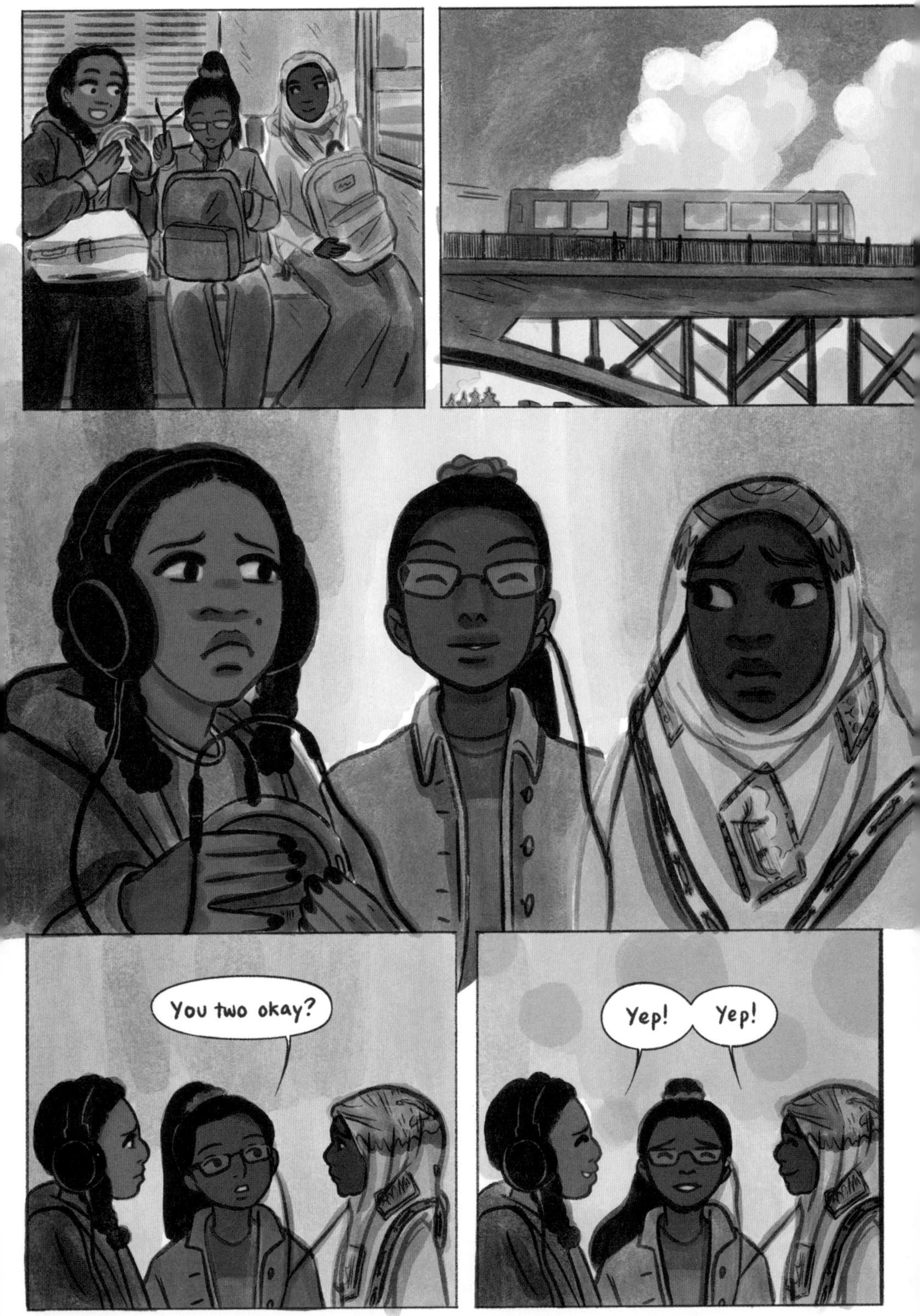
You two okay?
Yep!
Yep!

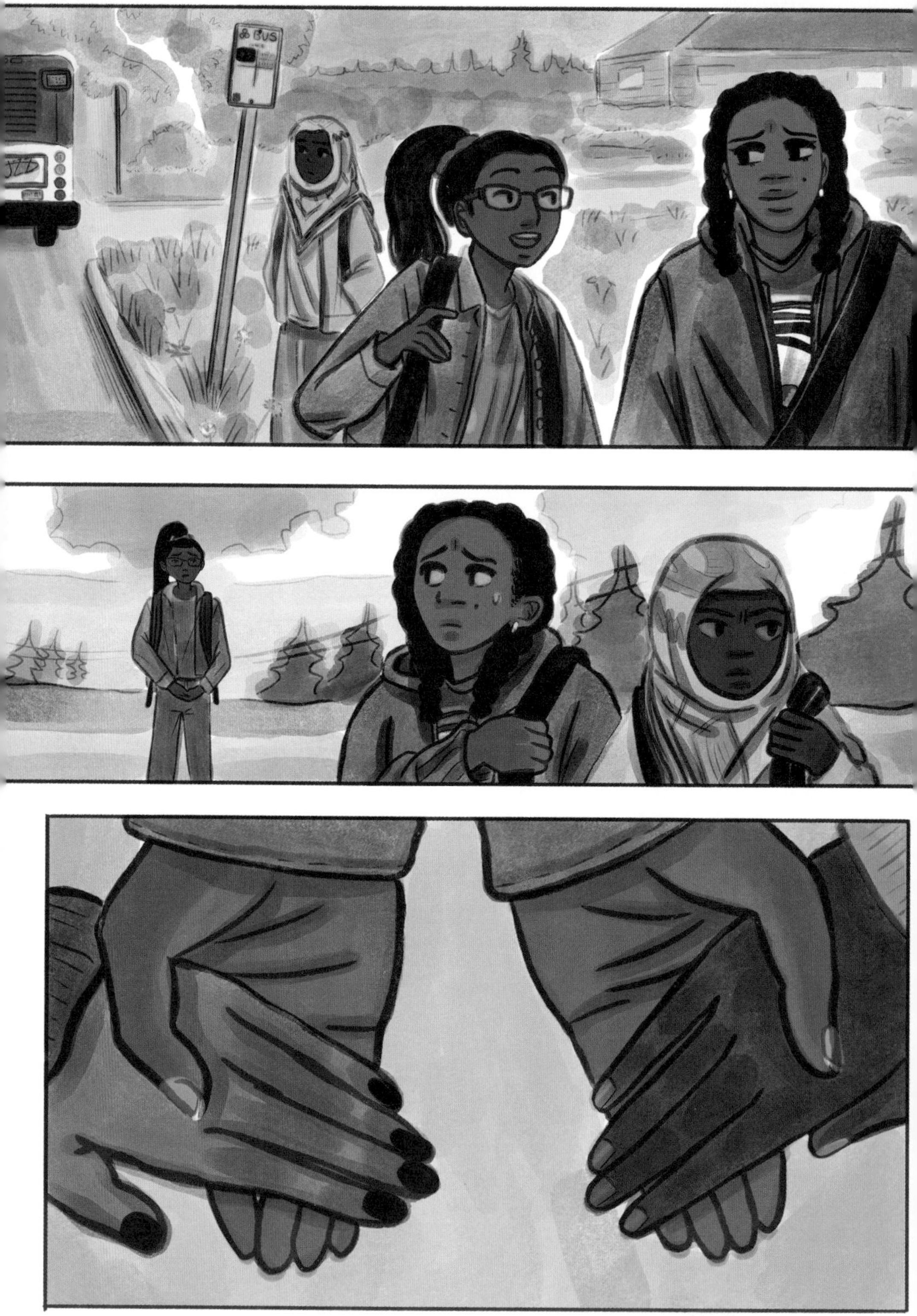
BUS

Let's stop at the café before we go home.

I'll buy, I've been saving up.

Hi, can I get—

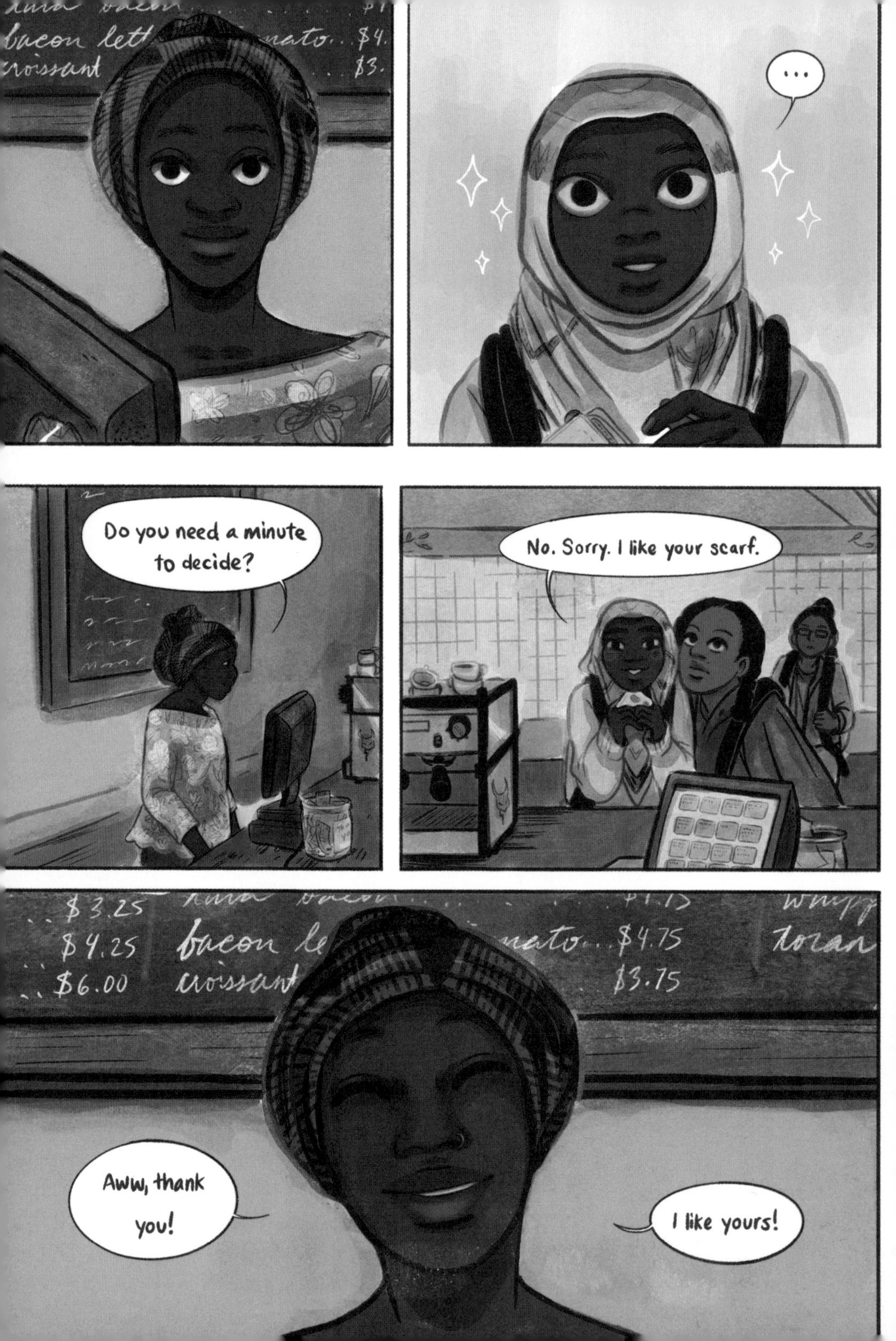
...
Do you need a minute to decide?
No. Sorry. I like your scarf.
Aww, thank you!
I like yours!

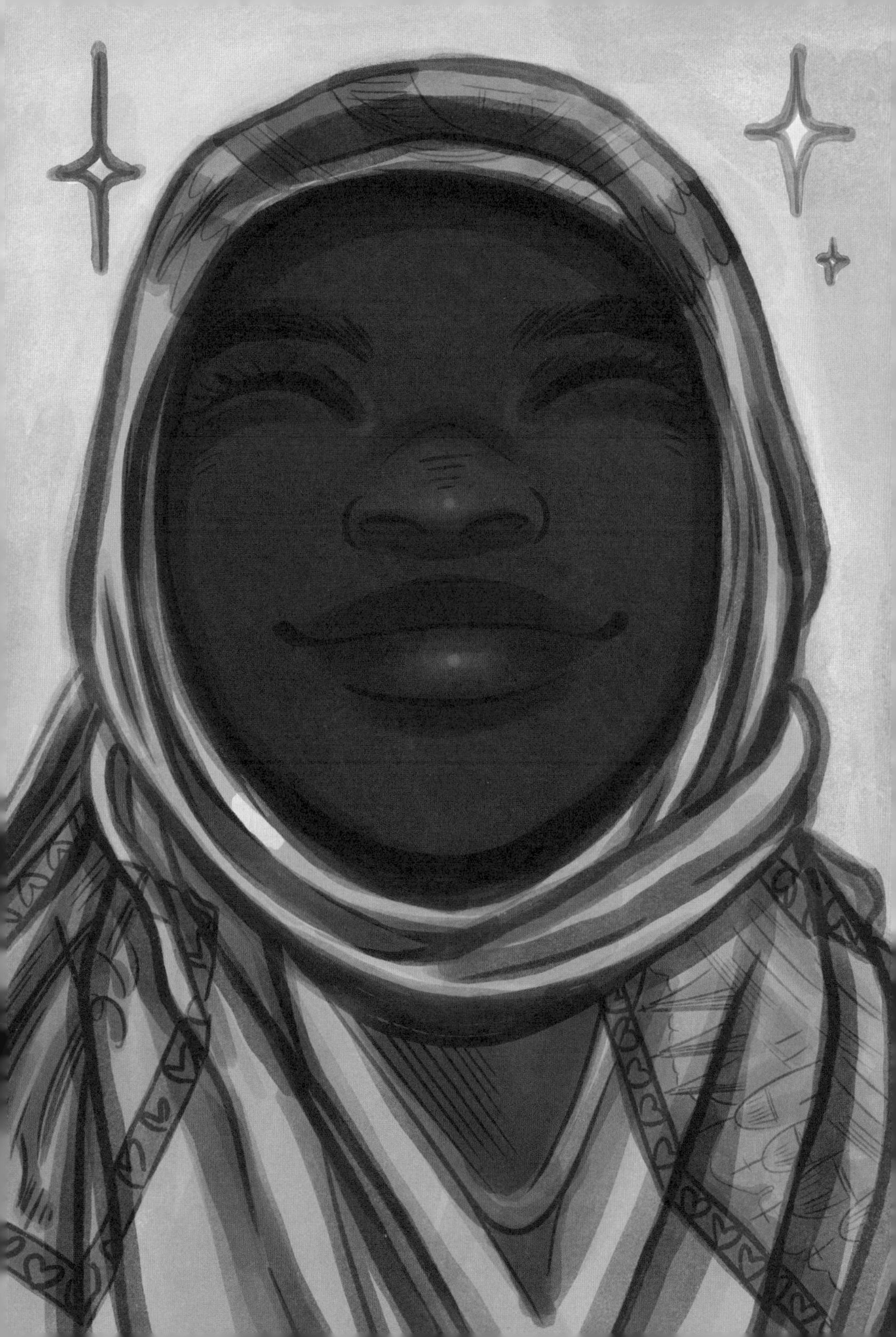

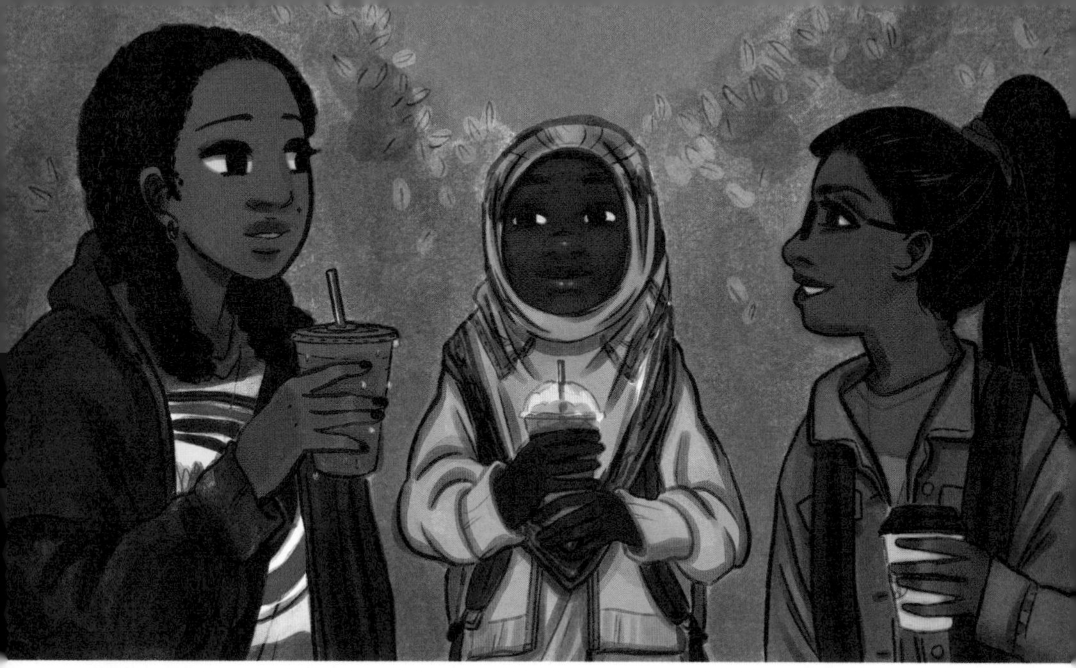

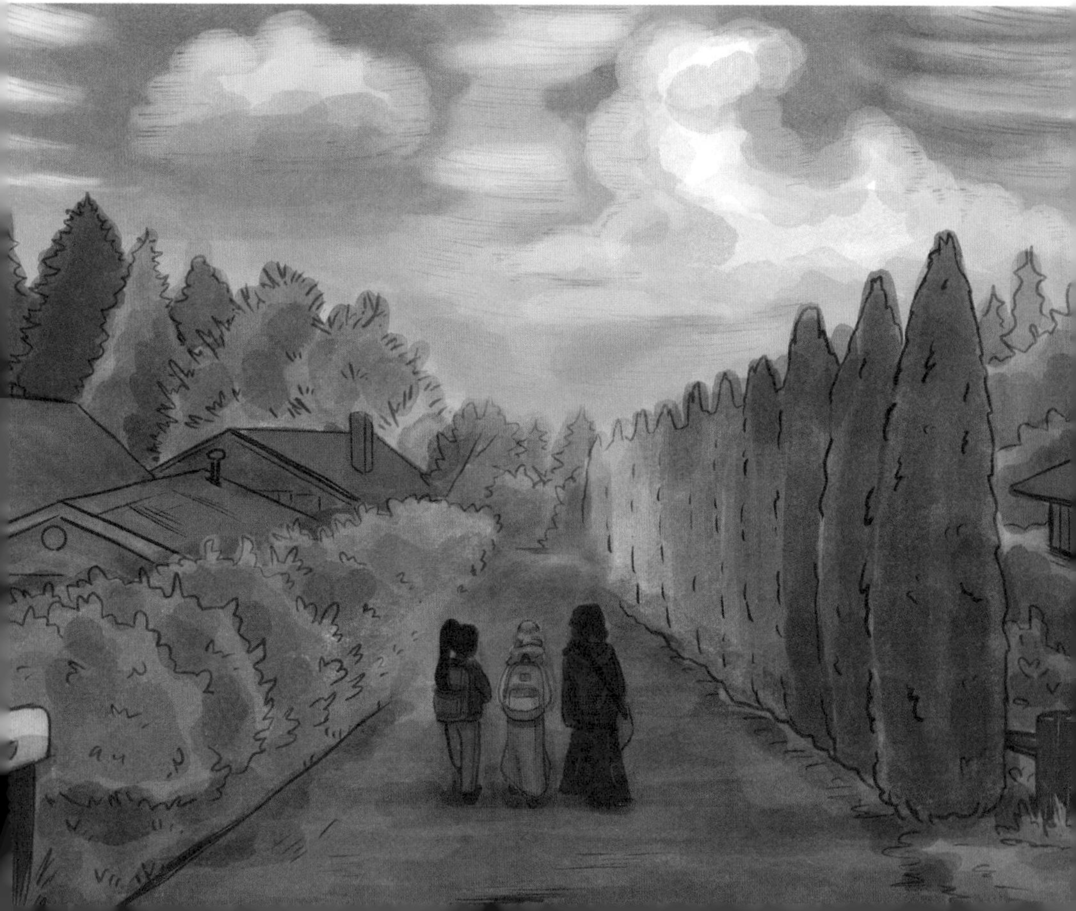

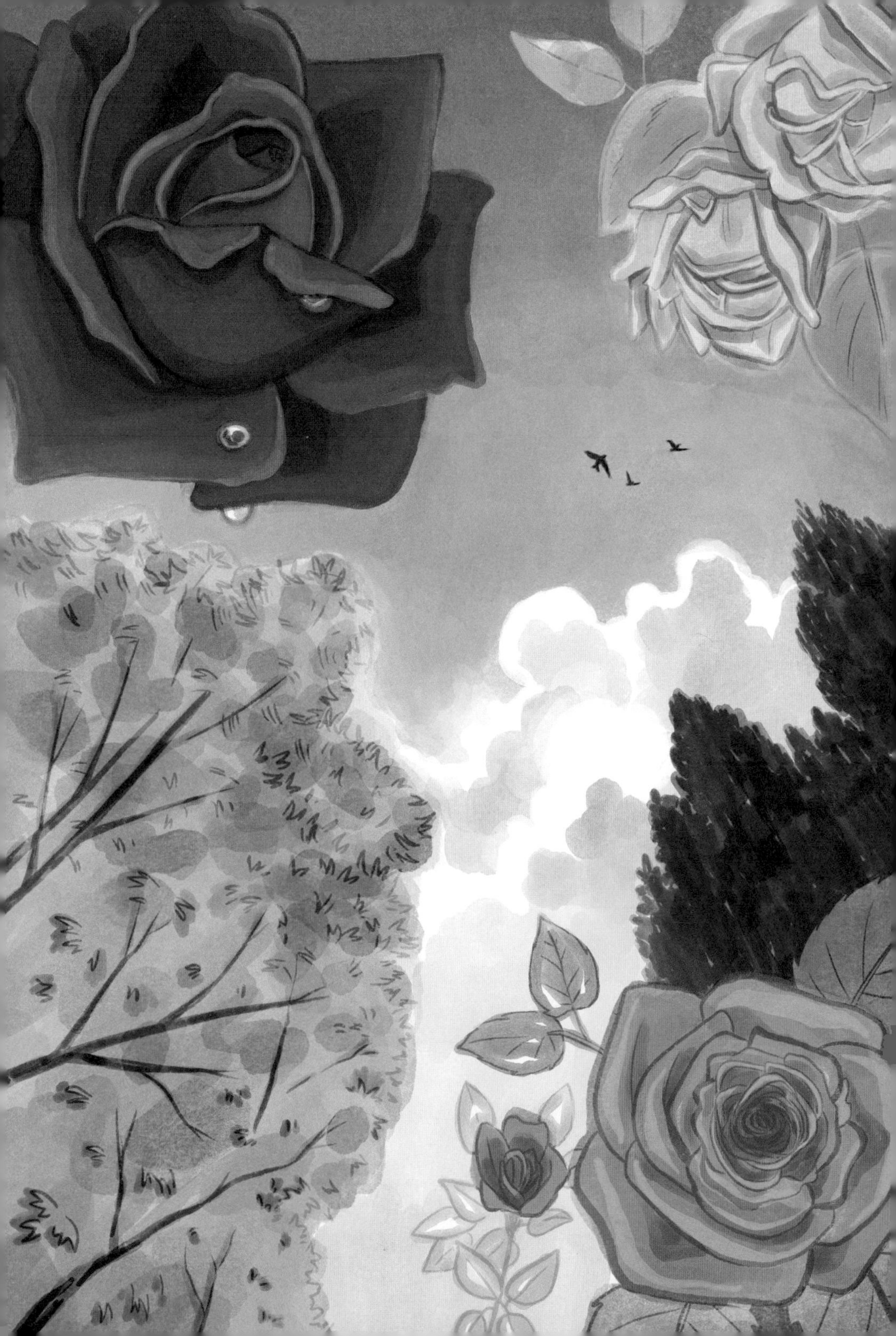

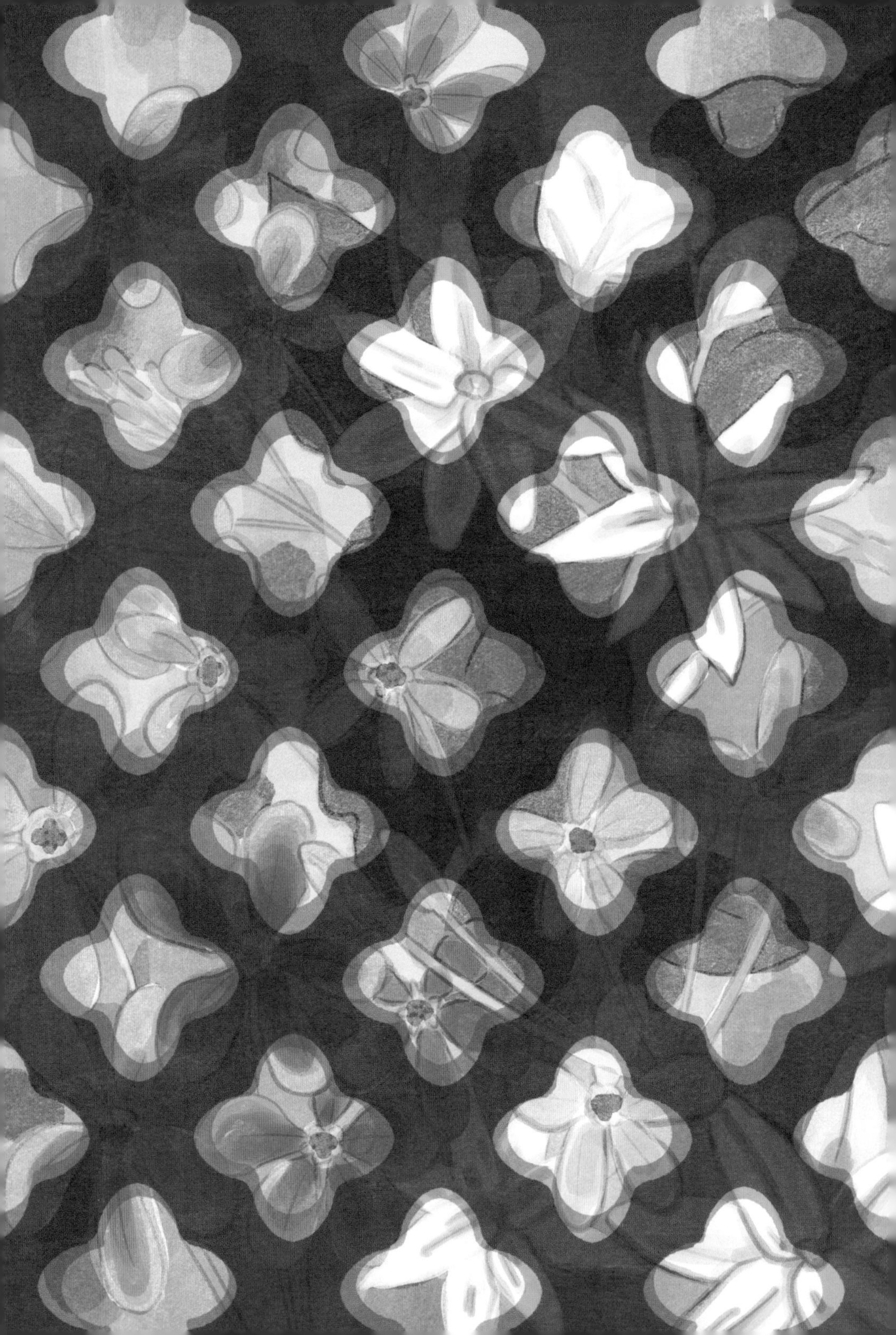

NISRIN MONIRUZZAMAN
GUIDE TO
BANGLA
DESH
105/100
Nisrin-
excellent work
& esp love the
"kantha" work -
I hope to visit
someday!
Ms. M

BANGLADESH

Nisrin Moniruzzaman
Language Arts 8
Ms Mayorena
May 21st, 2002

Fig. 1

My family is from the People's Republic of Bangladesh. Bangladesh was established in 1971 and is nestled between the countries of India and Burma (Myanmar, Fig.1). The national language of Bangladesh is Bangla (Bengali). [1]

Bangladesh's currency is the *taka* (Fig. 2) and their GDP in 2001 was 2.9 trillion Bangladeshi Taka ($54 billion). [2] Bangladesh's main export has traditionally been jute fiber. However, in 2001 clothing accounted for 53% of Bangladeshi exported goods. [3]

Fig. 2

GOVERNMENT

The People's Republic of Bangladesh is a parliamentary democracy with an elected Parliament, President (elected by Parliament), and Prime Minister (appointed by the President).' The Constitution was ratified in 1972, but because of several military coups, has not always been historically enforced. In 1991, parliamentary democracy was reestablished and elections have been held since then.'

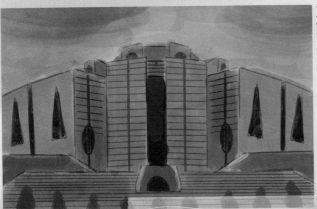

Bangladesh's National Parliament House (Jatiya Sangsad Bhaban, Fig. 3), located in the capital, Dhaka, is one of the biggest parliament buildings in the world. It was conceived while Bangladesh was still East Pakistan by Louis Khan and finished in 1982.'

Fig. 3

A note from Priya:

The Bangladesh Liberation War and 1971 Genocide

When I was growing up in the 90s, we did not talk about the war. I overheard my mom recording a speech for class in which she described experiencing it as a seven year old. I was around the same age when I eavesdropped on this and it stayed with me forever. She described hiding under a bed with her mom and baby brother, and how one of the Pakistan Army's rape squads tried to break down the door. They couldn't and eventually gave up. She considered this a miracle, because the door was not very strong. Later, when they escaped in secret, her mom (my nani) told her not to go above decks of the boat. My mom did anyway and the river was so clogged with corpses, she couldn't see the water.

Operation Searchlight

Later, I learned that my family had survived something called Operation Searchlight. In order to curb Bengali resistance against their rule, the Pakistan Army planned Operation Searchlight for March 25-April 10 of 1971. The President of Pakistan, Yahya Khan, said, "Kill three million of them and the rest will eat out of our hands." They especially targeted intellectuals and Dhaka University, where my nana worked.

More and more people have come forward with their stories and history, and there is much more information in English than when I (and Nisrin) was a kid. We will learn more as time goes on. To the genocide deniers: Your lies will never silence the survivors.

ENVIRONMENT

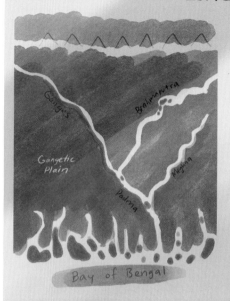

Ganges
Brahmaputra
Gangetic Plain
Meghna
Padma
Bay of Bengal

*Now known as climate change -p

Bandgladesh is a country of rivers in a tropical climate. It is a delta made up of the Ganges, Brahmaputra, and Meghna rivers and is part of the **Gangetic Plain**, which flows from Pakistan, across India, and into the Bay of Bengal. Flooding is common during and after the Monsoon season.[6]

Global warming*is threatening much of the Bangladeshi environment, not only through sea level rise but also through rising salinity, which kills crops and freshwater fish.[7]

Farming is very important in Bangladesh, and rice is grown throughout the country. Tea is traditionally grown in the hills of Sylhet.[8] While urban areas are growing, there are thousands of small villages, and the biggest city is Dhaka. Bangladesh's population in 2001 was 129.3 million.[9]

SEASONS

গ্রীষ্ম	Grissho Summer	mid-April to mid-June 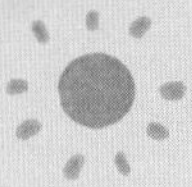
বর্ষা	Borsha Monsoon Season	mid-June to mid-August 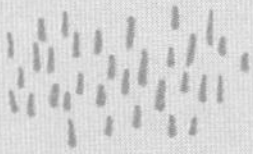
শরৎ	Shorud Fall	mid-August to mid-October 
হেমন্ত	Hemont Dry Season	mid-October to mid-December 
শীত	Sheet Winter	mid-December to mid February 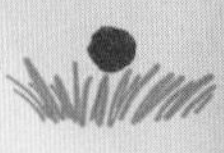
বসন্ত	Boshount Spring	mid-February to mid-April 

Bangladesh is the eastern part of the region of Bengal and shares many cultural characteristics, such as language and folk traditions. One of these folk traditions is the embroidery I used for the cover of this report. This embroidery is called kantha work and traditionally is used to decorate and even mend clothes!

PLANTS AND ANIMALS

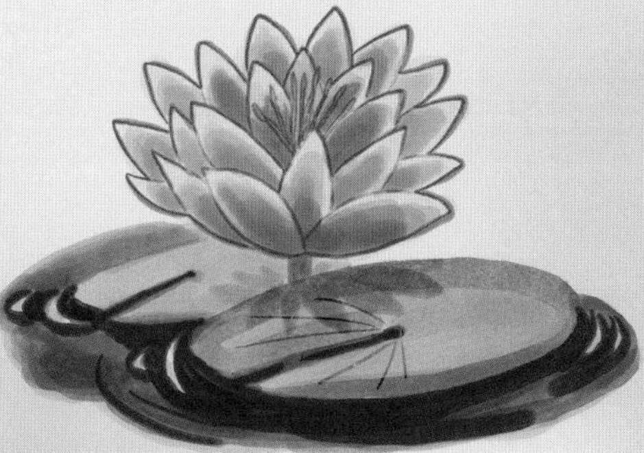

The national flower of Bangladesh is the water lily. The jackfruit is the national fruit, and the mango is the national tree. The national animal is the Bengal tiger.[9] Sadly, Bengal tigers are endangered![10]

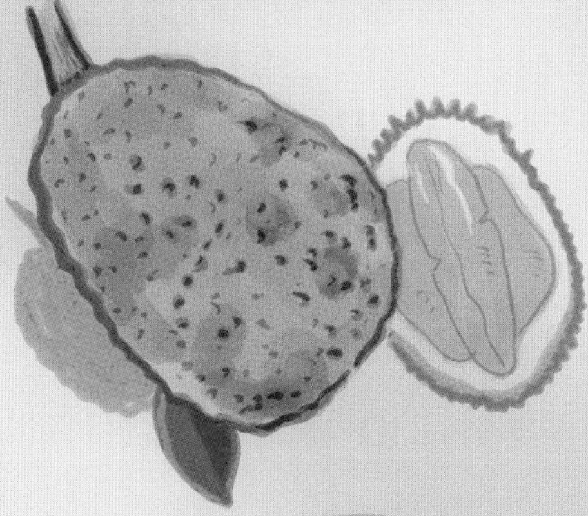

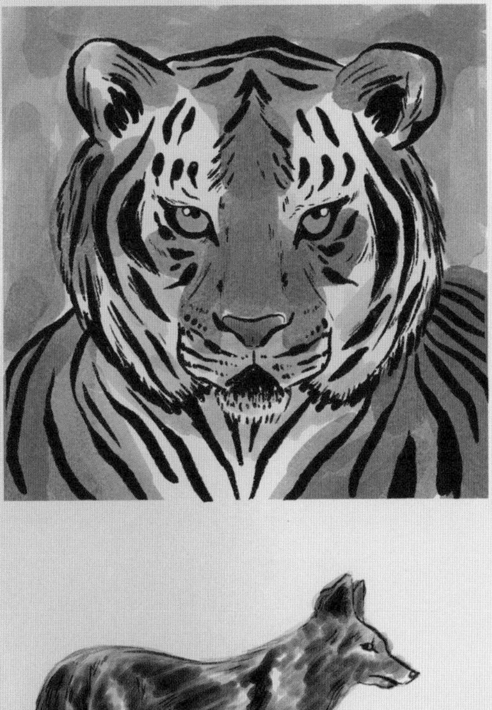

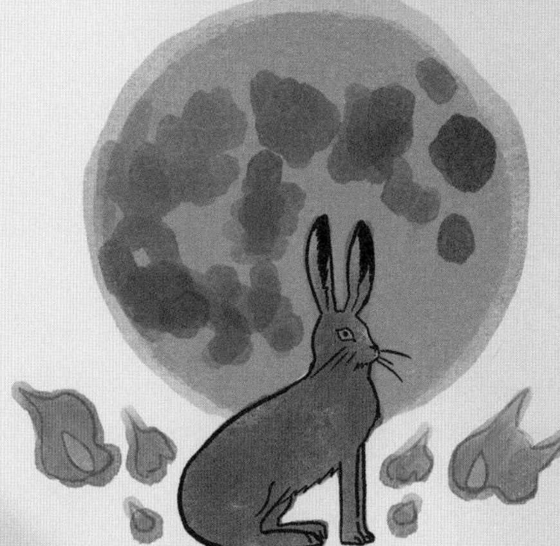

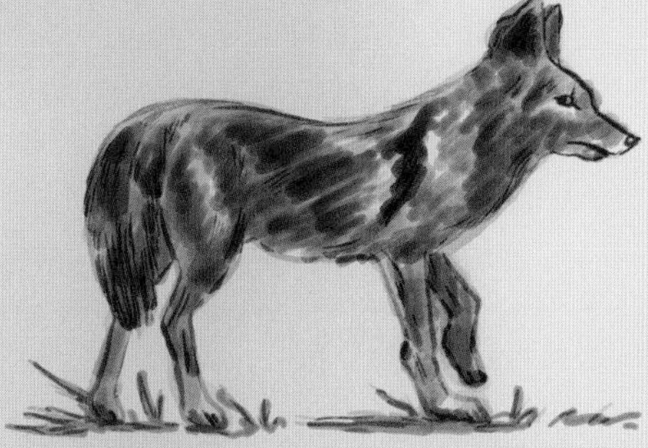

What stories did you hear about animals growing up? I learned about the noble hare in the moon, mischievious monkeys, and very stupid tigers. Tigers can be very scary in real life, but in Bengali folk tales they get into lots of trouble, tricked by other animals (usually a jackal).

BANGLA

The Bengali Language is known as Bangla and is the fifth most popular language in the world. Bangla is spoken by Bengali people all over the world, most commonly in Bangladesh and India. "

Some common Bangla phrases and words are:

Hello! (Hindu)
Nomoshkar

Hello! (Muslim)
Slamaleykum

How are you?	Apni kemon acho?
I'm good.	Ami bhalo ache.
What is your name?	Apnar nam ki?
My name is ____.	Amar nam ____.

Yes
Henh

No
Na

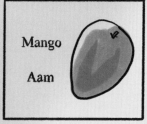

Mango
Aam

Me
Ami

You (regular)
Apni

You (intimate)
Tumi

MOTHER LANGUAGE DAY

Ekushey February (21 February) is Mother Language Day, celebrating the Bengali Language Movement (along with the preservation of all mother languages). On February 21st, 1952, several students were killed at Dhaka University. They were protesting the suppression of Bangla by the government. International Mother Language Day was offically adopted by the UN this year (2002). [12]

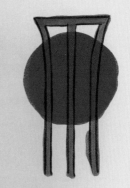

POETRY IN BANGLADESH

Poetry is incredibly important to the Bengali people. Rabindranath Tagore (pronounced "Takoor") is our most famous poet, and the first ten lines of his poem *Amar Shonar Bangla* is the national anthem of Bangladesh. [13] Poetry does not translate well from Bangla to English, so if you want to properly read Bengali poetry, my grandfather says you should learn Bangla first.

AMAR SHONAR BANGLA
(Partial)

Amar shonar Bangla, ami
tomay bhalobhashi,
Chirodin tomar akash, tomar
batash, amar prane bajay bashi.
O Ma, phagune tor amer bone
gharane pagol kore,
Mori hay, hay re— O Ma,
Oghrane tor bhora khete ami ki
dekhechhi modhur hashi.

MY GOLDEN BENGAL
(Partial)

My golden Bengal, I love you.
Forever your skies, your air set my
heart in tune as if it were a flute.
Oh Ma, the smell of the mango
orchard in Spring drives me crazy,
What a thrill— Oh Ma,
In the dry autumn, time sees sweet
smiles all through the ripe paddy
fields.

FOOD

Bangladesh's main crop is rice. Rice is harvested in all seasons and grows in paddies. People in Bangladesh eat lots of rice, lentils (dal), bread (parathas), fish, and vegetables like eggplant and okra. [13]

Rice paddy in Bangladesh

I love Bengali food! Here's a recipe for my mom's beef curry.

CLOTHING

shari

shalwar kameez

Bangladesh has produced textiles for the West since the late 1970s.[1] Our own style of clothing involves wrapping long pieces of cloth around the body in various ways. Many women all over South Asia wear the shari (sometimes anglicized shadi in Bangla),[2] a dress made by wrapping a long piece of cotton, silk, or nylon around the waist and draping it over the shoulder. Men wear a piece of clothing called a dhoti, which wraps around the legs and tucks into the waist. There are many ways to wrap these items, and sometimes women will wrap the shari like pants to make working outside easier.[3]

People also wear shalwar kameez, which was introduced to Bengal (possibly) by the Mughals in the sixteenth century and have become more popular since. Girls like me wear them to school as a uniform. "Shalwar" comes from the word for pants in Farsi.[4] "Kameez" means shirt. Girls and women wear a scarf called an "orna" ("dupatta" in India)[5] with shalwar kameez. It's both fashionable and modest.

orna

hijab

HEAD COVERINGS

Some women cover their head with the pallu (train) of their shari or with their orna, to be modest or respectful. An orna (or any scarf) can also be used for hijab (the religious head covering). The women in my family do not wear hijab, but I have cousins and aunts who do.

MY FAMILY

My mom's name is Rani Khan. She was born in Bangladesh in 1963 to Amira and Muzzammil Moniruzzaman. My mom moved to the United States for college in the 1980s and her parents followed when I was born in 1988.

Families in Bangladesh are traditionally patriarchal, but not the way Western European families are. A man controls the house but his mother runs it. If you are a girl, you marry into your husband's family and your mother-in-law has the final say in everything. Then if you have a son, you become the head of *his* household when *he* marries.

My family is not like this. For one thing, my mom is not married. For another, my grandfather (Nana) is a feminist. My grandmother (Nani) runs the household and my mom and Nana make the money. My nana is a sociologist and my mom is a financial specialist. Sometimes my nani works part-time at a department store.

My nani at her wedding in 1962.

My best friend Firuzeh Brown, my nani, and me at Oaks Park over spring break.

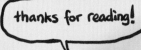
thanks for reading!

Mommy
Nani
Nana
me!

ACKNOWLEDGMENTS

Thank you Steenz, for knowing I could do this and believing in the project. Thank you Anjali, for your encouragement, enthusiasm, knowledge, and help. Thank you Charlotte, for fighting for this book and holding me to your highest standard. Thank you Wendy Xu, for insisting I get an agent. Thank you Shivana Sookdeo, for insisting I'm legit. Thank you Ashanti, Autumn, Bianca, Lin, Jade, Jem, Jo, Marian, Mikhaila, Olive, Shannon, Shing, and Sunmi, for your friendship and inspiration. Thank you Carrie McClain, Claire Folkman, and Kelly Phillips for giving me my first shots. Thank you Claire Napier, for doing the first edits and giving me the confidence to move forward. Thank you Morgan, for your invaluable hard work. Thank you Niki Smith, for making the "Literary agents who represent graphic novels" list. Thank you to every person who worked to get this book published, whether we met or not. Thank you Eri and Mary. Thank you E, e, M, and M for supporting me when no one else would and for keeping me fed, sheltered, and loved in my worst moments. ♥

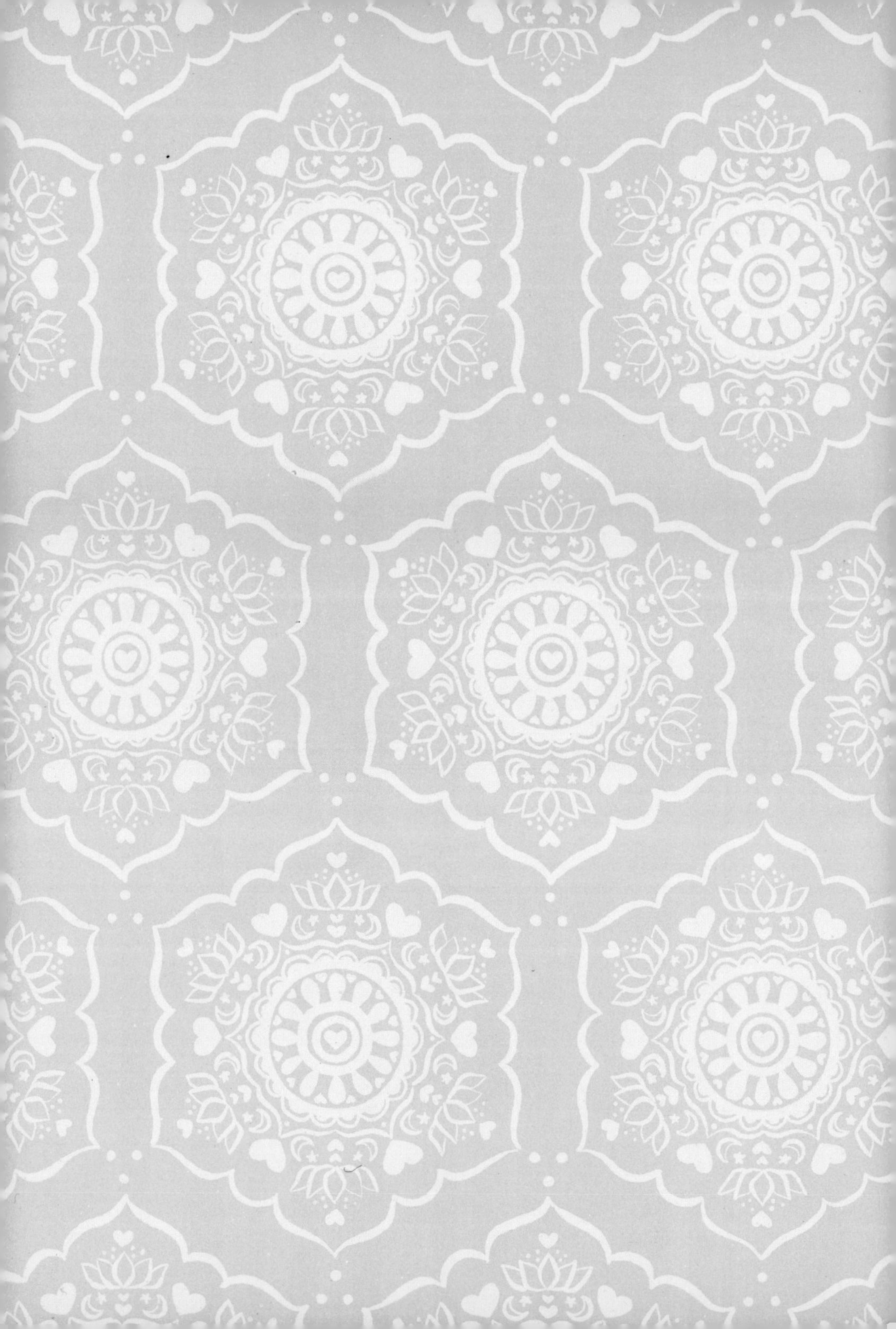